Owl at Midnight

A story of Gwenllian, the lost Princess of Wales,

by

Patricia Lennan

First published in 2017
Publisher – Little Knoll Press

ISBN: 978-0-9935078-3-0

Printed in Great Britain by
CPI Group (UK) Ltd.
Croydon CR0 4YY

This book is dedicated to

the late Mair Eluned Lennan (née Williams)
and John Douglas Lennan
with a lifetime of thanks

and to the late Thomas Owen
of Pen y Bryn, formerly Garth Celyn.

ACKNOWLEDGMENTS

I would like to offer my sincere thanks to:

The late Dr Gweneth Lilly, who provided in her booklet, *Gilbert and Gwenllian, a story of a nun's life at Sempringham*, a picture of how life would have been for Gwenllian.

The Princess Gwenllian Society/Cymdeithas y Dywysoges Gwenllian. Founded in the memory of Princess Gwenllian, the Society has members in Wales, Lincolnshire and many parts of the world.

The Lincolnshire library services for providing historical information.

Lesley Hughes for providing historical information.

Siân-Anghared Tovey, Welsh Language Translator, for her help and encouraging review.

Heulwen Roberts for her support and review.

Jenny Knowles, Little Knoll Press, for all her help with the editing and promotion of this book.

The Copper Writers - an excellent Anglesey writing group

All friends and family for their support, encouragement and patience.

AUTHOR'S NOTE

The inspiration for this book stemmed from a discovery in the late 1970s. My mother received a letter informing her of the death of a brother, a half-brother as it turned out, who lived in Abergwyngregyn, North Wales. My parents were living in England at the time, but my mother's family was originally from Abergwyngregyn and Llanfairfechan. We were intrigued; no one on my mother's side of the family knew about him. Only my Nain (Welsh grandmother) it seemed would have been able to tell us the full story, but she had died in 1954.

It would take too long to tell the story here of how we discovered fragments of his life and pieced together his history, so to be brief I will just explain that Uncle Thomas Owen was living at Pen y Bryn House, Abergwyngregyn, previously known as Garth Celyn, with his wife, Margo, when he passed away. This site has been identified for some time now as one of the original courts (Llys) of the Welsh Princes, mainly due to much hard work by historian Katherine Gibson and family.

When visiting the property much later on, I was shown the room where it is thought Eleanor de Montfort gave birth to Gwenllian and the tunnel which led to the sea, and other tunnels which once led to the mountains above. It was here too where my story was born. I was intrigued and set about to discover more about the life of Gwenllian. But very little had ever been written about her; there were only a few historical documents recording that she was taken to Sempringham Priory and spent her whole life there until she died at the age of 54.

I have developed my story on a framework of historical fact, especially regarding the events surrounding Prince

Llywelyn and his family, and I have tried to depict life in a Gilbertine convent in the late thirteenth century as authentically as possible to illustrate how Gwenllian's life might have been. However, this being a novel, the facts are also woven into fiction with hints at the possibility of what 'might have been'. As so little is known about Gwenllian, much is left to the imagination.

Wales has a reputation for being a land of myths and legends. She harbours magic in the hollows and hills, in secret places; the rivers and valleys echo with ancient tales. I invite you to step into the living history and share an adventure.

GWENLLIAN'S FAMILY TREE

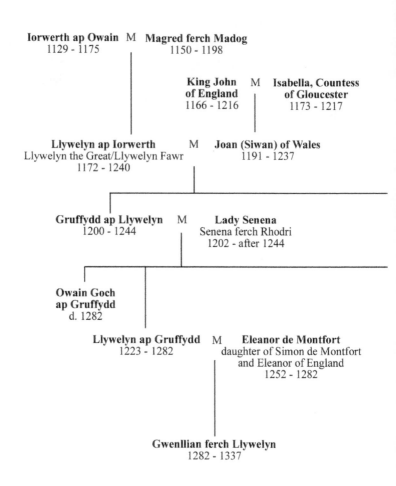

Iorwerth ap Owain M **Magred ferch Madog**
1129 - 1175   1150 - 1198

King John M **Isabella, Countess**
of England   **of Gloucester**
1166 - 1216   1173 - 1217

Llywelyn ap Iorwerth M **Joan (Siwan) of Wales**
Llywelyn the Great/Llywelyn Fawr   1191 - 1237
1172 - 1240

Gruffydd ap Llywelyn M **Lady Senena**
1200 - 1244   Senena ferch Rhodri
                              1202 - after 1244

Owain Goch
ap Gruffydd
d. 1282

Llywelyn ap Gruffydd M **Eleanor de Montfort**
1223 - 1282   daughter of Simon de Montfort
                             and Eleanor of England
                             1252 - 1282

Gwenllian ferch Llywelyn
1282 - 1337

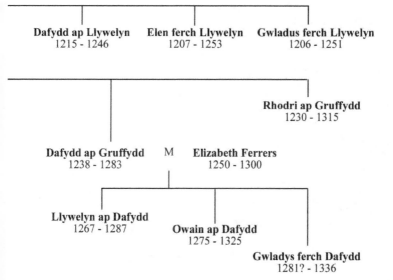

Dafydd ap Llywelyn
1215 - 1246

Elen ferch Llywelyn
1207 - 1253

Gwladus ferch Llywelyn
1206 - 1251

Rhodri ap Gruffydd
1230 - 1315

Dafydd ap Gruffydd
1238 - 1283

M

Elizabeth Ferrers
1250 - 1300

Llywelyn ap Dafydd
1267 - 1287

Owain ap Dafydd
1275 - 1325

Gwladys ferch Dafydd
1281? - 1336

THE BARD'S TRAVELS

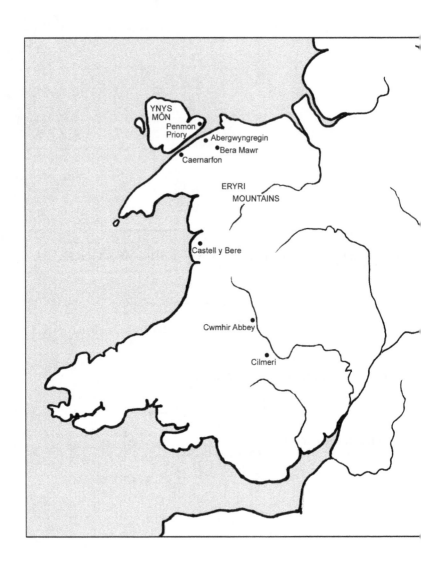

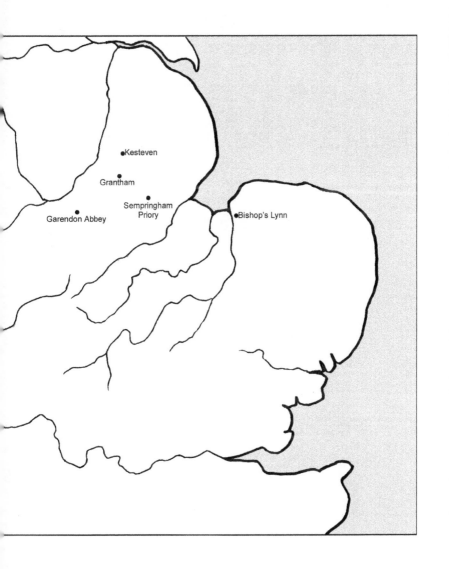

CHAPTER 1

Garth Celyn, Abergwyngregyn, Gwynedd
June 1282

The whole court was in panic. Olwen, the midwife, was desperately trying to display an air of calm and control, her Lady was slipping away and her Lord had not arrived. Lady Eleanor had been in labour for two days and still the babe was not born. Olwen had not left her side and was near to exhaustion, but how could she complain when her Lady was in agony and had barely the strength to talk. It had been a long hot night and the morning sun was beginning to filter through the high window, promising an even hotter day.

"The head is coming. You must push now, My Lady. Hold on, one big push and we should be there."

Celeste, Eleanor's faithful servant and friend, gripped her limp hand, soothing her forehead with a cool lavender-soaked cloth. "It's nearly over, Eleanor. The babe is coming, be brave."

The young maid, Catrin, hovered around the bed not knowing what to do or say, tears falling down her frightened face.

"Go and see if that physician is here, Catrin fach, and get more clean linen," ordered Olwen. "Lord knows, we can't do with tears at this stage."

Catrin scuttled off not quite knowing what to do first. She rushed down the stairs via the kitchen to the laundry room, hearing Eleanor's screams behind her. It was only a few minutes later as she climbed back up the stairs to the bed chamber

1

holding a pile of fresh linen that she was aware of how quiet it was. Then, into the silence broke the mewl of a new-born.

"Thank heavens, the baby lives," she muttered to herself as she crept back into the bedchamber.

Olwen sat on Eleanor's bed, cradling the baby in her right arm and wiping tears away with her other hand. "Lord be praised, it's a girl, a beautiful girl and she's fine."

But Eleanor lay still, she could barely raise her head or speak. Her fine golden hair was matted to her head, her face had the pallor of one leaving this world. Olwen placed the baby on her chest and Eleanor strained to hold her close between each faint and shallow breath.

"You just rest, My Lady, I'll see to her, you need your strength. Catrin, bring me that clean linen then go and see if the Prince is coming." Turning to Celeste and handing her the baby girl, she lowered her voice to a whisper. "Hold the little one for a while, I must clean Eleanor up before he arrives and please God may that be soon; I don't think she has long."

Catrin approached the bed. The sight of the blood-soaked silken sheets shocked her. Olwen's tabard was like a butcher's apron; only a short while before it had been pristine white. In the warm and airless room the stench was overwhelming. Never had she seen anything like this before and never, she vowed, would she lie with a man if this was to be the result.

Olwen, softening a little seeing her distress, placed a hand on her shoulder. "Go on, Catrin fach, I will deal with this. You go and check on the tunnel."

The tunnel was just along the corridor, hidden in a small chamber where the thick stone walls of the passage muffled any sounds. As she approached, Catrin could hear a scraping and shuffling noise. Edging her head shyly around the door, she could see two of the Prince's men trying to remove three heavy oak panels. The first panel was nearly loose and as one of the men turned to give her a dismissive look, the panel came free and he fell backwards, narrowly avoiding squashing his comrade. A cloud of dust blew into the room.

How exciting, thought Catrin, that the Prince would come

through the secret tunnel to see his new-born child, but she knew that this was no time for romantic imaginings. Eleanor was in grave danger. Danger was never far from any one of them these days; Catrin had heard the kitchen gossip. She knew that the Prince was using the tunnel, even though the word was that he was probably taking the mountain path from Caerhun. The King's men would be watching for him both on the coastal path and along the forested winding valley, which led down from the hills to the Llys at Abergwyngregyn.

As the final panel came loose, the Prince himself and his faithful bard, Cai, stumbled into the room. "Lord above, what a performance! We're like a pair of tumbling jesters," muttered Llywelyn.

"What timing! The dust in that tunnel was choking me," Cai spluttered, as he brushed himself down.

"Leave the passage open. Some of my men are following," the Prince ordered. Then, turning to address Catrin, he softly asked, "What news?"

Catrin's expression was enough to make him instantly concerned.

"The baby is born, my Lord," was the only reply she could muster, standing quickly to one side as the two men brushed past her.

Following them into the adjacent chamber, she lingered in the corner and saw that Olwen was just changing her apron and Celeste was still holding the baby, who cried softly.

As Llywelyn and Cai entered, the room fell silent. All faces were ashen and all hearts were thumping. Cai, standing beside the Prince, took his arm. "It looks like you have a healthy baby, My Lord."

Prince Llywelyn made straight for the large bed where Eleanor laid, his eyes searching Olwen's face for clues on his wife's condition. Olwen nodded her head towards the bed then looked down at the babe, her eyes misty with tears.

"Please woman, don't tell me I am too late."

"No, My Lord, she still breathes, but is very weak. She has lost a lot of blood. We have sent for the physician from Bangor."

3

Llywelyn rushed over to Eleanor, ignoring the baby, and sitting by her side he took her cold hand in his. "Cariad, cariad don't go from me, I need you now more than ever, I am so sorry I couldn't get here sooner."

Eleanor's voice was just a tiny whisper. "Have you seen her? She is so perfect. Take care of her, my little one. I want to call her ... the name we chose."

"We will name her that," cut in Llywelyn. "Don't talk, rest now."

He gazed upon her, wishing her beauty to stay for ever in his mind, his heart. He felt as if his body was paralysed and his head was on fire. The sight of Eleanor fading away stirred in him a medley of emotions so strong that he felt his entire being could shatter into a thousand pieces. In the last few months, while he had fought against the King, the sights of the aftermath of battle and the humiliation of defeat had sickened his heart, but nothing had prepared him for this.

"Where's that physician?" he barked. But, as he looked around, he found the room empty and knew the others had left to give him the last few precious moments with Eleanor alone. Celeste had laid the babe on the bed next to her mother. Llywelyn lay down beside them, taking Eleanor and the babe in his arms. These few moments would be the only ones they would ever have all together.

In the few days which followed everyone was affected by the cloud of grief which overwhelmed the whole court, from the stable boys and kitchen maids, to the men-at-arms and all members of the official household. Eleanor was loved by all of them. In the kitchens and the stables they muttered about how cruel life could be and how Eleanor, of all people, did not deserve to be taken by God when she had just become a mother, a mother to the heir of the Prince of Wales. Llywelyn shut himself in his small chamber in the West Tower, allowing only Cai to sit with him and bring him ale and food, which remained untouched. On the third morning, the Bishop of Bangor arrived and was reluctantly admitted.

"I will not leave until I have had her buried," Prince Llywelyn explained.

"It is not safe for you to linger too long," Cai advised.

"Then preparations must be hurried up. Surely the King will hold off his barbarous campaign for the burial; she was his cousin after all, even Edward could not be that callous. She will rest for eternity at the Llanfaes Friary alongside my grandmother, Siwan, a suitable place for my wife, the Princess of Wales and Lady of Snowdon."

The Bishop looked concerned. "You know Edward is amassing more troops on Môn daily?"

Llywelyn stood over the Bishop and looked down on him grimly. "Then I shall take my chance."

"As you wish of course. The people, your people, want to see you. They are all grieving; they need to know that you will not abandon them now … I mean due to your grief."

"We have come too far for that to ever happen, you should know." Llywelyn scowled at the Bishop. "I will deal with the King; you deal with your churchmen and the funeral arrangements."

"Of course, I shall see to it," replied the Bishop, and scuttled through the door, his skirts sweeping behind him.

With the Bishop gone, Cai poured two glasses of wine. As a bard he was normally eloquent, but now he was lost for words. Eleanor's death had affected him deeply and, although he shared a special closeness with Llywelyn, he did not know how to help him in his pain.

Llywelyn was the first to break the silence. "I want you to stay here, Cai, and make sure the baby is taken care of. When she is older, I want you to tutor her in all the ways we know. As it stands, she is my only heir."

"Of course I will, but don't you need me at your side?"

"It is more important for you to fulfil this task. You are the only one who can."

"I can't really do much at the moment, she just needs a nurse."

"I think the court needs your support, especially Celeste. She will, I hope, stay and help care for the little one, and there is much to oversee. You're not a fighting man and this summer could be the bloodiest yet. And, I need someone reliable. If my daughter is in any danger then you must take her to Denbigh, to my brother Dafydd's household to be with her cousins, and if there is danger there, then you know where to go."

Celeste, the thought of being close to her at court sent a thrill through Cai. He admired her so much, although he had never spoken of it to anyone. Had Llywelyn noticed his affection for her and was inadvertently protecting them both or was that just his hopeful imagining. He knew she was inconsolable since Eleanor's death; they had been through so much together, but he had not had time to approach her in the past few days. For now his thoughts must be with Llywelyn and the little babe.

"Yes, I know where to take her. That won't be an easy task, but I will protect her with my life. Are you going to name her before you go, have her christened to appease the priests and the bishops?"

"I will leave that to you, but we will call her 'Gwenllian', as her mother wished; that is the name Eleanor wanted."

"Gwenllian, that is a noble name," replied Cai, knowing that the name was rooted in a much older, darker time. But this was not the time or place to dwell on that. He would fulfil his duty and help his Prince to prepare to leave for the ongoing campaign against the King of England. Sometimes he wondered if Llywelyn was wise to continue, he had lost so much. It was his brother, Dafydd, who had dragged him in to this campaign, the brother who had previously betrayed him. Many of his supporters too had betrayed him, and now this, the loss of his dear wife. But these tragic events just made him more determined to reclaim his true title as the Prince of Wales. Cai knew better than to try and persuade him otherwise. It would be judged as betrayal; he would never be disloyal to his Prince and country, but at times he couldn't shake off a feeling of foreboding.

Eleanor De Montfort, Princess of Wales and Lady of Snowdon,

was taken over the Lafan Sands of the Menai Strait to be buried at Llanfaes Friary. She was thirty years old and had lived as Llywelyn's wife for only four years. The monks sang and Cai played his harp. It seemed the finest, most fitting instrument for a noble woman who possessed beauty, courage and refinement. Yet Eleanor had always been one of the people, caring for the needs of the poorest and talking to them as if she were no better than them. Many farm labourers, bondsmen, servants and their families had stood on the beach at Abergwyngregyn and Llanfaes bowing their heads in sorrow, just as they had waved their arms in joy when she arrived in their country those few years before. They had welcomed her and she had fulfilled all their expectations and more.

As he played, Cai glanced at Celeste, who stood with Catrin behind Llywelyn. Her head was covered by a black veil, but he could catch a glimpse of her lustrous brown hair which peeped out around her shoulder. Every few seconds she would place her hand under the veil to wipe away tears. As he looked around, he couldn't see many that were not openly crying, including Llywelyn, even the Bishop had watery eyes. Llywelyn's closest men-at-arms, Philip, Rhys and Owain, kept their heads bowed, their faces straining with the effort of holding back the grief. Concentrating on his music kept his tears inside him, but Cai knew that once he finished he would join in the torrent of grief which engulfed the whole community, in fact the whole of the Principality.

For several days the court was subdued. There were not many smiles and no laughter, although Llywelyn had stressed that everything was to carry on as normal; there was a war on and there was work to be done. Cai had been helping the Prince prepare to leave. Tomorrow he would be gone and this time without his trusted friend, clerk, counsellor and bard. Cai was scared for him; he had lost his dear wife and was holding his country by a thread. He would not care about his own life now; all his grief, anger and bitterness would be poured into this campaign. And Edward, especially with Eleanor gone, would not make any concessions, so determined was he to conquer the remaining stronghold of the Welsh Prince and take it for his own kingdom.

In his new role, Cai wandered around the court overseeing the organisation of the servants and the household, trying to keep up morale. He had been away so often with Llywelyn on campaigns that, apart from his clerical duties, he had rarely engaged with the day to day running of the court. He found Celeste sitting with Catrin in the solar, the baby Gwenllian sleeping in her crib close by. He thought he noticed a shine in Celeste's misty brown eyes as she looked up at him.

"How is the baby Gwenllian?"

"She's so well, she's a survivor that's for sure," Celeste replied in her native French.

"Have you employed a wet nurse?"

"Morwena – she arrived the very next day from the village. Her babe sadly died only a few days before."

It struck Cai at that moment how precarious life could be for a woman in childbearing, as it was for a man in war. He had always admired the strength and tenacity of the women he knew, and respected their wisdom and insight. How quickly they rallied to organise a situation with great efficiency. He wondered what Celeste intended to do now, with her mistress and dear friend gone, but it was too soon and he thought it would be impertinent to ask her.

Catrin picked up the baby when she started to cry. Catrin too had been close to Eleanor, arriving as a maid three years ago at the age of twelve, the daughter of a local maerdref tenant. Eleanor had grown fond of her and taken her into her small circle of women. Now she wondered if she would be sent back to her family, who really couldn't afford to keep her. Cai looked kindly at her as if reading her thoughts.

"You know that you have a home here for as long as you intend to stay, Catrin. You ...," he stuttered a little, "and you Celeste, belong here, and the Prince has asked for both of you to care for little Gwenllian, with Morwena of course. He also wishes me to stay to help and be more of a full time clerk and steward of the house, for the moment." With that he turned and left the room, feeling awkward, wondering how he could confidently sing and play to a room full of people, yet feel his cheeks burn when addressing Celeste.

So, several days later Llywelyn set off from Abergwyngregyn to his brother Dafydd's house in Denbigh to continue a campaign that he was secretly losing confidence in and wondered if he still had the stomach for. It was an emotional goodbye for Cai; he didn't know when or if he would see his Prince again. As they parted, Llywelyn handed Cai Eleanor's ring. "Keep this safe and in the event that I do not return, keep it for Gwenllian until she is at an age to marry." With those words he urged his horse forward and did not look back.

His time with Eleanor had been short on this earth. She had been a brave woman, suffering imprisonment by the King before they were allowed to marry, and now dying at the birth of her child. It seemed such a cruel fate. Maybe if his brother, Dafydd, had not acted so rashly by becoming involved in this new campaign, maybe if Llywelyn had not still had the fighting spirit to protect his realm from the Norman king, he would have been with her more and they would have spent peaceful days as a family. Now he could not even spend time with his little daughter. He had held her only once before he left. She had the same beautiful eyes as her mother, the same delicate skin and flaxen hair. He would love her greatly, but could not bear to look at her too much while his pain was raw.

He was riding back to his brother's house in Denbigh to discuss their next strategy, and from there, onward to slaughter the enemy. His closest men-at-arms rode with him, Philip, Rhys and Owain, keeping pace with their Prince, all silent sharing his grief, all uncertain of their fate and the fate of their nation.

The faster the Prince rode, the faster his anger started to gain pace. He would win back his lands for the memory of his dear wife and for his little daughter, who would one day be his heir. What did he have to lose? The wound he bore was deeper than any which could be inflicted in battle.

"Damn you, Edward, damn you to hell," he shouted for his men to hear him. "We're going to finish you this time."

CHAPTER 2

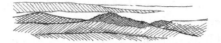

Nanhysglain
June 1283

Cai strolled in the midsummer sunshine. The scent of sun-dried sedge drifted from the bog and clouds of gnats hovered over the cotton grass. Tomorrow night would be the solstice. Cai thought of his kin in the mountains of Eryri, preparing for their midsummer celebrations. How he wished he could be with them, Seren and Cynan and the few surviving priests and priestesses of the grove, preparing his verses, gathering herbs for the rituals and kindling for the bright fires that they would burn in honour of the sun.

He looked up to the high peak of Bera Mawr that rose in front of him. Would he be able to find his people again? It had been so many years since he left them, but he knew they were not far away. Too long had he lingered here in Nanhysglain with Dafydd ap Gruffydd, now the leader of this fractured nation, and his family. How much longer would they be safe from Edward's troops? Castell y Bere, the last castle of the Welsh princes, had been taken at the end of April. On Dafydd's instructions they had fled, just in time, but their time of safety at Nanhysglain was running out and they had nowhere to flee to now, except to the last remnants of his kin. He had to get Gwenllian to safety before the nights started to draw in or the sickening thud of soldiers marching resounded in the valley below them.

A feeling of sickness was something that hadn't left him since his Lord Llywelyn had been ambushed and killed by King Edward's men, only six months before at Cilmeri. It was an ailment of the heart, he knew, but his body had succumbed too, with fever and a weariness that had weighed him down. He was now recovered, but was weak. Still, he assured himself, he was alive, unlike many of Llywelyn and Dafydd's men. He thanked his God and Goddess, and even the Christian God, that Gwenllian, whom he had sworn to protect, was safe. He could not entirely think the same of Dafydd, his rash actions had put them all in this dangerous position. It was only Cai's own loyalty to Llywelyn's wishes that had encouraged him to stay with Dafydd and his family. He should have taken Gwenllian to his kin before now and followed his own inner guidance. That thought had given him many sleepless nights and contributed to his illness, he was sure. His heart was torn; he had never really forgiven Dafydd for betraying his brother all those years ago by siding with the King, and now he resented him even more for leading Llywelyn into this last campaign which had led to his death and ripped him from his little daughter. Still, for now Dafydd was the reigning Prince, albeit of a mountain bog, and he owed him allegiance, but whatever the outcome, he would not linger here for much longer to be hunted down.

Walking back to the secret hiding place, Cai knew he had to act soon. He stopped and put his ear to the ground; as he did many times a day. This was something that Cynan, High Priest of the Mountain Grove, had taught him as a young boy. He had learnt to hear and sense vibrations in the ground, if soldiers were within miles of this marshy land he would hear them. For now they were safe.

He trod carefully across the boggy terrain, knowing that a wrong step into a sinkhole could be fatal. By the time he was returned to the camp, a mist had crept around the foothills of the mountain, shielding a hazy sun.

Within the scattering of silver birch trees that surrounded their rough shelters, he saw Celeste cradling little Gwenllian, wrapping her shawl around her to protect her from the evening damp. Catrin and Morwena sat next to her, pulling the skins off a couple of rabbits. Dafydd's boys, Llywelyn, a gangling lad on the cusp of manhood, and Owain, who carried his eight years on earth with a merriment that was infectious, tumbled in careless play on a small patch of clear grass. Their little sister, Gwladys, watched and clapped her hands in glee. Elizabeth, Dafydd's wife, was giving orders as usual, instructing Dafydd's older daughters, half-sisters to Llywelyn, Owain and Gwladys, to throw kindling wood onto a small fire.

Four of the men-at-arms were bringing in the horses from grazing, tethering them for the night. The other four, hidden from view, were keeping guard higher on the hill.

"Keep the smoke down, Elizabeth." Dafydd spoke sharply as he approached her, instantly regretting it and drawing her into his arms. "We don't want to send any signals."

"We have to eat, Dafydd. We are all sick of hard bread and cheese. Our supplies are running out. One of your men caught a few rabbits earlier. Catrin and Morwena are making a stew." She rested her head on his shoulder. A tear crept down her pale cheek. "I'm so frightened, scared for the children ... where can we go? How long can we stay in this god-forsaken bog?"

"I know, I know. I wish I could give you an answer. You must be brave. I will speak with Cai when he returns."

That evening Cai took out his crwth and sang very softly the lullaby he had sung to Gwenllian since her birth. Then he sang some of the ballads he had sung in the courts when he travelled with Llywelyn in happier days. His songs soothed the women, and as he scanned the faces of the men, he saw that they too were calm for a while, all but Dafydd, whose expression was tense as his eyes met Cai's. They both knew this might be the last time they would share these songs together ... a precious few moments shared.

Although they were fugitives on a damp Welsh hillside, they were not far from home, from where Gwenllian was conceived and born. Dafydd's home lay to the east; all this land had belonged to him and his brother; above all it had belonged to the people of Cymru, until Edward took it from them. Since that December day when Llywelyn had been killed, and it was thought most of his men with him, Dafydd had been hunted by Edward's men. They were hanging on to the last shreds of hope.

The morning mist cleared to reveal a cloudy sky. Cai awoke to the hungry cries of Gwenllian coming from the makeshift wooden shelter where the women and children slept. Dafydd's children were stirring too and it was all Elizabeth could do to keep them quiet. The boys, Llywelyn and Owain, were excited … this was just an adventure to them; they had no concept of the real danger that hung over them. The girls were quieter and obviously nervous, the older ones helping Elizabeth with little Gwladys, who was not much older than Gwenllian. Amongst the men who slept under the canopy of birches, only Dafydd and Philip were awake.

Philip paced restlessly around the grassy copse. Once Llywelyn's most trusted man, he looked worn and worried. It was not in his nature to wait and do nothing while enemies gathered.

Dafydd stood facing Bera Mawr. His features were obscured, a silhouette against the morning light.

Cai jumped up to join him, shaking out his damp cloak, brushing off the clinging leaves. "Dafydd, we must talk."

"We must. I was hoping to talk last night, but the mood was good and I let it be."

"Well, I fear we can't let it be any longer. Dafydd, My Lord, I must leave with Gwenllian and I must leave today. In my dreams I saw soldiers coming, and yesterday I knew we could not linger any longer."

"I don't think we need dreams to tell us that, Cai, but where should we go, that is the problem."

"There is only one place to go, Dafydd, to my kin, not far from here. The Eryri grove has been secret for hundreds of years and there they will give us shelter and food and Gwenllian will be safe. I promised my Lord Llywelyn I would take her there if we were not safe. I have waited too long."

"You are right, but I fear my time is short; they will hunt me down somewhere."

"Well, we should stick together."

"You go. Take my family. I cannot just give up and spend my years skulking in the hills."

"The Druids of Eryri are …"

Dafydd interrupted, "I know, Cai, they are highly regarded, wise people, but you and I are different. I will take two men only, with my sons, Llywelyn and Owain, and take my chances and maybe I will join you there. It will be safer to separate. You must look after my family and tell them I will be following. With all these children you cannot move fast. I want you to take Elizabeth and the girls to the nunnery at Gwytherin. It is to my own shame that I have not had them taken there before."

"It's too far and it means descending into the valley at some point, which is dangerous, and I promised my Lord Llywelyn that I would take Gwenllian to Seren."

"Our lives are at stake and promises sometimes have to be broken, Cai."

Cai knew it was no use to argue. His concern was to alert the women that they would be leaving that day.

Cai instructed Llywelyn, Dafydd's elder son, to summon the men-at-arms and prepare the horses. The eight armed men who had managed to leave Castell y Bere with them would not be much of a guard, but their lives would depend on them. Two were to go with Dafydd; Cai was not sure where to, but his greatest concern now was for Gwenllian and the other women. He would lead them to the safety of the Eryri grove; he had no intention of following Dafydd's wishes. He wondered why Dafydd had not sent his illegitimate daughters to the convent long before, or even back to their mother's house, for they would have found more safety there. Now Dafydd was placing them in more danger by asking him to take them to lower ground … and Gwenllian was certainly not born to spend her years locked away in a nunnery.

Cai walked with two of the armed men further up into the hills to warn the mountainside guards that they would be leaving. Nearer the top he would be able to see the surrounding land and get his bearings. The island of Môn lay behind him, and between Môn and the mainland, the glistening waters of the Menai Strait. Before him, to the distant south east, stretched the mountain range where he intended to lead the women to safety.

14

He stood for a moment to catch his breath. The mild breeze and green leafy landscape with pockets of broom and a few proud foxgloves, lulled him into a sense of security. The sun was warming his damp clothes. Scratching his stubbly chin, he felt at that moment that all would be well. It had to be.

The women did not panic, although each was silently hiding her fear. After Morwena had fed Gwenllian, Catrin wrapped the babe up tightly in the cleanest linen she could find. Poor Morwena, Catrin thought, caught up in this terrible drama after joining the court as a wet nurse. But then, she supposed, none of them had chosen this. She watched Celeste gather their meagre belongings into a sack. Celeste had come from a noble family; she had already suffered worse than this when she had been captured with Eleanor during their sea voyage to Wales and imprisoned for three years on the orders of King Edward. Elizabeth was as unfathomable as ever, fussing over the children and packing up the few bits of food they had. Now, all they could do was focus on their survival; their differences and family backgrounds were of no importance here. A strong bond had grown between them all, and Catrin was aware of the bond between Cai and Celeste as well.

The horses were ready. Young Llywelyn handed Catrin the largest mare. She was to ride with Cai, holding baby Gwenllian between them. Morwena, Celeste and Elizabeth would each take two girls behind them on their mounts. Philip would ride with them and the other five men would accompany them. Catrin hoped Gwenllian would not wriggle too much; she was starting to toddle now and was an active little baby. They would take their time, riding slowly, keeping as far as possible to tree-covered areas.

Cai rushed back down from the mountain to the camp, feeling encouraged. He felt useful again now that he was taking action and hopeful that they would reach safety. He stopped for a moment to breathe in the fragrant air and flung his arms out wide. "We'll be back some day; we'll be back to our sacred land."

His voice was restrained although he wanted to shout the words loudly out into the silent mountain range. But the heights still responded with a soft echo, the Gods had heard him, the Gods would restore this land to the Welsh. Then, in the silence he thought he heard a rumble and he felt a vibration beneath his feet. He knelt and put his ear to the ground. Something was moving and it wasn't far away, about a mile he thought.

He stood up and saw Geraint and Idris, the two men-at-arms who had been following him, break into a run down the mountain path. He hastened on his way towards the camp, but the men were soon at his side.

"Cai, a huge force of men is coming this way."

"The Gods preserve us! Could you see who they were?"

"Higher up, I just caught a glimpse of men marching and I could see others on horses in front." Idris, the older of the two men, trembled as he spoke.

"They must be Edward's men. Crouch down, we may be visible here. I'll run back to camp. You two stay here until you can identify them, then run back as fast as you can, keeping low."

Cai ran, tripping over brambles and tufts of grass, his heart thumping loudly, sweat pouring down his face.

Dafydd saw him approaching the camp and ran to him. "What is it?"

"Men, marching this way; they must be Edward's, but they were too far away to see clearly. Geraint and Idris are keeping watch."

"I feared this. Cai, you must go now; the women are ready. We will split. I'll take Geraint and Idris, with Llywelyn and Owain. The other men are ready and can go with you now. Go, and may God help us all. Elizabeth, make haste to go with Cai and the children."

Cai shook his head. "How far we will get with the children and a baby I don't know. I should have left earlier and not dallied here."

"That is my fault I know, Cai, but please go now. Make for

16

the forest, keep under cover as much as possible, you know these lands well."

There was no time, no time to make further plans. Their lives were all in danger. Cai doubted that Edward's men would even spare the children.

The women were hurriedly getting onto their horses, hauling the children up behind them, instructing them to hold tight, faces taut with fear. Philip held Cai's horse while Catrin mounted, and then passed up baby Gwenllian. He handed the reins to Cai and then swung into the saddle of his own horse.

They were ready to go when Geraint appeared, running into camp and shouting, "Edward's men, at least a hundred of them, if not more."

Within a flash Dafydd and Llywelyn had mounted their horses. Owain, whose lively mare was treading the ground impatiently, vaulted onto her. Geraint, ribs still heaving from his run, grabbed the reins of the two remaining cobs just as Idris appeared on the edge of the camp.

Dafydd's party waited until Cai, Philip, the women and children and the six armed men had ridden off towards higher ground, heading for cover in the deep forest which lay ahead.

Cai cursed the bright summer sunshine that left their party totally exposed on the open ground of the mountain slopes. Sweat ran down their horses' necks and the children's faces were red with the heat. They had started at a canter to put as much distance as possible between them and the King's men, but they could not keep this pace up for long. Exchanging a nod of understanding, Philip and Cai slowed their horses to a trot, and once behind the first slope to a walk, this way to preserve their strength and lessen the noise of their passing.

Alternating between walking and trotting they paced themselves until they reached the forest where the dark shade beneath the tress provided some camouflage. There they slowed their progress to a brisk walk, their horses treading carefully over the rough ground with not a whicker of sound as if aware of their need to hide. The children were silent, tensely peering into the undergrowth looking for eyes everywhere.

Cai felt disorientated, confused, angry that he should be forced to go into hiding like this in his own homeland and not far from Garth Celyn where he had spent many happy times with his Prince. Now, so he was told, his Lord Llywelyn's head lay on a pole outside the Tower of London, and here they were all running for their lives. He may never see Dafydd again and the Principality was doomed.

After some time, baby Gwenllian whimpered and Morwena brought her horse alongside Cai's. "I should feed her."

Cai was shaken out of his morose thoughts. "We will rest for a while, and then when the sun gets lower we will ride again, keeping to the edge of the forest as far as we can."

They reined their horses in and dropped down from their saddles. Unused to riding, the girls' legs buckled as they landed. Cai felt deep pity for them. This was not the life they had been born to.

Morwena reached for Gwenllian to feed her, but she felt weak and had little milk to offer. She wiped tears away with her apron. "I have barely any milk left; the baby will not survive such long hours of travel. What are we to do now?"

Cai tried to keep the weariness from his voice. "Deeper in the mountain range there are people who will shelter us. We will be safe there, but we have at least a day's ride ahead. Morwena, you must have the food we have left to sustain you to produce some milk. The children must be our main concern now. I will go and talk with the other men. You rest now."

So the women tried to rest, but none could sleep. Catrin wandered towards the place where the men sat and the horses grazed. "At least the horses can eat," she mumbled enviously.

Philip glanced at her sympathetically. "We can't risk hunting or lighting fires, Catrin fach, the men are too close. No doubt by now they have found our old camp, we had little time to cover our tracks."

Cai got his feet. "Someone must have betrayed us. Those men knew exactly where to find us. Idris said they were marching in line with purpose, not searching or scanning the land. I think we must prepare to carry on. When night falls I'm certain those men will not enter the forest. Courage, Catrin, have courage." Cai touched her hand as he spoke. He felt responsible that the women had been put in such a dangerous situation and could not help but admire their bravery.

"Philip, will you lead the horses? I will signal you the way from the rear so that I can best cover our tracks."

And so the last faithful defendants of Cymru trailed through the thick forest. Only the quiet squeak of stirrup on leather, a murmur from Gwenllian or the crackling of branches beneath their feet broke into the tense silence.

Cai with his exceptional hearing could hear distance voices, but he could not tell how far away they were. He knew distance and sound could be very deceptive in these mountain ranges. If there were a hundred men, then it would not be quiet until they slept. Hopefully by then their party would be far enough away not to be heard themselves. He prayed that a wolf or any nocturnal animal would not spook the horses. Their lives depended on it. Taking up the rear, Cai flicked back any branches that had been disturbed by their passage and brushed a leafy stick across the grassy patches to cover their tracks as best as he could. He worried that even he could be lost in this vast forest. They were not travelling in the direction he had hoped to go, towards his kin. From the camp he had planned out a different route, but now they would have to take their chances.

When the last light of day had died, Philip called the group to a halt in a small clearing. "We'll rest here for a while, then I will take two men to see exactly where we are."

The women, weary and shivery, collapsed onto the ground. Catrin took baby Gwenllian from Morwena so that she could rest. Luckily, the babe had slept for the last part of their journey, but Catrin knew she would be hungry when she awoke.

Exhausted, they managed to get some sleep before Gwenllian's cries disturbed them. Celeste got up in a panic, jolted from a disturbing dream.

"It was only a dream, only a dream," she assured the men who stood guard over them.

"Please be calm, Celeste." Cai rushed over to comfort her. "But dream or not, I feel we must move from this place now."

"I must feed the baby," Morwena insisted.

"Can she not be weaned now?" Philip asked briskly as he walked back into the clearing.

"And what are we to wean her on, pray?" Catrin snapped. "We have no food left at all, except a few pieces of dry bread."

What a pitiful situation they were in. Cai knew that they could not linger here for long. A full moon had risen while they slept and when the new day broke Edward's men would be marching. Perhaps they would encircle the forest, ready to capture them at any exit. Or had they followed Dafydd's tracks and would therefore leave them alone for now?

Cai turned to Philip. He looked scarcely less desperate than himself. "What did you see, Philip?"

"The forest edge is only a short walk away and then there is open land to a steep rocky path that leads to a forest further up. If we could reach that, we could breathe for another day. I spied a few scouts on foot, easily cut down, I would say."

"Philip, it's too risky to attempt to take the girls to the nunnery right now. We must go up and then across and seek sanctuary with my people. We have no choice now."

"You're right, Cai. If we are ambushed, you must ride on as fast as you all can. My men and I will hold Edward's men back as best we are able."

"Day or night, Philip, which is the safest time to cross the open path? Darkness would be better, but the track is dangerous with children and horses. Sounds travel further at night too."

"I think we should cross just before midnight. We will have to be as quiet as possible and take a chance."

It was not much of a strategy, but it was all they could do. Cai knew that Dafydd had gone a different way to try and divert attention away from them all, not because he was trying to save himself. Dafydd would fight to the death; he knew that, whatever he was, he was no coward.

Sometimes the mountains could be cruel. Even in the daytime at midsummer a burst of sunshine could be quickly obscured by a creeping damp mist, fooling the unwary traveller. But the group of desperate fugitives which crossed the open mountain path on horseback were glad of the night mist which shrouded them and veiled the moon.

Cai and Catrin led the train of horses across the uneven mountain terrain. Catrin held Gwenllian tightly under her damp and dirty cloak. Some of the younger girls whimpered. Elizabeth soothed little Gwladys. Cai was proud of them. Gwladys, together with Gwenllian, Llywelyn and young Owain, were heirs to the Principality and even if Dafydd was captured, one of them, one day, may reclaim this land again. That hope would never leave him.

He saw the steep rocky path ahead. If they could reach the forest above safely, they could rest until the next night. The moon, while it was up, would give them some light. They would follow a higher route deeper into the Eryri mountains to reach his kin. He imagined the warm welcome they would receive. They would be safe, for only a handful of people knew the whereabouts of the descendants of the Druids of Eryri.

Cai's thoughts were callously cut short as he heard the thud of horses' hooves heading towards them. He looked around in panic. Had he not been paying enough attention or had Edward's men crept up very carefully until they were near? He could not see through the mist and prayed that they too would not be seen, but then, as if the Gods were against them, the mist began to clear.

Cai jumped from the horse. "Go, Catrin, to the path, go!"

The company scattered. Two of the horses reared, throwing off Morwena, Celeste and several of the children. Cai was suddenly aware of ten or more men on horseback upon them. They seemed to have come from nowhere. He pulled out his knife, but it was no match for the English sword and mace. He saw Philip bravely trying to fight off three men, and then a blow struck his own head. He fell to the ground, his vision fading. He heard the screams of women, the yelling of the men, a loud shriek above him. Then all was black.

CHAPTER 3

Sempringham Priory, Lincolnshire
February 1300

Wencilian stirred slowly as the bell rang for Matins. Shivering, she quickly grabbed her tunic, scapular and headdress, slipping her feet into cold sandals. There was no time to put on the woollen stockings. Dazed and in a dream-like state, she slipped from her cell door into the line of nuns who were making their way silently along the cloisters to the night stairs which led to the church.

This was the service she hated the most. It was in the depth of the night and it disturbed her deepest sleep and dreams. The cold wrapped around her legs, creeping into her whole body as she made her way into the north end of the church. The only sounds were the shuffling of the nuns' feet and the heavier tread of the monks on the other side. They were like ghosts which she rarely saw but always heard on the other side of the wall which divided the church. In the semi darkness, the altar candles flickered and the few candles scattered around the church burned low, like the flame of life at this hour.

She had not completely roused herself from her sleep. In an almost semi-conscious state she was aware of the voice of Father Roger reciting prayers beyond the wall, while she relived the sequence of her dream, a dream she had had many times before. It was always the same, she saw a full moon in the night sky; she heard the thud of hoofs as a figure held her tight, tight against a hard body. Her whole being shook and vibrated, although she could not see her body, and then came the piercing screech of what seemed like a demon sweeping above her. Each time the dream came she would wake cold and trembling.

She could not understand why these images haunted her, for she had no memory of any life beyond this priory. Even memories of her early years here were blurred. She only knew that she came to this place when she was not much more than a year old. That much she had been told and no more, no details about whom her family were or why she was left here. Sempringham Priory, imposed upon the bleak fenlands of eastern England, was the only home she knew. They called her 'Wencilian', and since taking her vows she was known as 'Sister Wencilian'.

As the only child in such a large array of tall towers, arches and cloisters, she had loved to explore. When she could sneak away from the Sisters, she would run through the convent gardens with her imaginary friends, having adventures. Sometimes she would creep into the monastery, seemingly unnoticed by the monks going about their daily business. She would seek out the kindly Brother John, the cellarer, who would find her some bread and honey. Her guardian, Marie, would rarely scold her. She adored Marie, whom she clung to at night, who would soothe her and stroke her softly, as a mother would with her child. Marie was a lay sister though, her nursemaid, not her mother, and one day when Wencilian was twelve Marie was separated from her and returned to her duties as a lay sister. Then it was Marie who clung to her crying. She had been her constant guardian for eleven years. When they had been alone in the small room they shared, Marie would sometimes sing to her, although singing was forbidden for the nuns. Wencilian sorely missed her and her songs.

With Marie's absence, Wencilian's childhood came to an abrupt end. It was time for her to join the novices, for the more serious training to begin. On the day that Marie went, Sister Agnes had pulled Wencilian away from her and said with a voice as sharp as a butcher's knife, "You won't be needing her any more. You will be Bride of Christ soon and your life will be spent in devotion to Him."

These words had hit her like the hard whack of a cudgel. She did not want to be a Bride of Christ, but knew that any protest would be to no avail. And after that day her life changed. The stark reality of her existence began to increase, like the light of a new day beginning with the first glimmers at dawn. Then, when the light of the day reaches its zenith, darkness must descend, and so after a while she was plunged into that darkness, confused about her existence, angry at what had been stolen from her. Wencilian was turning into a woman, a woman with no past, no history, no family and a strange name.

Now she was in her eighteenth year and her footsteps paced along the cloisters and the paths of the Priory to the same obedient rhythm every day, but her mind and spirit were restless, and her feelings, well, they were well guarded, well hidden. The rhythm of the daily life within the Priory was all she had ever known, constant, enduring. Her yearning for any adventure was safely encased in her imagination.

While her life as a novice nun unfolded there was barely time to grieve the loss of her childhood, if a childhood it had ever been. The days were full of tasks, services and learning. The endless repetition of the psalter, hymns and canticles left her too tired for any play or much rest. No longer was she excused Matins to sleep in the deepest night. Now she had responsibilities. When Marie was taken away, her hair was cut from her head by Sister Agnes. As her lovely golden hair fell to the ground, she felt her life being ripped away from her and she had blamed Sister Agnes for this over the past six years. Sister Agnes was only doing her duty, but she did it with relish and without any compassion. Why, Wencilian wondered, had no one taken her away, why did her family not contact her? She could only assume that she was unwanted or her family were all dead, but she never let go of a tiny thread of hope. The few times she had dared to ask the Prioress, she had been given the same answer, delivered with an awkward smile. "I'm sorry I can't tell you any more, Wencilian. It seems that you were brought here as a young babe; that is all I know."

The Prioress Elizabeth had been in charge since Wencilian

was four years old. Her memories of that time were few and she barely recollected the Prioress Priscilla, who had preceded her. The Reverend Mother Elizabeth was not ever unkind to Wencilian, or in fact to anyone, but she had to maintain order and it was no small undertaking to run a convent of over two hundred women. A good business woman, sharp and organised, was how Elizabeth liked to think of herself. The two prioresses who shared the responsibility of the day to day running of the priory, Sister Agnes and Sister Marie Clare, mostly deferred to her for important decisions as they respected her good judgment. At the end of the day however, it was Father Roger, the Prior of Sempringham, who assumed overall responsibility, or at least thought he did. As Mother Elizabeth always maintained, what did he know of the daily administration of the convent? He was far more concerned with the outside world and the comings and goings of various dignitaries, not to mention unruly priests and canons.

At the age of roughly seventeen, Wencilian had taken her final vows. She was a bit younger than most, due to her years spent in the Priory. As that time drew near, Wencilian prayed that someone would come to claim her. Maybe a mother, father or a brother, who had been seeking for her since she was an abandoned baby, would hammer on the convent doors demanding to be let in to take her home to her family, whoever they may be. But no knock had come and the days went on.

Several weeks after Wencilian and her fellow novices' final vows had been taken, the Prioress Elizabeth had addressed all the new nuns in the chapter house meeting, reminding them of their responsibilities and designating tasks to each one. Wencilian was pleased that she was to be sent to the infirmary, where she had helped out on occasions before she took her vows. At times she had enjoyed helping the infirmarian. Although she secretly thought that Sister Beatrice was sour and embittered and slightly resembled one of the Priory sows in full gestation, she had learnt a lot from her and the patients about healing. It was one place where she felt really useful.

At the end of the meeting, the Prioress ushered Wencilian into a corner of the room. "I would like you to return to your room, the one you used to share with Marie. As a Sister with responsibilities, having your own cell would be more fitting. I know that you were fond of that room and it is free again now since, well, since dear Sister Francis passed away."

"Well, thank you, Mother, I would welcome the solitude for my devotions." Wencilian always had the right words for her Prioress that seemed to please her. Nodding her head in a stoic manner, she remained calm but she felt elated. For so long now she had craved some privacy and peace. Although she had enjoyed sleeping in the dormitory with the novices, at times she felt worn down by their childishness and their troubles. Having never had the company of other children growing up, she felt set apart from them. Many had come from good families and would talk about them when they had the chance. Wencilian knew nothing of family life and could not share experiences with them. She would listen though, eagerly soaking up all the details and sometimes sharing in the pain they suffered at being separated from their loved ones. The worst had been having to listen to some of them crying at night, trying to smoother their sobs under the blanket. Her pain was different. Hers was a deep emptiness which had always been with her; it wasn't raw like theirs.

Many women of different ages and backgrounds though also came to this place. Several widows and older ladies had their own rooms. Wencilian knew some of them, having been in the Priory practically all her life. But they were not seen very often, only appearing at certain masses. Wencilian guessed that these ladies, or their families, deposited large sums of money into the Priory coffers every year and for that reason they were not strictly bound by all the Priory rules. Rebecca, a widow from Lincoln it was rumoured, made regular trips outside to the markets, escorted of course by a barrage of lay sisters. She returned with the most wonderful cloths of deep rich colours, ribbons, combs and other items. She once gave a silver comb to Wencilian, and each night to this day Wencilian would run it through her imaginary hair when she took off her cowl.

The lay sisters were a great source of solace to Wencilian. They worked hard at all the practical tasks, with a cheerfulness that some of the nuns never displayed. Most of them came from poor homes and were glad to receive the warm clothing and food which was given to them at the Priory. She had a special fondness for Mira, one of the lay sisters who worked in the kitchen, and she would seek her out whenever she had to collect meals for the infirmary. Mira's family made a poor living on the fenlands. She would sometimes tell Wencilian tales of her life before she joined the Priory and Wencilian would soak up every word, feeling both shocked and fascinated by details of what seemed an often brutal existence.

It was a cold February day and in the infirmary Sister Beatrice urged Wencilian to eat the noon day meal with the Sisters in the frater. "We are quiet now, you take your meal with the Sisters; I'm sure you will be glad to resume the contact, it's been so busy here just recently."

Wencilian was glad of the chance to see Mira and her two closest friends, Alice and Isobel. They were the only two women in the Priory she ever had personal conversations with, other than Mira, and their times together were always restricted.

Alice was perhaps her dearest friend. The two of them had taken vows at the same time, and they shared from that day their deepest thoughts and feelings and a little frivolity, whenever they could, as this sort of friendship was not encouraged.

Isobel, a lay sister, always cheered Wencilian up when she brought linen to the infirmary.

While the infirmary duties often prevented Wencilian and Sister Beatrice from taking meals with the other Sisters, they also prevented them from attending all the daily services, which Wencilian found a relief rather than a disappointment.

During lunch in the frater, the Lectrix would read a suitable passage as an accompaniment to the meal. Today it was taken from the gospel of St John, but Wencilian was not listening to the words. As she ate, she thought of Brother John, dear Brother

John, who now must be getting quite elderly. Although it was possibly two years or more since she had actually spoken to him, he was now the Almoner, so she had heard.

Suddenly, the soft murmuring in the room had ceased and the Sisters were rising to file to the church for the service of Sext. Wencilian hung on to the end of the line, dawdling a little behind the others, when she noticed Mira, who was sweeping the floor nearby, clutch her stomach and bend over in pain. Wencilian rushed to steady her and placed a protective hand on her belly. She felt her belly hard and rounder than normal under her hand, but Mira stood up tall and brushed her hand away and when Wencilian looked into her eyes she saw fear and panic.

"What is it? What's wrong, are you sick?"

"I must talk to you, but not here."

"The bell rings for Sext and I must go, but the Sisters will be at rest for a while afterwards. Can you meet me? Gather these old rushes together and take them to the garden; we can talk then."

"I'll try, Wencilian, I'll try."

After the noon service, when most of the Sisters were retired for the hour before resuming their duties, Wencilian slipped into the kitchen garden. All seemed quiet and she had only waited a few minutes before Mira appeared, carrying rushes in her tabard.

"Here, let me help you, Mira."

They walked carefully, both carrying the rushes in their tabards, looking over their shoulders to be sure no one was following. As they shook the rushes onto a pile in the corner of the herb garden, Wencilian suddenly had a realisation. A baby grew in a woman's stomach. She had seen several pregnant women coming to sell wares at the kitchen doors, she had seen a statue of the Virgin Mother with child. She knew that when the curses came a girl became a woman and was able to bear a child. What had never been explained to her properly was how the act between men and woman created the child. She had used to giggle about it with the other novices, who even at their young ages seemed so much more worldly. Wencilian laughed with them, but felt ashamed at her own lack of knowledge. She felt so old sometimes, yet so young in the ways of the outside world.

"I think I am with child … well, I'm sure," Mira blurted out.

Wencilian was never lost for words, but she hesitated, she was not sure how to react at all. Her instinct then was to fire a barrage of questions at Mira, but taking one look at her terrified face, she just drew her close to her and hugged her.

"What will happen to me?" continued Mira. "You know what they do to nuns who are pregnant, it's unspeakable. You know the story the Sisters love to tell about the nun of Watton and the dreadful punishment she received."

"And I'm sure that in the telling it has been embellished. That was a long time ago, and you are a lay sister, they wouldn't be as harsh. You have your family outside the Priory."

"My family outside the Priory now consists of my uncle, he would surely banish me, my brothers, who would kill E … Eric if they knew, and my old aunt who is losing her mind," Mira sobbed as she clung to Wencilian.

"Well, Eric must marry you."

"My uncle would never agree, and Eric is apprenticed to a silversmith in Lincoln, his family have hopes for him to marry the silversmith's daughter, although that will never happen. Anyway, I would still need permission from the Prioress and they would know about the baby and consider it a grave sin."

Wencilian knew she was right and all that she could think at this tense, unexpected moment was that Mira had two options; both were extremely risky and one she could not seriously contemplate. Hearing footsteps coming from the path to the kitchen, she released Mira quickly.

"Someone is coming. We must talk later. Can you get to my cell after Compline? No, don't put yourself at risk, I will seek you out. Go, and don't speak to anyone else about this for now."

Wencilian felt increasingly frustrated and worried. She prayed that her conversation with Mira had not been overheard, especially by the young nun who had walked down the path, Sister Ignatius, whom she knew to be ambitious and the sort who would gloat in reporting any misdemeanour to Mother Elizabeth.

As she went about her daily chores, Wencilian searched the faces of all the Sisters, but not one showed any inkling of knowing her guilty secret. Equally, there was no one she could talk to or ask for advice without arousing suspicion. Her instinct told her not to reveal this secret, even to Alice, at the moment. Isobel, however, might be the one to help. Tough, practical Isobel would know what to do and as a lay sister had contacts on the outside. Isobel mostly helped in the laundry room, so she would need some reason to meet her. Moving her meagre belongings into her old cell might be the perfect excuse. She would fetch clean linen for her pallet and take her sheepskins to be thoroughly cleaned, if she could arrange that before Mother Elizabeth had a chance to.

Mother Elizabeth had found it an acceptable idea for Isobel to help Wencilian clean the cell and make her comfortable and it was an excellent opportunity for them to discuss the urgent matter. Isobel was surprised that Wencilian was not shocked by Mira's news, but seemed to take a very practical approach to it.

Isobel thought the best answer was to take the course that her mother had at times. "Pennyroyal, mix it in vinegar, water and snakeweed, if you can get some, but that doesn't usually flower till May. You are in the infirmary; you could do it, Wencilian."

"God in Heaven! I don't know if I could be responsible for that."

"Well, the only other option is to get her away. She needs to speak to this Eric. She must tell Mother Elizabeth that her aunt is ill and she needs to visit."

"I don't think she would be allowed to go on her own."

"The quicker something can be done, the better. It's too risky to wait."

"Well, it's sad to say, Wencilian, but the pennyroyal may be the best option."

"Then," interrupted Wencilian, "she may end up in the infirmary and it would be more obvious, as well as being dangerous for her, not to mention the sin on her conscience."

"I wouldn't worry about the sin, though I suppose you are

right. Leave it to me, I will find a way to get word to Eric and hope that he will support her and something can be done. Now I must go or I will be missed."

It was a relief for Wencilian to be back in the cell she had shared before with Marie. It was a cold February and probably the bleakest month of that winter so far. The cell was damp, and even in the summer months heat barely penetrated these thick priory walls. Excused from infirmary duties until after the next service of Nones, Wencilian wrapped her sheepskin cloak around her and sat for a while on her pallet. The straw mattress was spiky and uncomfortable, but she could enjoy some precious moments alone, moments to remember her early years in this cell with Marie, the life that had seemed safe and more carefree. Poor Marie had passed away only a year after they were separated, a year after her childhood was taken.

That time had passed. Now she was a woman and in danger of being a slave to her conscience and a servant, not only to God, but to the needs of the convent and those who relied on her. She worried for Mira and the danger she was in, but the thought of the new life inside her excited her and she wondered if she would ever feel a new life stirring within herself. While she was locked away from the world here in this place, she knew that would never come to pass.

A shriek, followed by a tapping sound jolted her out of her nostalgia. Lifting the sheepskin cover from the bars of her cell window, she stared into the round, grey, piercing eyes of a barn owl that was perched on the narrow ledge outside. The owl bent his head to let her stroke his fluffy neck.

"Boden, my dear friend, it's a long time since I've seen you, I thought you had deserted me, or suffered some injury, or worse. How is it you always come to me when I feel troubled?"

He must be old now, she mused. Years ago Brother John had told her the tale of when he found an injured owl, or rather the owl found him. It was soon after he had heard of a baby being admitted to the convent, he found the owl on the ground, near to death. Being the cellarer at the time, he took the owl into his office and nursed him. The Priory was a popular nesting site for barn owls, so Brother John was familiar with their habits. He had surmised that this was a young owl, one that had seemed exhausted from flight. The owl became tame in Brother John's care and bird and monk developed quite a bond. As the owl recovered, Brother John took him to the blacksmith where his foot was ringed so that he would be recognised.

It was the owl who cemented the friendship between Wencilian and Brother John and he had remained a frequent visitor to Brother John's rooms. When Wencilian first set eyes on the creature she was fascinated and learnt to feed him with her own hands. It took them a while though to learn that their owl was not a he, but a she, when several years later she proudly presented them with three little owlets. Only one survived. Wencilian nursed him and they named him 'Boden'. His mother had come to this place at the same time as Wencilian, but from where they both came, no one knew.

Boden was free to come and go, unlike Wencilian. Tamed though he was, at heart he would always be a wild creature. She watched him fly off again in freedom, his large wings spread barely making a sound, iridescent against the dark clouds of the sky. She lay down and rolled into her sheepskin cover, time to sleep, time to dream for a few hours before the bell summoned her.

Wencilian slipped again into the silent line of Sisters who filed out of the long church. She passed the shrine of St Gilbert that stood astride the wall between the canons' and nuns' chancels. Tomorrow was the feast of St Gilbert, the founder of their order, and she would be reminded of how he had provided sanctuary for women in a brutal and lawless age. She would be told that Gilbert of Sempringham was a model of piety, learning and selfless endeavour, and how all the people revered and loved him as a saint of God. She wondered what he must have been like as a man. Wencilian had only seen a few men in her life, the priests who administered the sacraments, the few who came to the infirmary, and Brother John.

Brother John had been like a father to her, although she only saw him now on rare occasions and those were precious times. She wondered if his feet shuffled along the other side of the wall with all the Brothers on this night, the ghostly footsteps of men she heard, but never saw, at every service of every day.

CHAPTER 4

Ynys Môn (Anglesey)
February 1300

The sea lapped soothingly upon the shore as Cai stepped off the ferry. His heart though was far from soothed when he stood before the castle. He looked up at the imposing structure, incomplete though it was, jutting out into the southerly end of the town he had known as 'Llanfaes'. The world had changed since Cai had last ventured onto Ynys Môn. Edward had taken control of the island since the death of his Lord and dear friend, Prince Llywelyn, and the construction before him was a testament to that.

Although he had seen the outline of the castle from the other side of the Menai Strait, to stand before it now was not only intimidating, but soul destroying. The only words in his native language he could hear came from the ferrymen. Around him a medley of French, English and Anglo-Norman dialects invaded his senses while soldiers, carters, masons and the new population went about their business.

He was dressed now as a Franciscan Brother in a simple grey tunic and no one stopped or questioned him, assuming him to be a simple friar returning to his monastery. He needed to gather his courage and remain inconspicuous. Seventeen years he had been hidden away and was older and thinner. It was improbable that anyone would recognise him, but he could not take any chances. Walking along the coast he could see Llanfaes

Friary where he intended to lodge for several nights.

He turned towards the Friary with a sinking heart. Only one thought consoled him, Edward I may have changed the landscape and the population, but he would never change the spirit of the Isle; that would endure forever.

The Brother who admitted him eyed him warily, noticing his shabby attire, his musical instruments tied together with old cloth and what he assumed to be a small bundle of meagre belongings. He was young and would obviously not know Cai as the bard and confidante of their Prince. Cai just hoped that Father William, the Guardian of the Friary, whom he and his Prince knew so well, was still there.

"Please take me to the Father, Brother. I can assure you he will welcome me. I just require lodgings for a few nights."

Father William did indeed welcome him after a few moments of uncertainty. "Cai, I could barely recognise you, but that voice is unmistakeable. How good it is to see you. What brings you here and in those monk's robes after these many years? I was not aware that you had joined our order."

"It is perhaps a good thing that I am not immediately recognisable, Father. As to what brings me here, that will take me a while to explain to you." Cai ignored Father William's last remark.

"Forgive me. Come and take some refreshment and you can explain at your leisure."

"Thank you, Father, I could certainly take some ale; I have walked for days."

Father William was an ally in a dangerous world which encroached gradually to the doors of the Friary. He would surely be eager for any news of the outside world. Cai expected many more questions.

"None of the Brothers venture very far from the Friary at the moment, unless it is unavoidable," Father William explained over a welcome cup of warm ale. "We feel threatened. Edward knows where our loyalties lie. They were and always will be with our patron, our Prince, God rest his soul." Father William crossed himself. "Edward has destroyed Llanfaes, removed all the local people, depriving them of their livelihood to install his English landlords on their land. He promises them all sorts, but we know those promises are hollow."

"They will be that, no doubt, but I fear that at the moment we are powerless. We will have hope, our time will come again. You and your Brothers will be safe here; he wouldn't dare attack a house of God. It is in his interest now to keep this friary thriving surely?"

"I wish I shared your optimism, Cai, or should I call you 'Brother Cai'? I know you are a wise man, but a little too trusting at times. The Welsh have been uprooted in more ways than one. Anyway, what brings you here after so long? It must be nearly eighteen years since you and our dear Prince, God bless his soul, paid us a visit."

Cai launched into his story. He found it painful; he had not discussed it with anyone except Seren and Cynan, the High Priestess and Priest of the Mountain Grove, the place where he had dwelt for the past seventeen years. It was a relief to talk about it, but he was careful about what he revealed to Father William.

"I went back home to my people. I was taking Llywelyn's daughter, the baby Gwenllian, and her women to safety, but I failed, failed in my duty and my promise."

Cai thought of the last time he had seen Celeste, Catrin, Morwena and the baby Gwenllian, a memory that kept resurfacing in his mind over all these years, no matter how hard he tried to push it away. He knew nothing of what had happened to any of them.

"Several months after the slaughter of my Lord, we left Abergwyngregyn to stay in Denbigh, but it wasn't long before we were in danger there. Dafydd moved us all to Castell y Bere, but as you no doubt know, the castle was eventually taken. Several weeks before that happened, a small party of us left to make for a safe haven in the mountains. I should have gone long before, but Dafydd was against it. We made a camp at Nanhysglain, but the camp wasn't safe for long and when we ran again into the forest, our progress was slow with the children.

Eventually, we were ambushed.

"I must have been left for dead. I have no memory of that at all. I awoke dazed and confused, with only the corpses of several men-at-arms for company in the drizzling mountain mist. Wandering alone, I eventually found sanctuary with my kin and settled to a life with them, a hard life after my time at court. It was a life in which you could imagine that no other world existed.

"I will tell you more another day, Father, but first I have an important matter to discuss – the matter of finding the Princess Gwenllian."

Father William looked confused. "Yes, I had heard rumours, but many rumours have circulated in these dark times. She was taken by the King's men I believe, but no one seems to know where, or indeed if, she is still alive."

"That is what I intend to find out. I hope you may help me, Father."

"I don't know what I can do, Cai."

"You have contacts. There are certain people concerned about her welfare who believe she is not in the tower. If she is alive, she could be imprisoned somewhere else, but it is not an impossibility that she is in a convent somewhere."

"If, and that is a big if, she is in a convent, you would not get anywhere near her."

"But Father, we would know she still lives."

"Who else is involved in this? I will not be party to any plots or subterfuge. You know our position here."

"I can assure you there are no plots and I will not involve you in any way. I just seek some information for my peace of mind."

Father William hesitated. "As I said, not many of the Brothers are venturing far these days, but I will do what I can. I think it best though if on the morrow you make your way to Penmon Priory and lodge there. Father Iorwerth will receive you, I'm sure. You will be safer there and it is near enough to send a message with some haste. But I will not let you go in that tatty dress; you will give us all a bad name."

"Thank you, Father." Cai smiled. "You have still retained your sense of humour."

The following morning was fresh and mild for February. Before Cai left Llanfaes Friary, he walked to the cemetery to pay his respects to dear Eleanor and to Llywelyn's grandmother, Siwan, who was buried next to her. A solitary bunch of snowdrops grew between the graves.

Cai knelt on the sodden ground. 'Times are changing, Eleanor, I don't know if I will ever be back this way. I swear I will find your daughter, Gwenllian, if it is the last thing I do on this earth. If she lives, if she is imprisoned, even if I cannot free her, then I will tell her somehow of her heritage, of her brave and beautiful mother and how her father fought to the bitter end for his people, for his land, for her.'

It was a sombre walk to Penmon, and tiring. Cai had been offered a comfortable bed at the Friary, but had been obliged to attend Compline, after which he sat up until Matins with Father William. There had been much to talk about – the old days, the times he had visited the Friary with the Prince, the battles, the death of Eleanor and the birth of Gwenllian.

Penmon Priory
The Brothers at Penmon Priory kept their own council and their own secrets, and Cai, although pleased to wait there, hoped it would not be for too long. He felt a sense of urgency now that he had decided to pursue this mission. Too long he had hidden away in the mountains of Eryri with his kin who kept in the mountains protected from Christian zealots who would persecute them. Very few knew how to find them. The old hill folk and the farmers who surrounded them would protect them even if it cost them their own lives. But there were not many old hill folk left now; many had left the mountains, tempted by the easier life near the sea or on the lower farmlands. Of these, some had infiltrated into the Anglo-Norman society in an attempt to preserve the old ways and bring comfort to the people of Cymru who kept the ancient ways.

Cai was now returning to a world which had much changed

during the seventeen years he had been away. The wise folk had reminded him that hatred would only eat at his soul and that he should not bear malice to those who were only pawns in the game. For Cai it was hard not to hate and almost impossible to forgive, even seventeen years later. The death of his Prince, the subjugation of his people and the demise of society as he knew it, had been, and still was, devastating. But life had to go on, he was stronger now and determined to complete what he had started years before.

Life was busy at Penmon Priory, but simple, and even though not luxurious, the Brothers ate well and the rules were not as strict as he had been led to believe. He shared in their tasks and often entertained the Brothers with a song or two after their supper. He knew he would have to be patient and he was grateful for his time at the Priory. It had given him a chance to re-adjust to a decidedly more hectic life than he had experienced in the mountains of Eryri, but he was getting restless and needed to concentrate on his mission. He was expected at Cwmhir Abbey, in Powys, by mid-April, Easter time.

He had been content while there in Penmon, and although restless for news, had been lulled into a sense of timelessness. February had passed already, he realised, as he took a walk away from the confines of the Priory along the beach early one morning after the service of Prime. Enjoying the solitude he rested for a while on the stretch of golden sand which faced across the Menai Strait. From there he could see the outline of Abergwyngregyn where nearly eighteen years ago he had made that promise to Llywelyn. King Edward had taken over the Court there now and he could only imagine that all traces of the life he knew had been erased. He averted his eyes from across the water for fear of stirring memories that were still too painful.

A noise behind him startled him. He was relieved to see it was only Moses, the Priory sheep dog, who had followed him. Moses nuzzled up next to him, and no sooner had he raised his head than a messenger came running up, a young novice, Brother Gwynwyn, waving his arms and shouting, "Brother Cai, the Prior wishes to see you. There is some news."

Cai felt a lurch of excitement, expectation and fear in his chest. He stood up and wobbled a little.

"Are you well, Brother? Please lean on me. I hope it is not bad news you were expecting."

Cai looked up at the young novice, who was expressing genuine concern. He could tell from his eyes that he knew more than he would admit.

"I am fine, thank you, but we will walk back together, all three of us. Come on, Moses, or you will be in trouble for neglecting your duties."

The Prior was waiting for him in his small chamber above the refectory. Always one for his comforts, Prior Iorwerth had chosen the warmest room in the building with easy access to food and drink, although he complained it could be noisy at times when all the Brothers were gathered there – the rule of silence during meals was not strictly observed.

"Please, Brother Cai, be seated." The Prior sat opposite him at the small table and leaned over, lowering his voice.

"I have received news from Llanfaes that the young lady, indeed the Princess of our beloved land, of whom we all seek news, could, and I stress, could, be enclosed within the walls of a Gilbertine priory many miles from here. It is a priory known as Sempringham, in eastern England."

"Oh, thanks to God she is alive as we believed, but you say you are not sure if it is her."

The glimmer of hope was enough to shake Cai to the core. So many years had passed since he had last seen her as a small baby, so many years and he had done nothing, nothing to find her.

"We think that she may have been taken there as a young child, or babe even. Only a few, if any, there would know her true identity, and nearly eighteen years have passed. There is no one who could swear to recognise her as Gwenllian, our lost Princess." The Prior sighed. "She may not even know her true name. In fact, that is most likely the case, as records do not show anyone of that name at the Priory."

"How did they …?" Cai started.

But the Prior continued, "It is best that you don't ask too many questions, but according to Father William, the information about the Priory records is accurate. Please hear me out. He writes here that it is known roughly the date that she was taken by the King, as you can verify yourself, Brother."

Father Iorwerth continued, passing over the letter to Cai, "It seems to have been discovered that around that time a child was registered at Sempringham Priory under the name of Wencilian. It is a most unusual practice for a Prioress to admit such a young child, and the name, surely the name is very similar to, or a distortion of, Gwenllian?

"We have since also discovered that Sempringham Priory receives a sum per year from the King's chancellor for her keep. Now, what reason would there be for a King to offer that amount of money for a girl child, unless she was a threat to him or she was related to him?"

Cai could remain silent no longer. "Well, Gwenllian is both. But of course, if she were just a relative, why not take her into the royal household? My God, at least Edward had the heart not to kill her and let her live, yet for the poor life she has she may as well be dead, cut off from her true existence. Sorry," Cai added, "I did not intend to insult the Church, Father."

Father Iorwerth ignored Cai's last remark. "I have a report that this Wencilian, if she is our true Gwenllian, is still living and well cared for. The King must have had a pang of conscience to spare her, if only for the memory of her mother, his cousin Eleanor, but he has made sure that she will not produce any children of her own."

Cai slumped back into the chair, hope and despair both clouded around him and in the cloud he saw the face of Eleanor, whom cruel fate had torn from the bosom of her Lord and her country in her prime, as little Gwenllian, just born, lay across her breast.

"I shall go there and find her, although I have little knowledge of that part of England and even less of the Gilbertines. I shall bring her back to her country."

Father Iorwerth faced him over the table. "To even get near

her would be very difficult, if not impossible. I don't know much about the Gilbertines either, but I believe it is a strict order and the women are never seen."

Cai wrestled with his thoughts. How could the Prior suggest they do nothing now that they were getting close to the truth? Cai knew a place where she could hide, a place where she would belong.

It was too dangerous to reveal his true thoughts, even to those he trusted. He had not told Father William or Father Iorwerth the whole truth, but there was no other way. He was travelling as a Christian Brother, and in this he was already engaged in deception. Assuming this identity was a relief, it was simple and straightforward, placing him in a position to seek shelter and refuge as a Brother of the established Church which had become such a powerful political force. He would have no trouble passing as a man of the Church. He had spent many years in a Christian court; he was learned and spoke Latin, French and his native Cymraeg. He was not a respected bard of the court any more, as the Court didn't exist. He had little to lose and his main objective was to find his little Princess, who would now be a young woman. And how apt was her name. He thought back for a fleeting moment to when Llywelyn asked him to christen her 'Gwenllian'. Had he somehow sealed her fate?

"Cai, I sincerely hope you will not do anything rash. It may even be better if the poor girl knows nothing of the death and destruction brought down on her family. She can do nothing. Is it not kinder to let her live her life in peace? She may even have taken vows by now. Her life is with the Church."

Cai knew he was on shaky ground. "You may be right, Father, and it gives me great peace of mind to know that she may be safe, but to be totally sure I need to travel there and find out the complete truth. You have my word that I will not implicate you or your Brothers in any way."

"I will not stand in your way. As far as I am concerned the matter is over and this letter will be burnt."

"Father William must have trusted someone to seek this information."

"Well, Cai, I think all you can do is trust that it will never be spoken of again. I don't think there could be any proof."

"I am so grateful to you, Father."

The two men embraced, two faiths merging and understanding at that moment. Cai knew however that the moment would not last for long. Their differences ran too deep.

The Prior stood back and walked over to the window. "May you travel safely, my friend, and know there is always a place for you here."

Cai was eager to leave now, both from the room and the entire Priory, for he needed time to contemplate this incredible information. Travelling alone would give him time to think.

Two days later he was on the road with a pony from the Priory, supplies for a few days and some letters he had obtained from Father William to verify his identity as 'Brother Gregory from Llanfaes Friary'. He would need some safe places to stay on his route. Most of the time, he thought, he would sleep in the wild and keep low. The spring had been warm so far, so food would not be hard to find. He had been a bard in the court of Llywelyn and not the hardest of men, but his time in Eryri had taught him survival skills that were better than any military training he could have had.

He'd had no wish to discuss more with the Prior. He knew it would serve no further purpose and he could not tell him anything of what had been told to him whilst in his mountain sanctuary. In any case, none of it would be believed and the less the Prior knew, the better for his own safety and peace of mind.

The day was fresh and clear, it was the middle of March in the year of our Lord, 1300. Cai set out on a course which he thought may reunite him with a part of his past which he had thought lost. He took the path which led away from the coast and making his way slowly through the forest tracks, descended again towards the sea, hoping to catch the ferry back across the Menai Strait before darkness fell. Once across, he would blend into the mountain pass where he felt at home, and with the blessing of the Gods, would travel safely.

Father Iorwerth poured himself another goblet of his finest mead, although he felt he had already had too many and it was not quite noon. He was sad to see Cai leave. He had become quite fond of him and enjoyed his songs and poems, which had brightened up many a dreary supper time. But he thought he was a fool and did not share his optimism. He also felt that he himself was a fool for conspiring in such a ridiculous mission. Surely no good would come of it.

CHAPTER 5

Sempringham Priory
March 1300

Wencilian was helping in the infirmary when Sister Martha, the old apothecary, an elderly nun with few teeth and a rasping voice, came and caught her arm.

"Wencilian," she blurted, handing over a bunch of early marsh marigolds. "There has been a skirmish; well a bit more than that, outside the monastery gates."

"What happened?"

"Two beggars were knocking on the gates. Brother John had let them in and asked them to wait whilst the Brothers finished lunch in the frater. When he turned his back, they pounced on him, pushed him to the ground, ripped his rosary from his hands and took two gold coins from his purse."

"Make way, make way," shouted a tall thin monk, who was helping two others carry in the injured man. "Brother John is hurt. Sister, prepare a bed for him," he barked at Wencilian.

The few monks she had ever spoken to all assumed a superior attitude, apart of course from dear Brother John, who was at that moment being placed on a nearby pallet. She was shocked to see that his head and face were bloodied and he was groaning incomprehensibly.

Sister Beatrice rushed over. "What's all the fuss? Oh, dear Lord, it's Brother John. You can't bring him in here, it's forbidden. Why is he not with the Brothers?"

"Their section of the infirmary is full and it's on the orders of Father Roger," replied the tall monk.

"That has never happened before. Well, you can't linger here, it's not appropriate. We have a full room of women. Put him in the back, in my sleeping quarters, for now."

Sister Beatrice turned to Wencilian, "I have never heard of such a thing in all my years. What happened?"

"I don't know exactly. He was attacked from behind, so Sister Martha said. He breathes, but will not wake up."

Wencilian shivered. How she had longed to talk to him, for so long.

"Well, we must treat his wounds and keep him warm, then wait, just wait."

"Please let me tend him, Sister Beatrice," Wencilian pleaded, thinking of how kind Brother John had been to her as a child.

"You may dress his wounds, but it is not appropriate for you to be alone with him," Sister Beatrice replied, mistaking her eagerness as a keenness to learn. There is some angelica and moonwort ready mixed for a poultice in the still room; you can prepare that and then bring it in to my room. Perhaps a little pitch with vinegar will stem the bleeding on his head and keep the wounds clean."

Sister Francis, who had recently passed away, had been Sister Beatrice's main assistant, and as the infirmary was exceptionally busy at the moment, no one could have slipped into her role as easily as Wencilian. Wencilian thought it very opportune. She was anxious to be there when Brother John roused. He would surely be glad to see her and she would have a chance of contact with, or news from the outside world. The infirmary was also one of the few places in Sempringham Priory where she could think clearly. In the dispensing room she felt a calmness not even felt in the church during mass. There were no voices, no distractions and the pungent aromas of the herbs and spices awakened her senses. Her head was clear, away from the constant repetition of psalms and prayers. There was time for inspiration to come to her here. When Brother John's injuries were treated, she would meditate on what to do about Mira, although it did seem that Isobel was organising it well so far.

Since the brief talk she'd had with Isobel in her cell, Wencilian had trusted her to find a way to contact Eric. She didn't want Mira to consider aborting the baby. That would have been putting Mira at great risk and would be a sin with grave consequences for them both. The lesser sin would be for her to abscond with Eric, or marry him. Something had to be done soon, as her pregnancy would become obvious and she was scared for her. She felt sure that Our Lady would not condemn her though. After all, Our Lord and Holy Mother would not want a young girl to suffer for the crime of falling in love.

The bell rang for Sext, the midday service, and at that moment, Brother John opened his eyes. Wencilian joked to Sister Beatrice, "That was a true calling."

Sister Beatrice was not amused and screwed up her deeply wrinkled face. "I shall go to service. You had better stay with Brother John, Wencilian. The lay sisters will help you."

Relieved to have respite from Sister Beatrice, Wencilian could now be in charge and have a chance to talk to Brother John whilst the two lay sisters were busy seeing to the needs of other patients.

"Brother John, how are you feeling?"

"Where am I? Wencilian, is that you?"

"It is me and you are in the infirmary."

"Oh, Lord be praised that I should see you again after so long."

Taking his hand in hers, Wencilian spoke softly. "I too am so, so pleased to see you, but I wish it were not because you were forced here by two evil men."

"Ah, I remember now. Godless beggars, have they been caught?" Brother John felt for his purse, which had hung from the belt on his tunic, and started to panic.

"It's been taken, according to Sister Martha, but she did find a gold coin on the ground."

Brother John drifted again into sleep, his breathing heavy, his chest rattling. Wencilian wondered, since when had the almoner been handing out gold coins?

"I saw Boden last night, Brother John," she whispered. "He

came to my window. I haven't seen him for a long time. You know he is so tame that he lets me touch his talons and stroke his plumage."

Hearing this, Brother John turned his head to look at her and tried to speak, but his voice was faint. "Really, that's remarkable that he is still around here after all this time. He must be getting old now. But how are you, my dear Wencilian, are you happy?"

Wencilian clasped his hand. "Often I feel sad, but I don't really have anything to complain about. I am fed, I am well." As she looked down on him, Brother John had again fallen asleep, their hands still clasped together.

A few hours later Isobel arrived, bringing fresh linen. Pleased to see Wencilian heading to the dispensing room, she rushed to her side whilst Sister Beatrice was nursing an elderly nun. Brother John still slept.

"Have you any news?"

"There are people in the fens who will shelter Mira for a while. We need to get her away on the next full moon. It is risky, but a darker night could be treacherous in the swamps and we would be seen with fire torches. I have spoken to Mira."

"What about her lover, Eric, will he help her?"

"I have sent a message to him, and as yet have had no reply."

"How can she get out without being seen?

Isobel took Wencilian by her hand. "By the tunnel with us. You have spoken to me once of a tunnel and swore me to secrecy, do you remember? We need you to show us the tunnel and stand watch at the other end ... besides Mira will not go without you."

"But it's too dangerous for me. I want to help Mira, but it's dangerous."

"I will stay with you, there and back."

"I need to think about this."

"Well, there isn't much time to think, the moon is waxing and half way to full ... and now Sister Beatrice is coming." Isobel swept up the dirty linen into her arms and was gone in a flash.

Wencilian watched her disappear. Isobel was quick, nimble, confident and worldly, the ideal person to help Mira, but it seemed to Wencilian that everything was black and white in Isobel's world. She didn't ponder too long on a question or analyse her decisions once made. Her life had been hard before she entered the convent, one of fifteen children, ten of whom had died of disease or starvation. Isobel hadn't had many choices to ponder on.

"What are you staring at, Wencilian?" cut in Sister Beatrice. "There's plenty of work to be done."

"Yes, and it will be done in my own time," replied Wencilian calmly, silently pleased with herself that she could stand up to Sister Beatrice. The joy at seeing Brother John and Isobel's remarks had instilled in her a renewed strength. She had to be strong.

"Well, make sure it is. I will go and check on Brother John." Sister Beatrice disappeared into the drapes which separated her sleeping quarters from the back of the still room. A faint aroma of almond trailed behind her as her feet crunched on the meadowsweet strewn across the floor.

After Compline that evening the nuns retired as usual, but Wencilian found it impossible to sleep. In her drowsy state she was anxious yet excited. Even the recital of more prayers could not take her mind off the one time in her living memory that she had stood outside the tall imposing walls of her confinement.

That day, she had gone to market with Marie, having had special permission from the Prioress providing they had an escort of two older Sisters. What a wonderful medley of sounds, smells and people she had experienced that day; it was intoxicating. She had known nothing of the world and knew no one outside the Priory. The colour and the noise were overwhelming. Her eyes scanned the merchants behind their stalls and others parading along the cobbled square – the urchins and bedraggled women who crouched in doorways, curious eyes staring back at her. A young woman was feeding a child at her breast behind a stall selling linen and wool. She had looked up as Wencilian paused and for a moment their eyes met. Marie had kept her close to her, taking her arm and hurrying her along. That day had left her with many questions which she could not answer and would not dare to put to anyone else within the Priory.

Returning to the Priory grounds with Marie, she had absorbed the musty smells of the damp fenlands and the saltiness of the sea wind, feeling a little disappointed at the landscape, thinking it bleak and unwelcoming. The fields were dreary and flat and the clouds above murky and grey. She saw paths which weaved in and out of the misty reed beds and islands. Dim lights in the distance created soft patterns, a stark contrast to the sharpness of the Priory buildings. She knew this was where the fen people lived in their damp huts and she had wondered how different their life must be from her life in the Priory.

That seemed so long ago; she had not been out since then, for now it was forbidden. Nuns were not allowed beyond the walls of the Priory and rarely beyond the confines of the women's quarters, although the monks and canons were free to wander into the outside world. Some had even gone to the university in Cambridge and come back with vices, mostly ignored by the Prior. They never set eyes on the men of course officially, except occasionally in the infirmary, but the women had their methods of uncovering their 'secret' world. Information would always filter through from that mysterious domain of men on the other side of the wall.

Arriving back in the Priory, Wencilian had felt safe and secure, but at the same time her eyes had been opened, her vision widened. Why, she had asked herself, had she not been out before? It had never occurred to her on that day that she may never go out again.

Now she was preparing to venture out again, but this time into the dark mists of the fens where the paths could be treacherous. Her desire to help a poor girl could have unknown and disastrous consequences. Tonight a brilliant waxing moon shone through her small cell window. In less than a week the moon would be full and Mira would start a new life with Eric, while she and Isobel would return here. Isobel had made her choice to stay and be a lay sister several years before; she had had the chance to leave, but chose to stay knowing life on the outside could be a lot harder for a girl with no family and no status.

Why though had no one given her, Wencilian, the chance to stay or go before she took her final vows? If she had been unwanted, left for the wolves, cast out from a family too poor to feed her, who had there been out there to care? Maybe a poor fen family was still wondering what had happened to her. Somehow though she didn't feel that was the case. Many of the fen people worked for the Priory; surely someone would recognise a likeness if they were to see her? But the few fen people she had seen or talked to at the Priory, or those she had seen on that day out with Marie, did not have any similar features to her, in fact they seemed worlds apart from her.

Could she take her chance and stay out there alone? The thought had never really occurred to her before. It wasn't beyond possibility, but where would she go? She had taken vows before God and to break those vows would incur the wrath of not just God, but the Abbot, the Prioresses, the Bishop and even His Holiness the Pope, himself. She was sure God would forgive her, but not the others.

Deep into the night, the Sacristan rang the bell for Matins. Wencilian followed the nuns down the night stairs to the church. In single file each nun walked in silence carrying her dimly lit candle. This was the service which disturbed her the most, her mind and body deprived of the sleep she so craved. Sometimes she could escape it if needed in the infirmary. The service always passed in a haze of sounds and aromas, muddling her senses sometimes to the point of disorientation. After the service, if she was not needed in the infirmary, she joined the line of dutiful nuns who trod silently to the chapter house, where they would read by torchlight until daybreak and the service of Lauds. She pulled her cloak around her. It would be a long, cold night and a long day ahead.

CHAPTER 6

Sempringham Priory

Wencilian clasped her sweating palms together. She hated feeling anxious like this. For two days she had not had a chance to slip away from the infirmary, apart from to attend services, meals and sleep. Isobel had not been to see her. A young novice nun had brought the linen down from the laundry room today. It was as if Sister Beatrice was keeping an extra close eye on her, sensing her unsettled mood and nervousness. Or was it just her own guilt that made her think so? Her mind flitted from one possibility to another as she attended the patients, her nervous energy driving her on. Just as well, as the infirmary had been busy.

"We always seem to be busier when the moon is waxing to full," commented Sister Beatrice.

"I had never thought of that before," Wencilian replied.

Looking around her she realised that could be the case. There was Sister Juliana, curled up like an infant on her pallet, shivering when anyone went near. A 'disease of the mind' Sister Beatrice had said, but she was very elderly, over seventy years of age. Young Sister Monique had bad cramps every month and took to her bed with the bleeding time for at least two days, but this month she seemed worse than ever. Sister Beatrice dismissed her as a spoilt French aristocrat making a fuss about what every other woman had to put up with, but Wencilian making her tisanes and hot packs for her stomach was not happy about her condition. Two days ago, poor Sister Constantia had passed away suddenly. Maybe it was true. She remembered now that she had heard Sister Martha remark once that there were more deaths, births and injuries at the time of full moon than any other time.

Behind a wooden partition came groaning noises from two of the lay sisters, injured from over work, Wencilian knew – one with a broken wrist and one with a shoulder too painful to move or be touched. Yesterday there had been a flogging, for what sin Wencilian was not sure, but she nursed the Sister carefully, tending to the deep grooves in her back, feeling the pain herself each time the Sister winced or cried out. Whatever had the poor Sister done to justify this punishment, she wondered, but kept her thoughts to herself. She recalled others over the years; Sisters who had been punished for minor offences, especially by Sister Agnes who showed no compassion or mercy. In fact it was a miracle that she herself had rarely been punished in a harsh way.

She pondered on tomorrow's mission. It was more than rash and could incur the greatest punishment if it went wrong or she lost her nerve. Was she doing the right thing?

Brother John had returned to the monastery, nursing his wounds. He was lucky to have incurred just cuts and bruises, although Wencilian was worried that he seemed a little unsteady and his face was still very pale. She would have encouraged him to stay, but Sister Beatrice was convinced he was fit enough. She missed him now – he was the closest thing to a father she had ever known. He seemed to be the only one with whom she could share some childhood memories, the only one who even cared about her childhood.

The bell had just rung for Vespers. Maybe after that Isobel would be at supper in the refectory, but there would be a reading and she doubted that there would be a chance for the two of them to talk.

Sister Beatrice nodded at her; that was her cue to go to service. If needed, one Sister would stay in the infirmary and be excused services and today obviously Sister Beatrice wanted to stay behind. She would pray instead in the small chapel at the side of the infirmary with those patients who were able.

Walking briskly along the cloisters to the church, Wencilian paused at the entrance to the Lady Chapel where tomorrow night they would attempt to use the tunnel to take Mira to freedom.

The Lady Chapel was her secret sanctuary. Here she had often slid unnoticed, as a child, into the shadows under the altar where she sought the protection of the statue of the Virgin Mother. That was how she had discovered the tunnel. It lay behind the altar covered by a large stone which could be dislodged without too much difficulty, even by a child. She had little fear then and had crawled right through. A shaft of light had glimmered some distance ahead, so she had made her way towards it to find a crude wooden door at the end, not locked but bolted from the inside. She had emerged out to what appeared to be the side of the Priory, close to a forest and the marshy fen land. Scared to venture into the open space, she had turned and retreated back before she would be missed.

That was nearly ten years ago. At the time, the tunnel had seemed big enough for her to crawl easily through, but would it be as easy now and would it still be clear? The chapel was rarely used nowadays except by a handful of solitary nuns. Someone must know of the tunnel, or was it a relic from a more violent time when St Gilbert's dream of establishing a religious community for women was beginning to take form. A light still shone on the Lady Chapel altar, a light which stayed lit for Our Lady at all times. Wencilian crossed herself as her head whirled with memories and questions, then turned and walked to the church. She would return to check the tunnel later.

Vespers seemed exceptionally long and tedious. Over the years Wencilian hadn't minded this service so much; the work of the day was done and the Sisters could look forward to supper, which was always more than welcome. It would be seven hours or so since they had the meagre lunch each day and hunger usually wrapped around her stomach like a blacksmith's vice, but today she had no appetite; her mind would not settle.

After the service, the Sisters filed silently along the cloister to the refectory. Wencilian looked for Alice and managed to squeeze next to her at the long trestle table. They exchanged a smile and a clasp of a hand under the table. Meals were meant to be eaten in silence, although chances for a private whisper were always taken. For when it was needed, Alice and Wencilian had developed their own private language, communication by touch, gestures, expressions. They understood each other very well. Tonight, Alice sensed Wencilian's agitation and thought maybe she was overtired and strained from the duty of care, but something else nagged at her; she knew that.

As the nuns ate in silence, Wencilian saw Mira appear with a pitcher of ale and make her way along the table, serving each Sister in turn. As she slid alongside her, there was a clatter and a wail. Isobel had entered the room and slipped, dropping plates of bread on the floor. In the commotion that followed, as Wencilian went to stand up she felt Mira's hand on her shoulder and heard the words, "Tomorrow night, an hour after Compline, in the chapel," before she moved along the table. So, that had been a diversion … only one night to go. She noticed Alice's curious glance, but she could not tell her, not yet.

Sister Beatrice and the lay sisters usually stayed in the infirmary after Compline and they would retire to their sleeping area there, as all of the Sisters would to their cells or dormitories. This would allow them six hours of rest before the two o'clock call for Matins, their only chance for a deep sleep. Wencilian returned to her cell, knowing that should she be needed in that time Sister Beatrice would call her, although this didn't happen often. Sister Beatrice was getting older and resented having her sleep disturbed by needy patients. Whenever she could, she left that task to the lay sisters.

The next day, Wencilian could barely concentrate on her tasks and certainly could not eat a morsel. The night came too soon and she could not break her promise to Mira now. Going out of the Priory during this time was highly risky. The Sacristan could be prowling around and rumour had it that the Prioress Elizabeth often sat up and worked by candlelight on the Priory accounts and parchments. But the night had arrived and she could not break her promise to Mira.

It was the time when day merged into night; dusk was now falling. Wencilian could glimpse faint streaks of pink ripping across the fading light as the Sisters filed along the cloisters to the evening service.

Wencilian was careful to position herself so that she was not too noticeable. Listening to the chants of the priests and canons on the other side of the wall which divided the church, she tried to run over in her mind the moves she was to make in less than two hours' time. The 'Salve Regina' came through her lips, but the words were automatic. She prayed to the Virgin for protection and help on this fearful night. It was risky on a full moon, but its light was needed to cross the marshy lands which would take her, Isobel and Mira to the fen people.

Back in her cell, Wencilian waited until the Sacristan had completed her rounds and checked that the convent was settled. Taking her warm sheepskin cloak and removing her sandals, she then crept gingerly along the corridor and down the stairs to the Lady Chapel, thankful that it was situated discreetly behind the northern nave of the church. It was from this corner of the church that all the Sisters would enter for services, so there was no need for her to cross the church and be exposed. She slipped like a shadow into the small chapel where three candles flickered on the altar by the feet of the Holy Mother. The statue looked into her eyes as if she knew what she was about to do, but there was no recrimination, only pity.

Wencilian whispered to herself, 'You do not need forgiveness for you have done nothing wrong,' and hid under the altar to wait. She had crept back here on the previous evening after Compline. The entrance to the tunnel had been as she remembered it, apart from the cobwebs she had to clear. The stone now lay to the side revealing only a tiny glimmer of light in the distance. The equinox was a few weeks away; the days were stretching, but the darkness of that night was starting to descend. If anyone had followed her and found the chapel empty, they may have added fuel to the rumour of the ghost of the nun who had died at the altar many years before. The

56

thought made her smile, even though she shivered inside. Taking a deep breath she reminded herself that she was about to enter the tunnel to save a new life, which if discovered might be forcibly taken from the womb of its mother by the most terrible means, by those who would claim it was the will of God. Blessed Mary protect us.

Minutes seemed like hours before she heard the soft pat of sandals on stone. Her eyes peered beneath the altar cloth at the feet of two young women. She had told them she would not speak until they spoke first, just in case another Sister may have decided to enter the chapel. Mira was the first to whisper, "Hail Mary, full of grace." Wencilian lifted the cloth and ushered them in. They waited under the altar cloth for several seconds, barely daring to breathe. Footsteps approached, paused, then continued along the corridor. Silence returned.

"Come, follow me. Be brave, Sisters."

Her shift was dragging as she crawled through the tunnel. The dust smarted in her eyes and filled her lungs. In an effort not to cough and make a noise, she wheezed. It seemed that it would be nearly impossible to turn around ... but that was not an option. Mira followed, then Isobel. Fear was making her sweat as she crawled near the exit. The bolt was stiff, she pulled it hard. It shifted. The door was stuck tight though and she needed all her strength to force it open.

"Take my hand, quick, Mira." Feeling faint and trembling, Wencilian pulled Mira through the exit. Mira hugged her to support herself as she stumbled out of the tunnel.

The three hunched and hooded figures crept into a soggy field where sheep huddled together. There was no wind, so all sounds would carry that night. The tunnel had taken them to the outer perimeters of the Priory. Soon they would reach the treacherous marshes where even Isobel, their guide, could falter and lead them into danger. Even in familiar territory the moonlight may not be enough to guide them safely. The night sky sparkled with stars.

"Please God and Mother Mary let us be safe," Wencilian prayed.

Above them, ghostly white wings swept across the shadowy sky. It was Boden, Wencilian was sure; as if answering her prayer, he was following them. They reached the cover of trees and tracing a path which weaved along the outer edge of the forest, they were safe for now, but going back would be dangerous. A whistle in the distance made them stop in their tracks.

"It is well. It's Robert waiting for us. He's a friend." Isobel returned the whistle.

Robert, a sturdy fen man, was waiting for them exactly where the marsh land began. He guided them carefully; their steps were slow, the remaining daylight was getting fainter. Isobel had complete faith in him, but Wencilian was wary. She glanced at Mira, even in the half-light she could see terror in her eyes. She knew that must be more from fear of what lay ahead … her future, for Mira had been born in the fens; she would not be afraid of picking her way through the marshes.

They reached an expanse of water where a boat was waiting. Stumbling into the boat against the drag of her heavy robe, Wencilian caused several grebes to flee from the nest, flapping and squawking, nearly causing her to tumble into the water. Robert caught her arm. For a few seconds she felt his muscular strength hold her. "Sit down quietly, Sister," he whispered. "We are nearly there."

Wencilian could just see the outline of Robert's face in the moonlight. Here she was with a strange man in the middle of the night, outside in the world, a world at this time full of eerie shadows and unfamiliar sounds. The swish of the paddle against the water, the cries of small nocturnal animals were music to her ears. These were sounds she had never heard before and may never hear again, but she was not afraid out here, only afraid of what may happen when she got back.

Inside the hut a fire glowed, smoke surrounded them and a cluster of noisy barefoot children sat in a corner, dipping bread into a bowl. The fire and the rush lights cast shadows around the room. Wencilian was shocked to see the rough conditions this family lived in. One small room it seemed was all they had. A woman of about thirty years of age entered and shooed the children out. "Go to your homes now. Go on."

The woman ushered them to sit at a table. She looked directly at Mira. "You can stay here tonight, but at first light you must leave. It's not safe here; it's too near."

"Are they not your children?" Wencilian enquired.

"I have only one," the woman replied, nodding towards a corner of the room.

Wencilian looked around to see a young girl of possibly ten to twelve years of age crouching on a stool, her head bent between her knees. Her soft curly fair hair obscured her face but her body was thin and delicate. She looked like a fairy child on a toadstool, Wencilian thought, like a drawing Marie had once shown her."

"That is my daughter, Leoba," the woman added, staring intensely into her eyes.

Wencilian could not tell whether the mother's gaze was meant to intimidate her or scrutinise her.

Isobel broke the silence. "Hilda, this is Sister Wencilian. She agreed to help us at much risk to herself."

The woman, Hilda, nodded as if in acquiescence. Mira nodded too, but looked to Wencilian for reassurance. She was trembling, whether with cold or fear or both, Wencilian was not sure.

Isobel touched Mira's arm. "You will be safe. Don't forget that you must go at first light. Robert will guide you to meet Eric. Then you must stay within the forest and make your way to the river at Fosdyke. Ask there for the man named Aelred, the boat handler. We must go now. We will be missed."

"Can I be sure Eric will come?" Mira muttered. "Can you be, Isobel?"

Isobel handed Mira a bundle which she had carried under her cloak. "Here, a little extra food for you. I sent word to Eric to meet you there. He sent word he would meet you. I'm sure he'll be there."

Isobel looked away not wanting Mira to see any doubt in her

eyes. In truth, contrary to what she had told Mira and Wencilian, she had not received any message back from Eric and had guessed that he would have found it difficult to send any reply. She knew his family and thought him to be an honest man. She prayed he would do the right thing. She would never forgive herself if Mira was left alone, homeless and with child. As a contingency measure, she had instructed Robert in case Eric failed to turn up to take Mira to a woman she knew of near Lincoln. There was no other way; she could not have remained much longer in the convent.

With eyes full of tears, Wencilian put her arm around Mira and leaned close. As she glanced around the hut she wondered how she could cope if she had to live such a life as this. The fen people, she had heard, often went hungry or even died of starvation. Their roughly woven woollen tunics looked totally inadequate to keep out the damp mist which constantly pervaded the atmosphere. The hut was dirty and noisy, but there was laughter and chatter and acceptance. These people did not judge a young girl whose only crime had been to follow her heart and give in to her emotions and urges, such a natural thing in their eyes. They only lived within a mile or so from the Priory, yet what did they know of hymns and Latin chants? Their only concerns were with survival.

Some of the fen men and women would work for the Priory, the men digging ditches to drain the soggy land and the women doing laundry, spinning and weaving. They shared a mutual respect, but this did not usually extend to friendship. They had their own beliefs and their own ways. Wencilian felt deep inside herself that Mira would be safe despite the dangers of the outside world. She almost envied her.

Isobel interrupted. She looked apologetic, reading her thoughts. "We must go," she said softly.

"We will pray for you all the time, Mira." Wencilian hugged Mira's small frame and reluctantly turned to follow Isobel and retrace their path to the Priory.

As they were leaving, Hilda grabbed Wencilian's arm. Her eyes still gazed intently, but her face was softened, almost pleading. "My child, Leoba, has special gifts, but is too fragile for a life here on her own. It is good that you have come. I can see by your face that you are of noble birth. When my time comes to leave this world I want you to ensure that Leoba is taken into your care at the Priory."

Wencilian was startled. She had no idea what Hilda meant. "I cannot do that. You would have to approach the Prioress. Don't forget I am not meant to be here. You must not speak to anyone of my presence here."

"You have my word, and worry not, you will find a way to protect my girl."

Robert was waiting to escort them safely over the swamps. Wencilian shivered as she took his hand to step into the small boat. The cold and damp were beginning to penetrate even through her thick cloak. In the boat no one spoke. The man, Robert, she may never see again but she would be ever grateful to him. And the woman, Hilda; well she didn't know what to think of her, but she would always see the warmth of the fire in that small hut and imagine the warmth filling her when she sat in the cold church or her cold cell, for a fire was rarely seen in the Priory.

As soon as Wencilian was alone with Isobel, she wanted information. "Who was that woman and what did she mean saying I was of noble birth, and why does she want me to protect her child?"

"Hilda has the gift of prophecy. People come from many miles around to hear her. I can't explain what she says, but I do know you can trust her. She will not betray you. The daughter is strange and no one knows who fathered her. Be quiet now and concentrate if you want to get back at all."

They did not speak again until the Priory was in view, Isobel totally absorbed with every step she took. Wencilian followed every footstep, her heavy wet cloak weighing down her body and the sadness of leaving Mira weighing on her mind. Soon there was to be the re-entrance to the tunnel and the fear that she may have been missed. But these few moments of precious freedom were invigorating and she wanted to soak up every second.

In front of her stood the walls of the Priory, tall and imposing. She stood still for a moment in the light of the moon to view the structure, the prison which held her whole life and her memories within … all her memories, except her one previous visit to the outside world. At that moment in the silence of the night, a barn owl swooped before her, his wings iridescent in the moonlight. Was it Boden again or one of the many barn owls which nested in the walls and turrets of the Priory.

Isobel was suddenly holding her. "What is it? What is it? Dear Sister Wencilian, we must hurry."

For a brief moment Wencilian was tempted to run into the trees, disappear into the night. She thought she saw pairs of eyes watching her from the forest edge, but she felt no fear, only exhilaration and invincibility. Looking up at the stars, she just wanted to stare at the wonder of the sky at night, the beauty, the vastness. Only a fraction of this had she seen from her small cell window. What freedom the outside world could offer.

As if feeling her thoughts, Isobel took her arm and hurried her towards the tunnel entrance.

"Hurry, we could be seen, we may have been already …" she looked towards the forest and lowered her voice to a faint whisper, "… by those who gather in the darkness."

"Those! Who are they?"

"Those who the Sisters would tell you lurk in the shadows of the night forest to practise their dark arts. But they would not betray us for they would not want the priests to know what they do."

"But tell me more, Isobel."

"There is not much more that I know. Shh, we are nearly at the tunnel."

There was just time to change her woollen shift; the wet dirty one Wencilian hid under her bed. After Matins she would somehow get it to the laundry, but now she could hear the footsteps of the nuns going down the night stairs to the church.

Not at all tired and still exhilarated from her clandestine adventure, she hurried along the corridor and tagged on to the end of the line of weary Sisters disturbed from their sleep. She was sure that they would know where she had been, that they would read her thoughts, that she would stand out like a beacon, glowing amidst the rows of dark bowed heads.

For a while, the service passed as unremarkably as ever and although Wencilian was there in body, her spirit was elsewhere. The whole experience of the night had been so exhilarating that she could not calm the thoughts in her head. Isobel, she thought, had been remarkable to organise Mira's escape. Poor Mira, how her life had been so altered by one act: and, the strange woman, Hilda, what had she meant, would she ever be able to see her again?

Closing her eyes and trying to capture the memory of Boden flying through the night sky, she felt a throbbing sensation spread through her body and a jolt from behind as if someone had pushed her. She was looking down from the high vaulted roof of the church at the rows of nuns standing obediently in rows. The next thing she knew, she was being lifted off the floor, a Sister on either side of her, the nuns were filing out of the church. The Prioress Elizabeth was approaching her with a concerned look on her face.

"Are you unwell?"

"What happened?" Wencilian muttered.

"You swooned and fell to the floor," put in Sister Agnes who supported her right arm. "We had better get you down to the infirmary."

"No," Prioress Elizabeth cut across anxiously. "I think she would be better in her cell for the moment until we know exactly what ails her."

Not wanting to contradict the Prioress, Sister Agnes helped to escort Wencilian to her cell.

Becoming a little more coherent, Wencilian remembered the wet shift under the bed.

"It's all right, Sisters, thank you, I shall just lie down for a while."

"Did you have a vision?" asked Sister Agnes, excitedly.

Mother Elizabeth's face looked anxious. "It is perhaps the monthly curse; the moon is full and that is common," she said, trying to belie the worry in her voice.

"Oh yes, possibly it is near that time," replied Wencilian. "Please, just let me rest."

The two nuns reluctantly edged out of the cell. "I'll send for Sister Beatrice; I don't want to leave you like this," Mother Elizabeth muttered.

Their voices faded as suddenly a wave of tiredness came over Wencilian and she slept.

She woke to find Isobel shaking her arm. She was dazed. "Oh Isobel, thank God you're here."

"I heard you were unwell. The news has swept through the Priory like a pestilence." Isobel stopped and coughed. "I was worried at first that you had been found out and confined to your cell, especially as the Prioress, Mother Elizabeth, is meeting with Father Roger, and everyone has been told to stay away from you."

"What? No! I swooned in the church; that is all. What time of day is it?"

"It is the time all the Sisters are at lunch. I have duties in the laundry today, I cannot stay."

"In the laundry, of course, God must be with me." Reaching under the bed Wencilian grabbed the dirty tunic. "Take this quickly before the Prioress comes. I think she told me to wait here until she comes."

Isobel felt her forehead. "You do not seem unwell, but I must tell you that there are rumours of a type of pestilence in some nearby villages and I think maybe this is what the Prioress fears."

"Oh, holy sweet Jesus, and we have been outside."

"Well, there is nothing to be done. We must just pray and I must go."

Before Wencilian could gather her thoughts, Sister Beatrice entered her cell with a bowl of soup, fresh water and bread, eying her warily. "How do you feel, Sister Wencilian?"

"A little tired, but no more."

Sister Beatrice felt her forehead and her cheeks, and then examined her eyes. Although she did not do much to comfort the sick, she knew how to diagnose a fair range of illnesses. "Ah, mmm," she murmured as she carried out her examination.

"I am not ill, I don't think," Wencilian stated impatiently again.

"I agree. I will leave you to rest. You had better not resume your duties until I check you again though, Sister."

Wencilian had never before experienced what had happened in the church. She had felt rapture once or twice during worship, a heightening of awareness, a feeling of being filled up with a beautiful sense of peace, as if a warm light suffused her whole being body and soul. Many of the Sisters reported this, especially during Matins. Wencilian always thought that at that time of the deepest night, the veil between the worlds was thinner; the body and mind were tired and the mind more amenable to divine intervention. Sometimes, one of the Sisters would claim to have a vision, or one might swoon and fall. More often than not though, this could be due to exhaustion or near starvation because of penance, imposed or self-inflicted.

Last night during Matins, her mind had wandered off; she was thinking of Boden, imagining flying with him through the night sky when, without any warning, she found herself to be floating outside of her body. She felt her arms as wings, powerful, with waves of wind washing over her body; then something had jolted her body again and the next thing she knew she was being supported by the Sisters. She could not explain what had happened to her, but she was eager to know if it would happen again; if, in fact she could make it happen again with her will. To use her will in such a way must surely be sinful, yet it had felt natural and had given her a sense of freedom.

The fact that she was confined to her cell for the day gave her the luxury of mulling over the events of the previous night. Time for private thought was limited and not encouraged within the walls of the Priory. Her first thoughts went out to Mira. She hoped she would not feel too alone, and prayed that her lover would honour his promise, to meet her and, more importantly, provide for her. But how long would it be before someone noticed she was missing? Would they search for her, thinking her in danger or lost, or would they assume she had deserted her faith and her reason? Being a lay sister she had not taken vows, but still the punishment could be severe if she were caught. Wencilian went over the events of the night, which now seemed unreal. Even though there had been danger, the sense of excitement and freedom had been truly exhilarating. She would never regret the fact that she had done what she did. The danger she knew though, had not passed. There would be questions.

Wencilian clutched her rosary to pray. She uttered the words, "Hail Mary full of grace, the Lord art with thee," trembling with fear, guilt, trepidation. Yet in her own heart she did not deem what she had done a sin. Surely, if she had not helped Mira, the cruelty she would have suffered from those who profess to have moral superiority would have been a far greater sin. In their ignorance, they would condemn their own souls, so maybe by saving Mira she had saved them too, although they would never know it.

At that moment, there was a knock on her cell door. Sister Beatrice entered without waiting for a reply. The smell of lavender and marsh marigold drifted around her. Wencilian sat up sharply as if caught in a sinful act, restraining herself from saying, 'But it was only my thoughts; my thoughts cannot betray me, can they?'

"What is it, child?" Sister Beatrice lent towards her to feel her brow. "You are not hot. There is no danger; you would have been in fever by now."

"What do you mean?"

"A pestilence, child. There are cases in Lincoln and fear that it is spreading this way. The Prioress has declared that none shall enter or leave the Priory from sundown tonight."

There had been talk of some cases of disease and pestilence by travellers coming from the south, but none of them had actually seen a person with it. They said it caused a high fever, vomiting and swollen glands. It had killed some who were young, elderly or weak. Inside the walls of the Priory, gossip and rumours always managed to penetrate the imposed silence by ways or means. Sometimes in the chapter house when conversation was allowed, certain Sisters would be bursting to pass on snippets of information about the outside world. Some of it of course was not accurate.

When Beatrice left, Wencilian leapt off her pallet and paced the cold stone floor. Her thoughts raced. What if she had picked up a disease outside with the fen people or left Mira exposed to illness? But if she had not gone the night before, it would have now been impossible to leave. Mira is safe. The Lady will ensure that she will be safe. She closed her eyes and visualised Mira, hopefully now miles away with her lover, perhaps scared of what lay ahead, perhaps regretting that she may never see her family or friends again, maybe exhilarated by her freedom and the new life inside her.

Wencilian suddenly felt the need for company and went to join the Sisters in the spinning room. It seemed that the Prioress was not making an appearance and Beatrice had given the all clear. Spinning focused her mind. Although the Sisters and lay sisters spun mostly in silence, she could feel reassurance from the women around her. It was one of the lightest rooms in the Priory and the shaft of sunlight through the window dispelled some of the deep melancholy which overcame her at times. And most importantly, she knew that if there was any gossip or concern about Mira, the nuns would never be able to hold their silence for long.

CHAPTER 7

Sempringham Priory
March-April 1300

The next two days passed as the days usually did, bound by the rhythms of Priory life. Although the approaching spring was gradually warming the earth outside, the damp still seeped through the priory walls. Wencilian shivered as she walked to the church for the services of Nones. She thought it curious that there had been no mention of Mira or her disappearance. Neither had Wencilian seen Mother Elizabeth. She had passed Isobel several times in the cloisters and Isobel had nodded, as was usual behaviour, but had given no sign in her expression that she knew of anything unusual. Wencilian was eager to talk to Isobel and was waiting for the opportunity, but Isobel didn't seek her out, as if by doing so she would be admitting guilt or drawing attention to them both.

This was one of the few times in her life when she was glad of some imposed silence. Whereas she could not hide away in her cell, she could hide behind the convent rules which she had in the past so often liked to disregard. In the refectory, eyes met over the table asking questions, but she gave no sign that anything was amiss since her collapse at Matins. Most of the Sisters put it down to the moon flux or overwork. The worry of the pestilence had subsided, although there lingered a residue of fear which one could catch in the eyes of the Sisters from time to time during chores or in the chapter house.

It was on the next day, the day before Ash Wednesday, that

the Prioress sent for her. Wencilian felt the blood drain from her legs and her heart began to palpitate. As she walked along the cloister, she tried to convince herself that it could be to do with the preparations for the feast that evening. The Prioress had said that a feast before Lent would give the Sisters sustenance and would lighten the heavy atmosphere that had crept around the Priory since the restrictions following the news of pestilence.

In her room, the Prioress offered Wencilian a seat and a glass of warm wine, but she did not offer her usual warm smile. She sat opposite her by the hearth in which a rare fire had just been lit. Wencilian looked into her tired brown eyes, which today showed concern and fear.

"These are dark times." Mother Elizabeth spoke slowly. "I feel that in some ways we are not doing our duty to our faithful people. There could be illness, death and terrible suffering not too far from these walls. I feel that we should open our doors to those in need, but Father Roger has decreed that we should lock our gates and that none should come or go. What he does not know is that several of the lay sisters have gone out to the villages to take alms and medicines against his wishes and now they are stuck there and cannot get back."

The Prioress paused, then paced around her room uneasily. Wencilian always admired the way she would defy Father Roger over issues which quite rightly she should be in charge of.

"I did not realise that Mira had gone with them, but she has not been seen by anyone. She must have accompanied them. That would have been against my wishes, but it is typical of her concern for other people. Have you seen her? You are close to her."

Now Wencilian felt that God was really on her side for once, or maybe it was the protection of Our Lady. She was stunned for what seemed like several minutes. The Prioress tilted her head and looked at her expectantly.

"Oh sorry, Reverend Mother, I was trying to think when I saw her last. I think it was the night of the full moon," she replied honestly, praying she would not be questioned further.

"Well, it was the morning after full moon when the Sisters

left at first light, so it makes sense that she went with them. She has family on the outside, so let's pray that they will be safe with them. We can only wait."

"How long do you think we will have to wait?" asked Wencilian.

"I don't know, but I think it will be a long wait. You must not speak to anyone about this at all. We will dedicate a mass for them and we must carry on with preparations for the feast, otherwise a mood as malign as the pestilence will spread into the hearts of all of us in here."

The Prioress rose, went to look out of her window with her back turned and was silent. Wencilian knew that she would have that look that she had seen on her face before, a look of longing for something that was a distant memory that she would never share, as it was hers and hers alone. When she had said 'the hearts of all of us in here,' she was part of the communal heart of the convent on a level with all the other Sisters; when she turned her back it was a separation. That no doubt made her what she was, a leader, a pragmatist. It was also a cue for Wencilian to leave.

As she returned to her chores, Wencilian could not remember a time when she had been more relieved. No one would search for Mira, at least for a while. But she prayed that Mira and the other lay Sisters who had left the convent would be safe from pestilence and all the other dangers which lurked on the outside world. She had no appetite for the promised feast that evening and would need to force herself to eat some meat as she may not see any food to stimulate the palate before Easter.

Wencilian settled back into the routine life of the Priory, but she felt unsettled, worn down by the relentless duties and prayer and devotion. She had tasted freedom, a tiny morsel it may have been, but something had changed within her. The whole experience of the night of the full moon jolted forth memories of when she had ventured out before with Marie and now the dream she sometimes had was more frequent and vivid. She longed to write down these things so as to remember her fragmented thoughts, but writing anything personal was forbidden. She thought it strange how a person could become so accustomed to accepting things in life when that was all they knew, but she knew that she was changing and now felt unwilling to accept some of the restrictions placed on her. Maybe she would write some personal memoirs, but she would need to conceal them very carefully.

That evening, the extra food and mead warmed her and made her thankful that she was safe and sheltered with food in her belly, and although the Sisters had eaten mostly in silence, she was glad Alice was by her side and grateful for the company of the others. There were some, she knew, who must be out there in the cold with no food and no company.

For a while after Compline she had taken to staring out of her cell window instead of sleeping. Sometimes she would have a visit from Boden, and sure enough Boden came that night, perching on the sill, his strong talons gripping the ledge, pressing his heart shaped face against the bars, his huge eyes piercing straight into hers.

Wencilian reached out and stroked his forehead, tracing her finger around the shape of his face. He let her ruffle his dense plumage, bending his head towards her. "My little friend, how I wish I could fly with you or that you could tell me all you see as you fly over the fen lands."

How she loved to watch him fly. She would feel a fragment of the freedom he enjoyed, a sense of release from all her cares. Although, when he, or any of the other barn owls which nested in the Priory, let out a screech, a shiver would rush down her spine.

So many things had changed since the night she helped Mira. Never before had she felt such a need for freedom and to find out where she came from. Who were her family and why had they left her here? These questions arose again, without answers, only dreams and vague fleeting memories which confused her.

She knew she should not be ungrateful. The nuns had taken her in when she had probably been abandoned, exposed to the elements, left to starve and die of cold or be taken by wolves. Maybe that was where the dream came from. Maybe, left cold and alone, the fear, the memory of that night had never quite left her.

She did know that her life had been easier than many outside the Priory. The nuns always had food, even if it was meagre. They had warm tunics and cloaks, and sandals or boots. She had education and access to books and medicines, and always someone to care for. She even had more privileges than some of the other nuns. Her cell was furnished with a chest, a chair and several rugs, and amongst her treasured possessions, which she was not strictly allowed to have, were a mirror, a silver comb and a fine shawl of silk which she would take out of her chest when alone in her cell and wrap around her. This had been left to her by Marie. Wencilian thought of her often and relived the moments when she last saw her. Not many months after Marie had returned to her lay duties, she had been taken ill suddenly and died within days. Wencilian was allowed into the infirmary to sit with her for those last few hours of her life. Marie had been like a mother to her and left her so suddenly, ripped away from her cruelly, and for this she never forgave the Prioress.

Wencilian was starting to ask herself questions that had never occurred to her before, questions she would keep to herself, for there was no one who could, or would, answer them. Pulling the sheepskin cover over the window, she lay down on the bed and tried to rest, even if she could not sleep, for soon the knock would come on her cell door for the service of Matins when all the nuns would then have to stay awake and read by candlelight in the cold chapter house until daybreak and the service of Prime. It would be another long night.

Easter was only a few days away and it had become unaccustomedly warm for mid-April. Sister Ignatius was to deliver a reading and was rehearsing her words in the chapter house. There was to be the Veneration of the Cross on Good Friday, a serious mass, and on the Saturday a day of celebration. Guests were invited on Easter Saturday for a yearly visit and it sent many of the Sisters into a bit of a spin. The kitchen was frantic with preparation and Wencilian had been asked to help. Normally, she would enjoy the chance to be in the kitchens; it was one of the few warm places in the Priory, but today it was hot and the aroma of roasting meat was making her nauseous. Meat was a rarity in the Priory except on certain feast days and she was not used to seeing severed limbs of pigs and sheep dripping with blood. Trying to ignore the gruesome scene, she joined in the chat and laughter which all the Sisters were enjoying while they could, and it took her mind off the visitors' day, the day when the families would come to see their daughters, their sisters or their nieces, the day when she never had any visitors.

Attending the Easter mass would be many local dignitaries and wealthy sponsors of the Priory, ladies with elaborate head dresses and gorgeous robes, cloaks and jewellery. She would feel plain and ordinary, of no importance to the outside world. She would see pity in some of their eyes, even though the Prioress was always convincing them that the nuns of Sempringham were 'ladies of status'.

Everyone was occupied and most of the Sisters were excited about the forthcoming celebrations. The Prioress had even released many of them from the noon service at midday and Nones, the mid-afternoon service, so that more preparation could be done.

Wencilian wandered into the kitchen garden to collect herbs for the cook. It was so refreshing to be outside. The day was bright and sunny, and the air fresh and cool. Spring flowers were appearing all over the rough patches of ground around the carefully tended vegetable and herb patches. She decided she would take her time, instead of rushing as she was prone to do, and meander, taking in the pungent aromas around her, listening to the birds calling as they searched for food for their young. What a wonderful time of year this was; the earth was coming alive, being re-born after the dormant, cold winter. Colours, sounds and smells filled her senses. She thought that the earth was like a mother giving birth to her children, year after year, nurturing them, caring for them. What abundance there was, what beauty. Why had she never noticed this so strongly before? Surely, she felt, this is where God must be, not confined within the walls the church. Kneeling down to pick some dill, she felt the softness of the leaves and considered for the first time how such a beautiful and useful plant could grow from one tiny seed.

Walking back to the kitchens, Wencilian thought about the celebrations; they were always a welcome relief from the routine although tinged with sadness. Most of the Sisters would be eagerly looking forward to seeing their relatives. Even though the visits were monitored closely and restricted, she could see how much joy it brought to some of the Sisters. For others it was painful. She could see that too and knew most tried to hide the hurt it caused, knowing their siblings were living a family life in relative freedom, some having married and had children. Was it more painful, she wondered, than having no visitors like her, knowing that there was nobody out there who cared whether she was dead or alive, or if there were relatives who for some reason could never visit her. How she longed for someone to appear to tell her about her family, about the outside world, to embrace her, like a brother, a sister, mother or father.

In the light of common sense and compassion, rules were relaxed a little in the few days coming up to Easter, although food was still rationed as it was the Lenten fast. There was a rumour circulating that there would be music at the feast. If this was the case, then things were really changing for music had never been allowed before. The nuns were discussing this in the ambulatory after supper. Usually at this time there would be a reading and no conversation, but the Prioress had decided that final plans should be discussed for the Easter visits. Waiting for the Prioress to arrive, the Sisters could indulge a little in light-hearted banter on the ins and outs of priory life.

When the Prioress arrived, there was an atmosphere of joviality. Her entrance into the ambulatory caused many of the Sisters to look abashed and bow their heads, fearful of some punishment for their enjoyment. There was silence as the Prioress took her place by the unlit fireplace and gave all the

Sisters a small bow of the head.

"We must remember that we are but frail human beings about to enter once again into the most disturbing but also invigorating and enlightening time of the year. We mourn the death of our Lord Jesus Christ and also celebrate his resurrection to eternal life. This indeed stirs up many emotions within us and encourages us to strange behaviour. We must at this time, Sisters, support each other and pray for strength and obedience to follow the path which our Lord has prepared for us. When our visitors come, we must at all times remain humble and chaste in our thoughts. We must not allow any influences from the outside world to encourage any thoughts of envy or malice or greed. We must not engage in gossip. Whilst it is natural to rejoice in the salvation of our Lord, we must not take any pleasure from the misfortune of others. Before we begin our meeting, let us pray for our Almoners, Sisters who have been parted from us, but will re-join us tomorrow. They have been staying at the Bishop's castle and are now free from all harm. It seems that a type of pestilence only spread to the borders of the Fens, sadly taking the lives of a few families in that area."

Wencilian pulled her cowl around her, not wishing that any Sister should see her face for it had gone deathly pale. It was sudden shock. For days now she had not thought about the Sisters who went out on the same night as herself and Mira. Totally absorbed with the memory of her part of the escapade that night, she had pushed away thoughts of what the Prioress had related to her. Soon the truth would come out. Everyone would know that Mira did not go with them on that night. The rest of the meeting passed in a blur, for Wencilian could not focus her thoughts. The peace and contentment, and even moments of joy, she had felt in the past few days dissolved in seconds, replaced by a fear and guilt which spread through her body making her so heavy that she felt almost unable to move. When she lifted her head, it did not seem though that anyone had noticed. All eyes were focused on the Prioress, all ears soaking in her words.

Maundy Thursday came after a very disturbed night for Wencilian. Even without the normal disruptions of the Matins service, from which they had been excused to save energy for the Easter worship and feast, she could not rest. All through the night she tossed about on her pallet worrying about the possibility of being questioned about the disappearance of Mira, although she was at the same time intensely angry that she should be punished for doing what her conscience told her was right. In any event, if found guilty she would run away and take her chances with the brutality of the outside world, for the punishment given out within the Priory could be a lot worse. She resolved she must stay calm and logical until after celebrations, for surely nothing would be investigated until those were over.

On this day, once a year, after Terce, the main service of the day at 9 o'clock in the morning, the nuns would take part in the Maundy washing of the feet ceremony. The lay sisters would prepare bowls of warm water and following the mass, each Sister in turn, including the Prioress, would kneel to wash another's feet after a reading from the Gospel of St John. The Prioress reminded them of the virtues of humility and humbleness, and that in the eyes of the Lord no one was any greater or lesser than any other.

Wencilian normally felt a sense of peace and contentment at this ceremony and after the fasting of Lent it would make her feel renewed. Today it only added to her torturous thoughts about guilt and sin. She repressed an urge to giggle in spite of this when Alice sprinkled the water over her feet and looked up at her with a defiant glint in her eye. When she had first set eyes on Alice, she recognised a kindred spirit in her deep brown eyes which told of pain and frustration. But Alice also possessed a deep intelligence, humility and gentleness. Friendship like this was not encouraged of course, so they had to be extremely careful and devious to be able to spend a little time together. Today, before lunch they were excused some of their tasks in order to prepare for the following day, so snatching a few moments they sat in Wencilian's cell and removed the heavy woollen-lined headdresses. Alice noticed that her friend's head was red and sore. "It's the lambskin which itches," said Wencilian.

"Or it could be the mites. I will brush your cap for you," Alice offered.

"Let's do that after we have brushed our hair, Alice."

Wencilian treasured playing their game of imagining their hair was still long and thick, hers golden like it had been as a child, and Alice's deep brown with russet tones, like the earthy colours of autumn. Imagining they were preparing for a meeting with their betrothed, to be courted and to dance to the early hours, as ladies of the court did, so they had once been told. Imagining was all Wencilian could do. While she was emerging from childhood to womanhood, her desire to fly free was increasing, but she knew nothing about being a woman in the outside world. She treasured the snippets of information she gleaned from the novices and from Alice herself as they indulged in this small fantasy.

On this occasion though, instead of giggling, Alice became quiet and morose. "Let's stop this foolish game," she said tearfully, "for we know it will never happen and it is just torture to me at this time."

"Whatever is it, Alice? Has something happened?"

Alice turned to face Wencilian and wiping her eyes with her hand as her tears came gushing out, she gasped and stumbled over her words. "One of the lay sisters has a sister who is a servant at a house in the village where my father, mother and eldest sister are lodging, ready for the visit tomorrow. She overheard my sister and my mother talking about my sister's betrothal to MY Maurice."

"Your Maurice! I thought Maurice was your imaginary lover, like Simon is mine. Sit down on the chair and tell me what is going on."

Alice paused and looked down into her lap. "Look at me in these poor nun's robes, while my sister prepares fine silks for her wedding gown. And they told me my life would be always richer than hers for there is no higher path than serving God in this way. But it is not that which causes so much pain; it is the fact that they have both deceived me so much. When I left to come here I knew that I may not see him again and I was so sad, but consoled myself with the fact that he would pine for me just as much, perhaps even travelling far away to ease the reminder of separation for both of us."

"Then why is he marrying your sister? This does seem very unjust."

"Pressure probably. My father is not a poor man; he owns much land and Maurice's father was keen on our betrothal because of this. When I discovered that I had been promised to Sempringham from an early age, Maurice was devastated and I could see his father was angry and disappointed. No doubt he has not given him much choice but to marry my sister."

"Sometimes, Alice, I am grateful that I am not exposed to the inconsistencies of the outside world. Why would your parents agree to that?"

"My sister is no beauty, not to be unkind; she is also older than me and fears she may never find a husband. The thought of her giving birth to his children is too much to bear. I'll never know how that would feel, shut up here like a prisoner in a dungeon."

"Please, please," Wencilian said softly, taking her in her arms. "We are not certain, this could be a rumour. You must ask them at the visit and if it is true, then we must pray for some reason that the marriage will not go ahead."

Alice looked up at her in surprise. She had expected Wencilian to say the only words that all the Sisters would have said or indeed any lay person, that she was a nun now and had taken vows, therefore she would have to forget him and dedicate her life to Christ. There was usually no way out.

Wencilian however, might have said the same before she helped Mira, but now she knew that even in what seemed impossible circumstances, there was always a spark of hope. She surprised herself and hoped that she wouldn't raise Alice's expectations too much.

"Do you think that would be right, to pray for such a thing?" Alice asked.

"Do you think it right that your sister marries Maurice?"

"No."

"Then it is right to pray that she doesn't."

Wencilian left Alice reluctantly. She would have liked to comfort her more, but duty called and there was nothing to be done, at least not at this moment. She walked back to the infirmary with a heavy heart. Ah, she thought, there are so many reasons why women come to this place.

CHAPTER 8

**On the way to Cwmhir Abbey
Early April 1300**

Back on the mainland of Cymru, Cai kept Ianto, his pony, to inland tracks away from the coast. Before he began to travel eastwards, he needed to go south into Powys, via Caernarfon. This meant once again crossing the mountains to get to Caernarfon. The castle there had been one of Llywelyn's regular dwellings and the one he was most fond of, other than Abergwyngregyn.

He had heard many tales of Caernarfon since Llywelyn had died, but had not been back since that fateful year of 1282. He had been told that King Edward had torn down the original castle and built one of the biggest castles ever seen. Many of the local Welsh people had been dispossessed of their lands and forced to move, receiving little in compensation and even that didn't come until several years later.

Whilst dwelling in the mountains of Eryri, news had reached Cai of a revolt and the exciting prospect of the castle being re-taken. For a short while, the people of Cymru had dared to hope of reclaiming their lands and heritage. But it was not to be. Several months later, Edward's troops had once again defeated them. Such a needless loss of life, he thought. Hadn't enough blood been spilt already? Yet some part of him felt he should have been there fighting for his people.

Cai was imagining the fight, when he first caught sight of the tall imposing structure of King Edward's new castle at Caernarfon, a symbol of the arrogance of the Anglo-Norman invaders. He had never seen anything to compare with this in his life. Bigger by far and more sombre in appearance than Beaumaris castle, this had surely changed the lives of the local people beyond belief. A whole new world had emerged while he, Cai, had been ensconced in the hills. It was now so final, the loss of their country to the Norman warlords. While he had stood by the side of Llywelyn, there had always been hope. Even for years afterwards there had still been hope in their hearts, and the odd revolt, the occasional skirmish, always had the potential to stir up expectancy.

As he drew near the town he saw that it was busy with people going about their daily business. He dismounted and led Ianto up towards the town walls. Ten or so masons were busy constructing the walls, which seemed to be incomplete in parts. No one took any notice of Cai thinking him just a weary friar on his pony as they passed. Groups of traders, carters and town folk were standing casually chatting or going about their business. The languages Cai heard being spoken around him were predominantly French and English with only a smattering of his native Welsh. Then as he was nearing a tavern, he heard some men arguing in a language that was unusual, but nevertheless recognisable, to him anyway.

One of the men standing near the arguing group saw Cai approach and called out, "Father, perhaps you could help us sort out this dispute before it gets ugly." He spoke in broken French and went on to explain that the men involved were in dispute over some silver coins.

Cai, not wanting to draw attention to himself, thought if he did not respond they may become suspicious or run after him.

"What is the problem?"

"Well, Father, Finbarr and Seamus did a week's work for Peter Mason. They both did the same amount of work, but Finbarr got the work for them and thinks he should have a larger share of the wages."

The two other men had fallen silent in the presence of the friar and they looked at Cai expectantly to solve their problem. Identifying them by this time as Irish migrants, Cai knew that whatever he said as a priest, they would be likely to respect.

"Are you not all strangers here in this land? You should stick together, brother and brother. You say you both did the same amount of work, therefore you should have equal share. One day maybe Seamus will find the work and Finbar you will be glad; so now make peace."

The two men stared at each other for several seconds before Finbar said, "Yes Father, will you join us for some ale?"

"Maybe I will," he said, feeling a little affinity with these men, all strangers in what now seemed a strange land, and anyway, he needed to know about some of the things that were happening in this corner of what was once Llywelyn's stronghold, a place where at one time it was rare to hear any other languages than his very own.

Communication was not straightforward as they conversed in a smattering of French and English, but after a few ales and many laughs Cai thought it time to go. He had mused on the idea of staying in the tavern, but instead decided to leave the bustle of the town. He was journeying to Cwmhir Abbey. It was better to keep a low profile and he couldn't bear to remain long in a town so defiled. It angered him to see what a prosperous place it had become and know the price that had been paid by his people to make it so. In fact the boiling anger that he had once felt after the death of Llywelyn was bubbling up within him, hot around his chest. The anger, he knew had never gone away, however much he had learned to control it, he often felt it simmering deep within himself. He had to get out of this town.

As he set off from Caernarfon, he realised how much he had come to enjoy his own company. After years in the mountains and time spent at Penmon Priory, he craved peace and quiet. Or maybe he was getting old. He thought of Gwenllian as he walked along the road beside Ianto. He had a task to complete before he could set off for Lincolnshire, so he could not delay. Gwenllian would have to wait for a little while and he thought to himself that if she really was a nun she would not be going anywhere; she would still be there when he arrived.

He wondered if life in a convent may be preferable to a life outside. If Gwenllian was a nun, she would not see the death, destruction and suffering that he had seen, she would not see her homeland dominated by an alien force, her people totally humiliated and subjugated. He tried to picture her and imagine her going through the daily rituals of priory life. What would she look like, her father, dark and tall, or her mother, fair and graceful, with the aquiline features of the French nobility? He was sure he would love her as if she were his own daughter, whatever she was like. The biggest barrier would be getting close to her, to even see her if she was encased in a nunnery.

Each time he thought of Gwenllian or of her mother, Eleanor, he naturally thought of Celeste. The lives of all three had been so entwined that it was impossible to separate them in his mind, and his heart ached for all of them, Eleanor now dead, Gwenllian maybe shut away in a nunnery, and Celeste, well he just hoped that she would be safe in France if she had succeeded in getting back to her family. But how he missed seeing Celeste … those few months he had spent at the Llys of Abergwyngregyn after Eleanor's death, although tinged with sadness, were some of the happiest he had known.

Left in charge of the household, he had passed some precious hours with Celeste and baby Gwenllian, and young Catrin of course. They would chat, he would sometimes play music and sing, or recite to the ladies whilst they sewed or spun and nursed the baby. He and Celeste had grown close, walking outside together on the warm summer evenings. Then one night in autumn, sitting by fire in the hall until the early hours, singing and drinking a little too much of her own made mead, Celeste had fallen asleep in his arms. He had carried her to her bed and she had confessed her feelings for him, asking him to stay with her. He did, and he confessed his feelings too and that one wondrous night was the only one they had together. The next day a messenger had come … his Lord Llywelyn was dead and none of them would be safe again.

Thinking of that night, as he did most nights, Cai realised that it was about time he found some shelter. The sky was darkening, streaked with a rosy hue, and the air was chilling. A shepherd's hut, which appeared abandoned, beckoned him. It was the only shelter in sight. He would stop here, preferring to be alone with his thoughts than seek company. Before he slept he took his crwth and sang the melody that he had sometimes sung to little Gwenllian. There was no one to hear it and tears filled his eyes as he thought of what should have been, what could have been.

The next day was bright and sunny with a light breeze, perfect for walking. Offered cheese and ale at the nearest village, Cai blessed the family and the pigs and continued towards Powys. There were pilgrims on the road, for many people made the journey to Ynys Enlli at the end of the Llŷn peninsula. Many ancient races and tribes had made it their sanctuary over the years. He himself had visited the island once before when a young bard, fresh and eager. The place had so inspired him, poetry and music had just seemed to flow from him in a stream of bubbling creativity, unfettered by the worries and dark thoughts which plagued him today. Now that time seemed to him, not just one, but many lifetimes away.

He was buried deep in thought when he realised there was quite a hubbub of chatter behind him. He turned to see that he had gathered a little crowd of pilgrims, obviously following the good friar. He stopped, intending to share his food, but they crowded around him and offered him bread, cakes and some strange fruit he had not seen before.

"Give us your blessing, Father," pleaded a small boy who hobbled on a stick, holding out a piece of stale bread. A sad but proud young face stared up into his eyes.

Cai knelt down and spoke to the boy softly in his own language. "You keep your bread. I have enough for myself. But I will certainly give you my blessing. Where are you from?"

"From near Caernarfon, Father, but we have no home any more. Me tad's lands were taken, then he died. Me mam and me, we are going to pray on the island, then look for a new home."

"Well, may God bless you with that," replied Cai and meant it, more sincerely than he ever had when he had offered a

Christian blessing.

His next overnight stay was in the home of the parish priest of a small settlement near Mynydd Cilgwyn. He was a plump, friendly man of about his own age who offered him a bed, a meal and a lot more wine than he should have had. His housekeeper, Eluned, was also a little too friendly and he noticed that Father Idris kept a close eye on her, especially on her chest and slender waist. Cai wondered what would happen at bed time, but she retired early to a room on the far side of the kitchen and Father Idris later climbed a wooden staircase to his private room, although Cai felt they were being polite and that probably was not what normally happened. Cai was offered a pallet by the fireplace for which he was very grateful, but for some reason he felt uneasy all night and slept fitfully.

The next morning, after a good breakfast of wheat porridge, Cai prepared to leave. Father Idris supplied him with a quantity of food and ale, plus a little of his strong mead, which he was very pleased to report had turned out exceptionally well this year.

Cai felt a pang of envy for the life of Father Idris. His life was comfortable and straightforward, whilst he, Cai, had decided to venture far from his homeland on some mission which had little chance of succeeding and which could get more dangerous day by day. Was he mad, he wondered? Perhaps he was, after spending so many years in the mountains. However, what did he have here? He had no real home, no true identity. He didn't know where he belonged any more. So what was there to lose?

The invasion and victory of the Norman king seemed to have faded in some people's memory. A lot of folk, like Father Idris, had integrated with the Normans and the other nationalities which were swept in with them as workers, servants and farmers. Cai was somewhat shocked by this change of loyalty, but supposed that many had had no choice if they wanted to survive. And, he could not judge them, for he had effectively hidden out in the mountains for seventeen years. There was really no point in dwelling on his regrets now.

He patted his pony for reassurance. "Come on, Ianto, there is no turning back, friend, we must find our way to Cwmhir Abbey without delay, where there will be a good meal for me and a comfortable stable for you."

CHAPTER 9

Cwmhir Abbey, Powys
April 1300

Old oaks, pushed up through centuries, forged a canopy of spiralling branches overhead through which the dawn light flickered. Those creatures who roamed the forest floor during the daylight hours were emerging and the nocturnal creatures retiring to the safety of their hidden dens. Cai could not see them, but he could hear the scraps and shrieks of little animals and the howl of a wolf, which thankfully seemed far away. But it was not just these creatures he was afraid of. On the open road, although travelling alone he had not felt threatened. Most people were respectful of a travelling friar, as he appeared to them, and would ask for a blessing, Some would give him food or a bed for the night. As friars would traditionally have no worldly goods or coins, he was not in much danger of being robbed. In the forest, life was different and for this journey he was on foot the easier to hide his passage to a secret place. In here there were no laws and there were desperate people roaming who could rob him for his cloak alone. He carried a bag of coins hidden under his shift; always useful to bargain for his life should it be absolutely necessary.

As he got up from under the oak where he had fitfully slept, he shook out his damp cloak. One night in the forest and he was already missing the comforts, although meagre, of Cwmhir Abbey and now longing for a bed and a fire to sit by. It was early April and the days were warm, but the nights were cold. Three nights he had spent with the Brothers at Cwmhir Abbey. He was missing Ianto, with whom he had built a strong bond on their travels. Lodged with Brothers at Cwmhir Abbey until he returned, Ianto would be well fed and looked after, that he knew. He was not sure whether the monks had totally been convinced by his explanation of why he could not take Ianto with him. He had not mentioned his detour into the forest, for they would have warned him against it.

Cwmhir Abbey was a place which, next to the mountains of Eryri, felt like home for him. Set in one of the most beautiful valleys in Powys, it was somewhere that he could step out of the world again for a while. He felt close to Llywelyn there. The monks had carefully buried the remains of his body after his head had been taken and displayed on the tower, and his spirit lingered there, Cai was sure.

In that place were deep memories of the days that he had shared with Llywelyn when they were young and invincible, never to be defeated. Shrouded by extensive wooded hillsides, it had been a safe haven shared with the monks who would fight to the death to protect their patron, their Prince. His body, what was left of it, was now for ever under their protection.

Father Francis had been pleased to see Cai after so many years and even more pleased that Cai appeared to have joined the Christian brotherhood. "Why don't you stay here with us?" Father Francis asked. "You have no true home anymore."

Cai had expected such a question and was ready with an answer. "If I were to settle, Father, this would be one of the very few places where I would choose to be," he said truthfully. "But I made a promise to our Prince which I must honour, and after that one day I may return here."

Cai could see that Father Francis looked a little baffled. "I know you have been a travelling bard and confidant of Llywelyn. I suppose you won't change your nature now, but you may need to rest weary bones one day and that day may not be too far ahead."

"I hope not, Father," Cai had replied, a little put out. "I must admit though even a night on a monk's pallet would be most welcome."

He had not often slept well since he had left Eryri, not only because of the cold nights and damp, but because of haunting images both from the past and from what he had seen on his journey. He had spent that evening at Cwmhir Abbey in conversation with Father Francis and several of the other Brothers. They discussed how the land he was travelling through now was a different land from his youth. The whole of his native Cymru was now subject to the authority of Edward I, garrisons of Norman soldiers were a blot on the landscape and the spirit of the place and the people had altered. There was an air of defeat, disillusionment, mistrust and fear.

Father Francis had enquired no more as to his business or his promise to Llywelyn. He had never asked questions of anyone who sought shelter at the abbey, whatever their beliefs. He felt though that there were many things Cai had not told him.

The next morning Cai prayed and meditated with the monks to pay respects to his dear friend and Prince. He prayed that he would be guided to Gwenllian and that Llywelyn would forgive him for not saving her, and then he meditated in silence, listening for any guidance he might receive. In this holy place where his Lord was buried, there would surely be some answers, whichever God or Goddess one asked. He had taken a walk to the stables where Ianto was lodged. He seemed happy enough amongst the few horses belonging to the Abbey. Well, who wouldn't be, Cai thought, in this lovely place? He had friends and he would be well fed for a few days whilst he, Cai, ventured into the forest. No doubt, if Ianto could talk he would say that he would be glad of a rest after trekking for weeks from the priory at Penmon.

"A fine name for a pony." Father Francis's voice cut across his thoughts.

Cai turned towards him. "Yes, he came from the priory at Penmon; he was quite a pet of Father Iorwerth."

"Cai, I don't know where you are going or what you are planning, but take care; travelling alone these days, even for a friar, is risky. There are fugitives and all sorts of vagabonds in that forest." Father Francis pointed up to the dense woodland which sloped up the hills around them. "Lots of them hang around there because we put food out for them and sometimes provide shelter for those who are sick or old, but we can't shelter them all. In fact we would be unwise to. It is too dangerous, I will not put my monks at risk."

"What of the Norman soldiers, Father, Edward's men?"

"We have to subject ourselves as you know to Edward's rule, but with his attentions turned elsewhere at the moment they generally leave us alone. But we don't know who watches us. With our Lord Llywelyn buried here, Edward would not trust our loyalties I am sure. We have removed certain documents and manuscripts which may be considered, shall we say, inflammatory, both for their safety and the safety of the Abbey. We are a poor order and our survival is already under threat. I hope you understand that."

Cai was not entirely sure if that was a plea or a warning, but he understood Father Francis's intention. "Don't worry, Father, I would not do anything to endanger the Abbey. I am very loyal to you, and Cwmhir would certainly be a place I would chose to end my days if I ever have such a choice. Your survival is of great importance to me."

Later that morning, climbing the wooded hillside Cai reached the small crumbled stone tower. Llywelyn's men had used this as a vantage point previously. The tower, now covered in ivy and brambles, overlooked the beautiful valley in which Cwmhir Abbey nestled. It had taken him several hours to find it, circling around in the sprawling, dense forest. But now he was here it all seemed familiar again. He huddled up inside the broken walls to wait.

It had been true what he had said to Father Francis. Cwmhir Abbey would be a welcome place to spend his days as he got older. True, he was not of the Christian faith, but there were few places now which offered sanctuary for those of the old beliefs. He thought of the mountains of Eryri and those who had sheltered him, his kin; he would always be one of them. He would never betray them. He had vowed never to utter their names to any who were not initiated, but would he ever return to them, would he be able to fulfil his promise and take Gwenllian to them? And, if he found Celeste, would he be able to offer her anything? He had nothing, but he told himself sharply, he must not abandon his beliefs or he would abandon his reason for being. He had been summoned here and although he was not quite sure of what lay ahead, it was the only path to take now. His bardic training must not be forgotten; after all it was what enabled him to slip so easily into the role of a Christian Brother and in some ways that role was not too dissimilar from his life before. It was certainly an easier role to play in the world as it was today; he might otherwise be skulking in the woods wondering where his next meal was coming from.

He thought it must be about noontime when he heard a whistle. He hesitated; it could be a soldier or a robber.

"Cai, come out for heaven's sake." The voice spoke in Welsh and had a familiar lilt.

He poked his head warily around some overhanging ivy. It was a soldier, but one he had not expected to see, one he thought he would never see again.

"Philip is that you? Diolch byth. You're alive, you're well, and look at you, not even a scarred face for all your trials. Come here, brother." Cai embraced him with a ferocity which surprised Philip. "It is so good to see my kinsman again, believe me."

"So it is, so it is," replied Philip. "I am truly pleased to see you, Cai, but we must not linger. Follow me and try to tread as lightly as possible."

They must have walked at least a mile and had seen no one, although Cai could not be sure that no one had seen them.

At a point before a copse of large oaks, Philip stopped. "We have to wait here, Cai. Even we are not allowed to know the exact location of this meeting."

Two figures soon emerged from behind the trees, one from the left and one from the right. They stood before Cai, their heads bowed and shrouded by their white, hooded gowns.

"Welcome, brother Cai. It is many years since we met," cried out one of the men.

"Even though you are our brother, we must at this point blindfold you," said the other.

Cai nodded; he understood the need. The first guide took a cloth and covered his eyes. Cai felt a little of the vulnerability he had felt many years before when he and his Lord Llywelyn had undergone an initiation deep in the mountains of Snowdonia. He now remembered that was where he knew this man from. However, this was not to be an ordeal; this was to be a reunion which would bring him a step nearer to fulfilling his promise.

Stumbling through the forest floor, guided by the hooded man who held his hand, he certainly didn't feel as agile as he had done all those years ago. When his blindfold was removed, he was standing in the centre of a circle of men, and as his eyes accustomed to the light, he stared to recognise a few faces. One man with a badly scarred face stepped forward. "Welcome, brother," he said as he extended his hand. Cai took his hand to shake and noticed that he had two fingers missing.

"Norman soldiers," he explained, reading Cai's thoughts. "It's a thing they like to do if they catch you."

"Well, Owain, thank God you're alive," Cai replied, recognising Llywelyn's Captain of Arms.

"It is I, brother, together with Rhys and Ieuan ap Rhys."

Owain beckoned to the two other men, who came up and embraced Cai.

It was incredible to see them again, and together, safe. He had thought all three of them to be most likely dead. He had always felt a deep sense of guilt at staying behind in Abergwyngregyn in relative safety, whilst these men had risked their lives. But it was what Llywelyn had wanted and requested of him.

"This is good news; this is a miracle, Owain. I heard that you had fallen at Castell y Bere after we left. And Rhys, this must be your son, then. How time has passed."

"Sometime, Cai, I will tell you the whole story," Owain

replied.

They moved from the small clearing, through a tunnel of trees and into what seemed like a dead end. Large oaks blocked their way. Cai by this time was not at all surprised when one of the hooded men removed foliage covering the lower trunk of a large oak to see that the trunk was carved out to make a passage to the other side. With a squeeze, they all filed through into a larger clearing where there stood a wooden building, mostly camouflaged with leaves and branches. Inside, remarkably it was not quite as rustic; fresh rushes lined the floor and rugs and tapestries adorned the walls. In one room stood a table and roughly hewn chairs, a cooking fire at one end. The other room contained straw mattresses and blankets. Cai sensed a woman's touch, although he would not expect a woman to be here. An old man stirred a huge iron pot over the fire.

Owain pulled another chair, which was placed near the fire, over to the table. "Sit down Cai, we have a lot of talking to do."

Cai sat next to Owain and opposite Philip, feeling a strong sense of familiarity with his old comrades. The last time they had seen each other was the fateful night at Castell y Bere, the night a party of them escaped with little Gwenllian. Owain had been left in charge of the hundreds of men who had gathered there.

The men took their places around the table and the old man served up a pottage of rabbit and wild herbs and roots. He then took his place at the head of the table. Cai for some reason had not expected him to take his place with the others, as he thought him to be a servant, but he knew that in the forest normal rules of society did not apply, and this was not normal society. Even more strangely, a woman came and sat on the one remaining chair next to Philip. She appeared to come from nowhere, and although most of her face was obscured by her long brown hair, he felt a glimmer of recognition. Parting her hair and throwing it over her shoulder, she smiled at Cai. He knew that smile, even though it beamed from a face which was more worn and less carefree than when he had last seen it.

"Catrin? Is it you, Catrin fach?" He wanted to leap over the table to hug her and fire a thousand questions at her, but she put a finger to her lips to usher silence and then leaned over the table and placed her hand on top of his.

"It is so good to see you, Cai. Until a few months ago when we were summoned by Hywel, I thought you were dead."

"I thought you may be too. I had no word. How did you come to be here, cariad?"

"I am married to Philip now. I have so much to tell you, Cai, but we will talk later." Sitting back, she took Philip's hand and Cai noticed the unmistakeable affection which passed between them. He smiled to himself and was exceedingly pleased that two of his dear companions were alive and happy together. He dared to hope that Catrin may have news of Celeste, but knew that he would have to wait a while for that.

Cai leaned over to Owain and whispered, "I've been to Cwmhir Abbey many times, but did not know of this place. Is it safe here?"

"I believe this place was used by the monks of Cwmhir for storage of valuable items in times of trouble."

"And now they let those they consider ungodly use it?"

"They have always been tolerant of other beliefs. I guess we are the lesser enemy now. Anyway, we were united in our quest to help our Prince and their patron, Llywelyn."

Owain and Cai chatted like the old comrades they were, outlining the events they had both experienced over the past years. Cai was pleased at the spark of kinship that flashed between them.

As soon as the meagre meal was finished, the old man who sat at the head of the table banged it with his fist. He searched the faces that surrounded the table. "Have we all gathered our information?"

Cai was astounded that this man addressed them with such authority. He studied him closely, the long straggly grey hair, the bushy beard which obscured much of his face, the shabby, ragged clothes. Then he focused on the sharp green eyes which still held a sparkle, and a realisation dawned. Could it be, yes he believed it was, Hywel the Bard, once a bard who then became an Archdruid. Hywel stood to address them all.

"We have come together here today as brothers and sister," he nodded to Catrin, "to discuss two important issues. Welcome all. It is many years since most of us all assembled in one place and there are a few amongst us who have never gathered with us before, but all here have been and are willing to give their life for the guardianship of our late Prince, Llywelyn ap Gruffydd, and his sacred treasures. Some of you risked your lives for him, and some who are not with us, died supporting him. Let us send our blessings to those on the inner planes, departed from this physical life. Let us send our blessings to the Prince himself; may he be at peace, reunited with his dear wife, Eleanor."

A moment of silence followed before Hywel resumed. "There are not many of us now who continue to live their life by the old ways. The powerful influence of the Christian Church and now the ruling of the Norman warlords have almost obliterated any knowledge of us by the common people. Those of us gathered here today, and our few brothers and sisters scattered in the mountains of Eryri, are the only few who keep the knowledge in our native land. We have done well to survive and carry the light for so long. I spent some years in the Eryri grove with Seren and Cynan and their priests and priestesses. During that time, we discussed many things about our past and our future. There are some who believe we no longer exist in this world. But we know the truth. Our dear brother, Cai, who has joined us here, has now set out on a new quest. It is several years since I saw Cai, as I have been travelling, trying to piece together something of our heritage, to call as many of those who have been dispersed to gather here today. So to the matter of the manuscripts ..."

Hywel glanced and nodded at Cai. "The Llywelyn family manuscripts contain, as we know, ancient and not so ancient sacred knowledge drawn from many traditions of the world, together with the Llywelyn family history. The compilation of these has taken many years and much of my strength. They contain much wisdom and so they were named 'The Owl'. Today though, we are not here to discuss the contents of the manuscripts, but the protection of them. The Abbot of Cwmhir, Father Francis, agreed to keep these safe after Llywelyn's death, in this very place where we are, but when Edward laid claim to the Abbey, they had to be moved to a more secret location. There is only one person who should rightly have claim to these manuscripts and that brings us to our second matter; Gwenllian, daughter of the Prince and the rightful Princess of Wales, the only living heir to the Principality, Tywysogaeth Cymru."

When the word 'living' was said, several who sat around the table gasped, for they thought her dead.

"But," continued Hywel, "we believe she could be alive. I hope brother Cai has some information for us. Here I will ask our brother and bard, Cai, to tell us anything what he may know."

Cai was unprepared as he had no idea that he would be asked to speak of this matter in this company. He had thought that no one knew of his visit to Penmon Priory, except Seren, the High Priestess of the Druid Grove of Eryri. Now the pieces of the puzzle were coming together.

Cai explained to the company what he knew from the information he had gleaned about Gwenllian from Penmon Priory, although he did not say where that information came from. Even though all of those present had been summoned or invited here by Hywel, who would vouch for their sincerity, there were some Cai did not know. Scanning the faces of those present, he saw amazement, relief, concern and sadness in their expressions.

Philip then stood up and said he could verify Cai's words, as under Hywel's instruction and guidance, he had infiltrated Edward's army for several years now and discovered that Gwenllian was most probably at Sempringham Priory and that a sum was paid to the Priory by the King each year for her keep.

Hywel continued his explanation. "It will be Cai's task to travel to this place in England and try to make contact with the Princess before we decide what further action to take. Gwenllian will be of the age of eighteen now. She will now be able to understand the importance of her family heritage."

"But could it be too late if she has taken holy vows?" asked a red haired man Cai did not recognise. "Why has no one tried to free her before?"

"It is only recently, Simon of Halston, that we have known of her exact whereabouts and it is only now that our company, the only people left who are concerned of her whereabouts, have come together. Besides, our Princess would have been too young had we been able to pluck her from the clutches of King and Church earlier than now. Simon of Halston, don't forget that although we honour all beliefs, you too have been initiated into the mysteries of the ancient Druids. Gwenllian was not only destined for that too, and it was promised by her father, that although she was to rule a Christian country, she would also honour the old ways. She is the last of a lineage and at the whim of King Edward, who ordered the slaughter of her father, she has been locked away from life. The King has the power of her future in his hands and we have to tread very carefully.

"Gwenllian should rightfully be, as her name depicts, our Holy Priestess. In early times the name 'Gwen' encompassed the essence of blessedness, as in 'The Circle of Gwynfyd', which represents life as a blessed and pure force, where love, knowledge and justice become ever stronger. Although she is not with us and has been reared by Christians, Gwenllian will doubtless have some of the holiness, strength and discipline of a Druid priestess. All of us have been scattered for years in the aftermath of the fall of our country, but we have not been idle. Philip, myself, Cai and others have been gathering our strength and information which will serve us well, and now is the time, the time to act."

After these last words, Hywel walked away from the table and the whole company fell silent.

Cai studied the face of the man called Simon, who had spoken. He could not recognise him, although the name of Halston he had heard before somewhere, but where? Simon looked out of place in this gathering, yet Cai could not decide why; after all, they must have looked a very motley crew to anyone from outside.

The two white robed men, who had sat at the top of the table on either side of Hywel, rose to serve a pewter goblet of wine to each of them. Hywel then returned holding a golden goblet embossed with emeralds and rubies. As he stood at the top of the table his powerful voice cut through the silence and a few who stood for the toast saw the waves of sound which emanated from his whole being.

"This is indeed a magical day. We should thank the God and Goddess that we have all survived through dreadful times. Although we may appear to have been defeated, the spirit of our people will never be crushed. Blessed be!"

The men and Catrin all echoed 'Blessed be!' as they raised their glasses in a toast and embraced each other as was the custom.

Taking his position again at the head of the table, Hywel explained, "I hold in my hand the consecrated chalice from which Llywelyn himself first drank when he promised to honour and protect our beliefs, as we swore to be loyal to him and protect his Principality in every way we could. We have failed to defeat the might of the King through the sword and through our magic as our ancestors did against the Romans those many, many years ago. Sometimes you cannot defeat the tides of change; however, the seeds planted by our ancestors still grow and will never die. We need to replant them in a different cause and learn by what we have been shown. We will never die."

There was silence, followed by a banging on the table and cheering. Cai stood up, ashamed of his own failure. "I promised my Prince and the spirit of Eleanor that if it was no longer safe at her uncle's house, I would protect little Gwenllian and take her to safety in the mountains of Eryri to be cared for and taught by the High Priestess Seren. For those of you who were not there, I will briefly retell the story. When her father was killed, the baby Gwenllian was taken to Denbigh to her uncle Dafydd's house. We moved from there to Castell y Bere, the last castle to be taken by Edward. Hearing that his troops were on the way, I, with a small party, tried to take Gwenllian into the mountains for safety. We made a camp eventually at Nanhysglain, a boggy area near Abergwyngregyn, but we never made it to safety in the mountains. We were ambushed and the few armed men with us were killed, or so I thought. I was left for dead. Luckily no one had time or inclination to bury me, for I was alive and when I woke there were only dead bodies around me. I knew not what had happened to the babe, Gwenllian, her nurse or her guardians, Catrin and Celeste. Being injured, I continued on my way to the mountains. I must have wandered for miles then collapsed again later on, for I woke up this time in the arms of Seren, with the High Priest Cynan tending to my wounds. I am so happy to see Catrin here today. My only wish and purpose now is to find Gwenllian and bring her back to her true people."

There were claps and shouts from the company, but Simon stood up with a sombre face. "Hywel, you did not really answer my question. Why has she not been rescued before and what is the plan now to remove her from the Priory?"

"Simon, there are no direct answers to your questions. For many years, our company as exists here today, has been scattered, not just over the Principality, but over the entire world as we know it. The exact whereabouts of the Princess Gwenllian has only recently been verified, and this at a time which seems more fortunate, for she is now a woman and able to understand her position should we be able to make contact with her. We should be glad that at least she has been kept safe and well. After the fall of Llywelyn many of you here had been scattered for safety and survival. It has taken me years to locate all of you and bring us together on this day, if only to discuss this matter and renew our faith."

There was a tense moment of silence before Simon spoke again. "There are fighting men here, we should form an army to march on the Priory and bring Gwenllian to freedom. We are not all peaceful Druids who sit back and expect the Gods to intervene. Where were the Gods when Llywelyn was killed?"

"I understand your anger," said Hywel, now standing to face Simon, "but we must tread carefully. Firstly, we would not attack an undefended holy place, and secondly, at this stage we do not even know for sure which nun is our true Gwenllian. To seize her suddenly would be a great trauma for her. It is far better for Cai to infiltrate the Priory in his role as a monk and make contact with her to inform her of her true heritage. We had plans to admit Catrin to the Priory as a novice, but as she is now with child, that is no longer possible. We must not draw attention to ourselves at this stage. We must act secretly and carefully. And that is my last word on the matter."

Cai was stunned for a moment. His little Catrin with child; this was news indeed, but of course many years had passed. She was probably old to bear a child now; she would be over thirty years of age.

It was then that Hywel came to embrace Cai. "You have confirmed my suspicions that I am no longer the handsome beast I used to be. You did not recognise me, did you?"

Cai laughed. "Well I didn't expect you to be cooking and serving the food, therefore I took you to be a servant."

"Well, let that teach you a lesson. You of all people should know that you never judge a man simply by his clothes or the job he does, monk!" He sighed as he pulled at Cai's robe. "How is your bardic craft, have you grown in knowledge? These last few years have changed both of us. Let's go and sit together and tell me more of your years in Eryri and anything else you know of the Princess."

"You seem to know more than me, Hywel, about what Seren has planned."

"I sent a message to her several months ago saying I had uncovered some information. Her message back said that you were soon to be leaving. I replied and asked her to send you here before you ventured further away, possibly into England. I heard nothing back so was not sure if you had received the message. There are only a few who can be trusted with such information. And it is a long haul up into the western mountains. When I last visited there we spoke didn't we, of how we may find our Gwenllian. Now it seems we can put our plan into action. Seren is contactable from time to time on the inner planes, but it is up to us now. I want you to go with Philip and Catrin and wait in their house until I arrive, by the Solstice."

For a moment Cai thought of the manuscripts. Had Hywel left the manuscripts in Eryri, he wondered.

It seemed that he had read his thoughts, as he was often prone to do. Hywel started to explain.

"The manuscripts are safe with Seren, but she and Cynan are the only ones who know exactly where they are. Not even me, for I left them in their safe keeping. For a while I considered leaving them on Ynys Enlli with the monks who know something of our lineage, but even that was risky. The island could be attacked from the sea; unlikely, but it's a risk. It seems though that Edward is turning his attentions elsewhere these days, and, my friend, the descendants of our own people are the ones who should rightfully hold them. There is no way back now. We have to find a way to survive in the country as it has become. We cannot fight them now, but we can preserve the knowledge that we have and maybe our time will come again in the future. Let us get some rest, for tomorrow you will travel with Catrin and Philip to Philip's estate on your way to eastern England. They can help you. It is the ideal place for you to consider your plans to make contact with Gwenllian. Gwenllian is the only heir of Llywelyn, but you Cai, are one of the few heirs of the sacred knowledge of the Druids."

Cai nodded. It was good to be with his kin. He felt at home again. "Do you think we can trust Father Francis of Cwmhir?" he asked.

"He guarded the manuscripts well. We know that the Knights of the Red Cross have all the Cistercian monasteries in their hands and we know the work that they do to preserve ancient knowledge. Never forget Llywelyn's affiliation with the Knights and with us. Even though he was primarily a fighting man he knew the importance of saving the truth from the blind and ignorant. But we must never speak of this again."

When Hywel ended the conversation Cai knew it was pointless to ask any further questions. If he was travelling with Catrin he would have plenty of time for talking. Most of the men were heading to the sleeping area. The forest was darkening and the nocturnal creatures were awakening. Although he was looking forward to a more comfortable bed with warmth and company and felt very pleased that he was to travel with Catrin and Philip the following day, there were so many questions he wanted to ask both of them that he doubted if he could sleep at all.

He thought of Ianto and would not leave on such a long journey without him. He might never see him again so he would have to go again to Cwmhir before departing. Philip would not be happy about that he was sure, but he would insist on being accompanied back to near the Abbey in the morning to fetch him before they departed to Philip's house.

He closed his eyes and hoped sleep would come soon, and then the day would break and his adventure would begin. As he slowly drifted into slumber the shriek of a barn owl pierced the veil of night.

CHAPTER 10

Sempringham Priory
April 1300

The dark, the thud of horses' hooves and the shriek of a demon. Wencilian could not get much sleep that night. The dream had come again, and as always, it was fragmented; it made no sense. There were figures, their faces shadows; she could not tell if they were male or female or in fact even of this world. Thoughts of Alice and Mira then mingled with flashes of memory of her brief experiences in the outside world. The woman, Hilda, and her strange daughter were chasing her through a forest with a floor of slippery moss and leaves. She couldn't get a grip to run and was pulling herself along by the branches of the trees. She woke sharply, in a cold sweat. Then hearing the bell she sat upright, relieved that all was as usual in her small cell. It was quiet, very quiet. The Sisters would be stirring for the service, not yet fully awake. She was surprised to see light filtering through the window; of course, it was Prime not Matins. The extra time should have given her a restful sleep had it not been invaded by disturbing dreams.

Pulling off her nightshift, Wencilian stood naked, shivering. Normally she would reach for her small bowl of cold water to wash herself down without another thought. She stopped and looked at her body. Pale skin, she thought, but creamy, not pink or mottled. She noticed fine hairs of golden down, barely visible, covered her arms and legs, legs, which were thin but well defined by muscle. She felt breasts, which were well rounded and firm, and a stomach soft with a slight curve. It occurred to her then that this was a body in its prime, ready. Then tears filled her eyes. Her body might never have the promise of being ready for anything more than the daily worship of God and the daily slog. As soon as these thoughts had formed, she grabbed her shift around her and dressed quickly before guilt could seep through into her bones. It was a heavy burden, guilt, and heaven knows all the Sisters were weighed down by it.

During Prime, Wencilian thought again of Alice, of how, although Alice had felt ready for marriage with Maurice, her thoughts and feelings were disregarded and she was shut away from the world. The only choice a novice had when that thick oak door slammed behind her was to accept her fate gracefully or to fester inwardly with bitterness. Later today, Alice would see Maurice, who could be betrothed to her sister, and the pain she would feel would be a lot worse than the pain she had felt at losing him before. Was it worse, she thought than her own situation where she would scan the congregation just in case she met someone's eyes who would return her gaze and smile in recognition? This would not happen, because no one knew her in the outside world. If her parents, who had abandoned her, were still alive, maybe they could not claim her back for some reason; maybe they came every year just to try and get a glimpse of her. This was the fantasy with which she consoled herself each year. In a few hours' time, visitors would be arriving. Maybe, she thought as well, she shouldn't give Alice any false hope of being with Maurice. She could not repeat the experience she had had with Mira – it was too risky. In any case this situation was entirely different, Alice was from a wealthy family and Maurice was already betrothed to her sister; there was nothing to done.

Wencilian had been relieved from infirmary duties for the day to help the novices and designate tasks for them. She found the novices tried her patience, as some she thought feckless and giddy and not very bright. Of course this was no fault of their own. One young girl, Sara, she felt a great fondness for. Sara looked upon her almost like a mother, although she was not much older herself. She always seemed so cheerful, intelligent and brave. Brave, because when Wencilian checked their dormitory at night she could often hear her weeping for her family, yet she never mentioned them or complained about anything. Wencilian knew that her mother, father and two brothers had been killed by Norman soldiers. There had been some kind of dispute, Sara had told her; her father's land had been seized and all her family killed. She was the only survivor, so she had wandered for weeks in the forest until near starvation had brought her to the doors of the Priory where food was dispensed to the poor on a Friday. She had slept outside the Priory for a week until the Prioress relented and took her in. She may have convinced the Prioress that she had a true vocation, but Wencilian knew it was pure survival. However, she had adapted well to life in the convent and was eager to help and serve. Then recently, two years later at fifteen years old, she received a novice's tunic. Perhaps, Wencilian thought, she may be feeling guilt that she was the only survivor of such a terrible massacre. There are many reasons why women come to this place.

"Sara, could you make sure all the seats are clean. Then I think we are ready, our jobs are done."

Sara looked at her and smiled. "You have your introductions to do, so I will pray for you. I'm glad I shall be hidden away."

Suddenly, Wencilian felt this too. Normally nuns were hidden from view. Was it cruel or kind of Mother Elizabeth to expect her to introduce each visitor in the refectory after mass? Maybe she did it to keep her occupied, knowing that she felt disadvantaged, never having any visitors herself, or was there some other reason, a tinge of guilt perhaps? She had never stood so in public view before.

After the ceremony and the service, the time came all too soon. As she had practised, Wencilian proclaimed the name of each visitor as they entered the room. She felt that her first words had streamed out of her mouth far too fast, displaying her nervousness, but, after a little pause, she became in control and felt strangely powerful with hundreds of eyes starting expectantly at her.

The atmosphere was jovial whilst refreshments were served;

however, the usual strict surveillance was maintained. One of the Prioresses would lead the Sisters who had visitors to the hall where they could converse. Wencilian was trying to keep close to Alice, when Sister Ignatius took her arm and dragged her to one side. "Sister, we are to help now in the kitchen."

Wencilian just managed to glance back to see Alice's sister embracing her. By her side was a tall young man who looked ashamed, but also burning with desire to talk to Alice. 'Oh yes,' thought Wencilian, 'he is not doing this, marrying her sister of his own volition; he has no choice.'

Sister Ignatius was urging Wencilian towards the kitchens. "We have honoured guests dining with the Prioresses. We need help in the refectory before all the Sisters can eat."

"Yes, Sister Ignatius. I'll be glad to help, but first I must visit the latrine."

It was the first year she had noticed that Sister Ignatius never had visitors either, and a small stab of pity pierced her.

It was two hours later when the nuns sat down to their own feast in the refectory. Most of the visitors had departed, except for those who dined with the Prioress. The smell of roasted meat was overwhelming. It was not an aroma which drifted around the Priory very often. Wencilian tried to eat enthusiastically; she felt that she had become so thin since the beginning of Lent and it was not just the Lenten fasting, but the worry of the other events which had caused her to lose her appetite.

Over the meal, Wencilian sat next to Alice, but the little conversation which was allowed, being a feast, was restricted to comments on the day's events and performance. Nothing personal could be discussed. Wencilian was itching to know what had happened to Alice during her brief meeting with her family. Some of the lay sisters were serving wine and mead, so the Sisters were distracted as they had their glasses filled. Snatching the opportunity, Wencilian quickly turned to Alice and was dismayed to see real pain in her eyes. Without words, she took Alice's hand in her own and squeezed it gently. Her questions would have to wait. As she briefly held Alice's hand she felt something small and hard drop into her own hand. She glanced down to see a ring, pure gold; it glittered in the candlelight. Wencilian had never touched much jewellery, but this, she knew instinctively, was something special. Not only must it have cost a fortune, but more than that it was a symbol, a symbol of love, love which was forbidden and was causing a lot of heartache. As she passed it back, she felt Alice's hand shake, whether with guilt or pure emotion she wasn't sure, possibly both. Now was not the time for questions though.

Wencilian wondered how she could help Alice. At the moment she could think of nothing at all that would either ease her pain or help her reunite with Maurice. After the escapade with Mira, she concluded, it may be better not to think of it at all, but just pray for Alice that she may find peace. Many women in this place had no choice, like herself. Even though Mother Elizabeth repeatedly told the Sisters they were privileged women, privileged to have an education and food and clothing, she always told them with some misgiving. Wencilian always saw the doubt in her eyes.

CHAPTER 11

**Eryri Mountains
April 1300**

The mountains of Gwynedd were shrouded in heavy mist. To an unwary traveller, the paths would be obscured and to stray too far could be dangerous, unless one had a guide of course. The guide would be one of the hill folk, the only people who could safely walk through the mists. At times even they would be wary, for the mountains were the uncompromising lords of this harsh environment and if you did not pay them respect, you paid the price.

Even wise folk, known by many names, hidden in some of the densely forested areas of these hills, did not venture out in the mists without the hill folk to guide them. They respected the talents of these hardy people, without whose protection the wise folk would be in even more danger.

It was sad reality that many of the hill folk had taken to the valleys and the coast to be farmers and learn trades, and who could blame them for that. Some had been harassed and beaten by King's men in their endeavour to discover the whereabouts of the remnants of any heretics, but to turn their back on the old ways, the old beliefs, that was unforgivable.

It was these facts that Cynan was musing on as he walked to Seren's hut. Hidden well by the trees and camouflaged with other foliage, it was always a surprise to him that he hadn't missed it. Inside was welcoming; the fire was lit and the young initiate, Nerys, was stirring some broth. When he entered, she turned and made a small bow.

"Carry on, carry on, Nerys. Is your High Priestess not here?"

"She went to the cave by the waterfall to swim."

"Then I shall wait here. My legs are weary. I shall warm by the fire."

"You are welcome, My Lord."

Whilst Nerys busied herself around the hut, Cynan stared into the fire. He wasn't searching for anything; in fact it was many moons since he had divined or looked for omens in the fire. It had always been fire that held him and gave him the answers he needed. He never 'saw' anything in water, unlike Seren. She liked to be near water, bathing in it, scrying in it to glimpse the future, or just sitting praying and meditating by it for hours. The warmth of the fire was starting to cheer him and it wasn't long before he drifted off into a deep sleep.

Seren was shivering as she made her way back to her hut. She hoped that Nerys would have a good fire stoked up. It wasn't just the cold of the water that was making her body tremble, but something else, something that she had not felt or seen for a long time. Like the ripples of the pool where she bathed spreading like a fan around her, ripples of energy spread through her mind and body and she heard a voice from a distant place and she saw, saw a face she had longed to see, in the water below her.

When she came into the hut and reached for a sheepskin cloak to warm her, she was surprised to see Cynan. She walked over and kissed him on the lips lightly, as was the traditional greeting. "Blessings to you. What brings you here?"

"I was feeling restless and wondered if you had any knowledge of Cai."

Seren looked uneasily across at Nerys. "Nerys, serve us all up some broth and go to the novices and help with their studies."

"Novices. How many do we have now, three or four?" muttered Cynan.

Seren turned and looked at him sharply. "Cynan, I do not want any of your cynicism here. We are the ones who have to keep positive. It's painful I know, but we have six novices and they will lead the way forward one day. And there are others as you know, our brothers and sisters in Powys, in Ireland, in ..."

"Forgive me, I've lived too long and seen too much. We seem to be forever diminishing, skulking in the hills, driven further and further into obscurity. At least when the Prince was alive, we had some protection. Now Edward will make caeth of us all. What has a bard been reduced to, but singing verse to entertain the courts?"

"There are still some that spread the wisdom, as you well know!"

Nerys, looking relieved to be released from burdensome tasks, quickly served the broth, grabbed her cloak and set off the half mile or so to the house of novices.

Seren shook her long raven hair, now tinged with a little grey, and pulled the cloak around her shoulders. She beckoned Cynan to the table where they sat on the worn reed-woven chairs.

"Even though the day is warm, that pool is the coldest I have ever known."

Cynan made no comment. He was waiting, as he knew from her manner that she had something to tell him and would make him wait … that was her prerogative as High Priestess he told himself, but she could be annoying at times. He waited a few minutes in silence, and then she spoke.

"I have seen Cai on his path. He is heading south from Môn to Powys and Cwmhir Abbey. Our plans are as they should be so far. I sense that his mind is on the east though, but he needs to pass through Powys. He has a plan. He is confident. He must have had some news."

Cynan's eyes widened and his heart missed a beat as she continued, walking away from the table and standing with her back to him in front of the fire.

"I saw her. I saw her for the first time ever. Something has happened … she has always been hidden from me. I have worked out she must have lived roughly eighteen years now, so she is becoming a woman. It feels that her awareness has shifted. Until now she has always been hidden from me behind some tall imposing wall or structure."

"Do you think she felt you watching her?"

"No, but I feel she is starting to question who she is, where she has come from. Far memories are awakening in her soul."

"That is good. Will you try to contact her?"

"No, it would only disturb her at the moment. The time is not right and I don't even know if I would be successful."

"Well, there is no one else who could do so, not that we know of, not who can access the inner planes. Do you know where she is exactly?"

"No, but I feel she is being held prisoner somewhere."

"Well, at least we know she is alive." Cynan never really doubted for one moment Seren's ability as a seer, although his cynicism got the better of him sometimes. "I am glad, so glad," he continued, "that our Princess is alive. That gives us all hope, hope for the future. What should we do?"

Seren turned to face him and looked into his deep blue eyes. She saw in him the knowledge that he, their High Priest, would not be with them much longer.

"You, Cynan, could ignite fire out of the deepest rock. You can make the light sparkle within the deep womb of the earth. But I feel this is a job for the priestesses only, when the time is right."

"I am old, my strength is fading," he said as he read her thoughts. "Before I die, I would be a happy man to know that our true Gwenllian, our Holy Priestess and Princess, is with us in this land, her land. Her father promised us that she could train with us. How cruel that she has now become a prisoner, shut away from her people."

"A prisoner of the King, no doubt," mumbled Seren as she stared back into the fire. "I wonder how much Llywelyn would have kept his promise had he lived. The pressure of the Christian world upon the courts of Princes and Kings is too powerful for many to withstand, and some don't care; they will back whoever gives them the most land, the most power and people under their dominion."

"True, but there are some who have sworn, taken an oath and will be faithful to the old ways. And, there are some who are initiated and could not turn from the path for long before they are called back. Our Lord and true Prince was one. He always protected us, as we tried to protect him. Our mountains, our groves and sacred places have shielded him from the Norman king many times.

Seren looked forlorn. Leaning close to Cynan she took his hand in hers. "I am sorry; I did not mean him any disrespect. Perhaps we failed him. We should have tried harder to protect him from harm; our magic is becoming weaker."

"We cannot heal all the ills and evil in the world. All our magic, all our strength and weapons did not prevent the Romans from defeating our ancestors on Môn, now did it?"

"How different our country might be today if they had, Cynan. At times, I look over to Môn when the mists are clear and I can still hear the cries of the priestesses, the few who were left behind, the few who saw the aftermath of the slaughter. I wonder if they will always be heard by those who have the ears?"

"Are we sure they survived? It is so long ago, they are not even mentioned in legend."

"Cynan! What is happening to you? Where is your belief, are you so cynical in your old age?"

"I do not hear them, but then maybe it is only for the priestesses to hear."

"Maybe. Môn was sacred for its priestesses after all. Our ancestors, with all their knowledge and magic, did not neglect to conceal and preserve some secrets did they? Of course, some had become cynical old men who ignored the mysteries of the moon to their peril and grew too arrogant, like the priests of the Christians."

"Times were dangerous; masculine force was needed too, all the moon magic of the priestesses would not keep the Romans away." Cynan looked up at Seren a little nervously.

"I know that, Cynan, but all should be in balance."

"All those who would destroy us, they didn't defeat us entirely now did they, but how many do we have here now, Seren? You and me, several priests and priestesses, and six novices … once there were thousands of us, hundreds here in

Eryri alone; we were a force, a community. How much chance is there of our survival in the future, especially with our Prince gone? Maybe we should think again of joining our brothers and sisters in Ireland."

"We must have hope, Cynan. We must keep hope in Gwenllian. If Cai can find her, maybe somehow he can bring her here. I would not consider leaving this land while our Princess still lives. How could you even suggest such a thing, Cynan?"

"Will Cai meet with Hywel?" Cynan asked, trying to steer Seren away from a potential argument.

"I hope they have met already so he will have some protection."

The two sat in silence for a while, lost in their own thoughts. When Seren pulled her cloak closely around her, Cynan rose up to stoke the fire.

"I think I am worried, Seren, worried that when I go, who is ready to take my place?"

"The Priest Geraint is not far off being ready to become a High Priest. But your time has not come yet. The time of Calan Mai is approaching and we will lead the rites together. There is a lot to prepare; this Beltane ritual needs to be a powerful one. I can feel the tides changing. It is time for us to take a more active role, even though we may never be leaders of men and women again in our lifetime."

"Perhaps you are right, Seren. What short time on this earth I have left must be put to good use, but it needs a younger man now to lead the rites."

"You must gather all your strength and energy now, Cynan. We need you, you still have much to enjoy. It's so good to feel the earth quickening, the spring flowers in bud and the accursed cold and damp that wraps round these mountains in winter, breaking." Whilst trying to offer some cheer to Cynan, Seren tried to hide the foreboding she felt deep inside her and she hoped that the Beltane rites would not prove too much for him, and hoped she may not have to spend all her years in these mountains.

"Ah, I would welcome some warmth for my bones for sure,

and you, Seren, forgive me, but you are no longer the young priestess who could run like lightening across the mountain paths. You too need to rest before Beltane. We both know I will not be here much longer and you will need all your strength to lead the novices and help to find and free our Princess Gwenllian."

Seren looked at him softly, as a wave of sorrow washed over her. She would indeed, she knew, need all her strength to cope with the loss of him, her Priest, her dear companion, her one time lover at the Beltane rites when they were young.

"Will you stay, Cynan, and rest here tonight? We have a lot to talk about and I have some special wine brewed from last year's elderberries, just ripe for the drinking."

"Ha, Ha, Seren, blessed be! Let's be merry. After all we have had some of the best news and we cannot share it with anyone else yet. Wine and warmth by the fire will be very, very welcome tonight. We will make a toast to Gwenllian, our loved and lost Princess, who still lives!"

CHAPTER 12

Sempringham Priory

Sister Agnes was doing her rounds to check that all the Sisters were in their cells. The time between Compline and Matins was the only time for deep sleep, so she did not like to disturb anyone, if at all possible. The candle in Wencilian's cell was not flickering. No doubt she was asleep, as were all the other Sisters, save the new novice who was very unsettled. She had noticed Wencilian at Vespers; she looked very tired and drawn, worried. Maybe it was the extra work she had taken on in the infirmary, always one to help anyone in need.

Sister Agnes felt tired too and longed for her bed, but tonight she had been summoned by the Prioress. It had to be important for the Prioress to call her at this time. She approached the Prioress's room with some trepidation. She knew she had been overly harsh with some of the novices and some of the Sisters recently, but she felt it was only for their own interest. Giving them the benefit of her experience was a gift, even though deep down she knew sometimes it was tinged with bitterness. Tonight she was expecting a reprimand.

The Prioress Elizabeth was sitting with Sister Marie Claire by a cosy fire in her room, the room as usual littered with parchments and books of all kinds. The Prioress, waiting for Sister Agnes, was silent. Sister Marie Claire fiddled with her rosary, anticipating business of a serious nature. She was grateful for the warmth from the fire, but couldn't help but feel it was a little unfair that none of the Sisters benefitted from a fire, only on rare occasions in the depth of winter being allowed one in the chapter house or the refectory.

Perusing the tapestries which adorned the walls took her mind off mundane tasks. She loved to lose herself in these works of art. Donated by patrons of the Priory, each one told a story of a battle or a chivalrous deed that held secrets beyond her understanding. As the candle light flickered, the figures seemed to move around as if real. What an excellent opportunity for the Sisters it would be, she thought, if they could indulge in such a fine pastime, were it allowed. A knock on the heavy oak door interrupted her thoughts.

"Enter, Sister," responded Mother Elizabeth in a sombre tone.

Sister Agnes swept through the door, gathering her cloak around her. The Prioress stood and beckoned the Sisters to sit at her table. Sister Agnes, feeling the warmth of the room, let her cloak drop from her shoulders and waited.

"Two issues I need to discuss with you of great importance and I don't want any interruptions. That is why I chose this time to meet." Mother Elizabeth poured some wine for them each, and then continued. "Firstly, one of the lay sisters, Mira of Stamford, seems to have disappeared. I now know that she didn't go with Sister Mary Almat and Sister Francis to help the sick and I have enquired in the village where her family live and no one has seen her. Her father sent word to Lincoln where he feared she may have gone to meet a sweetheart, but it was discovered that he was missing too. So what are we to think; that she has run off with a lover to heaven knows where?"

"Has she taken anything?" enquired Sister Agnes.

"Do you mean stolen!" put in Sister Marie Claire.

"No, nothing seems to be missing, Sisters, but Sister Ignatius did see Wencilian and Mira talking secretly in the gardens before she disappeared."

"Maybe some harm has come to her," suggested Sister Marie Claire.

"Then, have you questioned Sister Wencilian?" asked Sister Agnes.

"Not yet. I wanted to discuss this with you first. Also I have had some incredible news." Mother Elizabeth paused before continuing. "This information is strictly confidential and must never be uttered to anyone. You must both swear on your life, in the name of the Father, Son and Holy Spirit."

Sister Agnes and Sister Marie Claire both crossed themselves. "We do, Mother," they both echoed.

"An agent of the King came yesterday with the usual matters of state ... taxation mostly, although they have no right and the Pope has again decreed it illegal to take from the priories, as it was before Edward starting taking extra for his campaigns. The agent gave me the usual sum for the keep of Sister Wencilian."

At this news, both prioresses looked stunned. Neither had any idea that such a thing ever took place.

"Sister Wencilian! Why on earth would the King pay for Sister Wencilian, an orphan with no family?" blurted out Sister Agnes.

If her voice were any sharper it would cut her tongue in two, thought Sister Marie Claire, remaining silent.

"Since she was admitted as a baby, before I came here, you will remember, Sister Agnes, the Priory has received a sum for her keep. I was sworn to secrecy and have never dared asked why. In my own mind I assumed she could be an illegitimate daughter of the King, who he wanted for some reason to hide away."

"Why are you telling us this now then, Mother?" interrupted Sister Agnes.

"Let me continue, Sister. It came to my notice by accident. The agent was a bit careless with his papers. I happened to see as he turned away that on the parchment was written, 'The sum of twenty pounds for the keep of the Princess Gwenllian'." She paused, "I'm not sure how it is pronounced."

"What sort of name is that?" put in Sister Marie Claire.

"I am not sure, but it confirms my suspicions that she is a daughter of the King, if she is a Princess."

"But if he wanted to hide her away, why refer to her as a Princess? Surely he would want to keep her identity completely hidden."

"Maybe she could be a captured foreign Princess who posed a threat to him," said Sister Agnes. "That name does not sound English or French."

"Well, whatever, it looks as if we have a Princess in our midst," continued Sister Marie Claire.

"We are all equal in the sight of God," snapped Sister Agnes. "No one has preference here."

"Now, Sisters, please none of this must ever be repeated outside of this room or it could have serious repercussions for the Priory," warned Mother Elizabeth, wondering if she had been a bit foolish to tell them.

"Do you think Father Roger knows?" Sister Marie Claire asked, nervously.

"Huh! I wouldn't be surprised at all," Sister Agnes exclaimed. "Certainly Philip de Burton, the Master of Sempringham, must know; he has ultimate control. Why are you telling us this now, Mother?"

"We all have to make a decision about what to do with this information. Now that you have become joint treasurers with me, since the death of Sister Abigail Francis and the failing health of Sister Constantine, I think I need to share this with you." The Prioress Elizabeth crossed herself. "As you know it has always been a rule of St Gilbert that any money given on the admission of a nun was to be devoted to their needs; yet it seems unfair to devote so much to one and a pittance to another."

"She knows nothing of her true birth or any money provided for her needs. Maybe it is better that way." Sister Marie Claire shuffled in her seat.

"And what would we tell her? We still don't really know who she is." Sister Agnes yawned; it was too late into the night for decisions, but she knew Mother Elizabeth never seemed to tire, so she needed to prepare herself for a long night.

"Whoever she is," Mother Elizabeth continued, "she should be grateful that due to our holy Saint Gilbert she was not cast out into the evils of the world, but given sanctuary."

The three prioresses had not drawn any conclusions by the time the Sacristan rang the bell for Prime, but Mother Elizabeth had decided that she would question Wencilian again about the disappearance of Mira. During the service, she thought of the last time she had spoken to her. Wencilian had been a little on edge, and then there was the episode when she had collapsed during Matins; that was unusual, for in her eyes she had always seemed level headed and strong, never prone to delusions or hysteria like some Sisters. But who was she? It seemed to Mother Elizabeth now far more important to discover the truth about Wencilian, than the whereabouts of Mira, only a lay sister after all. She didn't like secrets in her convent, but she would have to be very careful; she was up against the most powerful man in the land, the King, the man who had the power to dispose of her and her priory should he choose to. His reputation was not one of kindness and humility. She also knew that there was a danger of her own deeply hidden secret being revealed.

Alice stared silently into her soup. She did not feel like eating, with the knot in her stomach tightening more every day. Even the thought of some of the fine foods she used to eat at home could not stimulate her appetite. Home, thinking of the once happy family of which she was part, made her tears well up. To her father, she was always the apple of his eye, the most fragrant and beautiful rose in the garden, he had once compared her to. A practical man, not prone to expressing his emotions or indulging in song or poetry, she had been delighted at this. Then, why had he sacrificed her beauty and her life? She would never blossom like a rose any more.

On the visiting day, he had been very distant, but she read his face – it was a mixture of guilt and shame. Her sister had almost gloated, dying to flaunt her fortune in her face. Her mother had tried to soothe her and win her round with flattering comments and questions about her life in the Priory. Maurice, well, he just stood for most of the time looking embarrassed, but once or twice tried to catch her eye with a look which said 'forgive me'. But, could she forgive him now? How did she come to have the ring? He must have passed it to her, but it was all a blur now; her strong emotions seemed to have blotted out her memory.

She did remember having told them never to visit again and insisting that the Prioress would not admit them. If she was to spend the rest of her days in this place she had to forget them or she could not bear the pain.

"You must eat something," Wencilian whispered. "You have barely touched your food for days."

"I cannot. What is the point?"

Wencilian could not think of an answer which would sound convincing, genuine or particularly useful. "Whatever happens, Alice, you must look after yourself. You must not let them all defeat you. You know whatever happens, he loves you; the ring proves that."

In the silence which followed, until after the lunchtime reading in the frater, Wencilian thought about the fact that it was unusual for all three prioresses to be absent from Matins. This worried her. She could not remember a time before when that had happened; something was brewing and somehow she felt it could involve her. It was odd that not much had been mentioned about the absence of Mira. Looking down into her bowl of soup, she too suddenly had little appetite. She needed some news on Mira, but how could she get that. Isobel was her only contact, unless, she thought in a moment of dubious inspiration, contact could be made with the woman, Hilda. Hilda may have heard of the whereabouts of Mira, and if not, her gift of prophecy might be put to use. Maybe the woman Hilda would help Alice too, but no doubt there would be a price to pay … Hilda, she guessed would not do it from the goodness of her heart. Wencilian herself had little to offer, but perhaps she could obtain medicines from the infirmary or food from the kitchens. Would that be stealing or giving to the poor, she wondered? Either way, it would be considered a sin and eschew a punishment. It was a risk she had to take. She would not mention it, even to Alice, but she would need to speak to Isobel.

CHAPTER 13

On the road to Lincolnshire

Three figures on horseback made their way across the Welsh borders into the flatter plains of the English countryside. They had avoided the open land as far as was possible. Philip felt a little nervous and vulnerable with a pregnant wife, a friar to protect and no armed men. He had become accustomed to referring to Cai as 'Friar Gregory' since they had left the forest above Cwmhir Abbey, and thought he fitted the role very well, jogging along at the rear on his little pony which he refused to exchange for a faster steed.

Cai too was feeling nervous. It was many years since he had travelled into England and he wasn't sure what to expect. Staying at villages along the way, with those who had offered shelter, they had tried not to draw attention to themselves. Philip and Catrin had mostly spoken English, but their accents sometimes attracted strange looks. They travelled slowly, mostly to protect the child Catrin was carrying. This was the third night of their journey and they needed somewhere to stay.

"There is a monastery I know of not far ahead; we could stay there," suggested Philip.

"I will be glad of that, and some warm food. I think I could sleep for days," Catrin sighed. "What shall we tell them? We look odd travelling companions."

"We will tell them what we had decided to say at the inns if anybody asked, which they didn't. They may well want to know at the monastery as we will have to ask for their free hospitality."

The monastery, Garendon Abbey, was well camouflaged by trees and the monk who opened the hatch on the heavy outer door was not immediately welcoming.

"What brings you here?" he fired sharply at the travellers.

"We are travelling to Grantham. We just require some rest and food for one night. My wife is with child; we would be grateful for your hospitality."

"Who are you and where do you come from, and who is the monk on that scraggy creature?"

"I am Philip of Grantham. This is my wife, Catrin, and the monk is Friar Gregory. We are returning to my estate after visiting my wife's family." Philip thought that the monk may think that a sufficient explanation, even though he really had told him very little.

The monk slammed the hatch shut. The three sat down on the grass and just as Philip was wondering what to do next, the hatch reopened and another face peered through.

"I am Father Thomas. You may enter, but leave any weapons on the ground behind that tree."

"Certainly," replied Philip, "but I would like my sword kept in a safe place. My wife and the friar have no weapons."

The heavy door opened and they were ushered into a courtyard where two young monks took the horses. Father Thomas beckoned the three to follow him.

"I will show you to the guesthouse and ask for some food to be sent. If you wish, you and the friar may attend mass, but the lady must remain within the guesthouse."

Catrin was relieved to hear that she would be excluded from mass, even though in principle she could have made a fuss. All she cared about tonight was rest for her and the baby, in warmth and quiet. She did not want to listen to some priest rambling words she barely understood, in Latin in a cold church.

The guesthouse did not look like it would offer much comfort. It was dark and contained a few pallets covered with sheepskins, a chair and small table. In one corner, a curtain had been erected, behind which there was a larger bed and chest.

"You and your husband can sleep here." Father Thomas smiled at Catrin as if he was doing her a great favour. "Behind that small door on the left are the latrines. I will send a Brother to set a fire."

Well, that would be fine, thought Catrin. At least we are safe and will be fed. She shook out her damp cloak and smoothed down her dark blue linen shift. Philip and Cai had returned to their horses to see them settled, not trusting the monks to do the job.

Catrin lay on the bed and rubbed her hand over her belly feeling a small rounding and hardness. How well life had turned out for her, she thought, from very poor and humble beginnings to the wife of a captain, and a happy wife. Philip was a good man, a considerate husband and they laughed a lot together, although he could be abrasive at times, as was often the manner of a soldier.

She had become used to life in England, even though she felt she had betrayed her own people sometimes, but what could they do? The King had restored Philip's father's lands in Powys several years after the conquest of Wales, on the condition that he swore allegiance to him. Philip himself had resisted for many years, living as a mercenary, but when his father was dying, he returned and made a promise to look after his mother and sisters and protect their lands. That was where Catrin had seen him again.

The years at the court of Llywelyn seemed like a lifetime away, but she would be ever grateful to Eleanor for taking her in and making her into a lady, and grateful to Cai for looking after her when Eleanor died and Llywelyn left to fight the last campaign. They had not talked about that on their journey, or of the night when little Gwenllian was taken by the English soldiers. Philip had made them promise not to discuss anything until they were in the safety of his house, for he said even the trees may have ears; you never know who could be listening, anywhere. She knew that Cai was dying to ask about Celeste, but that would have to wait a little while longer.

The meal came with apologies from Father Thomas. Rations were scarce, he explained, since King Edward was demanding more dues from the church. Every priory and religious house was suffering and the previous cold winter had killed off some of their livestock. Philip promised to supply them with extra livestock and several gold coins, at which Father Thomas seemed to shake off his sombre expression.

"Where is Grantham?" enquired the Father.

"In between Nottingham and Lincoln, you could say," replied Philip.

"Do you have lands there?"

"I have some land, but I am not a rich man. I am a captain in the King's army."

"Then why are you abroad with no escort?" asked the Father suspiciously.

"I asked for leave. My wife needed to visit her family. I chose to travel unescorted and the King can spare few men now that he is busy on campaigns."

"Indeed!" scowled the Father, keeping his thoughts to himself. "You are welcome to our hospitality. I will leave you now to eat and rest. Are you coming to mass, Brother?" he added, looking at Cai.

"Of course," Cai replied, unwillingly.

When Father Thomas left, Catrin turned to Cai, but before she could speak, Philip pressed his fingers to his lips, then whispered, "We should be home in a few days and there we can have plenty of discussion."

"I was merely going to enquire how Cai was and if his pony was settled," snapped Catrin.

"I think we are all tired," Cai sighed. "A good night's rest is what we all need, but it will be a while for me if I must attend Compline."

Philip slapped him on the shoulder laughing. "You're a good friar, Cai, a good friar."

It took two more days to reach Grantham, and there Philip led them to what Cai thought looked like a fine manor house, not large but impressive enough for one who used to be a Welsh soldier and then a mercenary who fought against the King. For a moment, Cai wondered whether he could trust Philip, but he had been assured by Hywel that Philip was still as committed as they were to their promise to Llywelyn. Cai saw two well dressed women rush from the house to welcome Catrin and she had barely dismounted before they swept her inside, laughing and chattering. He dared hope for a moment that Celeste may be here, safe and waiting for him.

Philip put am arm over his shoulder. "Let me show you around, brother."

Over the supper in the hall, served by two young servant girls, Cai was introduced to the household of Philip and Catrin.

"Rhiannon and Arian, my two sisters," Philip explained, "and my mother, Gwyneth, from Powys, are staying with us for the summer. Hervé oversees my lands and household while I am away and when I'm here, he helps me with almost everything. Elsie and Margaret here run the kitchen and the household. We are all one family, I have no need for many servants. Oh, of course, there are Jack and Henry who look after the horses and stables."

Cosy, Cai thought, and friendly. It was what he would expect from Philip and Catrin's household. But how did they come to be married? He hoped he would be able to hear the answer to this and other questions during the evening. As they ate convivially of the simple but ample meal of fish, vegetables and bread, he felt comfortable with his company. Rhiannon and Arian chatted, giggled and enquired about his family. There was not much to say about that. "I have no family, I have never married. My parents were from a small village in the mountains of Gwynedd. I had three sisters, all who sadly died quite young." Of course, Cai thought, they would not think him married being a friar, but he was not sure how much they knew, if anything at all, of his true identity.

The mother, Gwyneth, was silent. An attractive woman, like her daughters, her dark hair was swept elegantly into a coif under a thin black veil. No doubt still in mourning for her husband, it occurred to Cai. Her clothing was not ostentatious or colourful, but befitted her demeanour as a woman of some standing in the community. Her face had the plump softness of a Welsh country lady, but there was sadness in her hazel eyes.

Hervé kept silent, but Cai noticed that he observed every detail of what went on ... a keen shadow watcher, ready to spot any misdemeanours against his master. Cai saw that he walked with a limp when he left the table to serve the wine ... an injury perhaps? He was French. Had he served with Edward at one time? Cai wondered how he came to be in this household.

Eventually, the three were left alone and Philip suggested they retire to a small solar at the far end of the house, where a fire was lit but no one could overhear them.

"So please," asked Cai, "tell me how the two of you came to be wed."

Catrin spoke first. "I knew I would have to tell you this sometime, but I don't like to speak about it. In fact there is not a lot I can remember about how I came to be in Philip's household in Powys. That night, when we were ambushed trying to take little Gwenllian to safety, I was left injured on the ground. I crawled into the forest that was close by, but kept to the edge, moving when I could muster the strength, hoping to find some settlement. I must have fainted. When I woke up, I was being tended by an old woman and her son in a small stone house they shared with chickens and pigs. They were kind and wanted me to stay, but I couldn't stay, although I had no idea of where to go. I was desperate to find out what had happened to you, Cai, and little Gwenllian and all the others. I walked for days, then found some work as a maid in a house near Caernarfon. It was there that I heard the news of Dafydd and his terrible fate and the taking of his sons. No one seemed to have any news of Gwenllian and I could not make myself too conspicuous or ask too many questions. I thought no one would know me in Caernarfon, but I had to be careful. There were a lot of soldiers there; the King was starting to rebuild the castle. There were lots of rumours also circulating. I somehow discovered that Celeste and Morwena must have been taken with Gwenllian. Why I was not taken I don't know. I have no memory of that time at all.

"After several years my mistress died. She had no relatives, so I walked southwards hoping to reach the area near Castell y Bere. I just thought that maybe I would discover some clues of your whereabouts, Cai, or Gwenllian's. But I found nothing. After a while, at a market I was hired as a maid and very fortunately by Philip's mother, although I was not to know that until several years later."

Catrin stood up and went to sit next to Philip. Taking his hand, she continued, "I had only seen Philip once or twice before, with the Prince and his men, in the Llys at Aber. When he walked into the hall in his father's house in Powys, I was astounded. I had no idea that this same Philip that his sisters talked about was the very one who had fought with my Lord and lived almost side by side with me at the court. His mother and sisters had said he fought as a mercenary and they did not know where he was. It was a while before he recognised me and I kept a low profile for that time. But one day he took my hand and said, "Catrin fach, now I remember who you are, the little maid from Abergwyngregyn, who helped to nurse the baby Gwenllian. I heard how you bravely tried to rescue her from the King's men when she was taken."

Turning to Cai, she said, "Well, I don't think I need to tell you the rest of the story, except to say that I had no idea that our tale of the escape with Gwenllian had been told over and over again at that time, by soldiers, farmers, masons, fishwives and in all the alehouses."

"We can't say that we went unnoticed then, even though we failed," Cai said sadly. "I must dare to ask now, do you know any more of what became of Celeste?" He searched both their faces expectantly.

Catrin sighed, "I can't tell you any more, Cai. There were rumours that when Dafydd was taken to the King's camp at Rhuddlan there were several women with him. That could have been Elizabeth and his daughters, or it could have been Celeste and Morwena, and it is likely that Gwenllian was with them then. We heard that Dafydd had then been taken to Chester, then

Shrewsbury where he suffered his terrible death."

"Terrible it was," Cai echoed, holding his head in his hands, suppressing tears.

"I was injured and have tried so many times to recollect what happened that night," Catrin continued. "But all I have in my mind are flashes of the horror of that scene and sounds of screams and the thud of horse hooves. I was holding Gwenllian, and Celeste tried to help me push off the soldier who was pulling, pulling, at the baby."

Philip picked up the tale. "We have had no word of her since. When I joined the King's men, I tried to make some enquires, but did not want to arouse suspicion. Edward was doubtful of my loyalty at that time and I was being watched carefully." Looking at Catrin, he said softly, "Catrin fach, you go and get some rest. I don't want you upset thinking of that night so long ago."

"I think I will," she replied, patting her stomach. "It has been a long journey and the baby needs some sleep."

Cai was concerned. When Catrin had gone he poured some more wine. It had been a long, long day, but he needed to talk some more to Philip. "I'm sorry if I have upset Catrin, but I had to ask about Celeste. What about you, Philip? What happened to you on that night?"

"That night I would rather not remember, but for your sake I will recall what I can. I prayed that you and your small party would make it to safety in the mountains. We tried to fight the men off as best as we could when they came at us. It was chaos, we were all separated. I chased two men then cut them down. I was injured on the leg and dragged myself to the edge of the forest again. I have no memory of what happened next. When I woke all was quiet. I stumbled back to where we were attacked. All my men were dead and the women all gone. I couldn't find you, Cai, and I hadn't the strength to bury my men. I found my horse grazing and managed to mount him and made my way south.

"I sought shelter at Cwmhir Abbey for a short while, then joined a band of mercenaries, living wild, living rough. I heard that my father had made an alliance with Edward and had his lands in Powys restored, but I would not return home under any circumstances at that point. Word got to me much later that my father had died and I knew that my mother and sisters would need me, and to tell you the truth, I seemed to regain my rational mind. I think I had somehow lost my mind with the grief of losing our Prince, the struggle of the battle and the life I was living. So I went home."

"The pain doesn't go away even after all this time, Philip, I know. I thought you had been taken too. I must have left the spot not long before you came back. That is regrettable, but at least we have news that Gwenllian is alive. Edward must have had some pang of conscience to save her."

"But he has made sure the lineage doesn't continue ..."

"Not necessarily, if we can free her from the convent. How we are going to do that Philip? We must make some plans."

"Well, this is a good stopping point for you, on the way to Sempringham. Hywel is going to join us here before the Solstice night. In the meantime, Cai, I want you to rest a bit and have some thinking time and prepare yourself for the journey ahead, for we have no way of knowing what that will entail."

"Do you still practice the old ways, Philip?"

"I am a soldier. I have no time for religion, but I am loyal to the cause of Llywelyn. I have respect for the old ways and am no lover of the Christian Church, except for the monks of Cwmhir, who have sheltered me in hard times and asked no questions."

"And Catrin?"

"Catrin has grown into a strong woman. I love her dearly. I met her in this house, when I returned because my father was dying. She reminded me of that life I had tried to forget, but those experiences, after a while, forged a strong link between us. Over the years, Hywel has visited us here and she has spent many hours discussing life and the ancient ways with him. He has taught her a lot."

"I was so pleased to see her and see you two happy together. I would never have dreamt that I would be sitting here with you both. It would have completed my happiness to see Celeste of course."

"I shall make it my mission, Cai, to try to find her, but our first duty is to Gwenllian. Let's raise a glass to them both – women lost who will be found."

"Women we love," said Cai.

"We should get some rest and talk more tomorrow. I hope it won't be long before Hywel joins us, as I have a feeling I may be called back to service sometime soon."

"Philip, do you feel you are betraying your people by serving the King?"

"I do, Cai, but it is a means to an end and as you know I had no real choice, I had to protect my mother and sisters after my father died and now I have a wife and child on the way. The cause was lost when Llywelyn died, and nothing I could have done at the time would have changed the situation. I can do more good where I am now than living as an outlaw with a group of mercenaries, some of whom had no morals at all or concern for anyone. And, hopefully with you I can help to find Llywelyn's rightful heir."

Cai nodded his head and sat in silence for a few moments as Philip rose to leave the room. "I am with you and have complete trust in you Philip, and you're right." As he spoke Cai felt slightly uneasy and hoped he would never regret uttering those words.

CHAPTER 14

Sempringham Priory
Late April 1300

Wencilian thought it strange that Sister Ignatius had sought her out several times for conversation in recent weeks. She sensed Sister Ignatius was not overly fond of her, and the feeling was mutual. Maybe she was lonely, Wencilian thought, but she had never shown signs of enjoying any company before, preferring the quiet, contemplative life that was more the norm for the nuns of Sempringham. Wencilian didn't trust her; she knew she had ambitions to be Prioress, and there was nothing wrong with that, except that she felt Sister Ignatius would stop at nothing to get to that position.

The day was warm and sunny, and after the noon service of Sext there was time for a little rest, but Wencilian wanted to walk in the kitchen garden. She rolled up her sleeves to feel the sun on her arms and her face. It was the best medicine. It would perk her up more than a nap in her dark cell. Also she was hoping to make contact with Isobel. A few days before, in the infirmary she had asked Isobel to contact the woman, Hilda. Isobel had come to the infirmary that morning with linen and Sister Beatrice had stood with them talking, but as she left, Isobel gave her a wink, no doubt she had some news.

It had rained during the previous night. Moistness and strong sunlight diffused the potent aromas of the garden herbs around her. She really should pick some to make unguents and poultices, but today she just wanted to savour the delight of the warmth and the fragrances of verbena, thyme, marjoram, meadowsweet, dill and the moist earth. She sat for a while on a stone bench and hearing footsteps approaching behind her, she turned to see Alice. Pleased to have her company but disappointed it wasn't Isobel, she was even more disappointed when she saw Sister Ignatius walking behind Alice.

"Sit down quickly, Alice, before Sister Ignatius comes."

Alice sat close to Wencilian and Sister Ignatius did not waste any time squeezing herself onto the end of the bench.

"Good day, Sisters, what lovely sunshine we have today. I hope you don't mind if I share a little respite with you. What short time we have between tasks."

"Not at all," Wencilian replied warily, noticing that Sister Ignatius was displaying a rare smile with her mouth, which was not reflected in her eyes. Alice looked at the ground, not encouraging any conversation, but Wencilian could see a tear in the corner of her eye. No doubt she had wanted a private chat today and that was now impossible. She hoped Alice wouldn't give anything away unwittingly. Sister Ignatius, she felt, was hungry for information and she had found from previous conversations that she was clever at extracting confidences without giving away any of her own. At least Alice knew nothing of Mira, but it would not be wise to let her speak of Maurice or her family. Wencilian knew she must try to steer the conversation.

"I should pick some herbs for the infirmary whilst the young fresh leaves are sprouting. Would you care to help me, Sister Alice or Sister Ignatius?"

"Are your duties still keeping you in the infirmary, Sister Wencilian?" Sister Ignatius asked.

"Sister Beatrice needs my help since Sister Abigail Francis died. It's easier for me to be there as I have now acquired quite a knowledge of what is needed. I am happy to be there and it gives me the chance to enjoy the garden as well, on occasions."

"That's good. I would have no stomach for it," Sister Ignatius replied.

"It is hard sometimes, especially when dealing with those

who have inflicted dreadful suffering on their own bodies," Wencilian said with concern.

"But those very Sisters and Brothers should attract veneration and reverence. How sweet it must be to suffer with Jesus, to have courage to do that."

"I don't think it serves any purpose," Alice added, "to cause more suffering. Are we not meant to spread peace and love others as we love ourselves?"

"Women are made to suffer in one way or another," Sister Ignatius said, bitterly. "We are lucky here. Should we be married, we would have to endure all kinds of disgusting and demeaning activities. My mother always said that men pursue filthiness at all times. And a woman may be beaten and shouted at, treated like a drudge, constantly battling the exhaustion of childbirth."

Alice looked up, startled. She had never heard such a harsh, physical description of married life. "My parents' marriage is not at all like that. They are respectful of each other and always seemed happy together."

"What about you, Sister Wencilian?" asked Sister Ignatius. "What do you think?"

"As you may know, I have no knowledge of family life. The only life I have known is within these priory walls."

"What would you think of an unmarried woman or a nun who found themselves with child, Sister Wencilian?"

A strange question to ask, thought Wencilian, but maybe not so strange if she was searching for information of Mira. She must be in cahoots with the Prioress.

"I would have no knowledge of, or opinion of, such a thing either." she answered.

Relief, the bell rang for all Sisters to resume their duties until the mid-afternoon service of Nones. They made their way back to their work, silently, as was the rule. Alice was engaged in sewing the garments of the canons and Sister Ignatius returned to her duties of making candles and preparing parchments, overseeing the novice nuns.

Wencilian was glad to get back to the infirmary; even the

sick were a welcome diversion from the prying eyes of Sister Ignatius and whoever else may be watching her. As she worked during the afternoon, she wondered why Sister Ignatius had asked her such a question, which made it so obvious that she was seeking out information on Mira. Perhaps she was watching her reaction or maybe she had become tired of trying to skirt around the question during previous conversations. Well, as far as Wencilian was concerned, she could try all she liked but would be no wiser.

Back in the infirmary, Wencilian always felt safe. It seemed ridiculous she knew, as here she was exposed to all manner of illnesses, but here she had in a strange way some privacy and would be left mostly to get on with her duties, calmly, apart from the interference of Sister Beatrice, and even that had become less recently. Sister Beatrice seemed to trust her more, she respected her opinion and was quite happy for her to take on more responsibility, especially as she was ageing and Wencilian was growing towards her prime and was full of energy.

There were only three patients at the moment. Maybe, Wencilian thought, that was why Isobel had not come with any clean linen for a while. She would have to make contact, somehow, soon. Patience, Wencilian knew, was not her best quality, even though Mother Elizabeth had always encouraged her to pray for more of it. She laid some more sheepskins over a young novice nun, who was still shivering despite being layered in several woven blankets and skins already. She had been brought down by an elder nun earlier in the morning.

Feeling her brow, Wencilian was puzzled that she did not seem to have a fever or chill, yet she was very pale and her mind was drifting. Then she noticed blood seeping through her shift around her shoulders onto the bed where she lay. She said gently, "Can you turn over onto your side, dear Mary? I will help you."

The young novice groaned in pain as she turned. Wencilian lifted up her shift and, unusually, started to feel queasy. She was horrified by the deep grooves, torn into such tender flesh. "Who did this to you?" she demanded.

The young novice looked terrified and was unable to utter a word.

Wencilian softened her voice. "Don't be afraid, I am only here to help you. I will fetch some ointment for the wounds."

In the still room, she thought of Sister Ignatius and their conversation in the garden a little earlier. She had seen such wounds before, but not usually on one so young and a novice. Surely no novice would be so inclined or so yet indoctrinated to inflict such harm on herself. She had a feeling that Sister Ignatius was involved in this, somehow.

Wencilian bathed the wounds with an extra care and tenderness, and applied the soothing marshmallow ointment. The novice, Mary, winced and shivered at each touch. Something was needed to help her sleep, a little draught of poppy seed maybe. She would have to consult with Sister Beatrice. When Mary was healing and rested she would question her again and find out the truth of this matter.

A draught blew around Wencilian's ankles; her skirt lifted and fanned around her. Turning, she saw Brother John enter the infirmary from the small door at the north end which led to the part of the Priory always secret to her, the world of the priests and canons. The door was always kept firmly locked, unless a Brother would knock and ask for assistance in the infirmary when extra medicine was needed or their infirmary was too full. The only people to have keys were Sister Beatrice and Father Roger.

"Brother John, how did you get in here? Never mind, I'm so glad to see you." Instinctively, without thought, she rushed to hug him as she used to as a child. Luckily, there were no superiors to see her indulging in unseemly and forbidden behaviour.

"Bless you, bless you, Wencilian. I have not been able to make an excuse to see you since my injury, but now we need some supplies for the monks' infirmary and everyone else seemed too busy. How are you, my little one?"

"I am fine, Brother John, thank you."

"The look in your eyes belies your words, Wencilian. Are you troubled?"

"Well, there are always troubles in here, but they are of no consequence to any else, as we can do little about them." Wencilian would have loved to mention the trip with Mira, the woman, Hilda, Alice's heartbreak, and other problems that weighed heavily on her mind and soul at the moment, but it was too dangerous. Even though she trusted Brother John, she couldn't take the risk. But there was one thing she could mention.

"I am concerned about a young novice admitted today. She has injuries that I am sure could not have been self-inflicted."

"Who is responsible for her at the moment?"

"Sister Ignatius, I think."

"Well, Wencilian, if it is a punishment it will be difficult for us to intervene. But, it does seem a very extreme punishment for a novice."

"Extreme for anyone, I think. I cannot believe that such a gentle young girl as she is would do anything to deserve such treatment. Sister Ignatius has bitterness within her that I think could cause her to mistreat others."

Wencilian remembered what Sister Ignatius had said in the garden and wondered what her life must have been like with her family. Maybe she had been glad to escape into the convent. There were many reasons why women came to this place.

"I will do what I can, Wencilian, to find out, but with these thick walls which separate us from the nuns, I cannot promise to be able to do much."

"Now you are the almoner, Brother John, you must wander outside a lot and have tales to tell. Have you heard of a woman called Hilda in the fens?"

"I think most people have heard of Hilda, apart from, well, I am sorry Wencilian, those who are enclosed and cannot go outside." Brother John looked at Wencilian with care and compassion, but also with pity. "Why would you be asking about her?"

"Isobel was telling me about her and her gift of prophecy.

She had visited her before she became a lay sister."

Brother John wondered whether it was wise to say any more, but he would not deny Wencilian a little knowledge of the world outside. "Where is Sister Beatrice?"

"She has gone to discuss something with Mother Elizabeth. She won't be back for a while. No doubt they are enjoying some of the Prioress's fine wine."

"Come on then, we will go and prepare the medicines I need and I will tell you what I know, although it is not a great deal. I must be back for Vespers and my supper of course."

CHAPTER 15

Sempringham Priory

Poultices, hot and cold, purge the body and the soul, Sister Beatrice had always said. Wencilian though thought that a gentle warm poultice would benefit the novice Mary, to soothe her back now that her wounds were healing. She had tried her best to keep Mary in the infirmary as long as possible to enable her to heal and overcome the shock. She also wanted to try to find out more information about what had happened, but Mary was keeping quiet. The two young women, one a nun and one a novice, had built up a certain amount of trust, but communication was still awkward between them, as Mary barely spoke.

"It's time we discharged the novice Mary," said Sister Beatrice one morning as they walked back from the service of Nones.

"But I don't think she is ready. We can't let her go back under the care of Sister Ignatius for her to suffer more injuries. Besides we have only three patients in the infirmary at the moment," argued Wencilian. "Please let me speak to Mother Elizabeth. At least she may be able to put her in the care of another senior nun."

"Wencilian, you are making allegations against Sister Ignatius with no evidence. You need to tread carefully. I think it is my place to speak to the Prioress. I will agree to the novice Mary staying a few more days if I must."

Wencilian doubted that Sister Beatrice would plead Mary's case as well as she would herself, but she had little choice than to leave it in her hands. In one way it was a relief as she had a lot on her mind at the moment. Disorientated, confused and anxious, trying to care for those around her, Alice, Mary, as well as thinking of Mira, the strain was tipping her into a gloom she had not felt before.

The silence of the little chapel behind the infirmary where she sat on occasions soothed her, providing solace for the soul in the midst of the chaos in her mind. She liked to be alone with her patients and her thoughts, especially without the prying eyes of Sister Beatrice. But she had only been back a few minutes when Isobel appeared.

"I saw Sister Beatrice heading towards Mother Elizabeth's room, so I rushed down. The woman, Hilda, is coming to the Priory. She is unwell and is going to seek permission from the Prioresses to come to the infirmary."

"How do you know?" Wencilian asked her, her heart thumping.

"She knew she was unwell that night we went to her home. I think that's why she asked you to look out for her daughter."

"That makes sense, but why would she want her daughter enclosed in a convent?"

"I think she fears for her safety. I'm not really sure why, but I know they have no other family. It's true, her beliefs are of the old ways, but maybe she has no choice or there could be another reason that we don't know of. She is a mysterious woman."

"She certainly is mysterious. She makes me uncomfortable, but she is intriguing. Have you any news of Mira?"

"Her family have not found her and Eric is still missing, so they must have got away. Let's pray that they are safe. Have there been any more questions about her?"

"Sister Ignatius is prying. I think she is feeding back any information to Mother Elizabeth, but I have not said a word." Clearing her throat Wencilian asked, "When will Hilda come do you think?"

"I don't know, Wencilian, but it could be soon, if the Prioresses allow."

"What shall I do?"

"Just tend to her as you would anyone else. What else can you do? Dear Wencilian, you worry too much sometimes. We are stuck in here, we don't have much choice in what we do at all."

"You're right, what else can I do?"

That however did not put Wencilian's mind at ease while she waited for Sister Beatrice to return. She busied herself tending to Mary and the two other elderly nuns in the infirmary. When the bell rang for Vespers, she still had not appeared. Wencilian was unsure whether to stay or go. The duty of the service or the duty of the infirmary, which was more important? Seeing that the three patients seemed content and settled, and instructing the two lay sisters who helped, she walked quietly along the cloisters to the church to Vespers. She didn't want to miss the supper which followed, or the chance to see Alice or Isobel.

"Blessed are they that dwell in Thy house, they will always be praising thee," Sister Beatrice muttered. Her words were barely audible, but her anger was obvious to Wencilian. Her hands shook and her face was even more distorted than usual, as she shoved dirty linen brutally into the basket.

"Is something wrong?" Wencilian enquired, thinking that it must be to do with Sister Ignatius or Mary.

"SHE will not be praising him, that's for sure. She's a heathen whore," hissed Sister Beatrice.

Wencilian gasped, she was used to Sister Beatrice's acid tongue sometimes, but never had she heard her express herself so fiercely.

"The Prioress wishes me to admit a woman called Hilda to the infirmary and even worse her daughter is to be taken as a novice. They should not be admitted to a Christian house. Her daughter is a bastard and she is a she devil."

"Do you know this woman?" asked Wencilian.

"Of course not!" Sister Beatrice barked. "How would I know her? But I know those who do."

"Maybe these things aren't true. She may just be a poor

140

woman who needs our help."

"And what would you know about it?"

Yes, and what do you know, Wencilian thought; less than me that's for sure and I know little about her. But I have sat in her house, if I could call it a house, by a warm fire and witnessed her help a girl in trouble, and now you want to turn your back on her.

"I think it is our Christian duty to treat her, Sister Beatrice, regardless of who she is or what she believes."

"You better watch your step, girl, or I will have you out of here if you insist on being ..."

"Being what, Sister? Being what Our Lord Jesus would want us to be – compassionate, caring for our sick brothers and sisters."

"Well, maybe I am being a little harsh. Her daughter is called Leoba, so I believe, so her mother must have some Christian leanings or why would she call her after a saint?"

"I have not heard of Saint Leoba, Sister Beatrice. Who was she?"

"She was a Saxon nun, so I believe, born in Wessex. Her birth was supposedly a miracle. Her mother was related to Pope Boniface and she had a dream that told her that her daughter would lead a spiritual life and confer benefits on many people."

"And did she?"

"It was said that she consulted a woman who could reveal the future and this woman told her that she was destined to be a wise teacher and counsellor. That is all I know."

"That's interesting, that she consulted such a woman," Wencilian added without thinking.

"Is it, Sister Wencilian? Why would that be of interest to you?"

"Oh, no reason except that I do like a bit of mystery."

"Mmm, you like too much fanciful thinking, that is for sure. We shall see; no good will come of all this, I'm sure."

Prioress Elizabeth had received a messenger who had brought notice of a visit from the King's chancellor. In a flurry she called a meeting with Sister Agnes and Sister Marie Claire.

"We must have all our accounts in order, Sisters. He will be here within the week. I have asked Sister Ignatius to help with some of the paperwork."

"Well, I think our records are up to date," stated Sister Marie Claire.

"Why is he snooping around anyway?" Sister Agnes asked, heatedly.

"I don't know. It's a long time since a royal chancellor came here. The King probably wants to raise more money for his campaigns abroad, never mind about the poor and starving on his doorstep."

"Exactly, but what say do we have in matters?" Sister Marie Claire leaned in closely to the two other prioresses who sat around the table. "Have you found out any more about Sister Wencilian?"

"No, nothing at all, Sisters," Mother Elizabeth answered hurriedly. "Come on, now we must get down to the task in hand, our accounts, which may affect the future of this priory."

God forgive her for not telling the exact truth. She would have to confess this as a sin, but then the priest would be party to the information too, although of course she would have to trust him. Maybe she could skip the confession this once. Elizabeth had dismissed Sister Marie Claire's question too quickly; she and Sister Agnes may have been suspicious.

When they had left her room several hours later, she poured herself a glass of her finest wine and slumped into a large chair by her fire. She would love to share the information she had with her two prioresses, but she was not clear of any definite facts. She had indeed uncovered a little information on the nun, Wencilian, a little which may point to where she originated from, but it could never be spoken of, for what she had heard had put her life in danger. Now she had to compose a letter to a trusted friend.

Wencilian's heart seemed to miss a beat. Hilda was coming to the infirmary and her daughter had been admitted as a novice.

This was a strange thing to happen. How on earth had she persuaded Prioress Elizabeth? The woman did seem to have strange powers and Wencilian was eager to know more about them and to hear any news about Mira. If she was very ill though, she may not be coherent.

A bed was prepared for her and it was before dawn the next day when the knock came on the infirmary door.

With a look of disgust on her face, Sister Beatrice admitted the new patient. It was her task to settle her in and diagnose her illness. The disgust turned to anger when Hilda told her what was wrong with her and the treatment she required.

"Feel here on the stomach; there is a growth. It gets bigger, even with all the herbs I have used. I feel no more can be done. I can no longer eat, it is too painful, but I need some relief from the pain, with hot poultices and a draft to help me sleep. But first, I must see my daughter. Can you fetch her for me?"

"I am not used to running errands," barked Sister Beatrice.

"Please, Sister, I may not have long."

Sister Beatrice hesitated. She would normally have sent Wencilian, but she would be quite glad to get away from this vile woman and walk off a bit of her anger. "Wencilian, prepare some poultices. I will be back soon."

Hilda, greatly relieved that Wencilian had not been sent on the errand, called her over. "Come here child, quickly, while the dragon is away."

Wencilian smiled and suddenly felt more at ease with this woman, who looked now frail and in pain. She felt the urge to sit on the bed and take her hand. "How do you feel?" she asked.

"Never mind me, I have things to tell you. You must listen. My daughter, Leoba, is here. You must look out for her and protect her. She in turn will teach you things that will help you. Since I saw you, I have dreamt of you. I sometimes see the future, you see, and I know that really you do not belong here. I feel you were torn from a life far away, where you were, as I said before, of noble birth. I see a man who will come to find you. He is not family, but you can trust him. Your destiny lies elsewhere. Do not believe all the nuns tell you; you are far more powerful than them. I only tell you this for your own good, not to disturb you. Please, now prepare me a draught, for when I have seen my daughter I need to sleep. Make it a strong draught." Hilda squeezed Wencilian's hand, which made her tremble.

"Just tell me, how is Mira? Have you heard?"

"I think they are safe, the babe is not yet born, but all goes well."

Wencilian wanted to ask a dozen questions but she could see that Hilda needed some relief from pain. What did she mean, Wencilian thought, by a strong draught? Did she want some help to pass from this life? That would be a grave sin surely, but would anyone know? The woman was clearly dying and she had seen first-hand too many times the grizzly scenes of patients writhing in agony in their last days, their last hours. Surely it was kinder to help them on their way. She decided she would make the draught just a little bit stronger for now, but if she needed another later she would administer a stronger one.

Sister Beatrice entered with the fairy-like child. Although she didn't have the shimmer and glow that had caught her eye in the hut which was Hilda's home, Wencilian was captivated by her violet eyes and ethereal beauty. The dowdy black tunic and headdress looked so odd on her, but still did not diminish her inner glow.

Wencilian laid a warm poultice made of marshmallow leaf gently on Hilda's stomach as her hand reached out for the hand of her daughter. Even Sister Beatrice stood quietly by and time was suspended for a moment. It was like a dream. Wencilian could never recall the exact words or actions which flowed between the mother and her daughter on that morning, but when Leoba had returned to the main priory there was an atmosphere in the infirmary that Wencilian had never felt before. A reassuring calmness fell over the room as a trickle of light filtered through the small door which led outside. Wencilian, on Sister Beatrice's instructions, rarely opened this door, but she had a sudden urge for fresh air and light. She needed to just stand and think, think about what Hilda had said to her.

144

There was a small yard at the back of the infirmary, closed in by a high wall. Wencilian stood still in the centre. The morning sun was rising in front of her, the gentle rays warming her face. "Mother Mary, help me to make sense of what is happening; send me patience and guide me to do the right thing." How she wished she could take a sledge hammer and knock these walls down, but she just stood quietly and heard the sounds of the monks going about their business on the other side of the wall.

The monks were stoking up the fires in the bakery and the comforting aroma of the first batch of freshly baked bread drifted over the wall. She had been on the other side when she was younger and could visualize the activities which would be starting now, after the service of Prime, when the monks would go about all their daily tasks.

She only just realised that both her and Sister Beatrice had missed Prime, being absorbed with Hilda and her daughter. They had a good excuse; surely a penance would not need to be paid.

She had to speak to Hilda again. May God keep her with us for a bit longer, Wencilian thought, although she knew that was a selfish thought, for the poor woman must be suffering. Engrossed in her reverie she had failed to notice her little friend, Boden, on the wall. She held out her arm and he hopped onto her wrist.

"It's late, or should we say early, for you to still be out my friend. How has your hunting gone this night? I have no titbits for you today."

The soft-plumed owl nestled into her neck before letting out a loud shriek and flying away. His talons had left marks on her arm. Those would be hard to explain away, she thought. For a moment, again Wencilian envied his freedom. Each time he came to her she felt happy, soothed, consoled, but when he had gone she was left restless and slightly disturbed.

CHAPTER 16

Grantham, Lincolnshire

Cai was comfortable in Philip's house, too comfortable. He enjoyed the company of his close friends and their family and he enjoyed his occasional sojourns into the surrounding countryside and villages. The local people seem to have accepted him as the friendly friar with the strange accent. He missed his native land though, and the language, but he had the women of the household to talk to and Catrin to reminisce with. Catrin's pregnancy was now showing more, but she seemed to work as hard as ever, around the house and in the stables, feeding the pigs, sheep, goats and all manner of tasks. Philip had told her many times that she didn't need to, they had servants, but Catrin always said that all her life she had worked hard and she wouldn't stop now, unless she had too many children or got too old. Philip had been called back to his duties several weeks before, so now Cai was the man of the house, along with Hervé, the crippled Frenchman, who said very little.

The women though seemed more than capable of running the household, although sometimes they did request Cai's company in the evening, to sing and play to them and tell them tales. He enjoyed the company of Philip's sister, Arian. Her laugh reminded him though too much of Celeste. Then the pain would flare up. Amongst the frivolity and the nagging pain which never quite left him, he had never forgotten his mission. He had not been idle. His trips outside were more to try to glean information rather than for his pleasure. And, he knew that any day Hywel could arrive and together they would consolidate a plan to try and see their Princess Gwenllian.

The nights were shortening and the days warming. On May eve, Cai began to feel restless. He excused himself from supper and took Ianto for a trek along the edge of an old forest. There was a hill in the distance, a densely wooded hill, one of very few in that area. The sun was sinking behind the hill and what Cai first thought were the fading rays of sunlight were, he realised, the glowing sparks of a fire. A Beltane fire, could it be, he wondered. Were there still some folk here who kept the old ways, the Beltane rites. It was Beltane tonight and a fire atop a hill in his mind meant only one thing. He forced himself to reconsider and be sensible. He was in England now, a very Normanised England, but even after two and a half centuries of Norman rule and Christian domination, he could not believe that some of the old beliefs had been completely obliterated.

Tying Ianto to a tree, he crept around the forest edge and weaved in and out of the trees which ascended the hill. Nearing the top he hid behind a clump of ash trees. It did not give him complete cover, but in his grey robe he could merge into the copse. He saw a circle of figures standing around a fire, chanting. Some words were familiar to him, but some were hard to understand. It was a strange dialect in which he recognised a few threads of what he knew to be an older form of English. If this was a Beltane rite, it was surely different from the rituals of his native land. He counted twelve people, all hooded, three or four smaller than the rest; these he took to be women but could not see their faces. He knew he had to be careful; in his friar's robes they might take him to be a spy from the church, seeking out heretics. They would probably never believe that he had sympathy for them. They might even cause him great harm or worse.

In the dim light he tried to see their clothing. From the way they were dressed it looked as if these were country people, poor people, and from what he could hear and the little he understood, it seemed that they were carrying out a tradition that must have been held here on May eve for hundreds of years. They wanted the God and Goddess to bless their land and asked for a fruitful season of growth and successful harvest. But there were no cattle to drive between two fires, or young couples ready to jump the fire and make love in the open air, celebrating the spring and the season of fertility here. The people who lived in this land had been suppressed for many more years than his native Cymru. No doubt these were just a few who performed the rites in secret and the potency of those rites must have been sadly diminished.

As he crept down the hill he felt a spark of hope. The ways of these people were different from his, but they shared a common aim, a deep-rooted belief in the old ways which would not be shaken. He didn't want to delay much longer. His promise to Llywelyn must be fulfilled. There was no time to lose now. Somehow he had to contact Hywel and Seren and if he couldn't locate Hywel or get a message to Seren then he would have to try on the inner planes, something he was not that practised in, but tonight, May eve, would be a powerful time as any to try.

There was little privacy at the house, even in his own chamber, so he wandered a bit, enjoying the bright night sky, until he came to a group of old oaks through which the light of the rising full moon shone like a beam as if guiding him to the right place. Ianto nuzzled against him, confirming his feeling. They had grown close during these past months together and seemed to share a natural understanding. They looked out for each other.

Cai was getting hungry, but was glad he had missed his supper. Fasting was more conducive to reaching into the other realms. Closing his eyes and breathing deeply, he relaxed his body and prepared to go into trance. If anyone passing had glanced into that moonlit glade they would have just seen a weary friar resting from his travels while his pony munched contentedly nearby.

In the mountains of Eryri, the cold frosts had given way to soft spring warmth which nudged the hardy rowan and stooped

148

hawthorn trees back into life. The season of growth had returned and the Druids of Eryri were ready to welcome it and hail the new life which it brought. Seren had taken command. As High Priestess of the Grove, the few priests, priestesses and novices deferred to her, as well as Cynan, her High Priest, with whom she would perform the Beltane ritual, nos Calan Mai. She had been preparing for days; this one had to be powerful. Since the day that she became certain that the Princess Gwenllian was alive but imprisoned, she had waited for this moment to summon the aid of the Goddess and God in her search for her and to make contact with her. She hoped that they and her priests and priestesses would not fail her. She was not young anymore and had not coupled at the Beltane fires for many years. Nor would she this year; that duty was reserved for a younger priestess to ensure the fertility of the land and more importantly to preserve the ongoing flame of the spirit of their tradition. Beltane was the feast of Bel, the shining one, and it heralded the first beginnings of summer and the blessings of the God, bringing together the young God and Goddess in union. The wheel of the year was turning and the cycles of the earth were flowing, as they had done for thousands of years.

Seren walked alone by the shores of the mountain lake, treading carefully between the few bluebells which grew in her path. This was her private routine before a ritual; she needed time alone, it calmed her and helped to focus her thoughts. But it was always at this time that unwanted thoughts crept into her mind, thoughts of the past. The face of her daughter floated translucently on the top of the water when she looked towards the lake. Where was she now? She felt that she wasn't too far away from her, but why didn't she contact her or come home, home to where she was born. Luned, her only child, conceived at Beltane, a child of the God and Goddess. What a powerful priestess she could be if she hadn't turned her back on the old ways and denied her fate. How ironic life can be, Seren thought. Turning to stand by the lake she looked for the face again, but it had gone.

"I know you can hear me, Luned, even though you may not

want to listen. When the wind rustles, the leaves of the silent trees and spirit upon the water breathes, I will remember you with my cherished thoughts. Tonight, on May eve, I know you will think of us wherever you may be."

As she walked away, Seren thought for a moment that she heard the cry of a new-born, or was it just the call of the birds? Could it be that her daughter had given birth, could she dare to hope that? If it were so, it may bring her home to her family, to where she belonged. To hear of a birth on May eve would be indeed a good omen and a source of such joy, to be a grandmother. But now she mustn't dwell on that thought; there was work to do, she must return to her preparations for the night.

The procession weaved and curved up the forested hillside. The path, well-trodden, but known only to a few, passed secret shrines and groves where the initiated practised their art. Tonight, the procession wove more deeply into the tree clad mountain range to a place where nature would protect them from any distant prying eyes. Their fires could not be too obvious. It had been many, many, years since they could dance and jump the fires with uninhibited abandon. They were more guarded; their survival had depended on it. As darkness descended, they would conduct their rites under the veil of invisibility.

Seren led the dance with Cynan; behind her followed Nerys with Geraint. Priestess and priest formed a line behind, spiralling into the circle where a central fire had been lit by the two youngest novices who waited in attendance. Only twelve made up the circle within the mountain stone, the surviving Druids of Eryri, each one descended from those ancient ones who had guarded some of the most precious secrets of existence. Once Lords of their environment, they were held in high esteem equally by kings and farmers or fishermen, whichever they had then been. Now they were conducting rites in secrecy and only a very few others knew of their existence.

The quarters were cast, air to the east, fire to the south, water to the west and earth to the north. The veil of darkness descended, enfolding around them, while the spirit of Bel ascended as Seren invoked the God of the ancient ones. Sparks from the Bel fire filled the darkness with a gentle shower of golden light. But gentle this ritual was not to be, for Seren and Cynan it was to take virtually every dram of their energy to summon the powers to their aid, and pure their intentions and strong their will had to be, together with all those who worked with them in the circle. Seren knew they only had this one chance to succeed. And so into the night the ritual went on.

Cynan lay down on his bed as the soft rosiness of the dawn light turned into the greyish blue hue of daylight. He felt depleted, exhausted, but exhilarated. He was pleased that he had the energy to match Seren and be at her side as a High Priest should be. He was glad that he had fulfilled the task that he was intended to at his last Beltane ritual. He knew it would be his last one and Seren knew it too. She would not be resting like him now though, she would have gone down to the lake to wait for any messages from the inner planes, in whichever form they would come. That was her task now; he had completed his and would rest. The younger priests and priestesses would be coupling in the woods, or some may be meditating in silence. That was their prerogative; it was Beltane and whatever happened was sacred, whatever they did would be a sacred act. He himself would fall into a deep sleep and let his dreams take him where they would.

CHAPTER 17

Sempringham Priory

The angel in the corner bowed her head in silence. She was a steady and reassuring presence, but the angel who stood over her was disturbing. The Reverend Mother Elizabeth could hear her words echoing in her head, advising her not to meddle. It was a very hard task, she felt, running the convent, and she relied on her angels more than she relied on Sisters Marie Clare and Agnes. They should share the burden more, but somehow the angels where always there for her and she trusted them, even if there were moments when she wondered if they were just figments of her imagination.

Wencilian, oh what to do about Wencilian, the nun she now knew to be Gwenllian. But more than that she didn't know for certain. Wencilian was close to her heart, just a child when she first met her. She remembered how her pretty green eyes looked up into hers when she first became Prioress. Mother Elizabeth had liked the child straight away and understood her vulnerability and loneliness. She recognised a seriousness, a wisdom in those green eyes. Wencilian, she knew, had never really been able to be a child. Whoever she was or wherever she came from, the Priory was her only home, her only family. Elizabeth loved her, but had had no time to raise her, leaving that to Marie who seemed more than competent.

So, what did she know now about Wencilian? It occurred to her to make notes, but that might be too dangerous. She would think over all the facts, then recount them to the angels and they would listen and offer advice, even though it may be conflicting advice.

Firstly, Wencilian has another name, Gwenllian. Maybe it had never been recorded properly by the Prioress Priscilla, who had preceded her, or maybe it was intended to be a deliberate error. Why then did they not give her a name that was totally different and would not arouse any suspicion?

Secondly, the King paid a sum each year for her keep. That was highly unusual, in fact unheard of before. Why would Edward want to protect her, yet never visit or acknowledge her?

Thirdly, she had been placed in the Priory at nine months old, not yet weaned. As rumour went, by several much older Sisters, the nursemaid came with her and was dismissed when she was weaned and never seen again. One of the older Sisters claimed to remember the night the baby arrived. She was called to open one of the Priory doors by the kitchens and said she had seen Prioress Priscilla accepting a bundle. She was then dismissed, but she heard a lot of horses galloping away and later heard what sounded like a baby crying in the cloisters. These were not reliable facts though.

And then, the name Gwenllian was not one she had ever heard before. Reliable sources had confirmed that the name originated from an ancient language of Briton which was still spoken in the west, mostly in Wales. Wales she knew, although many miles away, had been conquered by Edward and he had built many grand castles to defend his new land and subjugate the people. She supposed it was similar to the Norman invasion of England, but on a smaller scale.

Fifth, she had been told that Gwenllian could mean 'white stream' or 'fair and flaxen or pure' in the Saxon tongue. One of the scholarly monks she had asked also reported that in pagan times, 'Gwen' referred to 'blessed' or 'holy' and 'Llian' could denote a Druidess of that time, but in present times related to a very similar word which meant nun. How strange, Elizabeth thought, that God must have blessed her with that name, for he didn't bless her with a family or a heritage of any kind. Or had he? She had heard something of the Druids, a few tales when she was a young nun; tales of blood, sacrifice and all manner of unholy things.

Lastly, if Gwenllian was conceived in Wales and was an illegitimate daughter of the King by a servant or local woman, would he bother to conceal her? Why would he care? Elizabeth wondered. But if she was the daughter of a Welsh noblewoman, maybe married, then he would want to conceal her many miles away from her homeland. She felt she was perhaps closer to the truth, and surely with the help of the Father Thomas from the Monastery at Garendon, she may discover the whole truth.

Father Thomas had been eager to help when Mother Elizabeth had written to him. Always one for intrigue and having lots of contacts, he was useful to her. Being a man, he could travel beyond the bounds of his monastery, if required for a good reason. But he had another reason for helping, guilt. It seemed now to her something confined to a misty bygone age, the days when they walked out together, young man and young woman in love. Their families had been close and from the moment they were introduced as children, Elizabeth had wanted to be with him, and as she grew up she realised she wanted to marry him. He loved her too, no doubt, but his love of God and the Church was stronger. When he entered the Church, she had been bereft, and although her family had been understanding and tried to console her, even introducing her to other possible suitors, she had refused all and claimed that she too would dedicate her life to Christ. Then she had found she was with child. But her parents had soon dealt with that. She was sent away to give birth and then dispatched to a nunnery.

She had poured all her energy into her training as a nun and eventually rose to be Prioress. Inside the church, she could also keep a vague but tangible knowledge of Thomas and his whereabouts. The only contact they had though was the occasional official letter discussing Church business. However, just recently she had plucked up the courage to write to him regarding Wencilian. She was not sure how he would react at her request for him to find out any further information about her or her heritage, but it was her only chance. She had been very surprised to receive a letter back.

The letter was less formal than usual. Father Thomas had agreed it would be a precarious business but that he would try although he could not promise any results. He also told her of some strange visitors he had received at the monastery just before her letter arrived. Although they were used to accommodating travellers from time to time, he stated that these seemed to him a little suspicious. There had been a man who called himself Philip of Grantham, of the King's army, with his wife who had a strange accent and was with child. With them was a friar who attended mass, it seemed unwillingly. He had written that he would enquire about the authenticity of Philip of Grantham and the friar.

Mother Elizabeth wondered why he had mentioned the visitors. Was it a bit of intrigue of his own he wanted to share or did he think it had any bearing on her request? She would have to be patient and wait. Meanwhile, she may keep Wencilian a bit closer to her.

She sat in silence, awaiting the response of her angels, but none came. Closing her eyes she became aware of the sounds and the aromas around her; the smell of dying embers in the grate blended with the sweet perfume of the marsh lilies Sister Marie Clare had brought her the day before; the birdsong outside was vital and fresh, like the soft spring breeze which drifted in from the small open window behind her. 'Lovely,' she thought, 'why do I not notice these things … always busy, busy, with Priory business, no time to sleep.'

It was a few hours later when Sister Marie Clare found her slumped in her chair. Her first instinct was to panic, but on realising she was sleeping, she was greatly relieved. That's what she needs, she thought, and creeping slowly out of the room she left her to her dreams.

CHAPTER 18

Sempringham Priory

Wencilian sat in her cell with Alice. They had enjoyed very few moments alone to talk recently, but it seemed Alice had little to say these days anyway. Locked in her own misery, she found Wencilian's company comforting, but could not find joy or relief in conversation. Wencilian had told her about Hilda coming to the infirmary and the words she had spoken. Alice looked up at her and reached for her hand without comment.

"I need to speak to her again, but she is too sleepy with the draught we give her and in too much pain without it," Wencilian explained. "I don't think she has long in this life. I shall sit with her tonight between Compline and Matins, and Matins to Prime, if I can escape other duties. That is often the time when life seeps away."

It was a short period of time between the noon service of Sext and work duties resuming at half past one o'clock in the afternoon when the nuns could rest. Wencilian had found Alice and encouraged her back to her cell. Knowing that she would not get any more response from Alice, she made space on her pallet for her to rest and curled beside her, making a pillow for her. She closed her eyes but did not sleep, a stream of anxious thoughts invading her mind. She thought of the novice Mary, who had returned to her duties with Sister Ignatius. She had not seen Sister Ignatius for a while; just as well, she hoped she had the sense to keep out of her way. She knew Mother Elizabeth had reprimanded her for her treatment of Mary, but would that stop her unleashing her temper and bitterness on the poor novice nun again.

She thought of Isobel and Brother John. They would be the people to talk to about Hilda, not that Brother John had told her much that she didn't know, when he had taken her into his confidence the day he came into the infirmary. Wencilian thought that she would learn some secrets about the mysterious Hilda from him, but most of what he had mentioned she already knew. Except one thing … Brother John had revealed the possible identity of Leoba's father. She was not sure she believed it. He had told her that Leoba was conceived during a secret ritual and was thought to be a child of the old Saxon gods or a fairy child from a man of the wild wood. Wencilian thought that these were superstitions entwined with myths and gossip. Nonetheless, it fired her imagination and gave her a sense of excitement.

Brother John had sworn her to secrecy. "If the nuns hear you talking of such things it could have dire consequences. I myself find it quite amusing. There are still some who practice the drycraeft of the Saxon heathens. They will believe all sorts of rubbish, but I have no objection if they harm no one else."

Wencilian had agreed with him, on reconsidering she felt there could be an element of truth in the rumours. She had certainly experienced some strange things in the past few months and was no longer sure that the world was as black and white as she had been taught. Rumours start somewhere, she thought.

At that moment her thoughts turned to Boden. When she was distressed or unhappy, or when her mind was overactive, she thought of him. Today she pictured him in flight in the night sky, swooping towards her, his wings silent, shining with an opal light in the moon's reflection. She thought she heard him screech and a shiver went right through her. This time, she knew where she had heard that sound before. It was the screech which ended her dream, the dream which reoccurred from time to time, the dream in which the horses' hooves thudded, metal upon metal clashed, men shouted and the moon was full. Why had she not realised that before?

Alice stirred. "What is it Wencilian? You seem very distracted these days."

"As do you, Alice, much more than me I think; but no, I must have been deep in thought for a moment. I recollected that dream that reoccurs, but this time, being conscious I realised that the screeching in the dream is the screeching of an owl, an owl, like Boden. Why I had never connected this before, I don't know."

"Perhaps because dreams always occur in the deepest sleep and being awakened suddenly for mass pushes it out of your mind. Then you're busy with tasks all day and you have little time to dwell on it."

"That could be right, Alice." She smiled at her. Alice was very astute, she thought, and a dear friend. She felt a little guilty that she hadn't confided in her about Mira and the trip outside, but the truth was she didn't want to burden her with secrets or guilt. Alice already had enough sorrow to cope with.

They discussed again what to do about Maurice after the Easter visit. They had heard that the marriage with Alice's sister was going ahead. Unless Maurice was to send word somehow, although that would be difficult enough, or her family and the Priory were to agree to release her from her vows, which may be impossible or involve large sums of money, there was no hope. Unlike Mira, who had not taken her final vows as a lay sister, Alice was a fully-fledged nun who had taken final vows. Her family too was of a higher standing and Alice knew that any improper behaviour on her part would cause them hardship.

"I am glad you are here, Wencilian. Without your friendship I think I would have found a way to end it all, even if I had to suffer in hell."

Wencilian didn't believe that a God would be so vengeful on one who suffered, but the thought of the sin she may commit kept Alice from doing anything rash at the moment. Mira had no choice, she couldn't hide her pregnancy for long and her sweetheart was there for her. Heaven knows what would happen to Alice if she attempted to escape from the Priory.

"In a way we are similar, Alice. We both have had no control over our fate. And there are many more the same in this place. We have to support each other and be glad we are blessed with friendship."

"Isobel and Sara chose to be here," muttered Alice. "They begged Mother Elizabeth to take them in."

"Yes, the outside world is harsh, their circumstances were different, desperate, in fact, very desperate. The bell is ringing, I must return to the infirmary."

"Back to work, Wencilian. I'm tired, so tired and I've barely taken my vows. How will I cope with doing these relentless tasks and services for years and years to come?"

Wencilian sighed. She had no words which would comfort her. Alice had had a happy family life, which she mourned constantly. She had been in love and that love was lost forever, to her sister, which made the pain perpetually raw. That was perhaps worse, she thought, than having no memories at all, no raw pain, just a dull emptiness, punctured by moments of content, amusement, boredom and, just recently, moments of strangeness which captured her imagination.

Walking back to the infirmary, Wencilian passed through the open cloisters noticing the fine masonry and intricate carvings which adorned some of the pillars. Perhaps she was lucky, she thought, to live in such a fine building. On her few sojourns to the outside world, she had not seen such architectural splendour, only houses of wood and a few of stone around the market place those many years before, nothing anywhere near so grand. She savoured these memories and those of the night she helped Mira escape; they were her only memories and impressions of the outside world. She stored in her mind any information she had been fed – snippets of gossip filtered through to the nuns, tales from Isobel, Alice and other Sisters, of their lives before the Priory, never forgotten.

It seemed to Wencilian that women outside the walls of the Priory sometimes had little more control over their lives than the Sisters. It seemed that some, unless high born, commanded little respect, and the high born were perhaps even more subjected to the wills of their fathers and brothers. St Gilbert, the founder of their order, the Prioress said regularly, promoted education for women, and that all the Sisters should think of themselves as 'women of status', privileged women.

Women in the outside world, she told them, did not have the benefits of education. They were exposed to turbulence and strife. The nuns, by contrast, would know stability, peace and safety in which to satiate their spiritual longings. They would know equality, even those from the most humble backgrounds. Relative equality, Wencilian believed, was more accurate, for the nuns from the poorer backgrounds were not so often offered their own cell, even though they might eat the same food and wear the same clothes. Alice and she, and a fair portion of the nuns did have their own cell. That was a privilege, she had always assumed, granted to her recently again because of her unusual circumstances, having been there since a babe. Maybe, just maybe though, it now occurred to her, there was another reason ... could it be that someone, somewhere, was paying for her keep?

The cloister swept around the eastern corner of the Priory to the place where the infirmary stood, a little apart from the other buildings, and Wencilian felt the chill of east wind catching her. The sky was darkening, portending that a storm was coming. The tension before the storm vibrated through her body, a dark shadow ushered her through the heavy infirmary door, which unusually stood open. Sister Beatrice, it seemed, had expected the warmth of the sun to trickle in, it was the day of midsummer after all.

CHAPTER 19

Sempringham Priory

Wencilian never had the chance to question Hilda any further. The mysterious lady had slept most of the following day and after waking to request a draught for her pain, had fallen into a deep sleep and passed away quietly into those other realms of which the living can only dream. Sister Beatrice had at once gone to seek out Prioress Elizabeth to ask her what to do in this unusual situation.

"We can't bury her in consecrated ground. She was a heathen, or worse," Sister Beatrice blurted out.

Prioress Elizabeth's spare thoughts, when she had the time, had recently been consumed in seeking out the real identity of Wencilian. However, she supposed she would have to pay attention to this matter, irritating as it was.

"Shall we ask Father Roger?" continued Sister Beatrice.

"No, he will ask too many awkward questions."

"Why did you admit her to the Priory, Mother? Did she pay you?"

"That, Sister, is none of your business and you will not question my judgment! Has her daughter been told?"

"I will ask Wencilian to inform her, when I return to the infirmary."

"Prepare the body in the usual way. She will be given a decent burial in the far corner of the common cemetery. There will be no mass, but a priest shall attend at the grave. After all, this is the usual procedure for travellers and others we have treated, of whom we know little of their origins or faith. We have a duty to give a Christian burial, we cannot condemn their souls. Indeed, we would be the sinners then."

"But Mother …"

"That's all, Sister Beatrice. It will be done tomorrow after Terce. You will be there together with me, the priest and, yes, Wencilian too I think."

"Wencilian!"

"Thank you, Sister, as I said that will be all."

Slinking off with her head down and muttering to herself, Sister Beatrice retreated to her room in the infirmary. It was an hour later when she emerged to give Wencilian instructions. "You will go and inform that daughter of hers, and then return to help me prepare the body."

"What will happen to her, Sister Beatrice?"

"She is to be buried in the far corner of the common cemetery."

Wencilian was relieved that she was to have some sort of decent burial. She did not believe that there was any evil in Hilda at all. In fact she felt that she could have come to admire her had she had the chance. Saddened and frustrated by the fact that she had not had longer to talk to her, Wencilian walked quietly along the cloisters to the novices' house to find Leoba.

She found her in the chapter house, where the novices were undergoing instruction from Sister Benedict, a kindly nun who was devoted to her charges.

"Excuse me, Sister, but Mother Elizabeth has requested that I speak with Leoba in private."

Sister Benedict cleared her throat. "Of course. Leoba, please come here." Turning to Wencilian, she said quietly, "You'll be lucky to get her to speak at all, she barely ever utters a word."

Wencilian took Leoba to a small chamber further down the cloister. It was not strictly true that she had been asked to speak in private, but she felt it was the right thing to do and she was eager for any information she could get from her about her mother, or in fact herself. That was not going to be easy she knew, especially at such a sensitive time.

But it was Leoba who spoke first. "I know what you are going to tell me … that doesn't take much foresight. My mother is dead. I felt her spirit pass."

Wencilian was unusually lost for words. The two sat in silence for what seemed an hour, but must have only been minutes. "I am very sorry, I would have liked to know her better," she then said, taking Leoba's hand in hers.

Leoba looked up at her and Wencilian could see that her eyes were misty with tears. "Really? There are not many who would say that, except for the fen people, and most of those knew her well anyway."

Wencilian hesitated before asking, "Do you not have any other family at all? What about your father?"

"I never knew my father. He was an outsider. The fen people are all my family, although I don't think they have ever totally accepted me as one of their own."

"Then why did you not live with them? Why did your mother want you to come here?"

"My mother's ways were not the ways of the Church, but she understood the way of the spirit. She was a healer and she had 'the sight'. She knew that it was near her time to go and she could not fight it in the end. She was sad that she had not taught me everything that I needed to know, but she taught me a great deal. I think mother felt I would be safe here. The fen people may have forced me into a marriage or worse, with good intentions, but she didn't think I would survive well and feared my gifts could be lost."

"Won't your gifts, whatever they are, be lost here, and your freedom too?"

"Let me tell you, there is not much freedom in the world outside these walls, unless you are very lucky to be born into a well-to-do family. Even then, as a woman you may find yourself with little control of your life and the constant endurance of childbirth, miscarriage, death of your babes. Here I will have education, food, clothes and security. I do not believe all that the nuns and the priests spout from their mouths, but I believe most of them are not bad people. I also think that by the time I have to take my final vows, my mother hoped that my father may come to claim me, thereby saving me from a whole lifetime here."

Wencilian was astounded at the maturity of this young woman who could not be more than twelve or so. She had appeared to her as a fragile creature, but was obviously very strong indeed. Realising their hands were still clasped together, she was aware of the bell ringing for Nones.

Leoba, hearing the bell, squeezed her hand. "I think my mother wanted me to tell you this because she saw that you too did not belong in the place where you are. She knew she could trust you. I would like to work sometime in the infirmary where I can help with my healing gifts and I can teach you things too, and no doubt you can teach me a great deal."

"I sincerely hope that I can arrange that, Leoba, and that our paths will be able to cross often. Again the bell calls us now to go to Nones, and then I have to help Sister Beatrice prepare your mother for burial tomorrow morning. We will send for you after Terce, to join us."

All through the service of Nones, Wencilian thought about the conversation with Leoba. She had never spoken to anyone quite like her. In her young life, she must have experienced the rawness and poverty of life on the outside, the life that she, Wencilian, had always yearned for deep down. But it was obviously not always as she pictured it; she knew that from visiting Hilda's hut, but still clung to an idealised image of what her life could be like. She thought of Mira, what sort of life she would have on the run, but she had had no choice in order to save her baby. Her man was with her, she hoped, to give her some protection.

Wencilian knew that at night she would have supper and a bed to go to, but a small part of her still envied Mira. As Leoba had said, she didn't belong here, but where did she belong? That was the question which always haunted her. Leoba was similar to her in that she didn't know who her father was, but she did know her mother who must have loved her dearly.

That mother was buried the next morning, as planned. The sky was pushing sunshine through darkened clouds, whilst a sprinkling of soft rain produced a rainbow overhead. Leoba looked up in awe, as if seeing more than anyone else could see, and as the priest committed the body to the earth, Wencilian wondered why Mother Elizabeth stared at her continuously; it was making her uncomfortable. Sister Beatrice was noticeably absent. Maybe that was why, Wencilian thought, Mother Elizabeth had asked her to attend. It was often the case that someone from the infirmary who had nursed the deceased attended the burial. She could not think of another reason, unless, God forbid, it just occurred to her, she knew of her connection to Hilda.

CHAPTER 20

The mountains of Eryri
June 1300

Seren clasped her cloak around her. Was it too much to expect a little sunshine for Midsummer Eve? They had enjoyed a few warm weeks in the mountains of Eryri and now the clouds and mist had descended on them. Seren was concerned. Cynan needed some warmth, his health had deteriorated in the last few days. Geraint had assisted her in nursing him, but even his adeptness in the healing arts and Seren's knowledge did not make any improvement in his condition. Seren knew that his time was near and if it had been winter, she thought, he would have departed before now. She would not take part in the midsummer ritual this year, even though she really felt she was needed. Cynan needed her more. Geraint and the Priestess Roslyn can lead the rite, she thought. Cynan may not have long. I need to be with him in his final hours.

As Cynan slept, Seren built a fire and thought of Gwenllian. A few days after the Beltane ritual, she had been meditating by her mountain pool when she saw her in a vision. The vision became more lucid as it grew in intensity, and she could see Gwenllian clad in dark robes, leaning over a bed tending to a woman. The woman had a strong aura around her, although it was tinged with grey and fading. This was someone who was leaving this world. She had seen a similar aura many times. But that was not her concern. Her concern was with Gwenllian. As she tried to hold the vision it faded, but she had seen enough to know that the robes she wore were those of a nun and the building she was in must be some kind of infirmary. How strange and how interesting, thought Seren, that she should be in such a place. At least she is safe and possibly by now Cai would know, she hoped.

Since that day, Seren had gone into trance several times, hoping that on the inner planes she would succeed in visiting Gwenllian without her being aware of her astral presence. Each time something seemed to block her … until this morning when she found herself floating from her body, following her along a long cloister, around a corner and through a heavy oak door. Feeling her energy fading, she had swept in front of her to see into the room where she was headed. Gwenllian had stopped and stared for several seconds, wrapping her arms around herself, as if feeling the coldness as she swept through and maybe catching a glimpse of something, which she may have seen as just a dark cloud casting a shadow. Seren had seen pallets lined along the stone walls in the dismal room and an elderly nun tending to a patient, and then she was back in her body, an exhausted body. Trying to control her breathing, she lay for several minutes. Her urge was to fall into a deep sleep, but she had to fight that and get up to tend to Cynan. "I am getting too old for this," she told herself aloud.

Cynan drifted in and out of consciousness as Seren told him about her astral visit to Gwenllian. Holding his hand, she excitedly recalled details of her experience, unsure whether he could hear her or not. "It seems, Cynan, that our Gwenllian is a nun, locked up in a convent. I doubt that she is there of her own free will, not after having been taken by the King's men. But she looked well and she is practising the healing arts, albeit in a dismal atmosphere, not very conducive to healing at all. You know, Cynan, that the nuns have to practice obedience, chastity, humility and love. Therefore let's hope that she is pure in heart like our priestesses should be. We are not bound by the same rules, but we understand their aspirations; they are not too unlike our own. It's a pity the Church does not see that."

Seren imagined herself in the convent. She had, many years before, visited a few priories whilst travelling and had to rely on their hospitality, posing as a poor widow. She had generally found the nuns were pleasant and educated women, content with their life. Although, she had come across some in whom she sensed a deep unhappiness or bitterness. Not surprisingly, she thought. She admired the buildings greatly; they had seemed palatial compared with her mountain shack, but she would never have exchanged her freedom to live in such a place. She would never exchange her beliefs for those of the Christian faith. The Christian God they worshipped cared not for the beauty of the Goddess, the mother who exists within every living being. She had been born into her faith and it was deeply engrained in her heart and soul. What if it was the same for Gwenllian, she thought, perhaps never having known any other way of life? What would they do then? Would all their plans come to nothing?

Cynan was fading fast, but at least Seren knew that she had told him the news he most wanted to hear, that Gwenllian was alive and that she had seen her. She stepped outside to collect some more firewood, which Nerys had been stacking at the back of her hut. When she looked around for Nerys, there was no sign of her. She had probably gone to join the other priests, priestesses and neophytes; it was Midsummer Eve and there was a lot of preparation to do. The mist was even lower now, she noticed, as she heard footsteps close by and the crunching of twigs and stones on the ground.

"Who's there?" she shouted. When there was no reply, her heart thumped in her chest. She could hear breathing coming closer towards her. Preparing to throw some heavy logs of wood in that direction and run back to the hut, where she had a sword and a knife, although she had never used them in violence, she stopped just in time to hear a voice.

"Mam, Mam, it's me, Luned."

A figure emerged from the mists with a large bundle strapped to her chest, and behind her strode a young woman carrying an even larger burden. Seren recognised the second woman as her daughter and heard the cry of a baby coming from the bundle of rags wrapped around her.

"Oh Luned, praise the God and Goddess, can I believe it's you?"

Luned took the baby from the sling and held her in her arms. "Mother, meet your granddaughter. I think she is hungry, as we all are; my friend here, Erin, as well."

"Oh blessings! Welcome little one and welcome back, Luned. I think I knew you would come and just in time. It is always said that birth and death follow each other."

"Death?"

"Your father, Luned. He lies in the hut and is not long for this world."

"Then I was brought back just at the right time, or I should say really, 'called back'."

Grantham, Lincolnshire

Cai paced around the courtyard, agitated. The two servant girls passed him giggling, carrying pitchers of water from the well. It was the early morning of Midsummer Eve. He had not slept well at all, partly due to the few hours of darkness and partly due to worrying whether Hywel would show up. He never normally doubted his own intuition; he had been certain he would have been here by now. He had even suggested to Gwyneth a few days ago that it may be a good idea to prepare for a visitor. She had wondered why, as there had been no messenger or word sent. However, she was used to the occasional surprise visitor or traveller passing by, although they didn't usually get past Hervé at the gate without a lot of persuasion.

It was just before the midday meal was being served when Hervé came to announce that there was a suspicious-looking beggar at the gate and he had sent him on his way.

"That was a bit harsh," Rhiannon exclaimed.

"Certainly you should have offered him some food," added Gwyneth.

"I did give him some bread and water," replied Hervé.

"Oh Lord, that sounds like Hywel," Cai shouted, jumping up from the table.

"Who?" Gwyneth asked.

"My visitor, I must see if he is still there."

Opening the heavy gate that enclosed the courtyard, Cai looked left and right and into the distance, but there was no sign of anybody.

"You took your time." A voice came from the ground below. "And tell that measly Frenchman that his bread is stale and his water stinks."

"Hywel, I knew you would have the good sense to wait. Come inside. I'm sure we can do better than bread and water. The midday meal is being served. You took your time too. I've been worried about you."

"Always worrying like an old woman. Help me up. My knees are creaking like an old dog."

"Come here, you old dog." Cai pulled him up laughing. "Come and meet the lovely ladies of the household. Mind you, I think we had better scrub you up a bit, first."

"If you insist, my dear friend. Let's get the food and the pleasantries over. We have a lot to discuss."

CHAPTER 21

Grantham, Lincolnshire

Philip's mother and sisters were sitting in the solar, working on a tapestry. The tapestry was a fine, intricate piece of work, which usually took all of their concentration. They hoped to finish it before Philip came home, but today the silence was broken by inane chatter, sighs and nervous laughter. Gwyneth was particularly distracted and kept glancing out through the window from the deep alcove where they sat.

"What do you keep looking at, Mother? Surely the mist is obscuring any view today?" asked Rhiannon.

After hesitating, Gwyneth spoke solemnly. "Indeed the mist is low and the day is chilly for Midsummer Eve. That's what makes me wonder why Catrin, Cai and that strange man, Hywel, are sitting outside in what appears to be intimate conversation. In fact they have been huddled together in quiet places ever since Hywel appeared. I am not saying that he is not sociable or appreciative of our hospitality, but it makes me wonder what it is that we do not know. I am worried about Philip; there has been no word."

"True Mother, I too am worried. But that is often the case with soldiers. Remember when we didn't know Philip's whereabouts for many years. As for those three outside, maybe they are planning a midsummer celebration to surprise us all."

"I'm not too sure about that, their mood is not one of joviality, but rather concern."

"Cai was up early this morning. I saw him pacing up and

down the courtyard. He looked distressed," Arian put in.

Gwyneth put down her tapestry and stood by the window. "I wonder what's going on."

"I don't know, Mother, but I think maybe we should find out." Rhiannon jumped up to join her.

The three women huddled together by the window, all watching Catrin, Cai and Hywel, sitting huddled together as if guarding a precious secret. Gwyneth had come across Hywel once before, she remembered now, a hazy vision floated through her mind of a younger Hywel staying overnight with her husband at their Powys home. He had sung to them and her husband had declared to her afterwards that he was an Archdruid and followed the old ways. Only now had the memory come back to her. With his long hair and ragged clothes he was hard to recognise, but she was sure it was him. The clear eyes still sparkled, even though the face had aged. The way in which he gesticulated with his hands; yes, it was him. The girls would not remember; Rhiannon was then a baby and Arian not yet born.

Gwyneth knew a little of the old ways. There were people in Powys and the deeper west who still kept a respect for the ancient beliefs of their forbearers and the power of magic. She had heard tales of them practising their arts and celebrating the seasonal rites as the year's wheel turned, but she had never known any of them personally, or taken part in any celebrations or rituals. They kept themselves secret, and with good reason, for the Christians would persecute them and have them tortured as heretics. A tingle went down her spine, and she was not sure if it was the thought of torture or the lure of magical rites that sent her into a shiver. The words 'Alban Hefin' danced in her mind.

"Mother, are you well? You look pale," Rhiannon said with concern. "Come and sit down. Arian, fetch some wine."

"I'm fine, don't fret. You girls go down for your meal. Ask Margaret to bring some up for me. I'll stay here and rest."

A little space to think was what Gwyneth needed. If Hywel was an Archdruid, why would he be consulting with a friar and why would Catrin be so interested in their conversation. She wished Philip was here, he would take command. She felt insecure, yet she had grown to trust Cai and she loved Catrin like her own daughters. What did Hywel want with them both? With Philip away she felt a little vulnerable. Strictly speaking Catrin was in charge of the household, but with her pregnancy advancing, Gwyneth felt that she needed to take over and show some authority. Gwyneth asked the servant who brought the midday meal to ask Catrin to attend her after she had eaten. There were a few questions she needed to ask.

Downstairs in the hall, the two servant girls served the midday meal. Cai was aware of a strange atmosphere as Arian and Rhiannon ate in silence. Catrin looked at Cai with concern. She couldn't understand why Gwyneth had summoned her up the stairs to the solar with an almost formal request. Hervé had not attended at all, apparently taking some food to the stable boys and eating with them. Hywel ate in silence, totally absorbed with his thoughts. He had a lot to think about.

Cai too was absorbed in his own thoughts. It was Midsummer's Day and his mind was wandering up into the mountains of Eryri. The night before Alban Hefin, as Midsummer Eve was called in his own land, Seren and Cynan would have been celebrating the summer solstice with the priests, priestesses, neophytes and young initiates of the Eryri grove. After his talk with Hywel, he now had preparations to make. He was to leave tomorrow at dawn, but had not yet told Gwyneth and her daughters. Catrin knew now that he would be leaving soon and she would be left behind. He was reluctant to leave her at this time, knowing she was fearful of the birth to come. She had been with Eleanor as she gave birth to Gwenllian and had been quite traumatised at the time, being so young. He did his best to reassure her, although he wondered what else he could do to help, knowing there was nothing. He had to leave now – the time was right; he had waited long enough.

Hywel had been to the place where Gwenllian was allegedly held, the convent at Sempringham in Lincolnshire. With the help of several others who had been at the forest gathering in the spring, and the help of some of the Knights of the Red Cross, known as the Templars, he had even more reason to believe that Sempringham was the place where she had been taken as a baby and had remained ever since. This verified the account he had been given at Penmon Priory. It seemed now that the information they held could be believed as accurate.

"We had to make sure," Hywel had stressed that morning. "Now we can proceed and attempt to make contact."

It had been Hywel's plan to send Catrin with Cai, and to persuade the Prioress to admit Catrin as a novice lay sister to enable her to be close to Gwenllian. With Catrin's pregnancy this was now impossible. Cai was to set off with Hywel, and then later, as a lone friar, to try to seek temporary sanctuary with the monks of Sempringham. This was not ideal, but was the most unobtrusive way of making contact with her initially. Even that would perhaps prove to be very difficult.

After the meal, Cai knew he would have to brace himself to look into the scrutinizing eyes of his hostess and tell a half truth about his reason for leaving. It would probably not be that difficult, he thought, after all a travelling friar never rests for too long in one place. She would surely understand, although he knew she had grown fond of him, a little too fond perhaps. No doubt she would make some fuss and be packing him up all manner of things to take with him. This time he would have to travel light, as they were to go on foot. Ianto was to stay behind. Their destination before Sempringham was to be at a Templar house, where Hywel would be based.

Catrin approached Gwyneth's room. She had always felt a little in awe of her, she being the younger woman and of lower birth, and of course Gwyneth adored her son, so Catrin had always trodden carefully, deferring to her in household matters when she stayed with them. But, strictly speaking, Catrin was head of the household when Philip was away, so she had no reason to feel nervous, except that she did.

Gwyneth made her welcome and offered her some wine. "How are you Catrin? It is getting nearer your time now; you really should rest more and not concern yourself with other matters, cariad."

"Other matters? What do you mean?"

"Well, I have seen you chatting a lot to Cai and Hywel. They are more than capable of sorting out any household problems with Hervé. Unless of course, I can help with anything. You know you can rely on me."

"Thank you, Gwyneth, but we were just reminiscing about the days we spent in North Wales and I was asking Hywel and Cai if they had any news of my family."

"Ah yes, I suppose they are often in your thoughts," Gwyneth replied, disbelieving all she had heard, but knowing it would be hard to find the truth. Nevertheless, she intended to keep a closer eye on Catrin and the two men whilst they were in her son's house.

Catrin left her, feeling unsettled. She had not been sure how much Gwyneth knew of the plot to free Gwenllian, but it seemed apparent that Philip had not revealed anything to her, although she was an astute woman and obviously suspected something. She would just have to be very careful from now on.

CHAPTER 22

Sempringham Priory

The days following Hilda's death passed unremarkably. Wencilian felt encased within herself, within her own thoughts. She had wanted to speak to Leoba, but the opportunity had not arisen. She had seen Leoba sitting at the novices' table in the refectory, as self-contained as ever, giving away no emotion in her facial expression.

On the fourth day, after Prime and the chapter house meeting, Wencilian slipped away through the cemetery and stood in the quiet of the early morning beside Hilda's grave. A wave of sadness washed over her – sadness that she had not known Hilda better. She could not really grieve, for she hardly knew her at all. She had come to the grave expecting something, she didn't know what exactly, perhaps a revelation or inspiration, or even a lovely rainbow like the one which appeared at her burial. But there was nothing, just the rustle of the leaves on the trees and the early morning birdsong.

It was a few days after midsummer's day and the early morning mists enveloped Wencilian. She stood shrouded, a faint silhouette in the quietness of the common cemetery, where those who lay were forgotten and footsteps rarely trod.

"I wish you could speak to me beyond the grave, Hilda, and tell me who I am … tell me who is this nun who stands here? I will keep my promise to your daughter as far as I can. Rest in peace, Hilda."

She was barely aware of having spoken out loud, when she

heard the faint crunch of footsteps on the stone path which led back to the church. It could not have been a coincidence that Sister Ignatius was standing at the church door.

"Good morning, Sister Wencilian. No duties to keep you busy this morning? I'm surprised you want to visit the grave of someone you barely knew."

Wencilian looked up at her. Trying not show her anger, she replied as calmly as she could, "You too must be lacking in duty, and indeed company, to spare time to linger with the dead and buried."

With a slightly sarcastic laugh, Sister Ignatius shrugged and walked away past the church in the direction of the east cloister, which led towards Mother Elizabeth's rooms.

Wencilian walked with her head held high, back to the infirmary. She was not afraid of Mother Elizabeth, but still, she knew questions would be asked and there was no explanation she could give which could be convincing. She had been at the burial, so Mother Elizabeth would wonder why on earth she had gone back to visit the grave of a woman she hardly knew and, worse than that, was a heathen. She could never tell her that she wanted to say goodbye in her own way; she could never tell her what had happened between them or that Hilda had used the 'sight' to say that she, Wencilian, the nun with no past, was of noble birth.

Sister Ignatius was indignant that she had to wait outside Mother Elizabeth's room. Sister Marie Claire had come out to explain that they were busy doing accounts for the expected visit from the King's chancellor. She sat on the bench outside, regarding the carvings on the heavy oak door, hoping to overhear snippets of conversation, but she could only hear low muffled tones and the rustling of paper. A young novice nun came out, carrying dirty plates, and still she was not admitted. Her temper was rising, but she knew it was mainly because of the way Sister Wencilian had spoken to her earlier. How dare she speak to her like that, when she was the one at fault? She was the one sneaking around up to no good at all.

Eventually, Sister Agnes and Sister Marie Claire came out.

"You can go in now," said Sister Agnes. "We are going, but don't take up too much of her time, she has been working all night, she needs some rest."

The Prioress listened patiently to Sister Ignatius's report of Sister Wencilian's activities. She did not have a great liking of Sister Ignatius, but knew that she was the ideal person to keep a close eye on Wencilian, although she did not entirely trust her.

The Prioress did not reveal any information she had on Wencilian, instead suggesting that Sister Ignatius was merely to observe. She disliked having to do this and in fact wondered if it was necessary, as Wencilian obviously had no idea of her true heritage, if she did have one. She had thought of having Wencilian closer to her, working alongside her, for she was well-read, bright and she was fond of her, but that could be a bit dangerous at this stage. Wencilian may discover something she would be better off not knowing. The Prioress resolved that until she had more information Wencilian was better in the infirmary, out of the way, serving the sick with her special talents.

Sister Ignatius's observations however were disturbing. Why should Wencilian be standing at Hilda's grave? Were there grounds for her doubts about Wencilian's involvement in the disappearance of Mira, who, incidentally had not been found? She thought it best not to question Wencilian; it would only arouse suspicion and maybe hamper her investigation. Anyway, the King's chancellor was on his way; Wencilian would have to wait.

Wencilian kept strictly to the infirmary when she was not attending mass or reading in the chapter house. Recently, the infirmary had become busier and she had taken to sleeping most nights on a spare pallet beside the patients. She did not want to arouse any suspicions or incur any wrath from the Prioresses. In fact she was surprised that she had not been called before Mother Elizabeth. Surely Sister Ignatius would have reported her presence in the cemetery. She was certain that Sister Ignatius was spying on her, but was it her own means or at the request of someone else? In all her time in the Priory, she had not felt such unease. Why would Sister Ignatius want information about her unless she knew something about Mira? Wencilian doubted that the Prioress Elizabeth would be influenced by gossip and the suspicions of a vindictive nun who cared only about her own promotion, but she knew that the seeds of doubt would be planted and that Sister Ignatius would be there to sprinkle them with water and nurture them.

Wencilian longed to speak to Isobel, Alice or Brother John, her closest friends and allies, but she thought it better to lie low, fulfilling her devout duties, for the moment. Hiding away in the infirmary, she would be more or less left alone, apart from the interference of Sister Beatrice. Not many wanted to risk exposing themselves to illness if they could avoid it. In time, she would think what to do, she was certain she would have to do something. She had a right to know who she was, where she came from. Maybe she should ask the Prioresses outright, but they may not know and then she would be accused of pride. It was best to bide her time. For all of her eighteen years it had not occurred to her to question her origins in this way, but now the desire to find her true heritage burned within her and consumed her thoughts, as if discovering the truth would heal the emptiness in her heart.

CHAPTER 23

Kesteven, Lincolnshire

The landscape of Lincolnshire did little to inspire Cai. It made him more homesick for his own country, and the language he found disagreeable as he sometimes struggled to remember words. Staying in Philip's house, speaking mostly his native language with Catrin, Gwyneth and her daughters, he had felt quite at home, but now on the road with Hywel he wasn't sure what would happen next. At one time this would have inspired him, sent hot blood running through his veins, but today he was apprehensive. The possibility of seeing Gwenllian, being in her presence, speaking to her, was becoming more of a reality.

The impressive building of their next host stood out like a majestic monument against the flat farmland and heath land surrounding them. Hywel leaned on his stick, "You must sharpen up your accent, Cai, before you go to the Priory at Sempringham."

"I think that maybe you should be the one to find Gwenllian, Hywel. I am not going to lose the sound of my native tongue, even when it speaks another language. You have spent more time travelling, more time in England than me." Cai patted the pony Hywel had reluctantly purchased on the journey. They had both found themselves becoming weary, so had agreed to share one pony, riding in turn. They needed to look like simple friars, unremarkable, unassuming.

Hywel glanced at Cai. "No, it should be you. You held her

as a babe; you nearly lost your life trying to save her. You were the closest person to her father, apart from Eleanor, and you can best explain who she is and where she came from."

Cai did not reply, he knew it was true.

Drawing nearer to the estate, they could see a large, round church with many buildings huddled round it, all enclosed by a defensive wall with a gatehouse. Several farmhouses and small crofts lay in the surrounding area.

Cai had enjoyed the company of Hywel in the days it had taken them to travel from Grantham to Kesteven, a home of the Grand Prior of the Temple Knights of England.

Riding and walking together, they had shared memories, sung old songs and composed new. Whilst Cai had spent many years in the mountains of Eryri, Hywel had travelled, mostly posing as a merchant, which gave him a good living and the chance to infiltrate many levels of society, gathering what Hywel sought most of all, knowledge – knowledge, which could be a dangerous thing in this day and age. His contacts served him well and he had secured them the help of one of the most powerful organisations in Christendom, the Knights of the Temple. And it was the Templar settlement which lay just ahead of them, where they were to discuss the next step of the plan to reach Gwenllian.

It was in truth a feast for the eyes, Cai thought. The inside of their host's house was rich in artefacts, craftsmanship, style and artistic skill, refined, decorative, elegant and tasteful. Cai found it hard to believe that it was inhabited solely by men, and soldiers at that. He had met Templar knights several times with Llywelyn at Cwmhir Abbey. The Cistercian order had been instrumental in the development of the strength and power of the Templar movement many years before, and Father Francis and his Lord Llywelyn maintained links which Cai was sure must have been most influential, and could still be. He had thought the knights austere in their habits and frugal in their needs. The opulent appearance of this house was far more splendid than any court of Llywelyn's, or any court that he had ever been in.

In the large dining hall that evening, their host, Sir William de la More, explained it had been a good few years for wool. The markets had flourished; in fact much of their income went to those in need – the poor, orphans and widows. Sheep farming was their main income here and all over the county.

Hywel and Cai were seated next to their host. As Hywel had explained to Cai earlier, they were very privileged to have the attention of the Grand Prior himself. He had warned Cai not to mention his quest until Sir William spoke about it. The hall was full of men occupied with their own business, Cai noted, but they were remarkably quiet for knights, squires and soldiers. The sprinkling of chaplains and priests amongst them may have subdued them somewhat, he thought.

"Brother Gregory, Hywel tells me that you are quite a hero and want to liberate the Princess of Gwynedd from the nunnery at Sempringham," Sir William stated in hushed tones.

"Well, no hero. There are not many who care what becomes of her now," Cai replied, taken aback a little at the directness and the slight condescension in his tone. "We would like her to be restored as the rightful Princess of Wales, but if that cannot be, at least to secure her freedom would be an achievement, for her to know her true heritage, that she had a family and was loved by many would give me peace of mind."

"How much of her heritage do you think she knows?" asked Sir William.

"Possibly nothing, for she is registered at the Priory under the name 'Wencilian', but we do not know for sure."

"Why do you care so much?"

"I saw her born, or immediately after her birth, and made a promise to my Lord Llywelyn, whom I served for many years and became, I believe, his closest friend and confidant. I loved her mother, Eleanor, and little Gwenllian herself. For the first year of her life I helped to care for her along with her nurses, Catrin, Morwena and Celeste – as steward of the household." he added, seeing the disbelieving look on Sir William's face. As always happened when Cai mentioned Celeste's name, his heart missed a beat. He added, "Princess Gwenllian is the true heir to the Principality, deprived of her true title, her true worth, by the King."

Cai knew he could be treading on dangerous ground. Speaking against the King could be construed as treason and he wasn't entirely sure where Sir William's loyalties lay.

Hywel saw his unease and intervened. "Sir William has agreed to help us, but will not take too great risks. He cannot be seen to defy the Church in any way, therefore not the King, in any way whatever. The future of their entire organisation depends on that."

"I have agreed," Sir William continued, "to ensure a safe passage and secret temporary dwelling place in France for the Princess Gwenllian in the event that you succeed in freeing her. But I will do no more. I am only doing this because I am aware that Llywelyn was a great man, a leader of men, and of course was the guardian of the Llywelyn family manuscripts."

"France!" Cai exclaimed. "Why not back to the security of the mountains of Eryri, where she can hide and be schooled in the old ways?"

"Think carefully, Cai. I have discussed this with Hywel. The world has changed. Don't you think that that would be one of the first places that the King would search for her?"

"He has never succeeded in finding those who keep the old ways. The mountains are extensive and the mountain people will not be found if they do not want to be."

"Gwenllian is a Princess, daughter of Eleanor de Montfort," continued Sir William. "Would you see her hunted down, living in fear and coping with the harsh winters of Eryri. She has, no doubt, no experience of the outside world; she would be better housed in a safe environment for a while, perhaps with a family or even a convent, but as a free woman, until she can adjust to the world and you can find the most suitable place for her."

"You could accompany her to France, Cai, and stay with her," Hywel suggested.

"I would have to." The idea of going to France quite pleased him for he would perhaps have a chance to search for Celeste. He knew that her family came from the area of Montargis, although he had no other information yet.

"What is your plan ... to make contact at Sempringham?"

"As a travelling friar I shall ask for their hospitality and then feign some illness or weakness so that I can stay longer."

"Umm," Sir William muttered, seemingly unimpressed.

"I know it doesn't seem much of a plan," Hywel remarked, "but we have to be very discreet. We don't want to arouse any suspicion, especially at this stage."

"What House of Friars are you from, Cai?" Sir William enquired with a mocking air.

Unsure whether Sir William knew his true status or was merely testing him whilst preserving his secret from prying ears, Cai tried to reply confidently, "The Franciscan Friars of Llanfaes."

The less he said the better. It was true that he had spent more time in the Augustinian priory at Penmon and was perhaps now more accustomed to their ways, but he did not want to implicate Father Iorwerth, and Llanfaes, after all, was close to his heart as it had been to Llywelyn's; he had made a promise to both of them.

"What do you know about the Gilbertine order?" Cai asked. "Do you have any dealings with them, sire?"

"Pilgrims pass this way to the shrine of St Gilbert. Of course they have our protection. Personally, I may deal with the Brothers from time to time for business. They produce a lot of the wool in which we trade. I deal only with the Brothers and the Prior. I know nothing of the nuns; they are rarely if ever seen. The place thrives at the moment and has a good reputation amongst all the local gentry."

"Can you help me gain entry?" Cai asked.

"Frankly, no. No one there is to know of our connection. I suggest you approach the almoner as a poor friar and ask for admission as a guest. I have spoken with the recent almoner, Brother John. He is an agreeable fellow and knows most of what happens behind those walls and outside of them. I can do no more than this. Now I shall bid you both to drink and eat while you can. Here's to your health and the success of your venture."

It was a warm, sultry morning on the next day when Cai set off accompanied by Hywel, who was dressed as Cai had not seen him before, as a smart merchant. Sir William had provided them with a fine horse, which they shared until they parted near to Sempringham Priory. Cai was glad of the good weather and was relieved that they had not attempted this journey in winter. The tracks skirted the edge of dreary fenland intersected by straight cut dykes and drains in long parallels. But in some areas the summer had blessed the population with miles of ripening corn. On the fringes of higher ground, sheep grazed contentedly. They had taken a well-trodden Roman road until they came to the rougher tracks where Cai was to continue alone on foot. Hywel would lodge close to Sempringham to connect with Cai whenever he had the chance, whilst trading his spices and cloths at the local markets and possibly at the Sempringham Priory itself.

As the Priory came into view, Cai's dream that he had cherished for so long, of finding Gwenllian, the true heir of the Prince of Wales, could at last become a reality. He had come this far; he could not fail now.

The priory buildings looked impressive. He could see men working in the surrounding fields. It was a place bustling with life. He took a deep breath. If his Princess was hidden within those walls, he would need all his ingenuity to uncover her whereabouts. Would he now honour his promise to Llywelyn or would it be too late?

CHAPTER 24

The Mountains of Eryri

Luned rose early and nuzzled the baby Elena against her breast. She watched Seren and her maid and companion, Erin, sleeping peacefully on the other side of the room. It was often at this time when she fed Elena that she thought of Cynan. She was thankful that she had arrived back in time to be with him for his last moments, but sad that she had wasted so many years apart from him and that he had not spent any time with his granddaughter. She was glad to be home, although as she glanced around her, she wondered how she would manage living in such conditions. Since she had left this mountain enclave, she had become accustomed to more refined, softer living, and how she missed it, and her husband, Ithel. Since his death, his family had made life very uncomfortable for her. They never liked her, calling her a wild child, trying to control everything she did and worst of all, trying to take charge of baby Elena.

One night with Erin she made her escape, taking just a few possessions. She knew that she would never have a chance to claim the small property her husband had left her, without a great deal of wrangling and sacrifice. She just wanted to be home in the mountains of Eryri, where she belonged.

As she watched Seren stirring, she felt an overwhelming love and gratitude to the mother who welcomed her back without bitterness, without question. Having a baby herself now, she knew what her mother must have felt when she left without almost a backward glance those eight years ago. Her mother needed her now more than ever, with Cynan gone.

Seren searched for a shawl, shivering in the cool morning.

Looking over to Luned she could sense her thoughts. "Everything happens at the right time, Luned. Don't worry yourself about the past. We have to look to the future now. Except, when you feel ready I would like to know more about your life in these last years and why you came back. I'll heat some cinnamon porridge to warm us. Hywel left me a stack of exotic spices on his last visit."

"Hywel?" asked Luned.

"A travelling bard and merchant who once led one of the best teaching groves in Britain, but you will learn more about him later on."

"I'll heat some water for washing," Erin said, jumping from her pallet eager to help. She was glad to be by Luned's side, treated with respect rather than like a slave by Ithel's mother and family, although as yet she was not sure what to make of her new home. It had been such a gruelling trip to get here that she was glad to just have rested for several days.

Seren cast Luned a genuine smile. It was lovely to have her daughter back and with a trusted friend. She realised how often they laughed together and how little she laughed herself these days. There would be a lot of grieving to do, she knew, but Luned's presence would ease it a great deal. She was eager as well to tell Luned about Gwenllian and the plan to bring her home to the mountains of Gwynedd but had not yet found the right time. Her joy at being a grandmother to little Elena seemed to have taken precedence over anything else since Luned had arrived.

"Even with the heat of the summer sun, this water never warms, Mother," Luned called to Seren as she swam in the deep mountain pool, Seren's bathing pool.

"But it's wonderful to lie in the warm sun afterwards, while we can, while the sun blesses us," Seren replied, rubbing her long hair with a faded linen cloth. Feeling the sun's rays penetrating her thin robe and heating her bare arms, she stretched out on the grass, relaxed and content. "It's not often in these hills that we get such intense heat."

"Are you coming into the water again?"

"I had a long swim before you joined me. I'll lie here and wait for you. Then we can share some wheat cakes I've brought along."

Seren had planned this moment, just the two of them alone by the pool. Hoping to talk to her daughter without any interference, she knew this would be the best place. She watched while the tension and anxiety visibly dissolved around Luned as she swam and splashed in the water. The pool always had that effect, soothing the emotions and calming the mind. While Erin minded the baby, the two of them could have the heart to heart they needed.

Seren knew that what she heard that day would be etched on her memory forever. Luned answered her questions with total honesty.

"It wasn't just that I had a yearning to leave and see the world outside; I felt I couldn't live up to what was expected of me." Luned explained. "To be born as a child of the God and Goddess was a great responsibility, one that I didn't want to aspire to, at that time."

"You were conceived in a sacred ritual it's true, but Cynan and I raised you as our natural child. I gave birth to you and tried to give you a childhood that was free from too many expectations, whilst instructing you in the ancient ways of our people, so that one day you would be a competent High Priestess, passing on wisdom and knowledge. There are so few of us left now to pass on our traditions." Seren turned to look into Luned's eyes and saw tears gathering.

"I now know that is true, Mother, and I have come back in time to help you, but I don't know if I am worthy."

"You had a right to make decisions about your life; I would never have blamed you. Things work out as they should in the end, whichever path you choose. You've suffered sadness and maybe you needed to experience something of the world. Perhaps there was not enough here for you, but I have worried so much since you left, not knowing where you were."

"I know now I have a child of my own what it would be to

188

lose her. Ithel's family are not her true family. She belongs here. I would have liked her to visit them, but that is impossible, they would only try to take her away from me."

"What was he like … Ithel?"

"A fine man. I was working as a maid in his household. We fell in love and married, much to the disgust of his parents and brother who thought I was beneath him. When they had to accept me as mistress of the house they found it intolerable but didn't dare defy Ithel, and when they found out where I came from they called me a witch and heretic."

"How did they find out?"

Luned rolled up her sleeve to reveal the crescent moon tattoo etched deeply on her upper arm and the sign of Awen, the moon and the sun. The very same symbols Seren displayed on her arm. "I usually kept them covered, but only for safety reasons," she added, seeing dismay on her mother's face.

"We should be able to display it proudly on our forehead as all the Priestesses did in ancient times, not hide it away." Seren felt the familiar pain in her heart when she thought of the ancient times, times when Priests and Priestesses were revered and respected, times when there were Druid colleges spread across the Isle of Britain. "Even the early Christians who came to these shores lived in harmony with us until the Church of Rome drove us all into secret enclaves, had us hunted down, spreading lies of sacrifice and idolatry. How many innocent lives did they take?"

"I need to learn more of our history, Mother. Will you teach me?"

"If only you knew what joy it is to hear that request, for even though you are my daughter, I have no right to force the knowledge on you. I can only impart it if I am asked, for that is our code. Unlike the Church, we do not impose our beliefs on anyone, even those born of our blood. We need to keep the knowledge and the traditions alive throughout the centuries even though at this stage in time they must be hidden. One day, the world will know them again. Meanwhile too we have work to do. Our Prince Llywelyn protected us and we must prepare to welcome and protect his daughter Gwenllian who is imprisoned far away from here."

"Gwenllian? I remember I think, you used to talk about when she was born. It is a fragmented memory, I could only have been about six years old."

"Most memories are fragmented, Luned, often like dreams; we remember the parts which are more important to us."

"What has happened to her, Mother?"

Seren sighed. "I wish I knew for certain, but we are getting closer to the truth. Cai, you will remember him I'm sure, has set out to find her and will bring her home, home to her people. He was to meet with Hywel and some others of our kin plus some of Llywelyn's men who survived. It seems that memory of her has been almost relegated to history now even though only eighteen years have passed. How quickly the world moves on. We must remember her always, together with those who have honoured the name 'Gwenllian' in previous times.

"Tell me about that, Mother. I do seem to have a vague memory of stories when I was small."

"Stories they were to you and they kept you enthralled on cold nights by the fire, but we committed them to our memory and to our songs and poems. I have no time to retell their stories now, but you shall learn of them, Gwenllian, the warrior Princess, and Gwenllian, the Priestess who fought the Romans, and now we have Gwenllian, heir to the Principality.

CHAPTER 25

Sempringham Priory

Wencilian was in the still room, biding her time whilst preparing elderflower water. The infirmary was unusually quiet. Apart from two elderly nuns, who slept most of the day, all the beds were empty. This gave her time to catch up on other duties, especially while Sister Beatrice was out of the way discussing the running costs of the infirmary with Mother Elizabeth.

"We must be frugal." These were the words Sister Beatrice had used that morning to warn her of being too extravagant. "The Prioress is expecting a visit from the King's chancellor any day now. He will be inspecting all the accounts."

"Haven't we been expecting his visit for a long time now?" Wencilian had replied.

"The King's men are no doubt too busy with court business and overseas campaigns to give us priority," Sister Beatrice had called over her shoulder as she swept through the heavy oak door leading onto the open cloister.

The gentle aroma of the elderflowers diffused into the atmosphere around her. She would prepare a bottle of the water for Alice she thought and maybe one for herself. Elderflower soothed the head and dispelled gloom and melancholy, and above all softened the skin. Some of the older widows in the convent requested it for their skin, when Sister Beatrice was out of earshot, but now she would have to be extra careful and economical. She would see Alice in the chapter house that evening. It was days since she had managed to have more than a scant conversation with her, but she noticed that she was still enveloped in an air of despondency, aloof, fading as a flower whose full beauty was passing.

The door to the still room creaked as it opened slowly. Wencilian jumped and nearly dropped the bottle she was holding.

"Ah, up to no good whilst Sister B is away!"

"Brother John, don't creep up on me like that or I will be lying in one of those beds in there."

"Sorry, Wencilian, I didn't want to shout and wake the sick."

"How did you know she wasn't here?"

"I saw her going towards the Prioress's office. I was taking coins there from Father Roger, but that can wait for a few minutes while they are busy."

"It's so good to see you. How are you and how is your work?"

"It's been a busy day; poor pilgrims passing, asking for food and water, and coins of course. We are preparing the guest house for the King's men and on top of that, three travelling friars have turned up requesting bed and board. One has a very strange accent and carries a musical instrument, so we may have some singing in there."

"You're lucky, I would love to hear some music and do some singing."

"I'm so sorry it is forbidden to you. It surely does uplift the soul. Why it is not allowed for the nuns I really don't know. I'm sure you must all have voices like the sweet nightingale."

"Alleluia! You are a man after my own heart, who agrees with me."

"Bless you, Wencilian. I must go, but I will be back when I can. Have you seen Boden?"

"He comes to my window sometimes. His wings are so silent that I often don't hear him approaching. Whenever I see him, he fixes me with his piercing eyes and lingers for a while as if checking that I am alright. Recently though I have slept in the infirmary, so he may be missing me. I am missing him."

"You are doing your job too well, Wencilian. Either that or

the pleasant weather is keeping everyone healthy."

"I think I am just doing my job exceedingly well, Brother." Wencilian replied laughing.

"God bless you, my dearest Wencilian. I shall speak to you soon."

Cai put his sack and crwth on the pallet he had been allocated. He understood that some of the King's men were visiting so all the available space in the guest house would be taken. He had been put, with two other travelling friars, in a small damp room in a dilapidated building next to the guest house. "It is just a temporary measure," the pleasant Brother who called himself John had told him. But he would have suffered a pig sty if he had to. He was in; he was here after years and miles of separation. Only walls now lay between him and his beloved Gwenllian. He prayed that Father Iorwerth and Hywel had not been misled and that his Princess was really here. But he would have to be discreet and lie low for a while, especially if the King's men were snooping around. The Brothers of the Priory would not expect him to stay long though, not more than a few days, so he would have to move fairly quickly or feign illness as had been his plan. He would need to appear ill enough to be put in the infirmary, but well enough to take a few sojourns into the fresh air.

Brother John appeared, to invite him and the other two friars into the refectory for the main meal of the day and to show them the church and where they may stand for the service of Sext. As they walked along the cloister, Cai seized a chance to ask a few questions.

"How many Brothers do you have here, Brother John?"

"At the last count there were forty canons."

"And nuns?"

"They outnumber us, there are around two hundred I think, but we rarely see them."

"A lot of nuns," Cai commented. His heart sank wondering how he would find Gwenllian in a community of two hundred women, all locked away from the sight of men.

"Where are you from?" asked Brother John. "I can't place your accent."

Cai was prepared for this question and had decided that he would have to be at least partially honest. If anyone recognised his accent as being from Wales and he had told them otherwise it would arouse suspicion. "I was based at Llanfaes, the Franciscan house on the island you may know as Anglesey, and then I spent some time at Cwmhir Abbey, the Cistercian house in Powys. I had long heard and read about St Gilbert. Gilbert's Rule, as you are no doubt aware was a revision of the Rule of St Benedict, which also very much resembles the Cistercian Rule. I heard that Gilbert himself took advice from their great leader, Bernard de Clairvaux. I wanted also to visit the shrine of such a great man who promoted the education of women in Norman Britain where women are often viewed as unimportant and incompetent."

Brother John eyed Cai warily, although he felt sympathetic towards him. He was certainly not used to such comments from a friar. "I tend to agree with you; although Gilbert lived over a century ago, his ideas were quite revolutionary. He also accepted the poor and the rejected – serfs and fugitives alike. Mind you, of the few nuns I have contact with, I can certainly vouch that none of them are feeble or incompetent."

All the women that Cai had known in his life had certainly never been either, far from it, he thought to himself and smiled as they entered the refectory.

During the meal as the Lectrix read a passage to the silent canons, Cai thought about what he had said to Brother John and hoped that his comments on women's education would not be misconstrued in any way. He always felt lighter when he spoke from his heart and felt uncomfortable with concealing his true views. His training as a bard had taught him to be audacious in that way, but also he knew to achieve what he intended, he had to be not only careful but devious at times. He had told a half truth. He knew of St Gilbert and admired his belief in the intelligence of women, even though he shut them away from the world, supposedly 'for their own protection'. What a lot they

194

could offer the world though, Cai felt, like the Priestesses of old did. His thoughts turned to Seren. He had not tried to contact her on the inner planes for a while. Perhaps he should try, he had no idea what to do next and needed her help.

Cai barely recalled the service of Sext. The droning of the priest, the chanting of the canons and the strong incense which swirled around the church pervaded his senses and sent him into a state of trance. He saw Seren cradling what appeared to be an infant. Her face turned towards him and smiled, but there was sadness, great sadness in her eyes. He wanted to ask her what he should do, but he could not burden her; she had her own troubles. But he did not need to ask, a voice spoke clearly in his head. 'Do what you do best, Cai, and you will succeed.' Then the vision faded and he realised the canons were filing out of the church.

The hour following Sext was an hour of rest before the canons resumed their duties. The two travelling friars had gone to lie down. Cai walked around the Priory whilst all was quiet. He pondered on his experience during the mass. What did he do best? he asked himself. Maybe Seren had meant that he must be strong. She had always told him that his inner strength was one of his best qualities, but that was really not very helpful at the moment. He needed to plan and take some sort of action. It worried him that Seren had such sadness in her eyes. What had happened to her and if it was a baby she was cradling, whose baby was it? Surely she was past child bearing and if not, he would have known of it before he left.

As he wandered around the collection of priory buildings, keeping silent, he could barely believe that he walked in the very building where Gwenllian had spent her days as a child and now, as a young woman, carried out her duties as a Sister of this Gilbertine order. A huge yearning came over him. It was yearning to be home in the mountains with his kin, but also a yearning to see Gwenllian, to hear Gwenllian and tell her of her true heritage, her true family, for she was also his kin. For the moment though he would have to adapt to life in this Gilbertine priory and tread carefully until he could plan her escape.

CHAPTER 26

Sempringham Priory

The following morning, after the service of Prime, Cai took the opportunity to explore the priory grounds more extensively. It was already very warm outside and the day had barely begun. Behind the guest house he stretched his body to salute the morning sun. The dampness of the hut where he slept was seeping into his bones causing his back to ache. The Brothers were mostly assembled in the chapter house where the Rule would be read and the business of the day discussed. Cai was glad he was excused from this. It was tedious enough, he thought, to be obliged to attend the eight services of the day without having to attend other meetings. He knew though that he would be expected to work for his keep and would soon be allotted some duties to perform.

Passing the bake house, Cai inhaled the comforting smell of newly baked bread. He had not found anything else very comforting about this place so far, except perhaps for the friendliness of Brother John. Suddenly he missed the warmth and humour of the Brothers at Penmon. This priory was not a place where he could feel at home, as organised and very efficient as it appeared to be.

He nodded to several lay brothers who were working as stonemasons and carpenters. He had decided to keep his distance from most of them to avoid any gossip or suspicions, but he desperately did need to find out information about Gwenllian, and with the nuns rarely seen, this was not going to be easy.

Before he had any further thoughts, he heard a lot of noise across the courtyard. An elderly monk was opening the south gate of the Priory, with difficulty; men were shouting on the other side and horses scraping their hooves on the dusty gravel path outside. Cai rushed to help the monk pull the heavy gate and was then joined by several lay brothers. As the gate was pulled open, men on horseback carrying the King's standard thrust through. The elderly monk fell to the ground. Cai helped him rise up with a speck of dignity, while his own anger rose up through his body. The arrogance and carelessness of these men would always enrage him.

As the men steered the horses into the centre of the courtyard, one of them spoke. "Forgive me, Father," he said, addressing the elderly monk. "My men can be too enthusiastic sometimes. I hope you are not injured."

Cai looked up, stunned. It was Philip's face he was staring into and next to him was a red haired man he recognised from the forest meeting, but could not place by name.

Philip's stony face did not show a glimmer of recognition. "I am escorting one of the King's chancellors. Can you direct me to the Prior?" he continued whilst dismounting.

Cai counted seven men in the party. Several more lay brothers appeared and started to lead the horses towards the stables.

"Make sure they are well cared for," Philip shouted at them.

The elderly monk, rubbing his back, signalled Philip to follow him. Cai would have offered, but he didn't yet know where the Prior's office was, so he crept along discreetly behind the men as they filed along the cloisters. He just hoped Philip had arranged to be here for the best of reasons. Then it came to him, the name of the red haired man, Simon of Halston.

"Please wait here." The elderly monk beckoned the men to sit on the benches outside the Prior's office. "Prior Roger will return soon from the chapter house meeting."

"The chancellor and his assistant can wait," Philip said impatiently. "You can show the rest of us to the guest house and perhaps some refreshments can be provided. One of my men here has cut his leg. He will need to visit the infirmary."

"Let me help you, Brother," Cai interjected, scowling at Philip for his brusque attitude. "I will go to the kitchens, whilst you go to the guesthouse."

"The infirmary is just behind the kitchen building," the elderly monk explained. "You could take the injured man with you at the same time, then direct him to the guesthouse if you please, Brother …, sorry I don't know your name."

"Brother Gregory, at your service."

"Thank you, Brother Gregory. I am Brother Michael. I think I might need the infirmary myself later," the elderly monk replied, still rubbing the sore spot on his back.

"Well you should. These King's men have no care," Cai whispered.

Brother Michael hobbled off with the soldiers following. As Cai turned to lead the red haired man towards the infirmary, Philip caught his eye and nodded, his lips curling into a slight smile. What did Philip's presence here mean? Cai wondered. Was it chance or was it a deliberate manoeuvre on his part to help?

As he walked, Simon of Halston placed his hand on his shoulder. "It was good chance that brought us on this mission. Philip will seek you out later. Are you staying in the guesthouse?"

"Well, not in the more comfortable lodgings that you have, but just behind in the dilapidated shed of a building. How long will you be here?"

"Until the chancellor has concluded his business. That could be up to a week."

"I think this is the infirmary," Cai murmured as they approached a heavy oak door with a grille at eye level. Before he could raise his hand to knock, Simon's fist banged heavily on the door. "Open up. We can't wait all day."

"There are sick people in there. We should have some respect."

Cai thought Simon of Halston arrogant and too impulsive, but Hywel had accepted him at the forest meeting. There must have been a reason for it, Cai assumed … he would have to trust him.

The door was opened by a tall thin Brother with sharp green eyes. "What on earth is the commotion? Is somebody seriously hurt?"

This is a fine introduction, thought Cai. He wanted to make a good impression in this priory or it could ruin his chances of getting close to Gwenllian. This man Simon was an oaf, one to tread carefully with.

"I beg your forgiveness, Brother. I am Brother Gregory and this is one of the King's men. His injury is making him a little hot tempered. He has come here to escort the King's chancellor."

"I can see by his livery he is from the King. Who you are I don't know, but you had better come in. Let's take a look at the injury."

"A raggle taggle group of vagabonds tried to attack us as we rode here through a forest path," Simon explained. "We saw them off quickly, but some fool shot an arrow at my leg. It wasn't deep. We pulled it out and stemmed the bleeding, but now pus oozes out of it. I wouldn't have bothered much with it, but now we are here my captain insists I have it seen to."

The tall thin Brother and Cai peered at the wound.

"That's as well," said Cai without thinking, "for it looks as if the blood could be poisoned. But I think we have caught it in time."

The tall monk eyed him with suspicion. "And where do you get that knowledge from, Brother?"

Cai thought quickly. "I helped in the infirmary at Cwmhir Abbey, a Cistercian house in Powys."

"Do the Cistercians have superior knowledge?" the Brother asked with a sarcastic tone.

Ignoring his remark, Cai tried to appease him. "What would you suggest, Brother? The apothecary at Cwmhir would use a mixture of salt and poppy seed poultice."

"We have a similar mixture we use here. I shall fetch some."

"Whatever, but hurry up, my stomach rumbles more than my

199

leg hurts," Simon moaned.

"Be patient," Cai snapped, beginning to lose his usual calm. "The monks are here to help you. I don't have to do this. I am here for one reason and one reason only. Remember the forest house and what we are all trying to achieve."

"Of course," Simon relented a little, "but on this occasion I am here to escort the Chancellor and have had a tedious journey. Philip chose me to accompany him. It was not my choice. I would rather be fighting with the King."

"Tell me, where is the King at this time?" Cai whispered.

"He is ..." Simon started, but stopped abruptly when the tall thin monk came back with the dressings and poultice.

"This should help. In this hot weather the sore has festered. I should bathe it first," the tall monk explained.

"Are you the Infirmarian?" Cai asked.

"I am indeed. Brother Gilbert is my name."

"Do you work here alone?"

"Brother Dominique usually attends me, but he has just left us for a while to study in Cambridge. Father Roger has not yet arranged a replacement."

While Brother Gilbert continued tending the wound, Cai glanced around the infirmary. His thoughts raced ahead of him as his eyes took in the scene around him. The long dark room had three patients, two sleeping and one sitting up drinking from a goblet. At the end of the room was a door with a heavy key in the lock and bolts on top and bottom. Cai jumped when as he was staring at it, someone knocked from the other side.

"Excuse me, if you will," Brother Gilbert said, surprisingly politely as he walked towards the door.

Cai watched him carefully. He was eager to know every passage, door and corner of this priory if he had the chance. Any bit of knowledge could lead him to Gwenllian. Brother Gilbert was talking in hushed tones and it was a female voice which answered him, but not clear enough for Cai to hear the conversation. After a few minutes, Brother Gilbert locked the heavy door and returned to his patient.

"Are you staying here long, Brother Gregory?"

"I'm unsure at the moment." Cai thought quickly. "Do you need help here? I have some knowledge of healing. I could perhaps be of use to you while I am here."

"If you are willing, Brother, it may help. You seem to have some knowledge of healing the sick, more than most of the Brothers here."

"I'd be pleased to. I suppose we must defer to Father Roger first."

"Leave that to me. I don't think we'll have a problem. Now you can take this cantankerous soldier to the kitchens and get him fed."

Cai felt a wave of gratitude sweep over him. He was not sure what to make of Brother Gilbert but so far things were going his way. Maybe some of Seren's magic was working. He would be pleased to help and impart some of the healing knowledge he learnt with his kin in Eryri, but more than that it could help him get closer to Gwenllian. Whatever lay behind that heavy oak door at the end of the infirmary was a link to the nuns, the mysterious women kept hidden from view, hidden from life.

CHAPTER 27

Sempringham Priory

There were few truly silent moments in Sempringham Priory. The time between Compline and Matins was the only interval when weary nuns and monks could catch five to six hours of precious deeper sleep. Even then, some who could not sleep might wander the cloisters or some may keep an all-night vigil in the church. And, of course, Mother Elizabeth may be straining over her papers in dim candlelight. Father Roger too, often worked during these hours when he would have no interruptions.

It had been a taxing day in more than one sense of the word. The King was demanding money and Father Roger had been forced to show the Chancellor all his accounts. The accounts showed a good profit from wool sales, but trying to convince the chancellor that they needed this profit for building work, feeding guests, alms for the poor and a hundred other things was proving fruitless.

"This priory is a centre of spiritual and social activity. We have to be prepared for all eventualities, including a bad year," Father Roger had argued.

The Chancellor had grunted and said he was retiring and would see him promptly after Prime in the morning. At least he had the decency to wait until after the service, Father Roger thought. Restless and annoyed, he decided to take some night air and then see if Mother Elizabeth was working in her study. They needed to confer and stick together in the face of this intimidation from the King, even though, more often than not, they disagreed on matters.

The Prioress Elizabeth was still awake knowing that the chancellor had requested a meeting with her the next day after the noon service of Sext. Sister Marie Claire and Sister Agnes had just retired. All their accounts should be in order now she felt, as she poured herself a well-deserved mug of ale. Now she needed to think. Sister Wencilian was very much on her mind and she had got no further with her investigations, especially with all the accounts to occupy her. She needed somehow to get hold of some of the Chancellor's private documents, but how to do that was not clear to her, yet.

Father Roger made his way past the novice monks' dormitory and the cells of the older monks. All was quiet except for the snores coming from Brother John's cell. The Sacrist's door was open, maybe he was checking all was well, he thought. His sandals trod carefully along the eastern cloister until he reached the open courtyard. Dusk was fading into night. The light of the rising waxing moon guided his steps towards the nuns' buildings. No other man but himself would ever be admitted at this time of night and certainly no one but himself had any keys to the sanctuary of the Holy Sisters.

Elizabeth was startled by the knock on her door. She opened it cagily, assuming it to be Sister Agnes coming back for her cloak which she had left hanging on a chair. Picking it up, she thrust it through the partially opened door. She didn't want any more disturbance tonight. She wanted to be alone with her thoughts. When a male voice cried, "What on earth!" Elizabeth jumped back and screamed.

"It's just me, Father Roger. I'm sorry to startle you, Prioress."

"By all the saints! What is wrong to bring you here at this time?"

"Would you allow me in to talk? It's imperative to discuss some matters before we see the Chancellor in the morning. I had a feeling you might still be up working."

"I had just finished," Elizabeth emphasised sternly. "But I suppose you'd better come in, although it is really not appropriate. I'll pour you a mug."

Father Roger had never seen the Prioress without her headdress. He had never realised that her hair, although cropped, was a lustrous copper colour. Her face in the candlelight looked soft and young, like a novice nun or a young bride. He had always thought her looks to be a bit harsh, worn with cares of running the house of nuns. She looked so much younger tonight, but then he guessed she must be about thirty five years old, not yet quite passed her prime.

"What is it that is of such great concern, Father?"

"Well I think you can guess … the Chancellor. He wants more money for the King, more than we can afford. He doesn't realise all the hidden costs we have."

"You're right, but I don't think we have much choice, do we?"

"They give on the one hand and take it away with the other. I think we could be more economical with the truth." Father Roger cleared his throat and waited for a response. He was treading carefully. "It was unfair of the Pope to issue such a vague papal bull allowing the King to tax the clergy in case of emergency. What defines an emergency? More of his wars, which seem never to cease?"

"You are right, Father, but are you suggesting that we should be dishonest? It's a bit late for that; all my accounts are finished and ready – there is no time now to alter them."

Anyway, Mother Elizabeth thought, I have already taken care to make sure my accounts don't include all my incomings. But this was information she would not share. Father Roger should see to his own accounts. She wondered whether it would be a good time to mention Sister Wencilian, but then decided against it. She was not ready to ask him yet, if at all.

"In that case I suppose you have a point, but I think from now until the Chancellor's next visit we should be altering the accounts a little. We cannot afford to lose money like this. Pope Boniface has left us vulnerable. The last papal bull was too ambiguous; agreeing to the taxation of the clergy in cases of emergency lets the King basically do want he wants. The King with all his wars is always in a state of emergency. And it's been such a good year for wool. As soon as we get our head well above water it seems we are being pushed down under to drown again."

"Exactly. When this Henry Coverton, accountant, has gone, Father, I suggest we put our heads together and make a plan for the next year," Elizabeth replied, hoping that would keep him happy for now, she really didn't want to deal with this now. She would be polite and then say she was retiring. "How are things on your side, Father?"

"Not good. Several of the canons have left us to study at Cambridge. We now have only thirty five, and half of those are inexperienced novices and need training. Some of the lay brothers have sustained injuries with all the hard work they have to do and we have only Brother Gilbert to run the infirmary. He came to me today to ask if a passing friar, Brother Gregory could help him as he seems to have a good knowledge of healing, although he is not trained in medicine. I will see him tomorrow. In the meantime, would you agree to Sister Beatrice and Sister Wencilian preparing some of the necessary medicines for Brother Gilbert to alleviate some of his tasks?"

"I'll check with them in the morning. We do have two hundred nuns in our care you know. They are kept very busy. If you don't mind, Father, I need to catch a little sleep before Matins."

"Of course, forgive me for intruding at this time. We'll talk again soon."

The Prioress curled up on her makeshift pallet in the corner of her room and pulled a sheepskin over her. It was warmer here and there was barely time to return to her sleeping cell and settle before the bell would ring for the service of Matins. She had rarely been to her cell in recent months; it would be bleak and cold, even on these summer nights the damp from the fens seeped through the thick stone walls which surrounded her. Her last thoughts before she drifted into a fitful sleep were of Sister Wencilian. She had intended to remove her from the infirmary to help her with administration, once the Chancellor had gone, so she could keep her close by her. Leoba was to be her replacement, but now it seemed as if she may need both of them still in the infirmary, for the moment at least.

Father Roger retraced his steps across the courtyard. He was too agitated to sleep. He looked up at the night sky; the moon had risen, casting its strange otherworldly glow over the contours of the turrets and arches of the Priory. He had rarely been alone at this time, in this place. The immense beauty of the stars sent a shiver through his body; for a few minutes he felt rooted to the spot where he stood. It was a moment, but it was a glimpse of eternity, until the silence was pierced by the shriek of a barn owl close by.

He wrapped his cloak tightly around him for comfort more than warmth; the night was not cold. As he returned to his duties he felt vulnerable and alone. For a few brief moments standing under the stars he had felt free, in awe of the natural world, like a young boy before the weight of the world hung on his shoulders. Entering the cloister leading to his rooms he thought he heard footsteps behind him and turned to see two shadowy figures disappearing along the path which led to the guest house.

CHAPTER 28

Sempringham Priory

Cai waited patiently behind the guest house outbuilding where he was lodging, not too comfortably. Philip was taking his time. The waxing moon was rising but there was barely a glimmer of light where he stood. Would Philip see him? When he heard footsteps he would peer out carefully, he thought. He had poked his head around the building a few minutes before and seen a cloaked figure heading towards the nuns' buildings. Could a nun be out at this time, he wondered. They were rarely, if ever, let out at all. Judging by the size and stature of the figure he had concluded that it must be male. He thought it mildly amusing that maybe one of the Brothers or Sisters was conducting a clandestine affair and then a stab of regret hit him. He thought of Celeste again and prayed that she was alive and safe. When this mission was over, he would dedicate himself to seeking her out.

The slap on the shoulder jerked him out of his thoughts. "Good God, man, don't sneak up on me like that."

"It's a soldier's trick to take you unawares. Aren't we meant to be invisible, at the least very discreet?" Philip whispered.

"It's safer, don't you think? If we are seen talking together it may arouse suspicion. Someone might wonder why a travelling friar is meeting with one of the King's men. And there are few private places in here."

"Agreed, but if we are seen talking in the dark furtively it could look more suspicious," Philip replied, keeping his voice still very low.

"We can't risk talking in my lodgings. The two other friars could overhear, even above their snoring, which, if any louder could bring down that old barn of a dormitory. How did you come to be here anyway, Philip?"

"Hywel got word to me that you had arrived here. Fortune was on my side. I was serving at Harby and was summoned to accompany the Chancellor on a tour of the priories to conduct his business and collect his taxes. Cai, I have discovered that the cousins of Gwenllian are in the nunnery at Sixhills, not far from here."

On hearing this, Cai almost sunk to his knees. He clung on to Philip's arm, his heart pounding, his breath rasping. "Oh, God and Goddess be praised. I thought they were dead. Llywelyn's brother and dear wife, Elizabeth, if she still lives, would be greatly relieved to know that. But we have not really given them much thought have we? We were only thinking of Gwenllian. Those girls were older. Surely they would have some memories of their life before they were captured. What of the young Llywelyn and Owain? Is it true they are still in the castle at Bristol?"

"I believe so, but cannot be sure. Pray they are still alive. But we must focus on Gwenllian, at least for now. Her freedom is paramount – she is heir to the Principality. Let's hope she has the fighting spirit of her namesake."

She was to be heir to a lot more than that, Cai knew, but now was not the time to talk about that and if Philip didn't know already then it was best he didn't know at all.

"Give me news of Catrin, Cai. She must be near her time now."

"Catrin was well when I left her. She's a strong woman, Philip. The women will care for her."

"I must try to get home soon. I may have a son or daughter already."

"I'm sure they will get word to you, Philip, when it's time. But tell me, what is your plan, now that you are here?"

"While I'm here I'll assist you however I can, but we cannot be seen to confer together."

"Brother Gilbert from the infirmary has requested me to help him. I was there earlier and discovered that there is a door which may lead to the convent adjoined to it. That could be very useful, but I need a bit of time yet. We now know that the King pays the Prioress here a sum for the keep of Gwenllian – well of Sister Wencilian, as she is known here. Whether the Prioress knows of her true origins is doubtful, but we can't be sure of that. We need somehow to see the Chancellor's records, see what is listed. I don't think I am in a good position to do this, but you could be."

"I'll try, and as a King's man I should be able to gain access to the nuns' quarters with the Chancellor. He is due to meet with the Prioresses in the morning after Prime. You have arrived at the right time, Cai. I may only be here for a few days, but I will do what I can. We'll meet again tomorrow night at this time, here."

Philip returned to the guesthouse to find Simon still awake and the other men asleep. They call it a guesthouse, he thought, but it's more suited to lowly servants than King's men. For such a rich priory they don't invest much in their visitors.

"A fire would be good," he grumbled to Simon as he climbed carefully into his bed, checking for anything crawling.

"Are you getting soft? What were you doing out there for so long? You won't get any joy out of those black-robed virgins, even if you could penetrate the defences."

Philip gave a wry smile. "I was thinking, walking for a bit. I reckon sitting around too long in this place is making me restless. How is the leg?"

"Painful. Did you see Cai?"

"No, I may catch him tomorrow." Philip preferred not to disclose too much to Simon at the moment. He was not sure how much he trusted him and he was known to be hot headed and arrogant at times. He drifted off to sleep thinking of Catrin, hoping that the birth, if it hadn't already happened, would be as good as it could be and safe. He couldn't bear to lose her now, or his child. He knew that her pregnancy had somewhat thwarted the original plan of her joining the novices, but he was pleased, so pleased, to be on the brink of fatherhood.

Cai lay awake, unable to sleep at all. Not only was the snoring of the friars disturbing, but his thoughts about Gwenllian and now her cousin, Gwladys, churned over in his mind. How close to each other the girl cousins had been all these years and so completely unaware of the fact. How they could have given each other comfort and friendship if they had been given the chance.

Gwladys must now be just a little older than Gwenllian, he surmised. Would she remember her father, Llywelyn's brother, Dafydd, and her mother and brothers? Would that be crueller than the fate of Gwenllian, who would in all probability remember nothing at all?

He was overwhelmed with sadness and anger. Where were the true people of Wales? They had all been uprooted, many not only from their home and lands, but from their culture, laws, families, history. But most of all they had been torn from the heart. He tried to sleep, but it seemed he had barely closed his eyes before the bell tolled and the two friars rose for service. He followed, not wanting to draw any attention to himself. They filed through the darkness into the cold church, where they stood in silence until the patter of the nuns' feet on the other side of the wall ceased. Then the service began.

CHAPTER 29

Sempringham Priory

Cai made his way to the infirmary after the noon service of Sext. He had almost lost track of the days since he had arrived at Sempringham. The constant round of services, muddying the division between night and day, had disorientated his thoughts and definitely confused his physical time clock. He couldn't remember such a strict regime at Penmon Priory; the monks there seemed to be a lot more flexible and of course Father Iorwerth had been a lot more lenient with him, being aware of his true circumstances. Here he was obliged to attend every service without fail, and so he did, not to draw attention to himself. When Father Roger had called him earlier at Brother Gilbert's request to ask him to help in the infirmary he was delighted, hoping it may exempt him from some of the worship but above all hoping that it may lead him nearer to Gwenllian.

Brother Gilbert accepted him reluctantly though. He needed help, but he certainly gave the impression he didn't want anyone, especially some strange travelling friar, interfering in his administration of the infirmary. Cai really didn't care. He was occupied, keeping busy, and maybe he would gain more knowledge of, or access to, Gwenllian. He was more than satisfied for the moment.

Brother Gilbert set him the task of cleaning the still room and sewing strips of linen and lining them with moss for bandages. The room was at the far end of the infirmary close to the heavy oak door which he had previously seen opened. There were only four patients at the moment, all of whom appeared to be asleep, so when he had a chance he caught Brother Gilbert and asked him, "Where does that door lead to? If someone knocks should I answer it?

"It leads to the nuns' infirmary. Sometimes we have to ask them for help or medicines, and vice versa. No doubt that now they have been asked to help prepare some of our medicines … they may knock. Sister Beatrice, myself and Father Roger are the only ones to have a key, but Sister Wencilian who helps Sister Beatrice may knock on the door."

On hearing the name 'Sister Wencilian,' Cai pricked his hand with the needle he was holding and felt his knees nearly give way.

"Are you quite alright, Brother Gregory? You suddenly look very pale."

"Yes, yes, sorry. I'm not really very experienced in sewing. I lost my attention for a minute."

Cai couldn't believe that she was only a door away. A heavy oak door, which led the way into the mysteries of the hidden women, was the only barrier to Gwenllian, the only physical barrier, Cai thought, but there was a lot more to overcome. Even if she were to knock on that door and he was to open it, how could he even begin to talk to her and how could he ever gain access into that most secret and guarded part of the Priory, obtain even a glimpse of the lives of the hidden Sisters. He sharply told himself to pull himself together. It was a stroke of luck, much more than he had bargained for, to find Gwenllian so close, if it was her of course, but with a name such as Wencilian so closely matching her own, he was nearly certain that it had to be.

He would know when he saw her if she was Gwenllian. He had never doubted that fact all these months since he had heard she was alive and safe. He would, he felt strongly, surely recognise Llywelyn or Eleanor in her features, in spite of not seeing her hair, with the enveloping headdresses the nuns wore. He would know her.

Philip escorted the Chancellor to the Prioress Elizabeth with Father Roger. Respectfully keeping his head bowed as he trod quietly along the nuns' cloister, he furtively tried to glimpse the faces of the few passing Sisters. He couldn't miss any chance of seeing Gwenllian although he thought it nigh on impossible that he could identify her even if he had the whole convent lined up closely in front of him. Unlike Cai, he had only seen her once as a babe, just a few days old. And who could tell one nun from another in their black robes. He doubted he would even recognise his own sisters were they here. That thought made him shudder. He would never send his sisters to such a place even if they never made a good match in marriage. When he returned home, that would be something he would have to think about, finding husbands for them. He would soon have his own child to worry about, if it wasn't already born, and many more to come he hoped.

Father Roger was ready to stay with the Prioress Elizabeth, but she made it quite clear that she would rather speak to the Chancellor alone. He had learnt over the years that she was not one to argue with. Philip had hoped that he would have been asked to remain outside the office. That way he may have had more opportunity to catch a glimpse of passing nuns, but for him it was back to the monks' quarters.

Elizabeth served the Chancellor a goblet of her strongest wine, reserved only for special visitors. He however, was sipping it very slowly, wary of any attempts to distract him from the serious business of the accounts. This is going to be a difficult one, Elizabeth thought, tapping her fingers on the table in anticipation, please God, pray all goes to plan.

It was half an hour later with the Chancellor in deep concentration, when a huge clatter and bang arrived just outside the door, followed by screaming. Elizabeth rushed to open the door to find Sister Ignatius and Sister Agnes sprawled across the stone floor amongst an array of broken dishes and spilled food. "Oh, heavens above, can you help me, sir," she called to the Chancellor.

"What on earth is it, Madam?" he asked, with obvious

annoyance.

"My ankle," cried Sister Agnes, in between gasps of breath. "I think it may be broken."

"She slipped and just crashed straight into me," Sister Ignatius said, looking for once genuinely upset. "I'm sorry, Mother."

"Never mind, Sister Agnes needs to go to the infirmary. Sir, could you carry her? Sister Ignatius, you go with him. I'll call for help to clean all this up."

"This is really irregular, Prioress," the Chancellor stuttered, but found himself picking up Sister Agnes and following Sister Ignatius to the infirmary. It all happened so quickly that only when he reached the door to the infirmary did he realise that he had left important documents exposed. He doubted it would do much harm though. The Prioress would be occupied with clearing up the mess, but a quiver of suspicion passed through him. Eager to return, he deposited the Sister on the nearest bed and left her with the younger nun, then retraced his steps.

He must have taken a wrong turn somewhere he thought; this part of the convent was not familiar at all. He was beginning to feel uncomfortable, a man alone in this house of Holy women. Henry Coverton, one of the King's respected accountants, was a precise man, a man who excelled in his work, but he did not like to feel out of his depth. "Damn women," he muttered, fiddling with his beard. "I never wanted to come here and I will be very glad when I can get out of here."

"Can I help you, sir? Are you lost?" Sister Alice asked tentatively, seeing an elderly man muttering to himself as she turned the corner leading to the chapter house.

"Well yes, Sister, thank you I am, but no doubt you could point me in the right direction for the Prioress's office. I am the King's accountant. I had to make a dash to the infirmary and am having a problem re-tracing my steps."

"Follow me and I will show you." Alice hoped she would not get in any trouble, and more than that, that he was no infiltrator or murderer. She certainly wasn't used to bumping into men in the convent but any distraction from the routine was welcome, even if only for a few minutes.

The scene outside the Prioress's office was calm and orderly. Mother Elizabeth smiled as Henry Coverton walked in. "You were a long time. How is Sister Agnes?"

"I don't know. I just left her with the nuns in the infirmary and came straight back. Well I did get a little lost," he added clearing his throat, realising that he would possibly have to account for the time it took him to return. "A young Sister guided me here. I'm glad all the mess has been cleared. We had better resume our business."

"Yes of course." Elizabeth was eager to finish what they had started. She had seen what she needed to see and everything had gone according to plan, apart from Sister Agnes falling – it should have been just Sister Ignatius; she hadn't intended for an elderly nun to risk injury. There would be time for questions later, but for now she was satisfied. A warm glow of contentment spread through her.

CHAPTER 30

Sempringham Priory

There had barely been time to catch a bit of sleep before Matins. Cai was kept busy with a monk who had been admitted with severe stomach pain. Brother Gilbert had woken him in his small room adjacent to the still room. He was far more comfortable in his new surroundings and had made himself a homely corner with a bed and chair and small table for writing. It was however more difficult for him to slip away from the watchful eyes of Brother Gilbert. He had been helping in the infirmary for over one week now and had only seen Philip once since his initial moonlit meeting. He thought it must be time for Philip to leave, if he hadn't done already, although he was sure Philip would find a way of letting him know.

Matins and Prime had come and gone when Cai and Brother Gilbert had settled the new patient and the others who had been woken up by the noise of his night time arrival.

"Perhaps we should have a rest before Terce, Brother Gregory."

"I don't know if I can settle now. I may take a breath of air, Brother Gilbert."

"As you wish. I shall rest for a bit, if there is no more disturbance."

Cai longed for some air. At the rear of the infirmary was a small yard with a high wall on one side and a fence on the other. He took his crwth and sat against the high wall. The day was breaking. Cloudy skies were softening into interwoven layers of

216

pink and blue as the light increased. It was warm already; it promised to be a hot day. Cai loved this time, untainted by human presence; it appeared magical and mystical. It was always a time of promise and anticipation, nature awakening. He knew that Seren would say it was indeed a time when magic happened.

Without thinking, he found himself singing the lullaby that he would sometimes sing to Gwenllian when she lay in her crib at Abergwyngregyn. He didn't hear the owl approach, but just caught the movement of its large wing span in the corner of his eye. Coming home from a night's hunt, he thought. He had noticed the barn owls roosting in the turrets, roofs and barns of the Priory. They hunted with an eerie silence, but could let out an even more eerie shriek when they wanted too. This particular one perched on the high wall behind him and Cai saw something glittering on his ankle. He turned to see it was a ring of some kind. Maybe the bird had been tamed and was attracted by his singing. He felt a shiver along his spine as if some memory from long ago stirred but would not become clear. He heard Seren's voice in his head urging him to sing on, sing, sing, sing. Yes maybe that's what she meant when she said to do what he was good at – sing.

Wencilian had seen Boden sweep down onto the high wall at the back of the infirmary. She had flung open the door when Sister Beatrice went to the service of Prime. The night had been hot – she was restless. Several of the patients were not settling and when she did lie down on one of the empty pallets, the strange dream had come to her. Except she had not been asleep, so she thought, only very tired, but the images seared across the dark screen in front of her eyes – men on horseback, trees, the bright moon and the sounds of thuds and shouting, and the shriek, shriek of the owl. It haunted her not just in her dreams, but in the night even when she was awake. But there was another sound, of music, someone singing that was not there before. 'Where am I? Where am I?' she silently cried.

She sat up with a jolt. She must have been asleep for a few moments. But no, wait, she could still hear the music now.

Drawn by the sweet notes she walked outside to see Boden perched on the wall looking down the other side. Waves of sound reached her ears of a type she had never heard before. A male voice singing in a language she did not know, yet something about the song and the voice seemed strangely familiar.

She had no idea how long she had been standing there, when the voice of Sister Beatrice broke the spell.

"What on earth are you doing, Sister Wencilian, standing as if entranced?"

Wencilian turned, startled. "Mmm, I was just taking some air and thought I heard a strange noise."

"I hear nothing. Come in. We have work to do."

Maybe I was dreaming, Wencilian thought. Maybe it was a type of sleepwalking or a trance like the one that I had in the church that night Mira left.

Cai heard the nuns' voices on the other side of the wall where he sat. He dropped his instrument and stood up, but the wall was too high. It had not been too clear, but he could swear that he had heard the name, 'Sister Wencilian'. Of course, he realised, the other side of the wall must be at the back of the nuns' infirmary. The Gods were on his side. Feeling a bit shaky, he sat back down with his back against the wall.

The music, he knew, had drawn her outside. What was so natural and habitual for him must have been very strange for Gwenllian to experience, he realised. She would not be familiar with men singing, only the monks in the church, and she would certainly never have heard the Welsh language since the fateful night she was captured as a babe. Nuns were not allowed to sing at Sempringham, that much he knew, but he had no idea why and was baffled by the rule. But now he knew that singing could be a key to opening a door that would enable him to make contact with Gwenllian and maybe a door to her heart and mind.

He would need to tread so carefully through that door. He wished Seren was here with him to advise him, she would know what to do. His voice had guided him towards Gwenllian and maybe that was what Seren was implying when she said, "Do what you do best."

Singing had always been his love, but he had not done a great deal of it since he left Abergwyngregyn, partly because of lack of opportunity, but mostly he knew because it stirred up too many painful memories, memories of Llywelyn, Celeste, Eleanor and a little baby he had loved more than life itself.

He was aware of the bell peeling for Terce. Thank you Seren, he mimed to the morning light which now had cleared the grey streaks of what he had thought was an impending storm. The day begins, Seren. I have found Gwenllian, I have found my voice and the rest of the mission begins. Give me strength to do what I have to do.

CHAPTER 31

Sempringham Priory

Wencilian woke with a jolt. She had felt her stomach tearing apart, but touching it with her hands, it suddenly felt calm. Another dream, she mused, I am having another strange dream. She put her hands to her face; it felt wet – she was sweating. Well, it had been a hot night and she had fallen asleep on the nearest pallet with her headdress still on.

She tried to recall her dream as she walked the cloister to the service of Terce. She had images of lying down on a bed, writhing in pain. She recalled a time when she had been eleven years old and one of the fen women when delivering fish to the convent collapsed in agony. The older nuns took her into the infirmary and she had followed them in, watching from behind a screen as the woman writhed and screamed for what seemed like hours. That was the only time she had seen a woman in childbirth. The pain she had felt in her dream had brought up that memory, one that had long been buried.

All through the service Wencilian thought of Mira. Maybe she had given birth, but it was too soon, much too soon. She felt so helpless trapped in here; she wanted to go to her, comfort her. Mira was like her little sister, although only a few years younger, but she couldn't be with her and would never be with her and possibly never know where she was. At least Mira was free, but she, she was caged like a songbird without a song.

The chanting of the monks drifted over the high wall which

divided the church and she was reminded of the song she had heard the night before when Boden had appeared. I must have imagined it, she told herself. I must have imagined or dreamt it, for no music like that has ever been heard here before. It would never be allowed.

She had loved the sound of that music. It was something so new, so refreshing, but more than that it stirred something deep within her, within her soul. It had started a thirst for more that needed to be replenished.

It was sometime later after the service of Terce that Prioress Elizabeth came into the infirmary. Leoba trailed behind her, head bowed, picking up her novice robe in both hands.

"I have brought Leoba to help you, Sister Wencilian. Where is Sister Beatrice?"

"I think she has gone to the kitchens to organise some broth for Sister Agnes. She has not done well since her fall and barely eaten. "

"Well, that's another reason I came, to see Sister Agnes. Leoba will come after Prime each day to help you here. She tells me she has some knowledge of healing and you could do with some extra hands, what with Brother Gilbert on his own next door too. Although I heard yesterday that a travelling friar is helping him for a while. Perhaps you could show Leoba what you do in here."

"Of course, Mother."

Wencilian was elated to have Leoba near her; she felt drawn to her and she would have a young woman to share things with, although at the same time she was slightly wary of her wistful otherworldliness. She had missed Alice recently. Their duties seemed to be keeping them more and more apart and when she did see her, Alice was sombre, morose. Wencilian knew she was suffering, but could not quite reach her.

Wencilian immediately whisked Leoba into the still room and hugged her close to her. Leoba, startled, blushed, but couldn't stop her face from creasing into a genuine smile.

"I am so pleased to have you in here, Leoba. I'm sure it was meant to be. God has designed it that way, for us to learn from each other and be true friends."

A tear dropped from Leoba's eye. "No one has ever wanted me as a true friend before. I was always shunned, except by a few, because of the way I look or because of my mother."

"But folk went to your mother for help, for advice, she was surely respected amongst your people."

"She was respected by some, but also feared for her powers, and I … I was only really protected when she was there."

"But why? Is that why she wanted you to come here? And as for the way you look, you are certainly beautiful."

"You are kind, but I am not really one of the fen folk. I don't really belong here either. I am content to be a novice, but I have no intention of taking my vows. Please keep this between us. I know I can trust you."

"You can trust me. Come, let me show you the lotions and potions we have and how we work here, before Sister Beatrice appears."

Wencilian wished to know more, much more.

The Prioress Elizabeth did not return to her office straight away as she had planned. Her overwhelming guilt at having inadvertently injured poor Sister Agnes led her to the church to seek confession. The church was quiet. Everyone was busy with their work until the next service of the day.

She knocked on the confession box, which was built on the side of the long wall dividing the church. No one answered, but she could hear a shuffling on the other side of the wall. Knocking loudly and calling, she eventually drew the attention of the Brother on the other side.

The monk slid back the wooden panel to reveal the small grille on the wall. He was startled to see the Prioress facing him.

"Can you please fetch someone to hear my confession, Brother …?"

"John, Brother John."

"Of course, forgive me, Brother John."

"There is no one here at the moment, Mother. I am

collecting the alms boxes and cleaning them. All the Brothers are busy. Do you want me to fetch Father Roger?"

"No, no. Is there anyone else?"

"I can fetch Father Francis. He is in the vestry."

"He'll do then. It can't wait."

Brother John was flustered. He wondered what was so urgent and had never seen the Prioress so agitated, but then he never saw her much at all.

"Very well, Mother, please take your seat while I ask him."

Father Francis was not pleased to be disturbed. When he had started on the accounts, he liked to immerse himself and not be interrupted. Nevertheless he considered it his duty. Had it not been the Prioress herself, he would have told the nun to come back later.

The Prioress took a deep breath and prepared herself for her confession, not knowing quite how to start. Panic had made her rush into this so she needed to calm herself down. She was a pragmatic woman, not normally so emotional.

"Forgive me, Father, for I have sinned. I, I created a situation in which a Sister was injured. My intention was to find out some information from the King's chancellor, so I diverted his attention away from his papers by planning a small accident, but no one was meant to be hurt. I am truly sorry for this and all of my sins."

"Oh," replied Father Francis, secretly both surprised and amused. "Well, Mother, we have to be vigilant about our finances. We do not know that we can trust our King Edward implicitly, so I don't think that is a great sin. But tell me who was injured, and what manner of injury it was?"

"It was Sister Agnes, and I think her ankle is broken. You see, it wasn't information about our finances that I wanted; it was information about a certain Sister, who I have been harbouring doubts about for a long time."

"Doubts! Doubts of which kind? Has the Sister in question been corrupt or immoral?"

"No, no, I am not sure that she is who we think she is, Father."

"An imposter?"

"I don't think so. I don't think she could possibly know who she is really, because she came here as a babe only. As far as I know, she has never had any visitors."

Brother John, who continuing with his tasks had moved away a little from the confession box, was still in earshot. He felt a thumping in his heart which he was sure must be loud enough for the Prioress to hear within the soundless church. The Prioress could only be talking about one nun, Wencilian, the one who was like a daughter to him. He remained quiet, not daring to make a sound until the Prioress had spoken.

The Prioress was unsure whether to reveal any more, but she felt she just had to tell someone. She had kept her feelings to herself for too long. Father Francis would be under oath not to reveal any of this conversation. She need not mention her name, but was sure he may know.

"Her real name I am sure is Gwenllian, maybe I do not pronounce it properly, for I think it comes from the land of Wales. She was brought here, not as an abandoned orphan, as I had previously believed, but to be hidden away. The King pays a sum for her keep each year, so she must be someone of importance. I wanted to know who she is. She has been in my care since I came here when she was just four years old. I was told she had no family, no family at all. No one has ever visited. I am not sure if the Prioress Priscilla knew of her identity."

"I see. Does anyone else know of this situation, Prioress?"

"No, not really. I have mentioned my concern to Sister Agnes and Sister Marie Claire. That is all."

"Well, I certainly know nothing of this myself, but women come here for the strangest of reasons."

"She was only a babe when she came, not even a year old. She would know nothing of her life before or where she was born."

"If the King is involved, I don't think we should meddle. I would strongly advise you not to interfere in this matter. We don't know what we are dealing with. She has taken vows, she knows nothing of her family. It may even be very unsettling or even dangerous to let her find out her true identity."

"Father, I am sure she must be an illegitimate daughter of the King. But I cannot understand why he would want to hide her. He has several illegitimate daughters who live at court, so I hear. Therefore I think the mother must be a prominent person, or a married woman who would fall into disgrace if the truth became known."

Father Francis suddenly remembered some rumours he had heard years ago but at the time had taken no notice. He was not prone to gossip and was not interested in women's business, but now he was more than a little intrigued.

Brother John very nearly dropped the alms box he was holding onto his foot. He had forgotten his duties and was totally absorbed in their conversation. "Holy Mary, Mother of God, my little Wencilian could be the King's daughter!" he mumbled to himself.

The Prioress wanted to strongly disagree with Father Francis, but realised that she must tread very carefully. This issue could be extremely inflammatory and she was here to confess, no more, she had already said too much, but words could not be retracted now. She crossed herself and prayed Father Francis would take this no further.

He thankfully diverted the conversation back to the confession and continued with the business of absolution.

"Let us pray for the forgiveness of your sins. Give thanks to the Lord for He is good. His mercy endures for ever. The Lord has freed you from your sins. Go in peace. Thanks be to God."

At this point, Brother John crept out of the church into the sunlight. He crossed the courtyard and opened the gate with the help of the gate keeper.

A family of beggars were huddled against the wall. They looked up at Brother John, almost apologetic for their very existence. His heart glowed with compassion when he saw their dirty faces and the rags which clung to their malnourished bodies.

They have each other though, he thought, they have a family. My poor Wencilian knows nothing of where she came

225

from and who she might be. What shall I do now? What shall I do with this knowledge I have learnt today? I cannot repeat what I have heard in the confessional; I should not have even been listening. But I cannot let this go either.

CHAPTER 32

Sempringham Priory

Philip winced and held his breath as he cut a deep groove in his arm. It was only a bit of blood, he had suffered a lot worse and no doubt his dear Catrin had. Catrin was very much on his mind as he wrapped a rag around his wound and made his way to the infirmary.

Cai was relieved to see him. He had intended to seek him out this very day. He feared Philip may have already left the Priory. Brother Gilbert was occupied with a lay brother, so he swept Philip into the still room.

"I'd feared you had gone, Philip. How have you injured yourself?"

"Self-inflicted, to get in here to see you without suspicion. I have to leave tomorrow at dawn. The Chancellor's business is complete. I have had word. Catrin has given birth, to a girl. We have a baby daughter, Cai."

Cai could see the genuine delight in his eyes and was pleased. He knew Philip, as a soldier was hoping for a son, but that he would not reveal that to Catrin in any way. He would love his daughter equally and, as Cai suspected, would soon be totally in love with her when he held her in his arms.

"Blessings Philip, that is excellent news. I'm really pleased. Is Catrin well?"

"I hope so. I will be home as soon as I can, but I have duties in the meantime. Cai, have you made contact with Gwenllian?"

"Nearly, I was singing the other night outside the infirmary and I know she was listening on the other side of the wall. Then an older nun called her in. I'm sure now that she works every day in the infirmary and I can make contact soon. It's so difficult here to approach a nun. The women are so restricted in their movements. I don't want to scare or shock her. I need to approach her very carefully."

"That's right, Cai. It's a delicate operation and one with an unknown outcome. Things are not easy at the moment for the Templars and I fear their help will be limited."

"But will they still help to get Gwenllian to safety?"

"They will provide safe passage. I cannot say any more. One month from now, on Lughnasadh Eve as we know it, or Lammas to the Church, Hywel will be waiting for you and Gwenllian outside by the forest edge on the western side of the priory buildings. We cannot delay any more than that. You must win her trust and make plans to get her out of here at that time. It's an onerous task for you alone, but there is no one else who could be trusted or who would not arouse suspicion."

"It will be done. I can hear Brother Gilbert approaching. Take care. Let me bind that arm."

"What goes on in here, Brother Gregory?"

"This soldier has cut his arm, Brother."

"How did that happen?"

"Oh, you know, practicing a little sword play while we await the Chancellor, Brother."

"Soldiers! You must fight even in God's house."

"Forgive me, Brother, I mean no offence. We have to keep in practice for your safety. I hear there are marauders about outside the Priory," Philip replied, hiding his amusement.

Brother Gilbert flinched and merely murmured, "Well I wish you well, sir. Brother Gregory, I have a task for you when you are ready."

"I am done, Brother." Cai looked into Philip's eyes, trying to convey that all would be done.

"Thank you, Brothers, for your help. We shall be leaving tomorrow so you should not need to administer to us again."

"You're welcome, sir," Cai replied, as Philip left the room.

He wondered when, or if, he would see him again. And his dear Catrin, would he ever see her again or see her little daughter for the first time? In one month he could be sailing to France, to an unknown destination. How would he then get Gwenllian to their folk in Eryri? Only two thoughts consoled him – Gwenllian would be free and he might be able to find Celeste when he was done with all this.

Cai had become quite accustomed to life at the Priory. It could have been monotonous, but his work in the infirmary kept him busy and there was enough to keep him interested. He had learnt a lot from Brother Gilbert in his short time here and hoped Brother Gilbert had benefitted from some of his knowledge too. They seemed to have developed a mutual respect for each other, even though he would not call it friendship. The only other Brother he had talked to, beyond a polite greeting, apart from the patients, was Brother John, who had shown him to the guest house when he arrived. He struck him as a friendly, genuine man, with a sense of humour, unlike most of the other Brothers here.

Brother Gilbert had agreed to him playing his crwth and singing to some of the patients in the evening. Reluctant at first, he had acquiesced that it seemed to soothe the men and help them sleep. On those occasions, Cai had opened the door at the rear of the infirmary as the evenings were so warm, his main motive being to reach Gwenllian in the hope that the sweet sounds would drift across the high wall which divided the infirmaries at the back. He even sang some songs in his native Welsh, especially the lullaby, optimistic that it may stir some deep memories within her. Seren's words were always in his thoughts … 'Do what you do best, Cai.'

Cai was however careful to attend the services, as was his duty. Sometimes the work in the infirmary prevented him. Father Roger was quite tolerant of this, for which he was greatly relieved.

Brother Gilbert's words cut sharply through his thoughts as he prepared some salves for a lay brother admitted with cuts and bruises. "You go to Nones today, Brother. I'll stay here and pray with the patients."

For once, he was glad of the respite and a chance to explore outside a little. As he walked the cloisters, he scanned the courtyard. He could see the stable boys helping two lay brothers groom the soldiers' horses. Getting them ready to leave in the morning, he thought. The yard was buzzing with activity and chatter, and the crash of the blacksmith's hammer resonated around him. Pleasant aromas drifted from the bake house. A heat mist hung low at the far end of the yard near the entrance to Father Roger's quarters. It struck Cai that this place could offer a lot, especially to a man from a poor family. It offered security, regular food, care when sick, work and education. This community was a self-supporting unit where each person had a place, a dignity. The lay brothers worked as stonemasons, carpenters, dug ditches to drain the land, farmed the sheep, built bridges and fulfilled many other tasks. The canons could study and even attend university in Cambridge, offering them some freedom in the outside world. The sacrifices they had to make though; for some he thought must be hard, a life of constant devotion, eight services a day and of course a life of celibacy.

And what of the nuns? he surmised. They had less freedom, shut away from the outside world. He found it strange that the men and the women were so segregated. Back in the mountains of Eryri, Seren would find that incomprehensible. There, men and women, priests and priestesses, needed to work together, to honour the balance in nature, the balance in the universe. The qualities and strengths of both male and female were conjoined. Both were treated equally; this was vital to the harmony of the community and the faith as a whole.

How would his Gwenllian feel, unhappy and trapped or happy and secure? She had never known any other life. Would she be a devout and faithful nun or a bit of a rebel? The time was approaching when he would have to find a way to talk to her and tell her of her true heritage. He would need to win her trust and time was short.

His train of thought was cut into by Brother John arriving at his side as he came near to the church.

"How are you, Brother Gregory?"

"Well, thank you, Brother John. It is good to see you."

"I must commend you on your singing. On warm and balmy evenings, the sounds travel."

"Oh, I hope it has not disturbed anyone. It benefits the sick, helps them sleep."

"On the contrary, I myself enjoy it, but I cannot speak for everyone. Tell me what language is it that you sing in sometimes. I know the English and the French, but there is one I do not recognise. Is it your native tongue?"

"It is. It's the language of Wales, which was once of course the language of the Britons, the original inhabitants of our island."

"You are well informed on your history, Brother. We must talk later sometime."

They entered the silence of the church. As they merged with a line of other monks who filed in, Cai wondered whether he would regret his last statement. Brother John did not strike him as someone who would consider that blasphemous, but some might, even though it was the truth.

Brother John had just needed confirmation. After witnessing the confession of the Prioress, he had thought of nothing else but Wencilian and the possibility that she could be the King's daughter. A singing Welsh Friar appearing at this time, he knew could just be pure coincidence, but he had a strong feeling that it may not be. He needed to keep a close eye on Brother Gregory and get to the heart of this matter, before he, the Prioress or anyone else involved in what appeared to be a developing conspiracy, could break the heart of his dear Wencilian.

Chapter 33

Sempringham Priory

Wencilian unbound the blood-soaked bandages from Alice's arm and handed them to Leoba who placed them in a bucket. Alice had been admitted to the infirmary with severe cuts on her arm, although she had not told anyone how she became injured. Wencilian was pleased to see her, but upset and dismayed by her wounds. As she applied the new bandages, she sent Leoba to the wash room behind the still room to start washing the old ones.

"For the sake of our dear Lord, Alice, tell me how you got these injuries."

"I would only tell you, Wencilian. Swear to me you will not tell anyone else."

"I swear. You don't need to ask me that."

"I … I did it to myself."

"Really, but why?"

"I really don't know, except that I do know I wanted to end it all … leave this world. I felt so desperate. I don't want to be here in this place any more. But it is a mortal sin to kill oneself, so I stopped, stopped in time."

"Oh, my poor Alice, I knew you were sad, but not in such utter despair. I am so sorry that my duties have not left me time or opportunity to see you very much since Easter time."

"You are my only friend in here, Wencilian. I don't want this life. I wanted to be wed to Maurice, have children, live a life like my mother and sister. I would run away, but where do I go? My family would send me back here again. It would have been better for my sister to be here; she didn't love Maurice, nor he her. She has no taste for luxury, silk dresses; she doesn't even like fun. What a miserable life Maurice will have too."

Wencilian looked down into her beautiful face and the tiny wisp of auburn hair which peeped out of her head dress and couldn't admit to herself that Alice was wrong. She was not made for this life any more than she was, but Wencilian knew that she had no one on the outside, nor did she have a sweetheart or know any other way of life. Alice, she felt must be suffering a great deal.

"I am here now and I will try to keep you in here as long as possible. You must tell Sister Beatrice that you cut your arms some other way. As for your family, you must be strong; show them that you will not be defeated. You know, Alice, I have been in here all my life so I try not to think of the past or the future. I think only of each day as it passes. You must try to do that too. It will not torment your mind or soul so much. What have you been doing in the past few days?"

Alice looked up at her puzzled. "I have been helping Sister Marie Claire preparing cloths and cutting garments. She is a dear soul with such a talent with a needle."

"Yes, and you haven't, so you tell everyone that you have cut yourself whilst cutting cloth. Was Sister Marie Claire with you all the time?"

"No she left me alone most of the time, coming in to give me instruction."

"Well, there we are then; that can be your story and no one can prove otherwise."

"Oh Wencilian, I really don't know how I could manage without you. Bless you for your trouble. I'll try not to be a burden on you."

"Just get better and I'll be happy. We have a helper in here now, the postulant, Leoba. I'm sure she will be a good friend to you too. She is wise beyond her years, but fragile too. She seems to me like a fairy child. It's as if she knows everything that I am thinking."

"A fairy child?"

"Yes, I will tell you, but you too must swear not to tell anyone. Her mother was Hilda, a woman who could prophesy, a woman of knowledge. She lived with the fen people, but was not really one of them. That is a mystery, but she told me I was of noble birth."

"How did you meet her, Wencilian?"

Wencilian was careful not to reveal any details of the night she escaped with Mira. She would have loved to share it with her dearest friend, but it was too risky even now. She felt though that she wanted to tell her this; it may even take her mind off Maurice and her despair.

"She came into the infirmary. Sadly she passed away. But she knew she was near her end and asked for Leoba to be taken into our care, to protect her."

"What did she mean by noble birth?"

"I don't know and now I may never find out."

"Can you not ask Leoba?"

Wencilian thought about this for a moment. It had somehow never seemed right to ask her, but she supposed it would do no harm, now that they had developed a friendship, even though a little tentative. There was of course no guarantee that she would know anything about it.

"I may do that sometime. You rest now. Sister Beatrice will be back from Nones shortly. Pretend to sleep, even if you can't, then she will not question you too soon."

Alice lay down, more content than she had been since the visit of her family that dreadful day. She felt secure with Wencilian near her, but sleep she couldn't. Her mind was racing, so intrigued by what Wencilian had told her. She didn't regret cutting her arms for one minute. Our Lady had delivered her from a grave sin, but delivered her into the care of her dear friend. The thought that Wencilian could be of noble birth excited her; it pierced the dullness of this place with a sparkle of light. As she heard Sister Beatrice enter the infirmary and call out for Wencilian, she closed her eyes.

Leoba too felt more content. Even with her hands immersed in cold water stained with stale blood, she felt happier than she had since her mother died. The peace and calm of the convent suited her, although she could never be at one with their beliefs, which seemed alien to her. She kept to herself and spoke very little, attending the services and doing her duties. After the night Wencilian had come to their house with the young lay sister who was with child, Hilda, her mother, had told her that her future was entwined with the Sister Wencilian and that she would be safe in the Priory. She must have known then, Leoba thought, that she was ill and her time on this earth would not be long. She knew she had the sight, like her mother, but her mother had warned her not to speak of it or practice it whilst in the Priory.

"You will have your chance in the future," she had told her, "Just always remember what I have taught you." As she had lain dying in the infirmary, Hilda had whispered, "Stay close to Sister Wencilian. It will not be difficult to persuade the Prioress to let you help in here when she discovers your healing knowledge, but don't tell her too much."

She had pleaded with her mother to heal herself; she was all she had left in the world.

"I am old, Leoba," her mother had muttered. "I have succeeded in keeping myself alive for many years now, but it is my time, my time to let go, dear child. You have a bright future ahead I am sure. Wait here. You will know when it is time to go. You will be safe here."

Leoba took the bandages outside to dry in the sun at the back of the infirmary, thinking only of all the questions she wished she had asked her mother. Who was her father? Why hadn't he come for her? Why couldn't she see at this moment her own future? The sight came at odd moments, but it was always about others. Sometimes she saw the souls of those who had passed away in the infirmary, leaving the body. She wondered whether Wencilian could see them too, but no words had been spoken.

She felt the warm sunshine on her wrist and remembered the times when she would play outside her hut as a young child, loving the feel of the sun. Then Hilda would come and usher her inside and cover her arms. "Your skin is so pale it burns and it will hurt you," she would say gently.

Seeing the other fen children running around half naked without a care, their creamy or darker skin glowing, made her feel an outsider. And she had felt like that all her life. Even her name was considered odd. The other children would make fun of it. Now she was covered in the dark robes of a postulant nun. Not for long, she thought. I shall run free some day. I pray to Woden that one day I shall be free.

An unusual sound made her turn as she re-entered the dimness of the infirmary. It was music, a melody not unlike some of the fen men would play from time to time. It drifted over the high wall which separated the men's and the women's infirmaries. She stood in the door for several moments, then went to fetch Wencilian.

"Sister Wencilian, come quickly."

"What is it Leoba?"

"It's music, music playing over the wall. Come and listen."

"Then, let's go quickly."

As she stepped outside, Wencilian recognised the music she thought she may have dreamed a few nights before. Then the music became louder. The player was just right by the wall and he started to sing, sing so beautifully in the strange language that she heard before.

She clutched Leoba's hand. "I was not dreaming; I heard it before, Leoba. I know now it is real."

'Very real,' Leoba thought, as a shiver passed along her spine. The sight was coming upon her, but this time it was not a vision she saw – it was words that she heard. The musician sang in a language that she had never heard before, but it was as if she understood the meaning of each word in her head in her own language.

CHAPTER 34

Grantham, Lincolnshire

Catrin laid the sleeping baby carefully in her crib. She seemed a happy, contented baby and Catrin was a happy and contented mother, greatly relieved that she had given birth safely and the baby was well. After only a week of lying in she was feeling restless, although still sore and a little weak. The women of the household insisted she remain in her chamber for at least another few weeks and were about to send for a wet nurse, until she put her foot down and said she wanted to nurse the baby herself. Catrin thought of her mother who had given birth to twelve children and had no time to rest after each birth and no servants to help her. Here she had her mother-in-law, sisters-in-law and servants on hand. She supposed she was lucky, but she felt lonely. Philip had not returned yet to see his daughter and she had no word of his whereabouts.

As she lay back down on her comfortable bed and arranged the blue silk coverlet covering the crisply laundered linen, she remembered the day when she was the one bringing fresh linen to Olwen, the midwife, as poor Eleanor lay dying. That day had instilled in her a deep fear of giving birth and her happiness at knowing she was with child had been tinged by a constant anxiety. When the time drew near, she had been secretly terrified, but tried her best not to let Gwyneth and her daughters see her fear. Thankfully, the baby was born within a few hours, during which she had no thoughts at all beyond the searing pain which engulfed her. Now she felt a deep sadness for Eleanor, more than she ever had, knowing now how overwhelming a mother's love could be and how it must be totally devastating to know that you were dying and leaving your helpless child alone in the world.

Poor little Gwenllian, so cruelly torn from her mother, and then from the people who had cared for her – herself, Celeste, Morwena and Cai. She wondered how Cai was progressing in the Priory and hoped that somehow she would be able to see Gwenllian when she was freed. There had been no word from Hywel either. Catrin hated being so useless; it should have been her in the Priory, but fate had decreed otherwise. She was needed here now with her child.

The servant girl, Margaret, came into the chamber bringing warm milk and bread. "Are you comfortable, Ma'am?"

"Perfectly, but you could ask Hervé for some parchments and pens. I need to send a letter."

"Very well," Margaret replied, leaning over the crib, preoccupied with the baby, tucking the sheepskin around her. "Have you thought of her name yet, Ma'am? The mistress is coming to ask you today. They are all getting impatient."

"I have, Margaret, I have just decided on a name. She will be called Eleanor, Eleanor Gwenllian."

"That's a lovely name, Ma'am. I'm sure the mistress will be pleased."

The baby stirred and gurgled. Catrin leaned over to rock the crib and softly chanted a lullaby, the one she had always remembered Cai singing to baby Gwenllian at Abergwyngregyn. She had never forgotten the words. Singing in her own native language released many more memories of those days and she had time now to sing and remember as little Eleanor fed and slept.

She thought of the last time she had briefly seen her family. It had been the day before they had left Abergwyngregyn for Denbigh. Her mother, father and two sisters wept when she left them, all knowing they may never see each other again. Her three brothers were out working in the fields; she never had the chance to say goodbye. Nearly eighteen years had passed. She

238

had no idea if her parents were still alive or if she had nieces and nephews. She had wanted to travel there when they met Hywel and Cai in the forest house above Cwmhir Abbey, but Philip had said there was no time and it was too risky. Surely, now the land had settled and they could make that trip sometime before long? What would it be like now though, Catrin wondered, now that Edward had domination over the whole of Cymru? The thought of Edward and his troops taking over the Court at Abergwyngregyn made her shiver. It was not grand, but it had been her home and it had such a rustic beauty all of its own, nestled between an array of ancient trees in the foothills of the Carneddau.

Eleanor had made the Court come alive with colour and music, and her sweet temper made all that knew her happy to serve her. They were happy days. Catrin sighed. She loved her family but being at court had given her so much more in life to enjoy and experience. Without Eleanor, she would have remained poor with no status, on the lowest rung of society with barely nothing but the ragged clothes she stood up in and some days barely any food in her belly. She was grateful to her and glad she was naming the baby after her.

Then she had found her way to Philip's house, unknowingly, years after that terrible night when Gwenllian was abducted. It seemed that fate took her there and onwards to this place in England, and now she was married to the man of the house who perfectly understood her background and loved her. They used to sometimes speak of those days with Prince Llywelyn, but Philip rarely mentioned them in recent times. It seemed like another life they had lived. She guessed too that it was painful for him to recall. When Philip had first brought her to this house in Grantham, she had entered another world; she had never set foot in England before. The language was strange, but she was relieved that most of the small household could converse in French, a language she had heard at Abergwyngregyn, most often between Celeste and Eleanor, and had become familiar with. Although she struggled to express herself in it, she at least could understand. Sometimes in the early days after her marriage, in the privacy of their chamber, she could chat with Philip in Welsh. Philip had told her old tales from the locals, passed down through many generations, of the Norman invasion of England and how life had changed, the old laws and customs gradually eroded and replaced with alien Norman ways. They discussed how the very same thing would be happening in the land of their birth now and how Prince Llywelyn had fought for so long to keep a hold on his lands, his culture, his family heritage. Then feelings of guilt and sadness would well up inside her.

After her marriage, there were long periods when the women were back in Powys, Philip away on duty and she was alone with Hervé and the other two servants. She thought of the times Hywel would visit on his travels with his merchandise. He would often present her with little trinkets or cloth to sew for new dresses for herself, Margaret and Elsie. But it was his books which intrigued her. She would sneak a read of them, but her reading was very basic and she struggled to follow them. That was until he offered to teach her more and she then couldn't get enough of them. Nor could she get enough of his wonderful tales of Druids, Priests and Priestesses in the mountains, all of which she regarded as his fanciful imagination … until she knew better.

CHAPTER 35

Sempringham Priory

Brother John was sweating in the hot early July sunshine. His tonsured head had burned as he stood distributing the alms by the south gate of the Priory. There was a line of beggars today and he was impatient to get through them. He wanted to concentrate on what he should do about Wencilian. As soon as his duties were over, he planned to skip Terce and find somewhere to be alone and think. As the line moved on, a little beggar girl handed him a posy of sweet smelling flowers and herbs.

"A gift for a gift, Brother," she said, looking up at him with large, innocent, deep green eyes.

What a beautiful child, he thought. She looked very similar to Wencilian at that age, which he guessed must be about ten or eleven.

"Thank you, child, you are very kind. What plants do we have here?"

"There's rosemary, sir, celandine, coral wort, lady's mantle, lavender and wood sage."

"That's a fine selection. Some of these are hard to find. Where did you find them?"

"On my travels, sir."

She smiled sweetly as Brother John pressed a coin into her hand.

"You have indeed given me a gift today, child."

The girl ran off, but he had a feeling she would be back

another time. He would remember her.

Brother John knew that this could be the worst month of the year for the poor. Grain stocks were low until the harvest time, the fruits of the hedgerows were not yet ripened and all last winter's meat, if they were lucky enough to have any, would have been eaten. Food could be sparse at times in the monastery, but he would never starve or know the meaning of true, biting hunger.

Coral wort, he had remembered Sister Martha saying years before, was a rare plant that they would always be glad of in the infirmary if anyone were to come across it. He would take it to the nuns' infirmary and hope to see Wencilian.

As the bell rang for Terce he slid into the cloister which led past the monks' infirmary to the nuns' buildings. The coolness of the shadows soothed his head. It was quiet. Most of the nuns would be in the church now, he knew, and hopefully Sister Beatrice had left Wencilian alone in the infirmary.

When he passed the entrance to the monks' infirmary, he was startled to encounter Brother Gregory, face to face. "Good day, Brother."

"Good day, Brother John." Cai was pleased to see the cheery monk, whom he had found very congenial when he had first arrived. "Have you been collecting some herbs from the garden?"

"No, they were a gift from a little beggar girl. One of them I think is a rare plant that they may have use for in the nuns' infirmary, so I thought I would take it along while it is still fresh."

Sensing a golden opportunity, Cai was eager to keep him talking. "Let me see, could that be coral wort there? That has many uses and you are right it may be of more use to women than men."

"There is an elderly Sister, Sister Martha. She was the apothecary before Sister Beatrice, she certainly knew a thing or two about herbs and healing, but sadly she is losing her mind these days. She always said to pick some if ever I saw it growing, as they could use it well."

242

"Would you mind if I accompanied you, Brother."

"Well, it really is irregular for monks to enter the nuns' infirmary, except in exceptional circumstances, but I could say that you are helping me with some tasks. If Sister Beatrice is there however, you may have to wait outside."

Brother John was as eager to find out more about this 'musical' monk with the strange accent, as Cai was about him, so was keen to keep his company. He didn't believe that Brother Gregory was just passing through and wanted to visit the shrine of St Gilbert, and since he had overheard the Prioress during her confession, he was starting to believe that he could be there for a totally different reason. The Welsh connection seemed more than coincidence.

As they walked, Brother John asked, "Do you intend to stay here for a while yet, Brother?"

"I think I am being of use helping Brother Gilbert. We are both learning from each other. Maybe this is where God intends me to be for the moment." Cai replied without turning to look Brother John in the eye and hoping that the evasive answer would suffice for now.

"Well, there is talk of your music soothing the sick, although I don't think the Prior quite approves."

"Nor did Brother Gilbert at first, until he saw the results of my singing. The patients slept better and seemed more content."

"I see. Well, there is a type of logic in that no doubt," Brother John replied as he knocked the brass gargoyle face on the heavy oak door which led to the nuns' infirmary, and both men exchanged a look which left them both knowing that there was a lot more to say.

Cai's heart was thumping as he stood in front of the door. He could not believe how easy it was at this point to enter the nuns' infirmary. Brother John had just come along and now he was here. Of course, Gwenllian could be at Terce, but at least he was one step nearer to her.

A young postulant shyly peered around the door. "Can I help you?"

"I am here to see Sister Beatrice or Sister Wencilian. I am

Brother John and this is Brother Gregory."

"Please wait here."

'Which one would it be?' Cai wondered, 'Gwenllian, or the Sister Beatrice he had heard of and would rather avoid.'

The young postulant came back again. "Come in quickly, Sister Beatrice is at Terce."

The nun who approached them was wiping her hands on a linen cloth. Her face broke into a huge smile when she saw Brother John, but she restrained from embracing him in front of the stranger.

"Brother John, what brings you here?"

"Herbs, Wencilian, … and to see how you are, of course. I have brought you some coral wort, which old Sister Martha always said was rare and extremely useful."

Wencilian laughed.

Cai was rooted to the spot and found his body paralysed. This was his Gwenllian, standing, living and breathing, laughing with joy in front of him. A single golden hair protruded from her black headdress. In her green eyes and fine nose he saw Eleanor, and a touch of Llywelyn in the more squared chin; a perfect blend of the two. There was no doubt in his mind now.

"Wencilian, let me introduce Brother Gregory. He is a travelling friar from Wales, who is staying and working in the monks' infirmary for the moment."

Cai's voice was frozen. He could not address her as 'Sister Wencilian' and he could not address her as 'Gwenllian' and he couldn't take his eyes off her as he gave a short bow and mumbled, "Sister."

Brother John was watching and noting Cai's unusual reaction. "We call him 'the musical friar' now. He soothes the sick with his singing. Although we cannot understand much of what he sings, it being in the language of Wales."

Wencilian spoke gently and coaxingly, aware of Cai's awkwardness. "I have heard you sing, Brother, outside the infirmary, although I could not see who was singing for the high wall which divides us. Your music was especially soothing."

"Thank you, Sister. Did you understand any of the words?"

"No. That is a strange question, Brother. You sing in a language of which I have no knowledge. I have rarely heard any music in my life, apart from the singing and chanting of the monks of course."

Cai was about to try and engage her in further conversation, but Brother John interjected, "We must return now. Sister Wencilian, I am glad to see you well and content."

As the two Brothers made their way back to their duties, Cai was eager to delve a bit more, unsure how to start.

Brother John was the first to speak, regarding Cai carefully as he did. "Ah, she is like a daughter to me, Sister Wencilian. Do you know, Brother, that she has been here all her life, well almost. She was brought here as a baby and no one has ever been told where she came from. The previous prioress may have known, but she never revealed it as far as I know. When I was a cellarer and she still a child, she would sneak in and sit with me, talking about anything and everything, always eager to learn, especially about the birds and the animals, the stars – you name it."

Cai flushed a little. This was the total confirmation he needed. Brother John had spilled out the information he needed to hear, no doubt completely unaware of the effect of his words. He was convinced now that this was Gwenllian, the true Princess of Wales. It made him happy that Brother John had been like a father to her. Maybe Brother John would be someone he could trust in the future. But the future was short.

"Do you think she may have been abandoned by a poor family, Brother John?"

Brother John cleared his throat. "That does seem to be the most likely explanation, but babies are often abandoned and not many of them end up in nunneries. I think there could be more of a story to this one."

He searched Cai's face, looking for any more signs that would indicate that this travelling friar had something to hide.

Cai felt uncomfortable for a moment, sure that Brother John was suspecting him of some unrevealed motive, or that he knew more than he was saying.

"Come into the infirmary, Brother, and I will find you a salve to soothe your head, or it could blister."

It wasn't possible to continue any conversation as Brother Gilbert was irritatingly hovering around them inside the infirmary, even though the beds were all full. However, the busyness of the place excused Cai from services until evening Compline. He carried out his duties, mostly in silence, unable to think of anything else but Gwenllian. The memories of Abergwyngregyn flashed through his mind again – the night of the escape from Nanhysglain, Celeste, Eleanor and Llywelyn.

Now, after all these years, he had been led here to a nunnery, a place where Gwenllian had been kept in ignorance all her life and, like him, she was working in the infirmary, cheerfully doing her duty. Tears filled his eyes. How would she react he wondered, when he told her the truth? She might not believe any of it; she might scream for help and he would be carted off to be questioned, possibly imprisoned or worse. Then he would never see her again. Did the Prioress know, was she in league with the King? Whether she was or not, it was dangerous to question her he surmised, but maybe he could seek an audience with her and glean some information surreptitiously. Whatever his plan of action, he had to formulate it soon.

The singing had enticed Gwenllian, perhaps it could entice her some more. Seren would help him he was sure, even though she was many miles away, hidden; he felt her presence alongside him often. It was a while though since he had gone into trance and heard her voice; he had not really had any privacy to do it in the Priory or really any need until now. He had trained with the Druids and in the bardic arts. He had power within him he could summon, although he had always been warned to use it only when other methods had failed, and then only for the highest good. Seren, he knew, would be making her own plans and he wasn't sure if Hywel had been able to contact her to tell her that plans for Gwenllian had now changed, for a while at least.

In the community within the Priory, all his needs were met – food, clothing, a bed to sleep in, tasks to complete, company, protection from the outside world. The only onerous duties were the repetitious services. It wouldn't be a bad life at all if he had never known the freedom of his previous life. He wondered if it would be cruel to tear Gwenllian away from all that she knew and take her out into an uncertain world, a world which could be dangerous for her. But how could he live with himself if he didn't tell her who she really was and who her family were. He couldn't just let the story of the Welsh Principality, her heritage, float away as if it had never been and no one cared.

CHAPTER 36

The Eryri Mountains

Finally the snow had melted from the caps of the mountains. Seren looked up towards the highest peak of Eryri. She would always be in awe of these hills, their beauty, their majesty, and would never take them for granted. She had been here so long that she knew almost every joint, fracture, colour and tone of the rocks which surrounded her. The previous winter had been tough and she was glad of the warmer July sunshine. Her bones ached and she missed Cynan, although the return of Luned and her baby had done a lot to ease her heart and give her joy which she was so grateful for. The midsummer solstice had passed and preparations would soon have to be made for the Lughnasadh festival. She must start working soon. The younger priests and neophytes were busy building a new dwelling, a dwelling more fitted to a princess than their own timber buildings. Stones were being brought from all over the mountain range and that was a hard job with so few men.

As she watched Luned playing with little Elena, she was pleased that the baby was thriving. They both seemed so at home here. Her thoughts turned to Cai. She had dreamed of him the night before. She felt that the time was drawing near when his plan would be put into action. Gwenllian would be soon be free, but how she wondered would she and Cai make the dangerous journey back to Gwynedd? She had received no message since the spring equinox. In her dreams and meditations, she had seen Cai several times, and seen Gwenllian. They had made contact and this pleased her.

"What are you thinking of, Mother?" Luned asked. "You

look concerned and distracted."

"It's time I told you something, Luned. Do you think Erin could mind Elena for a while? I'll wait for you by the lake."

Luned returned to their hut with baby Elena, and then walked pensively to the lake to join her mother, dreading the news that she could be ill or worse. By the time she reached the lake, she saw Seren sitting in her favoured place and was relieved to see her smiling.

"Come and sit next to me, Luned. I need you to listen carefully. I haven't wanted to burden you with any of this information before. I just wanted us both to enjoy a happy peaceful time together after so long and for you to settle now in your new home."

"Mother," Luned placed her hand on Seren's arm, "What is it?"

"Shh. Just listen, Luned, don't worry. You know the story of our Prince? I know you were only young, but it was not so long ago. You have heard me mention Gwenllian, heir to the Principality. Well I shall tell you more about her. You know the story of her abduction by the King. No one knew what had been her fate, but it seems she may have survived. You remember, Cai, don't you? Well, he took Gwenllian to safety for a while to Dafydd's house, when Prince Llywelyn was captured. Cai then went with Dafydd and his family and little Gwenllian to Castell y Bere, but had to leave there because Edward's troops were on their way to try to take the castle. Luckily, they managed to flee well before, only to be fugitives in the mountains, where they sheltered in a bog at Nanhysglain. The King's men found them, someone betrayed them."

"Yes, I think I know, Mother, what happened to Dafydd and his sons, everyone talked about it for years after. But what happened to little Gwenllian?"

"We have never known for sure, but Cai has set off in search of her with the help of Hywel and others. He intends to bring her here."

"To us!"

"Yes, Luned. It would have been safe for her here. If only

they had brought her earlier, she might be here now."

"Have you any idea where she is?"

"I'm not sure, but Cai may know by now. I have seen that she is imprisoned somewhere. It could be a convent in England. I am waiting to hear from Hywel, but no word has come yet. After the ambush, when Gwenllian was captured, most of the party were killed. Cai eventually made his way to us in a bad state. You would have been about six years old then."

"I have some vague memories, but Cai never talked of that to me as I grew older."

"No, he rarely talked of it with me. He wanted to forget. He felt he had failed Prince Llywelyn, Eleanor and little Gwenllian. No one seemed to reach him. Once when Hywel came to stay, they spent a lot of time in discussion, and from then onwards he was determined to set out to find out what had happened to her. At that point we were not sure if she was dead or alive. The Prince had promised that his daughter would train here with us, for at least a while to understand her true family heritage and be schooled in wisdom.

"Eleanor and the Prince named her after an ancient Priestess who once led our people on Môn. Gwenllian, her name, encompasses the essence of blessedness and purity. There was another Gwenllian too, whom I had mentioned before. She was a warrior princess who fought the Norman King. There was an ancient prophecy which said, 'Thrice will come Gwenllian'. Cai would sing the words of the prophecy to us many a night, many years ago. So, she is the third Gwenllian to come to us to try and save her people. I don't know what her fate will be, but one thing I do know is that if Cai can manage to free her, he is bringing her back here to us. She has no family left but us. We will be her true family."

"That is so incredible. I had no idea about any of this that you tell me. What can we do to help, Mother?"

"On the inner planes I have been trying to track Cai and see Gwenllian. A few times I have made contact with Cai, but it takes a lot of my energy now. The new dwelling that is being built is for her, for our Princess and Priestess when she comes."

"It will be strange for her. I once visited a convent. Her life would be so different and of course, she may not know any of our language. Do you think she has been told anything of her heritage?"

"It is hard to say, but doubtful. I can't imagine what she has been told. I want you, Luned, to be ready when she comes, to care for her and teach her our language too. When Elena is a little older, you too can take up your training again, if you wish. I will not force it upon you, but I am not getting any younger. We must continue and preserve our knowledge, even though we are hidden away in these mountains. One day, we may walk freely again and not be afraid to spread our truth. I doubt that will be in my time or even many lifetimes ahead. It should never be lost. Gwenllian will be about eighteen years of age now; you are twenty-four, you are close in age; you should be friends and lead together."

Seren paused and stretched to reach a wild mountain rose which grew close by them. She touched it carefully and gently bent the stem towards them. "You see this flower, Luned; the rose, it is a symbol of the Goddess. See how frail its petals are and yet so sturdy is the plant. It will not bloom for long, not in this harsh environment, but when the flower has gone the plant will give us fruit to help sustain us through the winter, and next summer, the flower will bloom again. So it is with the Goddess, she never dies, she is timeless. How can the Roman Church believe they have obliterated the Goddess when she breathes and lives all around us. She is the living earth. You, Luned, were conceived in the sacred rite of Beltane and it is your birthright to lead our people. Soon you will need to prepare for this if you are willing."

"I think I have grown up a lot since I left here, Mother. Being back here has made me understand the value of my family and my heritage and how courageous you and the others here have been, to never give up and seek a more comfortable life. But Mother, I don't regret leaving. I have seen how people live a different life. I met my husband and now have little Elena. I promise you though that I will stay and care for Gwenllian, and you too should you ever need it. I'm sure I have a lot to learn and I am glad I was called back here at this time, I always felt that it was the right thing to do."

"It certainly was, Luned."

Luned looked at her mother, for the first time seeing what a beautiful woman she was; strong, wise, a woman who had been through many trials and never complained, a woman of unending faith in people and her own beliefs. She hoped she would grow to be like her. Right now she was eager to know more, more about the people she lived with, more about Gwenllian.

"There is not a lot more I can tell you about Gwenllian at the moment, but I can tell you what I know of Prince Llywelyn, Eleanor, her mother, and the history of our people," Seren replied. "So let's sit a while longer in the sunshine. I feel there are many months, years of learning for you ahead, so don't rush too much."

Dusk was falling when the two women returned to Seren's dwelling. Erin and Nerys had prepared food and baby Elena was sleeping peacefully. It seemed to Seren that all was just as it should be. She saw Cynan's face in her mind. He winked at her and smiled as if to agree with her. How grateful she was for these simple peaceful moments these days. This moment she would like to capture in time for ever, but that could not happen, even with their magic, time moved on and life was constantly changing. Although in the Eryri mountains many days seemed to be the same, nothing ever remained so.

CHAPTER 37

Sempringham Priory

Cai waited and waited, for what seemed an endless time. In fact it was only one morning, but it was the day on which he had decided to approach Gwenllian. Finding the right moment was paramount to success or failure. He knew it had to be this day from the moment he awoke, and then when he heard her voice humming a similar tune to the one she had heard him play, he was certain that he must make a move. The lullaby he had sung had obviously had some effect on her, however small.

Scrambling up the high wall which adjoined the two infirmaries, he suspended himself on his arms for a few seconds and caught a quick glimpse of Gwenllian and the young postulant who had opened the door of the nuns' infirmary to them, hanging out linen to dry in the warm sunshine. Knowing he could be seriously reprimanded if he were seen, he rapidly retreated to the still room. If he seemed busy and indispensable at this moment, he may be excused from Prime. He prayed that Gwenllian would also be excused.

Brother Gilbert peered around the still room door. "The bell rings for Prime, Brother. The patients are settled, shall we go?"

"I really can't leave these medicines, Brother Gilbert. If I leave them, I may forget the proportions and they need sealing as soon as the tinctures are blended."

"Very well, I'm sure you know what you are doing," Brother Gilbert muttered reluctantly. "I will leave you to your duties."

Relieved, Cai quickly finished what he was doing and crept

past the seven men who lay on the infirmary pallets. All seemed to be dozing or asleep. This was opportune. The time was right; Gwenllian had to be there.

He could hear movement on the other side of the wall, but no voices. This meant that possibly one nun remained behind alone. It was a risk; it could be Sister Beatrice, but he took his crwth from behind the infirmary door and let the door close behind him. Sitting on the floor with his back against the wall, he began to strum, and then to softly sing the lullaby. His voice floated on the gentle breeze and waves of sound enveloped Sister Wencilian as she tucked an elderly nun up securely on her pallet. Intrigued at hearing the sounds of singing again, she went to stand outside and crept nearer to the wall.

I will be bold, I will be bold, she told herself. She stood entranced until the music paused. She hesitated, then she spoke. "Is that you, Brother Gregory? May I be so bold as to ask the name of the tune?"

Cai shot up and faced the wall. "You may, Sister, indeed ask, Sister Wencilian. We met only a few days ago. I remember your voice, Sister. My usual name is 'Cai' and the name of the tune is 'Gwenllian'. It is one I wrote myself many years ago."

"Cai, Gwenllian? Those are strange names I have not heard before. Brother John introduced you as Brother Gregory only a few days ago."

Cai smiled at her clumsy pronunciation, but the conversation was flowing perfectly. He was tingling with apprehension, delight and a mixture of so many emotions, although at once he felt a sense of ease and relief.

"They are Welsh names, Sister. Wales is my homeland. Cai is my name in the Welsh language."

"I know nothing of that land, but have heard it mentioned once or twice."

"It is a fine land, Sister. It has such rugged beauty, full of mountains, hills, forests, lakes and waterfalls; a land of poets and singers, where ancient history survives in spite of the King."

"In spite of the King?"

Cai was stunned. Of course he was prepared for this, but

254

hearing it from her own lips was heart breaking. She knew nothing of her heritage, nothing of her family, and she didn't even know what the King had done to their country.

"King Edward had many battles with the princes of Wales and finally they were defeated and obliterated … well, almost. The land, like this land, is now ruled by the Norman overlords, except your England was lost over two centuries ago, ours only finally eighteen years ago."

"That is my age, eighteen, I believe. I would have been too young to hear any tales, even if any such tales would ever be told in a place such as this."

"Ah, that's true, and people soon forget, but I never will. There are some others too who would sacrifice their own lives for the memory of their beloved land."

Wencilian was finding this conversation fascinating. She had never conversed with a Brother, apart from Brother John, about anything but perfunctory matters, and that was very rarely. It was as if a conjuror stood before her invoking images of a magical land, one that, romantically, really existed. But she knew the reality of the wars must have been unbearably harsh.

"Your people must have suffered a great deal, Brother. Is that why you come to be here?"

"It is in truth part of the reason."

Wencilian knew she must go back inside. Sister Beatrice could be back with Leoba any minute. Leoba did not concern her, but Sister Beatrice could not catch her having this conversation or she would face severe punishment. But she felt rooted to the spot and wanted to hear more. "Tell me about the princes; were they brave?"

"Very brave. But Sister there is so much to tell about them. Can you meet me here again? I fear your Sister Beatrice and my Brother Gilbert will be returning. I would not wish to cause you any trouble."

"Yes, I should go. Oh, I do wish I could talk to you again, but I don't know when that will be possible."

"I will try to be outside here after Compline whenever I can. Come when you can; do so safely."

"I can hear footsteps. I must go."

Wencilian stepped in just as Sister Beatrice and Leoba came through the door at the other end of the infirmary which led to the cloisters. As her eyes adjusted from the bright sunshine outside to the darkness of the room, the two nuns walking towards her looked like ghostly shadows merging with the gloom of the interior. She felt energised, charged with a new purpose, to find out about life beyond these walls, however scary or dangerous that might be.

Leoba looked at Wencilian and saw that she was glowing. Something had happened, she was sure, but knew not what.

Sister Beatrice regarded her for a moment then turned and swept into her room, calling behind her, "Sister Wencilian, you have been too long outside by the look of your cheeks, they are burnt with the sun. What could you have been doing in the yard for so long?"

"Oh just the usual tasks, Sister," Wencilian replied, exchanging a smile with Leoba.

Brother Gilbert expressed surprise when he saw Cai. "You look very pale, Brother, and are shaking a little. Are you unwell or have you seen a ghost?"

I think I have spoken to one, Cai thought, ignoring Brother Gilbert's rare attempt at humour.

"I think I may need to lie down for a short while, Brother, then I will be fine I'm sure."

The first hurdle was overcome, but how, Cai questioned, was he going to tell Gwenllian who she was? How would she react … with disbelief, with anger? Would she trust him? He lay on his pallet, thinking how to approach the next meeting. He felt it would not be long for she was interested in his tale, enticed by something mysterious to her – life in all its myriad of passions and events. He would open a new world for her; let her know about her true family and get her back to the land where she belonged. Although there would be no parents, siblings, uncles, aunts or cousins to greet her, in the mountains of Eryri was another family waiting to welcome her.

CHAPTER 38

Sempringham Priory

Brother John was watching the Prioress leave Father Roger's office. She looked anxious he thought, but then on the rare occasions he had seen her, she had seemed worried or distracted. Perhaps, he wondered, it was due to the Chancellor's visit, or he thought more darkly, it could be because of Wencilian.

He was really concerned that now, since the Prioress had discovered the information about Wencilian, they might remove her from the Priory or take some other action. But then, he thought again, if the Priory was receiving money for her each year that was unlikely. He couldn't bear knowing all this and not doing anything about it. He wanted to tell Wencilian. It was her right to know, but would it upset her too much and how could he admit to knowing? He had overheard a confession and was bound not to reveal anything that was said or he could face serious consequences. It was a dilemma that had left him with sleepless nights. Should he seek an audience with the Prioress? It would have to be on the pretence of another matter.

It was later that day after the service of Sext that a chance presented itself. While distributing alms at the gate of the Priory, Brother John noticed the little girl who had given him the herbs. She was loitering at the back of the queue, hobbling with a stick. When it came to her turn, he noticed that her foot was very swollen.

"What is wrong, child? Have you injured your foot?"

"I can barely walk on it, Father. I fell down a hole in the

forest."

"Where are your family? Does anyone help you?"

"Huh, I have no family. There was a woman, Hilda, who used to help me and give me food, but she died not long ago."

"I have heard of the woman. I believe she was here in the infirmary for a while. Sit here a while and when I've finished I will see to your foot."

The young girl looked appallingly thin and dirty, but she seemed very bright and intelligent, despite her appearance.

The poor came in dribs and drabs and several hours had passed before he could speak again to the girl. He found her curled up asleep against the priory wall. He shook her gently, but she just murmured something incomprehensible and closed her eyes again. On impulse he picked her up and took her to the nuns' infirmary.

It was Leoba who opened the door. Before she could utter a word, Brother John placed the young girl in her arms. "She barely weighs more than a dram. Feed her and see to her ankle. I am going to see the Prioress to make sure there will be no trouble."

The Prioress was occupied with Sister Agnes and Sister Marie Claire, discussing a rota of new readings for the chapter house and refectory. Brother John slipped along the cloister which led to the main convent. He knew he would need to have a very good reason to be admitted and much depended on who appeared at the grille on the heavy locked door.

It was the piercing cold eyes of Sister Ignatius which greeted him. "What are you doing here, Brother John?"

His heart sank. This would be a tough one. "I need to speak to Prioress Elizabeth. It is a matter which will not wait."

"What or who does this matter concern, Brother?"

"I am not able to discuss that, but it is urgent. Please …"

"I will ask the Prioress. Wait here."

It was perhaps easier than he thought, but he surmised, knowing something of the nature of Sister Ignatius that he had gleaned from Wencilian, she may be keen to discover what brought him there.

After a few moments she returned.

"The Prioress will see you now. Follow me."

There was not far to follow, the Prioress's office being near the entrance, strategically placed for her to receive any visitors without them encroaching any further into the convent.

Unbeknown to him, the Prioress had a particular fondness for him. It was not just his cheery nature, but his care of Sister Wencilian when she was a child that had endeared him to her, although she had never admitted that she knew about that. Secrets, she thought, secrets abound in this place, some darker than others, some to be revealed and some never to be known.

"Good day, Brother John. This is a pleasure. What can I do for you?"

All three prioresses smiled up at him as they sat around the table amass with papers.

"Please sit down with us."

Brother John was openly surprised by the greeting, but he was hoping to find Prioress Elizabeth alone. It would be unacceptable to request that now.

"Thank you, Sisters. It is a delicate matter. During the course of my duties this morning, I found a little beggar girl, who I had come across before; in fact she brought me herbs for the infirmary. She is a most intelligent child, but this morning she could not walk well. She has sustained an injury and seemed emaciated, close to death I fear. I took her straight away to the infirmary. I know I should have sought permission from you first of all, but the matter was urgent."

Prioress Elizabeth hesitated. "It is irregular, but if we can't help the needy, especially a child, then we would not be doing as our dear Lord expects of us. How is she now?"

"I don't know. I just left her with the young postulant at the door, instructed her to fetch Sister Wencilian or Sister Beatrice, and then I came here. Sister Wencilian will know what to do."

As he spoke the name 'Wencilian', the Prioress noticed that he stared straight into her eyes with the most intense look. She

259

shivered, it was as if he knew something, but how could he; no one could possibly know, except maybe Father Roger. Perhaps, she thought, it was just concern and fondness for Sister Wencilian that she had read in his eyes.

"Why didn't you instruct the postulant Leoba or Sister Wencilian to come to me?"

"I didn't really think. I suppose I wanted to let you know as soon as possible."

The Prioress felt Brother John to be a bit edgy and sensed that there could be another reason for his visit. She turned to Sisters Agnes and Marie Claire. "Sisters, I think we have concluded everything here. Would you mind instructing Sister Ignatius on the new rota for the readings?"

Once they were alone, the Prioress poured two glasses of her strong mead, guaranteed to relax her visitor.

"Tell me, Brother, how is Sister Wencilian? I have been so preoccupied of late I haven't had a chance to enquire of her."

"She is well I believe, but I rarely see her, only when chance may take me to the infirmary."

"Oh yes, she does a good job in the infirmary. I am reluctant to take her from there."

"Why? Do you need to?"

Brother John could see that the Prioress was disturbed. It seemed that she wanted to tell him something, but was not sure if it was the right thing to do. He certainly wanted to tell her something, but he knew it definitely was the wrong thing to do.

He added, "She has a talent for healing that's for certain, just as does Brother Gregory who is helping in the monks' infirmary."

"Brother Gregory?"

"He is a travelling friar, Mother, from Wales; says he has spent time with the Cistercians at Cwmhir Abbey in Powys. Do you know of it?"

"Oh yes, I have heard of a travelling friar who sings. I know a little of the Cistercians, but have never met any myself. What else do you know of this Brother Gregory?"

It was only a very flimsy chance but, she wondered, could he be connected in any way to Sister Wencilian, coming here from Wales and working so closely in the infirmary.

"Not a lot, Mother. He seems very knowledgeable and genial in his manner. He sings to the patients and it seems to soothe them a lot."

"I would like to meet him. Could you bring him to me, Brother John, after Prime tomorrow?"

"Of course, Prioress."

Was the Prioress thinking along the same lines as he or was she intrigued by the travelling monk's singing? Doubtful, Brother John assumed; she was more likely suspicious of a link to Wencilian.

"Do you want me to check with Father Roger?"

"No!" she asserted, a bit too quickly. "No, not at the moment. No need to bother him with trivial matters. I shall go to the infirmary and check on our new patient shortly. You did the right thing, but I'm not sure how many waifs and strays we can take in these days. The King's chancellor puts ever more demands on our resources. You say this girl is intelligent; if she recovers, maybe we can find her some work with the lay sisters for a while."

"I would like to know how she is. Could you keep me informed, Mother."

He had to keep some communication open with the Prioress. He couldn't let this go now and he was also concerned about the beggar girl. She reminded him so much of Wencilian at that age.

"Come with me, Brother, and see for yourself."

They walked in silence along the cloister, each absorbed in their own thoughts. The Prioress held her head high and several Sisters stood aside as the two passed, bowing their heads in reverence at the presence of their superiors. From the edge of a passage leading from the cloister, a figure lurking in the shadows turned to follow them, discreetly at a distance.

CHAPTER 39

Sempringham Priory

The patter of rain drops broke the silence of the balmy afternoon. The convent was at rest after the noon service of Sext, but Prioress Elizabeth worked on, although thinking of nothing but Sister Wencilian.

Sister Wencilian tended the patients, but could think of nothing but Cai and his tales of his homeland, Wales. As Sister Beatrice retired to her sleeping quarters, Wencilian crept out to the back of the infirmary hoping that Cai may be on the other side playing his music. She knew he had said he would be there after Compline, but she was so eager to talk with him again. All was silent apart from the snores of a few monks in the infirmary, which drifted over the wall. Well, she thought, it was raining after all and it was rest time. She must wait until the evening.

The little girl called 'Margred', whom Brother John had admitted, slept soundly. Her leg was healing well. She seemed so happy to be amongst the Sisters and her scrawny frame had definitely filled out in the few days since she had arrived. Bless Brother John, Wencilian thought; he would save the world if he could. She missed him a lot; their snatched moments of conversation were few and far between these days.

Alice was still a patient, although Wencilian knew she could not keep her in the infirmary for much longer. Her wounds had healed and her spirits had lifted considerably. Sister Beatrice would soon argue that she was fit to return to the main convent to resume her duties, but Wencilian knew that it might not be long before she would again become so despondent as to injure herself. It was the company of herself and Leoba, the constant care and watchful eyes that kept her from harm. She watched Leoba sitting with Alice in one of the small recesses behind the main room where the patients slept. In there was a quiet space with a table and two chairs, where she sometimes sat herself to do the clerical work of the infirmary when time allowed. Wencilian crept towards them, carefully trying not to disturb the patients.

"There is something I need to tell you both. I can't keep it to myself any longer, but you both must swear not to repeat anything I have said."

Leoba and Alice nodded in agreement, both speechless with anticipation, their eyes wide, fixed on Wencilian. Any news or gossip would brighten up the dreary day.

"I have been talking to Brother Gregory, the friar who plays the music and he has told me tales of a beautiful far off land, Wales. He told me of princes and how they fought the King for their country, but," she sighed, "the last Prince lost the battle and was later killed. Now King Edward rules the land of Wales."

"What happened to the Prince's family and his people?" Leoba asked, feeling strangely faint. She hoped the sight was not coming on her now,

"I don't know. He wanted to tell me more, but we had no time. He wants me to meet him after Compline."

"Be careful, Wencilian." Alice said looking concerned. "If you are seen, there could be awful punishment."

Wencilian took Alice's hand in hers. "Don't worry, I will be careful. I just have to hear more of what he has to say. I can't stop now."

At that moment, a door opened at the far end of the infirmary. The three Sisters heard voices, one male, one female, coming towards them.

"Wait here, Father. I will find Sister Wencilian to prepare the patients."

Sister Agnes was marching towards her. "Ah, Sister Wencilian, Father Bernard has come to hear confession from the patients and yourselves. We have been a little lax with the patients recently, they will never find redemption or heal if they do not confess their sins more often. Can you prepare them?"

"Yes, Sister."

Wencilian shot a look at Alice. She hoped she would not weaken or be foolish enough to confess what she had just told her. Leoba she could trust; she would make up some petty sins to confess to placate the priest and find it amusing. Herself, she was flustered for a moment, but whilst preparing the patients, she had a few minutes to think and she resolved only to confess that she should pray more for her patients.

Sister Agnes left them alone with Father Bernard, as Sister Beatrice emerged sleepily from her room.

Brother John was about to finish distributing the alms when an elderly man, whom he took to be a merchant, approached. He pulled a small trailer which gave off a very pungent aroma.

"Brother, allow me to introduce myself. I am Harold from Grantham and I come to offer your priory a wonderful array of spices and herbs. Would you allow me to enter?"

Brother John regarded him a little suspiciously. He had never seen him before. He was not one of the usual merchants they saw from time to time; his accent was strange, but also familiar somehow.

"Let me see what you have," he replied, examining the contents of his trailer. "It is not for me to say. It will be the cellarer or the infirmarian who decides what we will have, but I do have experience in these matters, having been the cellarer myself at one time."

The collection of spices and herbs seemed impressive enough for Brother John ... nutmeg, ginger, the dried berries of juniper, black pepper, saffron, cloves, cinnamon, would all be useful in the kitchen. Raw frankincense was always required in the church, and black henbane, hemlock and tormentil were sought after regularly for use in the infirmary, but only to be handled by very experienced hands. He was surprised to see olive bark too ... highly prized.

"Wait here if you will, Harold of Grantham, and I will ask permission for your entry."

Brother John returned within minutes with the cellarer, Brother Francis.

"Let us go to the kitchens first and see what we need or what we can afford," exclaimed Brother Francis. "The infirmary can decide for themselves what they need."

Brother John followed, eager to see the result of this visit and, as Brother Francis and the merchant Harold chatted, he realised where he had heard that accent before. It sounded just like the accent of Brother Gregory, the singing friar.

When business in the kitchen was done and Harold, the merchant, had taken some refreshment, the cellarer left it to Brother John to escort him to the infirmary.

"Where are you from originally, sir?" Brother John enquired. "Your accent is not local to these regions, I feel."

"You are right, Brother. I am from Wales originally, but have lived in Grantham for many years."

Hywel knew it would serve no purpose to lie about his origins. He had changed his name, but could not change his voice so easily. He just hoped that it would not arouse any suspicion or cause anyone to link him to Cai in any way.

But Brother John already had his suspicions about Brother Gregory, and his suspicions were confirmed when the two men were introduced in the infirmary. They each made a small bow to each other and exchanged formalities, but Brother John was not unaware of the look which passed between them or the surprise on Brother Gregory's face, which he had tried to cover not too successfully. Brother Gilbert on the other hand noticed nothing, as no one else would who had not already gleaned an insight into some deep secret which was about to be uncovered.

CHAPTER 40

Sempringham Priory

Cai uncurled the note that Hywel had surreptitiously passed him whilst Brother Gilbert was perusing the box of powerful herbs and roots. It was now several hours later that he had a chance to read it while he walked to the kitchens to collect supper for the patients.

The instructions on the note were brief. He was to bring Gwenllian to meet Hywel by the edge of the forest which lay about half an acre from the Priory on the edge of the marshy fenland, just as Philip had told him. From there they would make their way to a boat which would take them out to sea to join the ship which was to offer them passage to France. And they were to meet on Lammas Eve. The question though, Cai thought, was how was he to get Gwenllian out of the convent? No one was going to help him.

He destroyed the note in the fireplace, where a young monk sat over a pot of bubbling broth. It was opportune that Hywel had found him in the infirmary, or perhaps not; Hywel may have planned that carefully. He knew that Hywel would not take any random chances on such a dangerous mission.

Cai carried a large pannier of bread and cheese back to the infirmary, accompanied by a young monk carrying a pitcher of ale and another monk who trailed behind carrying a pan of broth. Brother Gilbert liked all the sick monks who were capable to sit around the infirmary table for meals and for prayer, but they ate in silence, which for once Cai was glad of. He was in no mood for conversation; he had a lot to think about. He would have to speak to Gwenllian tonight. There was no time to lose.

The Priory was already starting to prepare for Lammas and the feast commemorating St Peter's miraculous deliverance from prison, which may cause them to be distracted. Most of the fen people though, Cai guessed, would be celebrating the harvest, which had not been at all bad this year. Most of those poor people would be eagerly awaiting a decent meal and some would be giving their thanks to the land on which their survival depended and on which the old pagan gods still stalked.

He thought of Seren and his kin. They would be preparing for Lughnasadh, their Lammas ritual, to offer their thanks too for the bounty of the earth and prepare themselves for the descent into the dark time of the year. That's where he should be, but now he wondered if he would ever see them again. How long would it be before they could get Gwenllian safely back from France? He may have to stay there for years. If that was the case though, he considered, all may not be lost; there was a glimmer of hope for him to seek his other lost treasure, his love, Celeste. All he should consider now was how to talk to Gwenllian and how to get her out of the Priory safely. His time was short. He should have acted sooner, he had been lulled by the rhythm of the day to day life in the Priory and time had escaped him.

After Compline, the Priory was quiet. In the monastery most of the canons retired to their cells and the novices to the dorter to grab a few hours of sleep before Matins. There were three however who could not settle: Brother John, Father Roger and the Sacristan. Sleep eluded them all, each wrapped in their own thoughts. Brother Gilbert retired to his quarters at the back of the infirmary. Cai went to his small room to wait. He had administered a sleeping draught to several of the more troublesome patients. When he heard Brother Gilbert's loud snores he would go to the wall to see if Gwenllian waited for him.

In the convent too, a blanket of silence fell. The Prioress Elizabeth however sat with a glass of her finest wine, surrounded by parchments that needed attention, but she had a more immediate problem to solve. The soft footsteps of Sister Ignatius crept along the cloister. She was almost practised in the art of invisibility; if anyone caught of glimpse of her she would appear as a shadow or a phantom of the night.

Sister Wencilian lay on her pallet until all was quiet. Alice and Margred were asleep, and the three other patients, elderly nuns, were dozing fitfully. She could hear the soft snores of Sister Beatrice drifting from her sleeping place at the end of the infirmary, separated by only a thick curtain. Only Leoba, who had now been given a bed next to Wencilian, lay awake, and although her eyes were closed, she had no intention of sleeping. Thinking all was safe, Wencilian crept out to the back of the infirmary.

Barely daring to breathe, she stood close to the wall. Then she heard footsteps approaching on the other side of the wall. She coughed to make her presence known. If it was Brother Gregory on the other side he might know it was her. If it was Brother Gilbert or another monk he would assume she was a restless patient. But Cai too had to take extreme care. It could be Sister Beatrice taking some night air.

"Are you well, Sister?" he enquired.

"I am feeling better now that I know it is you," answered Wencilian.

"Oh Gw … Oh, Sister Wencilian. Thank the Gods," Cai stuttered, feeling more nervous than he ever had done, even facing Llywelyn's enemies.

Wencilian giggled. He spoke in a strange way. She was glad that the wall separated them or she wouldn't know quite how to act in front of him.

"Have you any more tales to tell me, Brother?"

Cai relaxed a little and sunk to the ground against the wall.

"Tales, dear Sister, I have told tales much of my life and sang them too, to many people at many courts. But that was many years ago. Some were true tales of glory or defeat in battle, some were legends buried in antiquity, some were tales of despair and sadness, some tales of magic, immense power and inspiration. The tale I have to tell you, Wencilian, is a tale which combines all these elements, and it is true, more true than any tale I have ever told. I have to tell you now, Wencilian, because it concerns you, your family, your life that you should be living, your true heritage as a princess."

There was silence as Wencilian stood stunned on her side of the wall.

Cai continued. "Don't go. Please Sister, sit and listen to me. There may not be another chance."

Wencilian slumped down against the wall, transfixed. Whether this man was a madman possessed or true in his heart she did not know, but she wanted to hear, hear so much, about a family she may have, even if it be pure fantasy.

"I'm here, I'm listening, Brother."

There was really only one way to say what he had to say, and that was directly. "Your true name, Sister, is Gwenllian. You are the one and only daughter of the Prince of Wales and his wife, Eleanor de Montfort. You were born on 12th June 1282 at Garth Celyn, a court of your father's. And I was there."

Cai could now only bluntly tell Gwenllian the story of her birth, her parents' deaths, her capture, the plan to free her. There was no point now in softening or embellishing the truth. But he would not tell her everything; it was too soon and she was not ready. On their journey, there would be time, plenty of time to talk. He knew she would have many questions to ask. He told her a little of the dedication and bravery of her father, the special qualities her mother possessed.

Gwenllian listened as the words bounced over the wall and hit hard in her heart.

"I will only call you Gwenllian from now on, for that is your name, but there is no time to tell you more now. In four days' time we must leave this place. Please trust me, you will be safe. I cannot guarantee it will be easy, but you will eventually get back to the land of your birth where there are still people who will love you. You are a prisoner here, not a free woman."

"But if what you say is true ..." Gwenllian sobbed, tears streaming down her face, her heart thumping as loud as a thunder clap. "I will be hunted by the King, for surely he will not let me ever be free."

"We are to wait in France until it is safe. We have the protection of some powerful people."

"How do I know that what you say is not some wild fantasy?"

"Believe me, I would not be here if it were. I have no wish to be in this place. Although it is not unpleasant, it is a poor life compared to the life I had before. I want for nothing here except true nourishment of the spirit, freedom, life and love. I made a vow to your father that I would protect you and tutor you, and I will fulfil that duty, as I failed when you were a babe and for that I am truly sorry. You know that you don't belong here either. Can you say that you are truly devout?"

Gwenllian felt some compassion for this man who seemed to be dedicating his life to saving her from something she knew nothing about. "I can hear footsteps somewhere. I must go. How can you prove to me you are the man you claim to be?"

"I have this ring. It was your mother's; her name is engraved inside. I promised your father, before he departed for his last battle that I would keep it for you until you married. But I will give it to you now if it will prove my honour. Please keep this, whatever you decide you must do. Stand and I will throw it to you. Tomorrow night we must meet here again at this time and work out how to get you outside of these walls."

Gwenllian picked up the ring and saw that it was gold and was inscribed with the name of Eleanor de Montfort and the date 1278. A wedding ring, she knew, although she had only ever seen one before, and slipping it on her finger, it fitted perfectly.

"Beautiful."

A voice spoke from the infirmary door. Gwenllian gasped, but was relieved to see Leoba standing facing her.

"Oh, Leoba, how much ...?"

"Have I heard?" Leoba cut in. "Most of it I think. Forgive me, but I had a strong sense that something momentous was about to take place and this, Sister, or should I call you Gwenllian, is certainly momentous."

"Oh Leoba, what shall I do? I am too confused to think. He wants me to leave this place and he says that I am a princess of a country I know nothing of. How do I know he tells the truth?"

"Would he have much reason to lie about all that?"

"He could be mad or worse, wanting to abduct a maiden."

Leoba was silent for a moment, and then she took Wencilian by the hand. "Do you remember what my mother Hilda said? She said that you were of noble birth. My mother was never wrong with the sight. She knew that there was another life for you, that you were special, and that is one reason why she wanted me to stay with you."

"Did you know about any of this?"

"No, only what my mother said, but I do get the sight, like her. Sometimes I don't wish for it either. It can be a burden, but I have learnt to control it more now. If my mother was here, she would know what to do. I think you can trust him, but we need to know for sure."

"I have my mother's ring, Leoba, my mother's wedding ring. I was not abandoned, nor left for the wolves. I had a family, a brave and noble family. I shall treasure this forever."

It seemed to Leoba that Gwenllian had already decided her fate. Leoba hoped she was not already too enraptured by romantic tales.

CHAPTER 41

Sempringham Priory

The bell rang for Matins, jolting Cai from his dream. He had slept for only a short time after tossing fitfully, eventually succumbing to sheer exhaustion. In his dream he was in a dark and wild forest where Seren spoke to him. "Do not fail, Cai. You have nearly completed your mission. The true fulfilment is yet to come; remember your training. Know thy power, know thy wisdom, know thy time. You are not alone, Cai."

But Cai did feel alone. He had never felt so alone, even in this place full of monks and the ethereal presence of many nuns he never saw. No one, apart from Seren and Hywel knew what was in his mind, his heart, or soul for that matter. At the moment he had to act very much independently. Maybe he was mad, maybe he should never have taken on this task. His life could be at stake, and that of his Princess. He could put her in danger and take her from a life that was safe, albeit austere, the only life she knew. But she was young. She must have a chance; he knew he must also honour his promise. The old life had gone and there was always hope for the future. As the wheel of life turned, their chance would come again.

Brother Gilbert snored on, so Cai crept out of the infirmary, but not to tread the stairs to the church for the service; he needed to continue exploring more ways of leaving this place. He had not been idle. Whenever he could sneak a chance, he had searched for possible ways of escaping with Gwenllian. He was more or less free to go when he wished, but if he were to leave suddenly on Lammas Eve it would, without doubt, arouse suspicion. And he had to rescue Gwenllian from behind the locked doors of the nunnery. He had heard some of the older monks talking about a labyrinth of tunnels which were once used by monks fleeing danger or even injured soldiers seeking safety. He listened to their tales which had been passed down through generations of monks since the setting up of the Priory in the year 1135. They told of a lawless and brutal age during the reign of King Stephen when it was said 'God and his saints slept'. Whether any of the tunnels were still used, he didn't know, but they had talked of one which led off the granary and had been used in recent times by an errant monk escaping punishment.

The granary was still and quiet save for a few mice, and the only light was a shaft of the silver moonlight which gleamed through the open door. Cai fumbled a little in the half light, wondering where to start. Save for some sacks of grain stacked against the walls, the place was nearly empty, waiting to be refilled with the yield of the new harvest. He got down on his hands and knees and started feeling the floor when he heard a sound behind him. He stood abruptly and turned to see Brother John holding up a candle.

"I'm surprised you didn't bring one of these with you if you are searching for something, Brother Gregory, or could it be that you hoped no one would see you?"

Cai was stunned for a moment. "I was here earlier in the day and I dropped my knife. I don't like to be without it. I need it in the infirmary and of course for eating."

"I think you had better tell me what you are up to, Brother, and what business you have with Sister Wencilian, or Father Roger will get to hear of this."

"What do you mean, Brother John?"

"I mean that I have overheard some of the things you have told Sister Wencilian at the back of the infirmary. Sounds travel on a still night." He had only heard snippets of their conversation, but needed to bend the truth to get a confession from this friar, whoever he was.

The look of shock on Cai's face was enough to convince Brother John. He could not reveal to anyone what he had heard by the confessional box, but he had enough information to question this Welsh friar on what he now deduced to be an extremely grave situation.

"Don't worry," he continued sardonically. "No one else heard it, I'm sure. This is between you and me at the moment."

"Are you spying on me, Brother?"

"Sister Wencilian is very dear to me. She has been here since she was a babe and she has been almost like a daughter to me," he sighed, "and I hope she thinks of me almost as the father she never had. Even though now she has taken vows, I see her rarely. I am always vigilant and I have my contacts who keep an eye on her."

"Then if you treat her like a daughter, you must know that what you may have heard is genuine and I have her interests totally at heart."

Cai's heart was thumping; he had come this far and now this old monk could ruin all his plans, he needed to find out what Brother John knew.

"Who are you really, Brother Gregory? I know you are planning to escape with her, so you may as well tell me."

Brother John touched the knife in his pouch; he had never used it to harm another but he would defend himself if needs be.

Cai saw the threat in his eyes. He was stuck. The only way to redeem this situation was to sway Brother John with the truth.

"If you care so much for her, Brother, sit and listen to my story. I was her guardian, a close confidante of her father and mother, a bard of the court."

"The court?" Brother John wanted reiteration of what he had heard from the confessional. He needed to know the exact truth.

"The court of Prince Llywelyn, the last Prince of Wales, the father of Sister Wencilian, whose real name is Gwenllian."

And so Cai continued to tell how he tried to take her safety, how she was captured and a little of how the plan to return her to her homeland had unfolded.

Brother John listened in silence, enraptured by what seemed

a fantastic tale, and he found he could not doubt Cai's sincerity when he told it, although he reminded himself that this man was a singer and would have a gift for telling tales. But he had heard the words of Prioress Elizabeth and the facts fitted together. Thinking of his little Wencilian as a princess made his heart almost burst with emotion; he had always known she was special. Tears streamed down his face; the thought of losing her was tumultuous. He had never even considered that she would ever leave this place, having taken her vows.

Cai saw how this Brother loved Gwenllian and felt a pang of regret at tearing more lives apart. "I am so sorry, Brother. You obviously care very much for her, but she belongs in her homeland and deserves to know of her family. I hope you will honour that."

"I understand, but she will be put in danger and this is the only life she knows." Brother John almost choked on his words. "If what you say is completely true, then the King will hunt her down, and you need to take care because I think the Prioress has her watched carefully too, by Sister Ignatius."

Almost at once he thought he may have said too much in his emotional state.

"Why does the Prioress have her watched, Brother? What does she know?" Cai demanded, raising his voice.

"I really don't know, but I overheard a conversation between the Prioress and a priest. It seems she receives a sum from the King for Sister Wencilian each year. The King's chancellor left some papers on the table, which she saw, I gather. When I heard that I was intrigued and suspicious. As far as Wencilian herself, she believed, and most of the Priory believed, she had been abandoned as a babe by a poor family possibly. I don't think the Prioress knows the whole truth, but she is trying to find out."

Brother John knew he had revealed too much, but at least had not admitted to overhearing it from the confessional box.

"Will you help me, Brother John?"

"Help her escape? I don't know, Brother. If I don't, it will be for my own selfish reasons; to keep her here and prevent punishment for myself. If I do, I could put her in danger, but I think if it is what she wants, I could not deny her; after all I am old and may not be here to help her for long."

"I will not put you in any danger, Brother, just help me plan a way of getting her from behind that wall and I will do the rest."

"I need to speak to her first, then I will make my decision. This candle burns low. We must return or we will be missed."

Cai grabbed Brother John's arm. "Trust me, Brother, and I will trust you. We both want what is best for Gwenllian."

"She will always be Sister Wencilian to me."

Brother John closed the door of the granary. It was a heavy weight, as was the burden he now carried. Perhaps he should pray for guidance. He made his way towards the church, Matins would be over and most of the canons reading in the chapter house or sleeping. As he crossed the courtyard, silent wings, silver tipped in the moonlight swept over his head.

"Boden, my dear friend," Brother John muttered.

From behind an arch of the cloister, he glimpsed the white scapular of a nun. He could not see, but instinctively thought it to be Sister Ignatius, skulking, scheming, a deceiver.

Boden flew in front of him. Always the protector, he thought, and how the moonlight illuminates them both. If only the truth were so easy to perceive.

CHAPTER 42

Sempringham Priory

"Gwenllian, Gwenllian, Gwenllian." Gwenllian repeated the name to herself over and over again, trying her best to pronounce it the way Brother Gregory, or was she to call him 'Cai', had.

Her fingers traced the edge of the ring in her hand. She had sought permission from Sister Beatrice to return to her own cell after the noon service, but would have come there even if she had refused. This little room gave her some connection to who she was, or who she had been. She wasn't sure if she was crying or laughing as tears flooded from her, soaking her scapular, but she couldn't have held it in much longer. Eighteen years of pent up feelings poured from her.

"I have a mother, a mother who would have loved me, a noble woman, and a father who was a Prince," she blurted out loud, not caring who may hear.

The only one to hear was Leoba, who had followed her and waited discreetly outside the cell, but at this point rushed in.

"Please keep your voice down. I know you must be totally overcome with emotion, but it is too dangerous to risk being overheard, Wencilian, or should I say Gwenllian?"

"Oh Leoba, why would I be treated so? This Welsh man tells me that all my family are dead. I should be grateful to have been spared, but why would God himself let them all be killed and not me as well? If not for Cai, I may have gone all my life without knowing any of this. Do you think Prioress Elizabeth knows?

What should I do?"

"I don't know, dear Sister. I cannot answer any of these questions for you. If I were you and I could be sure it was true, I would go from the Priory, no matter how dangerous. I would not spend my life cooped up in here."

"You do not belong here, Leoba. I have been here all my life. I really know nothing of the world outside these walls."

"You do not belong here either, Wencilian. It seems you are a princess who has a duty to keep the knowledge of your family alive."

"Perhaps I do have a duty, Leoba. If I go, you too must come with me. It will break my heart to leave Alice, Isobel, Brother John and a few of my dear Sisters, but maybe my true calling is in that land far from here, not in the misty fenlands of eastern England. But Leoba, I know you are waiting for your father to come one day."

"My father, ah, I have doubts that he will ever come now. I will come with you Wencilian. I will not stay here without you."

"Who is your father? Have you ever known him?"

"No. My mother said he was one of the fairy people, but now I'm older, I think he may have been one of the travelling people who would stay with us sometimes."

Gwenllian looked into her delicate pale face with its elfin like features and ethereal beauty. If ever there was such a thing as a fairy child, she could be one. That thought had struck her that night in Hilda's hut when they helped Mira to run away. Mira, dear Mira, she went through the tunnel for her that night, so she could do it again.

"Leoba, I have an idea, but I need to speak to this Brother Gregory, or Cai, as he is called."

"I will be there, Gwenllian, whatever you decide. And that is the only name I shall call you now, your true name."

"You can't. No one else must know about this, not yet. If we are to leave, we must act as if nothing has happened. Brother Gregory says we must leave on Lammas Eve. It is only five days away. How can I be sure it will be safe?"

"I don't think we can be sure, we just have to trust in …"

"In what? Do I trust in God? Has God protected me so far?"

"Well, I don't know much about your God, only what the Sisters here drum into me, and most of it I do not hear. You must trust in yourself."

"I have never really learned to do that. In here we are told only to trust in God, or Our Lady, of course."

"You have a strong will, Gwenllian, and a strong spirit. Your father was a warrior, your mother a brave, noble woman. Stand up, Gwenllian, and show that world outside who you truly are."

Gwenllian looked into the elfin face of Leoba. Her delicate features hid a worldliness and wisdom way beyond her years. No one would ever guess her true nature, she thought, disguised as she was in her nun's robes. Not much more than a child, but more of a woman than herself.

"I want you to go back to the infirmary, Leoba, and tell Sister Beatrice that I have been summoned by the Prioress after cleaning my cell. That will excuse me for a while. There are a few things I must attend to."

"What are you going to do, Gwenllian?"

"Shh! I am still Sister Wencilian until I leave this place."

I need courage not tears, Gwenllian told herself as she slipped into the Lady Chapel and stood before the altar to pray. This was the only place since she had been a young child where she felt a true sense of peace and could enjoy a few precious moments alone. It was the only place where she felt her prayers were heard. The Lady had heard all her sorrows, all her rambling thoughts as a child that she could share with no one else. It had been a lonely childhood, with no siblings or friends of her own age. The Lady had shown her the tunnel concealed beneath her, now that tunnel could lead to her freedom. Scrambling underneath the altar, a place where no other nun would ever go unless they knew of the tunnel, she felt for the stone. The stone was loose, as she had left it the night she went out with Mira. That night was meant to be, she thought, for she knew the tunnel was safe, although the thought of crawling through it again filled her with horror. No one had been here since that night, no one knew.

The cloister was quiet, all the Sisters would be at their duties again after the noon service of Sext and their rest period. Gwenllian approached the Prioress's office unsure of what to say, but she had to cover her tracks. If Sister Beatrice questioned her she would not have to lie. Anyway it was about time she faced the Prioress, not revealing that she knew anything but looking for any clues she may pick up.

The Prioress seemed pleased to admit her although she stressed that it was unusual to see her at this time without a prior arrangement having been made that morning in the chapter house.

"Forgive me, Mother, it slipped my mind this morning after the reading, but I felt it could wait no longer. I am concerned about Sister Alice. She is now in better health, but is very fragile. Sister Beatrice wishes to send her back to her duties, but I fear she is not ready."

"Well, Sister Wencilian, it was only an accident that injured her, wasn't it? If she is healed then I see no reason to keep her in the infirmary."

Thinking quickly was a trait Gwenllian was always grateful for. "She has confided in me that she feels still very weak. She looks pale and can barely stand for long some days. I think there is something not right with her blood. Sister Beatrice thinks she is malingering."

"Very well, I will have a word with Sister Beatrice."

Gwenllian flushed. "I would be grateful if you could see her for yourself, otherwise Sister Beatrice would not be pleased with me at all, if she knew I had requested this."

The Prioress was silent for a few moments, thinking that this was a very unusual request. What was the real problem? Was Wencilian so obsessed with the girl? She had observed their close friendship and hoped it wasn't unhealthy. But at the moment she had bigger thoughts on her mind.

"Very well, I am due a visit to the infirmary; I'll see what I can do," she replied, feeling a pang of guilt.

"Thank you, Mother." Gwenllian was relieved.

"I am glad you have come, because I was going to send for you. I want you to leave the infirmary for a while and help me here. I have so much administration to do that I need some extra help and you are accomplished in that area. Your duties must be tiresome in the infirmary."

Gwenllian felt her stomach lurch. "Mother Elizabeth, I love working in the infirmary and I am sure that there are other Sisters who could be of more help to you than me."

"I didn't realise that you enjoyed your work so much. I think the change would benefit you, but I will give you another week to help Alice and I will find a suitable replacement. It is only temporary; you can perhaps return there before long."

Gwenllian knew it was of no use to say any more. No one argued with the Prioress. At least she had a week's reprieve, by which time she should be gone. Why did the Prioress want her so close? She knew something about her, that was certain, but how much she had no idea. A thought then occurred to her. This could be opportune; if she started straight away she could rout for information. But would it restrict her too much? In the infirmary, she had a little more freedom and that was vital to her escape, but the temptation to possibly uncover something in this office was enticing.

"Prioress, maybe I could join you for one day here before the next week to see if I am suitable."

"I am sure you are, but very well, I will agree to that. Be here after the chapter house meeting in two days."

With that she was dismissed and returned to the infirmary with mixed emotions swirling around inside her. She pictured her feelings like whirls of exploding colours, like the ones she had seen on the tapestries in the office. Soon her life could be full of colour and excitement, danger too, but it wouldn't be shrouded in black and grey any more. She smiled to herself, her confidence was growing. A figure was walking the cloister towards her, a male figure and she smiled even more when she saw it was Brother John. But Brother John did not return her smile; his face was stern and drawn as he pulled her gently into a side passage which led to the store rooms.

CHAPTER 43

Sempringham Priory

"Wencilian, I have been to the infirmary hoping to find you. You could be in great danger and I am so worried about you."

"Brother John, whatever is it?"

"I think you know well what it is. I have spoken to Brother Gregory and I know what he plans. You should have come to me."

"Oh, Brother John, all this has been an enormous shock for me. I have only just found out things myself which defy all reason but seem to be true. And I hardly get a chance to see you. What has Cai ... Brother Gregory ... told you, and why did he?"

"He didn't have much choice, but never mind that. You can't possibly leave here and go with this man; you are a nun who has taken vows." Brother John released the hold on her arm and took a deep breath. "Wencilian, what he told me may not be true, but if it is and all your family are dead, where would you go? You know you can trust me; I will not betray you."

Gwenllian took the hand of her dear friend. "Brother John, I'm relieved that you know and I would love to tell you more, but all I know is that he has to leave in a few days' time. It breaks my heart to leave you and the few that I love here, but it may be my only chance to ever see my home country, and there are people who will shelter me."

"Forgive me, I should kneel down to you, if you are indeed this Princess Gwenllian. I know it is not right that you are imprisoned here. I should not stand in your way. Maybe I am a selfish old man. I do not want to lose you, even though I may only ever have an occasional fleeting conversation with you these days."

The words 'Princess' and 'Gwenllian' had never been uttered to her before, together.

"Maybe God has protected me after all and saved me for this day to return to my people. I gather courage hour by hour and know now that this is the right thing to do. I must return now to the infirmary or I will be in trouble, and nothing must foil my plan now. Pray that I can see you again and talk before I go."

"I will make sure of it, Wencilian."

But Brother John walked away with a heavy heart. He needed to keep a close eye on this Welsh man. He could easily denounce him, but it may rebound on Wencilian and somehow he could not prevent his Wencilian from following her heart in this matter ... but should he let her be exposed to danger? Who knows where this man would lead her, and if she were caught either by the Priory or the King's men, there could be disastrous consequences. She was naive in the ways of the world. He himself had lived in the outside world until the age of eighteen and had regularly ventured out with other canons since then. Every day he witnessed the cruelty of poverty and disease as he distributed alms to the wretched people at the gate, and they were the lucky ones.

Cai kept low in the infirmary following his encounter with Brother John. He should have been more careful. He called on his God and Goddess to protect Gwenllian and to guide them both. If the old monk got in his way, he may have to do something drastic. He did not want to hurt anyone, but there was too much at stake. He knew that any act of violence would rebound on him at some stage, be it in this life or another, but it was a risk he would take to free Gwenllian. He had failed so far and what would his life be if he failed again to protect her? She was entrusted into his care as a babe and he had let her be stolen. The life she had been forced to lead had been his fault. Nothing would stop him now.

He waited until several hours after Compline. Brother Gilbert and the patients all slept, several helped along by his sleeping draught. As the shadow of dusk spread, eclipsing the daylight, he stood waiting by the wall. Time passed, but she did not come. Such was his faith that he had not seriously considered that she may disbelieve him, turn on him, denounce him. Then he heard a rustle of skirts and gentle footsteps on the other side ... and a cough, the sign they had agreed on.

"Gwenllian, there is so much I want to say to you, but it is too dangerous now; we could be overheard."

"That could be. I have spoken to Brother John today. Why did you tell him?

"I had no choice, but I pray he will not betray us."

"He won't betray me, but he may try to stop me."

"We must leave on Lammas Eve. I have been trying to explore tunnels, a way to get you out of here."

"Listen to me, I know of a tunnel I have used once before, it comes out by the west wall of the Priory. There is a path just beyond which leads to the forest, and one which leads into the deeper fen land. I can meet you there."

Cai was astounded that she had been outside before and that she had hatched this plan already. "Well, Sister, you do surprise me. Wait by the opening. I will lead you to the edge of the forest where we will meet with our guide."

"What about you, how will you leave?"

"I am free to come and go, but it may look suspicious if I suddenly leave after dark. Leave that to me. Don't worry, I'll be there."

"Brother, there is someone I must bring with me. She is special, she doesn't belong here. I cannot leave her."

"This could jeopardise our mission. Can you trust her?

"Can I trust you, Brother Gregory? You have fooled many here already?"

"You have my word; you had the ring, my Princess. I can do no more to convince you, only say that what I have told you is entirely the truth. I understand that you are wary and afraid."

284

Doubts crept up in her mind. Earlier in the day she had been so sure, but now it occurred to her that it could be a plot, a plot to kill the last surviving member of the Llywelyn family. But what danger did she pose to anyone, locked away in here?

"Gwenllian, we may not talk again until Lammas Eve, but be assured I will not let you down, and I have so much to tell you. You have cousins, Gwenllian, but they are imprisoned too. Maybe one day we can free them. I want to tell you about your mother, father, and the life they had. I could teach you our language. I will care for you, have no fear. "

"Cousins! Where are they? Listen … someone comes, I must go."

There was no time for a reply; Sister Beatrice was approaching the rear of the infirmary.

"Is that you, Sister Wencilian? What are you doing out here?"

"Er, I couldn't sleep, Sister. I needed some air."

"Well, you had best try. I am locking this door now. I think there is a storm coming; the air is heavy. We have a busy day tomorrow; the Prioress is coming for an inspection. It will be time for Matins before we can barely get our heads down."

Heavy and close was the atmosphere that night. Every day brought a new shocking revelation turning Gwenllian's life as she knew it upside down, disturbing her thoughts and her sleep. Now she had been told that she had cousins. Would she ever see them? There was no doubt more chance of that if she were to leave this place.

CHAPTER 44

Sempringham Priory

Prioress Elizabeth arrived in the infirmary with Sister Marie Clare after the service of Terce. Sister Beatrice had sent Sister Wencilian and Leoba to the service so that she could be alone to make some last minute adjustments to the infirmary records without interference. It was rare for the Prioresses to make an impromptu inspection in between the twice-yearly ones. This had made Sister Beatrice nervous.

The three nuns were pouring over the infirmary records when Gwenllian and Leoba arrived back and busied themselves with administering tisanes and draughts to the patients, where necessary changing linen on the pallets. Isobel had come early that morning with clean linen, and Gwenllian, being so pleased to see her and thinking she may never see her again, had hugged her close. Isobel, surprised and being sharp as she was, could recognise something was brewing.

Sister Beatrice looked pleased with herself as the two Prioresses moved on to talk to the patients. Tagging behind them, Gwenllian soaked up every word. There was an air of efficiency and calm, but she was inwardly trembling, trying to cover her nervousness. She kept a constant eye on Prioress Elizabeth, especially when she approached Alice.

She had battled with herself all through the previous night, wondering whether she should tell Alice or even take her with them. It could be too risky and Alice was quite fragile; it wasn't a total untruth that she had told the Prioress. If she said nothing, Alice would no doubt feel it to be a great betrayal when she realised she had been left behind. Alice had to stay in the infirmary until Lammas Eve whatever she was to decide.

She rushed to Alice's side as the Prioress began to question her, taking Alice's hand in hers.

"Sister Beatrice tells me that you are quite recovered and that you have been in here quite long enough, but how do you feel yourself?" the Prioress enquired.

Gwenllian cut across before Alice could answer. "She is so weak; I think there must be something else which ails her, and she misses her family so much."

The Prioress scowled. "I am sure Sister Alice can speak for herself, Sister Wencilian. Alice?"

"It is as Sister Wencilian says, Mother. I can barely stand some days and my body aches so. I have no appetite, but I am not afraid to work; I am not malingering."

The Prioress was undecided and really didn't have much patience for these matters. She was eager to finish this inspection and return to her office to attend to her piles of administration. Something told her that at this pivotal time she did not want to upset Sister Wencilian either. Was that guilt, she wondered, or the feeling that she was on the verge of discovering something hidden, some coveted information? A letter had arrived that morning from Father Thomas, but it lay unopened on her desk.

The Prioress spoke to Sister Beatrice. "I think Alice should stay here for a while, but she should attempt to attend mass. That will not impede her progress, only enhance it, and the walk to the church will gradually strengthen her limbs. She should be encouraged to walk the cloisters whenever she can and help with simple tasks here in the infirmary."

That was a good solution, Gwenllian thought, satisfactory for all, although Sister Beatrice did not look impressed.

When walking back from Terce, Gwenllian had been able to tell Leoba exactly what had transpired between herself and Cai on the previous evening. She explained about the tunnel and told her of her concerns about Alice. She left out her concerns about Brother John; the young girl had enough to occupy her thoughts.

"Are you sure, Leoba, are you really sure you want to come with me?" she had questioned her again, sternly. She had to be sure.

Leoba had replied that she would follow Gwenllian anywhere and that her mother must have foreseen what would happen and that was why she had chosen Sister Wencilian to be at her side.

"I only hope I am worthy of your faith," Gwenllian had replied.

Today, Gwenllian wanted to savour every moment in the infirmary. Tomorrow she would be helping the Prioress, and the following day would be her last, her very last day in the only home she had ever known. She talked to Alice as much as she could, but still mentioned nothing about the escape. There was not much time to decide what to do about Alice. It could be, she considered, that Alice, if told, might refuse to go anyway. It was doubtful that she would ever betray her, but they might put pressure on her and punish her, knowing the closeness between them. Was it safe to leave her? Was it better that she knew nothing at all? Or would she pine away and feel betrayed left behind?

"Oh Lord, please help me. What should I do?" she muttered as she tidied up the still room, thinking herself alone. But her mutterings had been loud enough for Sister Beatrice to hear as she entered the room.

"What is it that worries you so, Sister Wencilian, to call on our Lord so earnestly?"

"Oh Sister, I want to help Alice, but really don't know what ails her or what I should do," she replied, not dishonestly, bending her head to try and hide the flush which spread across her face.

"You worry too much about that girl. In my mind, it is not healthy. Other patients need your attention too."

"Yes, Sister, you are right. How is the young girl Brother

John brought in? What will happen to her?" Gwenllian asked, thinking any diversion was welcome.

"I spoke to the Prioress about her. She is willing to give her a position in the kitchens with the lay sisters when she is healed. That will be on trial of course."

"I am glad of that. I'm sure she will be suitable and very grateful. You know, Sister, that I am to help the Prioress tomorrow and she wants me to work with her for a while soon. I would rather stay here, Sister, but I have to obey Mother Elizabeth."

"I'm sure. I do not want to lose you, Sister Wencilian, for you are very capable and have a way with the patients, I must admit. Your knowledge is indispensable. It will take me a long time to train someone else. I am glad that Leoba has been a quick learner, but she is very young and only a postulant after all; she will have to return to her studies soon. The Prioress mentioned that Sister Ignatius would be helping me."

"She has no stomach for it," Gwenllian replied, tersely. "She has no way either with those who are sick and need patience."

She could hardly believe what she had heard. Why would the Prioress swap her with Sister Ignatius? Worried now, she was glad she had said nothing to Alice. Sister Ignatius had a way of gleaning and extracting information without her victims realising it, and Alice was not in the sharpest frame of mind.

"If the truth be told, I do not care for her manner overmuch," Sister Beatrice replied in a low voice.

No, Gwenllian smiled to herself, she won't be an easy one to manage. She felt an unusual pang of pity for Sister Beatrice. As the months had gone on she had become more accepting of her ways. She was, after all, fairly elderly and had taught her a lot. Working together their relationship had mellowed, and they had developed, if not friendship, a mutual respect for each other.

"You have taught me a lot, Sister, and I will always be grateful for that."

She took Sister Beatrice's hand in an unusual show of affection. Sister Beatrice's face glowed. Gwenllian had never seen her looking so pleased, starved as she probably was of any affection, like so many in this place.

For the rest of that day, Gwenllian could only think of what she was leaving behind. At lunch, at the services of Sext, Nones, Vespers and Compline, for she attended each one, she listened attentively to each word, scanned the face of each Sister and prayed earnestly. She wanted to remember every detail of the place which had sheltered her, educated her, nourished her. Even when times had been harsh and the routine punishing, she had been safe. There were some who had been kind; could she betray them so, leave without a word? But there was no choice if she was to ever see her homeland … and see it she would. She would cast off these nun's robes, grow her hair and let it flow in the wind, and one day she would ride on a fine horse into her native land, the land of her ancestors.

CHAPTER 45

Sempringham Priory

Brother John had to seek out Cai again. At least it was a lot easier to approach him than Wencilian, although finding privacy to talk was another matter. He found him in the infirmary, but Brother Gilbert was hovering nearby. The bell would soon ring for Nones, so he hoped one of them would stay behind.

"What brings you here, Brother John?" Brother Gilbert enquired.

"I came to see if you needed any herbs or potions. I have heard that the merchant is lodging nearby, so may call on us again. I should be prepared this time. It will create less bother for you."

"That is thoughtful. Do you want to wait with me while I make a list?" and turning to Cai, Brother Gilbert said, "Brother Gregory, you could go to Nones."

Cai put down the jug that he was carrying and prepared to walk to Nones.

"Thank you, Brother Gilbert," Brother John replied. "But I really don't want to miss Nones. I will return straight afterwards; it will give you time to check your needs thoroughly." Turning to Cai he insisted, "I'll walk with you, Brother Gregory."

Brother John opened the conversation as they strolled along the cloister. "I have spoken to Sister Wencilian, Brother. I am concerned for her safety."

Cai looked alarmed, but he'd had time to reflect since the encounter in the granary. He decided that the next time he was to face Brother John, he would appeal to his more charitable nature.

"I am at your mercy, Brother," he whispered, aware of other monks following behind them. "I would not encourage her to do anything against her will. It is right that she knows of her true heritage, but if she chooses not to come with me, I cannot or would not force her. What will you do, Brother? Will you help us?"

"I find it hard to believe all you told me. If it is true, then it is right for her to know, but I fear it has made her unsettled and turned the only life that she has known upside down. The thought of her out there, God only knows where, fills me with dread. I love her too much to betray her or stop her, but I will not be a part of it. Be careful, for I think the Prioress has been having her watched. Sister Ignatius is more your enemy than me, Brother."

"Unruly, unruly, to natter so Brothers," the Sacristan reprimanded them as they entered the silence of the church.

Here they parted company, as Cai, being a visiting friar, was obliged to stand near the rear of the church. He was glad of this, he could be less conspicuous and undisturbed with his private thoughts. Only when he took Holy Communion would he walk to the front, where Father Roger would stand, attended by his two most faithful canons.

Cai was aware of the shuffling of feet on the other side of the wall where the nuns entered. Which one was Sister Ignatius, he wondered, worried now, for how was he to tell her apart. He remembered a shadowy face he had seen when he left the granary, illuminated by the moonlight falling on her scapula. He had wondered for a fleeting moment why a nun would be in that area at all, let alone so late, but he hadn't given it another thought given what was on his mind.

The psalms recited by Father Roger seemed to reverberate in the distance as he thought of the hidden Sisters. There was no sharing between men and women here. He thought of Seren and the Priests and Priestesses of the mountain grove and how they would laugh or be totally incredulous to see such a thing. To them the passing of the chalice man to woman, woman to man, was paramount to creating a balance of the feminine and the masculine in the world and on the inner planes. The God and Goddess presided over their rituals. There was love and joy, not fear of hell or damnation.

Oh Gwenllian, he thought, let me take you back to your country and one day you shall share the knowledge and the joy, as is your birthright. Maybe you have become too Christianised, but it matters not, whatever your belief, you will be home where you belong. Your heart will never be bitter or afraid to love. In two days you will be free, Gwenllian, you were not born to be kept in this place.

Father Roger's recital carried on, but Cai heard little of the service, so troubled was he by the plan.

Brother John had made it clear that he would not help, but could he rely on him not to betray them? No one could answer that question. Now there was an added complication to this – Sister Ignatius, whoever she may be … unless, unless it was untrue and Brother John was deliberately trying to disrupt his plan.

Cai could be surrounded by insincerity, danger. He had to focus; only two days to go. He wished he could leave tonight with Gwenllian, get her to safety, but there was no way to contact Hywel now. Everything was set for Lammas Eve and everything had been made so much simpler by Gwenllian telling him of the tunnel which she had used before. She would surely then have the courage to do it again. She must have the courage.

Cai slipped out of the church as the monks rose when the service ended and before Brother John could catch him. Returning to the infirmary, he went through the motions of his duties, dismissing the doubts when they crept in like shadows to darken the clear surety in his mind.

Brother John had returned to pick up the list from Brother Gilbert, but had not approached him again. However Cai was sure he would see him again before the end of his time here.

As a friar, Cai could rightly leave this priory at any time, but he would be expected to give notice to Father Roger. If he left suddenly, it would arouse suspicion and immediately link him to Gwenllian once she was missed, but if he approached Father Roger or Brother Gilbert now they may question him too much or encourage him to stay. He couldn't easily claim that he had received an urgent message from any source, as all messages were normally passed through Father Roger. If they left after Compline on Lammas Eve, hopefully Gwenllian would not be missed for at least several hours, unless Sister Beatrice went to the service and left Gwenllian in the infirmary.

Cai hoped that Gwenllian would engineer her movements tactfully. He would pray that the Gods would be on their side. That was all he could do now, pray. He prayed in his own way to the God and Goddess he revered, kneeling in the small chapel at the side of the infirmary where the patients prayed if they were able. It was still, peaceful and empty. If anyone were to enter they would think him deep in Christian prayer, a devout Brother. They would not know, or ever understand the silent words he spoke. But Cai was devout and he had faith today that his prayers were going to be answered.

CHAPTER 46

Sempringham Priory

The Prioress watched Sister Wencilian as she sorted through the parchments on the table in the corner of the room. A princess indeed; she holds herself quite nobly, she thought. But would I think that if I didn't know, she asked herself. She would just be like any other ordinary nun to me. Now she has become an enigma, a fascination, a mystery. I needed her near me, but what am I to tell her? I only know that she has that title, 'Princess'. I know nothing of her true background for sure.

In her hand she held the letter from Father Thomas. She had read it and re-read it. It was as if events were synchronising to reveal the answer to the puzzle, but parts were still missing.

Father Thomas had written in reply to her request. It had taken him a while to do some research. He revealed that the name 'Gwenllian' did come from the Welsh language and so it followed that one of her parents or grandparents could be Welsh. It did not prove where she was born. He had not been able to uncover any illegitimate daughters of the King with that name, although that was not conclusive. He did however, write in his letter that the last Prince of Wales, who had been at war with the King and slain in the year 1282, had a daughter who was later taken by the King as a baby and imprisoned somewhere, placed possibly in a nunnery, but he had no idea where.

1282 – the Prioress held her stomach as she recalled that when she became Prioress, Wencilian was four years old … and now she was eighteen years of age in the year 1300. The name

'Gwenllian' was Welsh, and the name 'Wencilian' was so similar, a distortion of her real name. It must be her. The previous prioress had possibly tried to keep her name; maybe the nuns here couldn't pronounce it properly or maybe someone had changed it, too ashamed to obliterate her completely. Again there was no conclusive proof, but there were too many coincidences.

The Prioress thought of herself at the same age and the pain she had felt at her abandonment by the man who now wrote to her. He never knew of the child she had borne. Where was she now? Never a day went by when she didn't think of her. She only held her for a few moments after the birth, before she was ripped away from her. Her parents had made arrangements and it was never spoken of again.

That was eighteen years ago. Had she somehow hoped that this Gwenllian, whom she knew as Sister Wencilian, could be that daughter. Never could she have admitted it before. When she started delving into the background of Wencilian and discovered links with the King, she knew she couldn't be her daughter, but she was too involved; she had to find out who she really was. All her adult life had been a lie; she felt that she owed Wencilian the truth, if only she could be sure of it. She felt pity for Wencilian. Like her daughter, she may never know her mother or father. But if the truth would only cause more pain, some secrets were best left buried … and there were many women in this place who had buried secrets.

Wencilian filed the parchments carefully. No doubt if there was anything relating to herself, Mother Elizabeth would have concealed it well. Wencilian knew that she had been observing her closely since she had reported to her office after Prime, and she was sure it wasn't her work she was assessing.

Does she know where I come from, she mused. I must have been about four years old when she was appointed Prioress. Was she told, like everyone else, that I was an abandoned orphan? Because that is still exactly what I am, my parents are dead and the King and the rest of the world had abandoned me … until now, until Cai arrived here. Does she want to know more? Is that why she wants me close to her and has been sending Sister Ignatius to spy on me? Oh yes, I have been aware of Sister Ignatius lurking in shadowy corners; I have been aware of her clumsy attempts at friendship, belied by the coldness in her eyes. Now she is probably talking to Sister Beatrice, subtlety extracting information from her like poison, drip, drip, drip. I always thought it was because of Mira that they watched me, suspected me, but that must be of no significance to them now. How important is a lay sister to them compared with the Princess of Wales?

The bell rang for Terce.

"You go to the service, Sister, then take your lunch. I'll see you back here after the rest period."

"Thank you, Mother."

Wencilian had been taking the rest period after the lunch and the noon service of Sext in the infirmary since she had worked there, if patients allowed. Now, here was the opportunity to return to her cell for an hour. God was on her side. She would gather her meagre belongings ready for her departure and hide them under her pallet.

The cell was cold. Facing north over the fens, it rarely warmed even in the height of summer. Snuggling under the sheepskin she lay down and closed her eyes. It was going to be a problem to create time alone in the Prioress's office. She was relying on Leoba to create a diversion, a need for the Prioress to be called to the infirmary.

She was fond of the Prioress; apart from Marie she had been the nearest resemblance to a mother that she had ever had. She could be stoic, harsh at times with others, but she had always treated her almost like a daughter. Could the Prioress have lied to her having known her true identity all these years? If she had, Wencilian thought, it could only be because of pressure from higher echelons of the Church, or from the King himself.

She would feel a great sadness at leaving this place, even though to be free of the daily grind of work and services would surely be a huge relief. But what would she do in the outside world? Would she always be in hiding, or always lying about her identity? Would she ever be able to live as a Princess, with her people? She could not even speak their language.

Cai had not entirely promised her safety. How could he? But he had promised her a taste of freedom, a chance to see her homeland one day. Did he hope that by passing several years in France she would be forgotten and be able to safely travel to Wales? Would she be married off to someone against her will? Who were these people in the mountains who Cai had said would shelter her and instruct her in the ways of the wise? It would be hard, he had told her, but there would be love and laughter, and singing. To hear the voices and songs of her ancestors would be such a delight. The thought made her spine tingle. Would she be prepared to suffer punishment if all these plans failed?

Wencilian silently prayed. 'Oh, Holy Mary, mother of God, pray for me. Tell me what I should do. Although I think I know what I must do. How can there be any other way? How could I stay here for the rest of my life knowing what I now know? Guide me safely, Holy Mother, now and until the hour of my death. Pray for us all.'

The bell rang for work, the time when all the nuns, novices, postulants and lay sisters would return to their designated tasks, obediently, silently, until the bell would ring for Nones, the 'ninth hour' of the Gospels, when they would once again file in silence to the church.

Wencilian returned to the Prioress's office where she found the Prioress asleep over her desk. "Mother, are you well?" she asked tentatively, not quite sure what to do. The Prioress was not normally pleased to be disturbed even in such circumstances.

Mother Elizabeth looked up sharply, but her face softened when she saw Wencilian standing over her. "Oh, I must have just nodded off. Sleep caught me unawares, Sister."

Wencilian was not blind to the empty bottle of mead on her desk and she knew how strong that could be, although it was rare for the nuns to be offered any, except occasionally on feast days.

"Mother, forgive me, but you should rest more; you work too hard."

Expecting a terse reply, Wencilian returned directly to her table in the corner. But the response surprised her. "I think you are right, Sister, I will lie down on my couch for a while. Wake me for Nones if I fall asleep again."

Wencilian noticed that the Prioress was very unsteady as she walked to her couch in the opposite corner of the room, where a curtain had been erected around her make-shift bed. She rarely went to her cell any more; she just grabbed naps when she could. Wencilian knew that much – it was common knowledge in the convent, but how long had she been drinking like that, she wondered. This was not good; was she under so much strain?

Now however, if she was very careful, she had a chance to root through some papers. Only seconds had passed when she heard the snores. She could not believe her luck. Used to tiptoeing and making herself nearly invisible so as not to disturb the patients in the infirmary, Wencilian moved around the office silently, wondering where to look first. The Priory records would be the obvious place, but would she be listed as anyone other than Wencilian?

She reached up to pull down a dusty book marked '1283' from a high shelf. This is the year I was told I came to this place; there must be some mention in here. After a few minutes, she found what she sought, in bold script were written the words:

Wencilian. Admitted June 1283.
Orphan of no known parenthood.

Tears welled in her eyes. Was she really just an orphan? Had Cai lied to her? But why would he? Could it be though that the records had been written as such to avoid any detection of the truth? Or maybe the previous Prioress was just as ignorant about her as everyone else? There had to be more.

The Prioress stirred, but her snores continued. Wencilian peeped around the curtain. She was still deep in sleep. If there were any secrets, they would be well hidden. The Prioress would not have asked her to work here then leave obvious clues of her true identity, if there were any at all.

The Prioress's desk had a drawer and Wencilian noticed that the key had been left in the lock … a careless act no doubt, the sort that can often result from too much rich wine or mead. She fingered lightly through a mix of papers and small artefacts, and then she came across the letter. It had been sent from the Monastery of Garendon, addressed to the Prioress. She skimmed through it thinking it may be irrelevant, but when she saw her name, 'Gwenllian' in the black ink, her heart thumped. She started again and read it slowly, soaking in every word. It was all about her and what she read both shocked and delighted her. It was no absolute proof, but it was enough to convince her that there was a good chance Cai was telling the truth. The letter was signed by a Father Thomas. Whoever he was, he too had been searching for information about her, together with his accomplice, the Prioress.

Wencilian replaced the letter carefully in the same position. Sitting down, she recalled as many details of the letter as she could, so that she would not forget. Memorising was not a problem for her, how many psalms she had memorised over the years she could not even count, there had been so many.

Why, she wondered, was the Prioress trying to find out who she was now, when she had not done so in the fourteen years since she took over the office of Prioress. And, who if anyone else, knew of her clandestine quest; Sister Marie Claire or Sister Agnes who shared the responsibilities of running the Priory? Father Roger? Wencilian suddenly felt exposed. All her life she had been hidden away – a nobody. Now it seemed that she could be somebody, somebody of importance, not only to her own people but to the Priory itself. The letter mentioned that they thought she could be an illegitimate daughter of the King but no evidence could be found. Then, the stunning suggestion that she could be the daughter of Prince Llywelyn. If what Cai had told her was true and she was the daughter of Llywelyn Prince of Wales, then the King was not her father, but her enemy.

CHAPTER 47

Sempringham Priory

The infirmary felt cold and bleak after the relative cosiness of the Prioress's office. When Gwenllian returned, she found Alice sitting pale and shaken on her bed.

"What is it, Alice? You were starting to look so well?"

Alice trembled. "Sister Ignatius told me I must return to my duties and Sister Beatrice agreed with her. Sister Ignatius has upset several of the patients with her harsh manner. Praise God you are back, Wencilian, but what am I to do? I would rather die than spend another night back in my cell."

"Don't worry, Alice, you won't have to. I will talk to you later. We are both leaving here, but you must be brave and speak to no one of this. Trust me, you will be safe."

"But what …?"

"Shh, I will explain when I can."

That has decided it, Gwenllian thought. I cannot leave her behind now. At least I have been forced to make a decision. I think she would die if I was to leave her here, either from a broken heart or taking her own life, a sin she would be forever condemned for. But the Lord only knows how three of us will escape through the tunnel safely. Am I putting the whole plan in jeopardy? Will Cai agree? I shall have to insist, for I would never forgive myself if I abandoned Alice to such a fate.

Gwenllian looked around her. She saw how she could make the infirmary a more pleasant place for those who had to stay here. Tapestries on the walls, a fire in the hearth and even music to lighten the heart and the soul would surely help the body and spirit heal or make the passing of those whose frail earthly forms were fading more bearable. But it was not to be, and she would be gone tomorrow night, Lammas Eve.

Cai stalked up and down the still room in the infirmary. As a bard of the old ways he had been trained to use focused intention, but at this moment his attention was wavering all over the place. The monastery was preparing a feast for Lammas; so many of the monks were preoccupied, as he had hoped they would be. Brother Gilbert, however, was not so easily distracted and he noticed Cai's restlessness.

Cai had taken himself to the still room to be less conspicuous. There had been no further communication from Hywel, but then he didn't really expect it; he knew he wouldn't let him down unless something totally unexpected happened. It was more likely that something unexpected would occur within the Priory. Brother John might inform on him or the bitter Sister Ignatius might know more than he realised. It was best that Brother John did not know exactly when he intended to leave with Gwenllian. This raised a problem though. If he were to inform Brother Gilbert that he was leaving to return to Cwmhir Abbey or to travel back to Llanfaes Friary, as he was entitled to do as a friar, it would not necessarily arouse any suspicion. But to disappear suddenly would seem very impolite and unruly.

"Damn Brother John," he muttered.

This was not what Cai had planned, but there was really no other way. He would attend the mass on Lammas Eve tomorrow, then slip away as the monks ate and feasted afterwards. Most of them would be drunk on too much mead or wine to notice he was missing. He didn't imagine that this would be the case for the nuns however, but Gwenllian seemed to have her means of escaping through the tunnel figured out. There were still a few details to finalise with her.

During the Lammas mass, Cai planned to meditate and attempt to make a connection with Seren. At their own Lammas ritual, the mountain grove would be working with them. He thought of the many years he himself had taken part in their rites – Lughnasadh, the first harvest celebration when the Goddess took on the aspect of the Harvest Mother, her blessing manifest in the bounty and abundance of the earth. There were some who knew the harvest was bittersweet. Amongst the joy and fulfilment of the celebration was sacrifice too as the cycle of life continues. As the harvest is reaped, the Corn God is slain, his seed scattered upon the earth as the wheel of the year turns. There was a time when all the villagers of his native land would be dancing, making corn dollies and lighting fires. Now there were few who dared to offer a furtive remembrance to that time. He had heard talk from the monks that some of the fen folk still celebrated 'these heathen rites'. The Grove of Eryri had kept the old ways alive, offering the secrecy of forested glades and mountain caves. Their rituals may be felt by some, but never seen. Only Seren, and her Priests and Priestesses, in garlands woven with meadowsweet, mint and vervain, knew the true power of the magic they would weave that night.

How would the monks conduct their Lammas mass, Cai wondered? Where was their bountiful mother of creation? There were no fires for them, no dancing, no cheerful singing. But his time here was done now and he did not regret that time, both for the part he was playing for his country and for Gwenllian and the part of her life here he had shared. He would understand her better. This was his harvest time and he had dreamed so long of this moment … to free Gwenllian would be joy and fulfilment for many and he was willing to sacrifice his own life if necessary.

Brother John was never far away from Cai. When his alms duties had been done each day, he lurked around the infirmary building or made himself useful carrying messages to and fro across the whole priory, giving him an excuse to be wherever he was allowed access. He was one of the oldest monks, so no one took much notice of his activities. Father Roger let him please himself as long as he attended mass regularly. But Brother John had missed several masses recently, for while all the Brothers were occupied, he had more chance to snoop around a little. That was not the only reason though. He had difficulty facing his creator in church while he inwardly wrestled with his conscience. Several times he had knocked on Father Roger's door, only then to make up some excuse. He couldn't bring himself to reveal what he knew. He could not betray his dear Wencilian, but he had to protect her.

Father Roger was becoming worried. He had seen elderly monks confused, losing their sensibilities, knowing there was not much to be done, just to treat them with kindness. He would however, he thought, have a word with Brother Gilbert when he could. Brother John did seem to him unusually agitated, maybe a draught of something may help.

Brother John felt that he had to somehow seek out Wencilian today. He had made an excuse to call in the infirmary on the previous day, only to find Sister Ignatius administering to the patients. When he enquired why she was there in place of Sister Wencilian, she just eyed him suspiciously and grunted something incomprehensible. It was not coincidence, surely, that she seemed to pop up every time he tried to locate Wencilian. Did she know something or was she just snooping for the Prioress? It was well known that the two were in cahoots and that Sister Ignatius would do anything for the Prioress in the hope of obtaining a position.

Maybe it was the Prioress he should speak to, not Father Roger. If he voiced any concern about Wencilian though, they could punish her. She should never have even spoken to any Brother, let alone some unknown friar. If she really was this princess, surely they would guard her more. He wondered whether they were still not sure who she was, or had they become complacent. The nuns were all locked behind their high stone walls like hostages for salvation. He himself was only allowed near Wencilian occasionally as the Prioress knew he had cared for her as a child, but they had rarely been left alone together. Now that he had uncovered some truth on this bizarre matter, he was sure Brother Gregory would act without delay. He had to get near her soon.

Just before the bell rang for Nones, he gained access to the convent, carrying some tinctures which he had saved from the merchant. When the bell tolled, he was relieved to see Sister Beatrice, the young postulant and Sister Alice join the line of nuns filing to the church. Slipping as unobtrusively as he could into the infirmary through the side door which the nuns used for access to the kitchen, he found Wencilian alone in the still room.

"Oh, Brother John, what in the heavens are you doing here?"

"I think you must know that, Wencilian. How can I convince you of the danger you must be in?"

"You don't need to. I know myself, but you cannot stop me, Brother John, from doing what I must do. Sometimes I wish that I had never set eyes on Brother Gregory, but knowing what I know now, I have to go. I don't want to leave you and part of me wants to stay here where there is certainty, safety, even a small degree of comfort probably, compared with the world outside. I am scared, Brother. I am not doing this with an easy heart. Please don't inform on me. If you love me, pray for my safety."

"Scared you must be, but you are precious to me, Wencilian. I know I am a selfish old monk and I want you to stay, but I will not stand in your way. I will spend the rest of my short life praying for you. I will not ask when you are going or how; the less I know the better, but be careful. I feel that there are others keeping an eye on you."

"I spent yesterday in the Prioress's office. I came across a letter which she had received from a Father Thomas. Obviously she does not fully know my true history, but she has been searching and is getting closer to the truth. Why after all these years, is she taking the trouble to find out about me?"

"Ah!" Brother John recalled to himself the exact words he had heard the Prioress speak in the confessional box. "I think I need to tell you something I have also overheard very recently." He had to reveal this now, maybe it would change her mind.

"So," Wencilian gasped, after listening to Brother John's story. "All this time the Prioress had received money for my keep from the King and you are saying she did not know, nor did she know why. If I had not already decided to leave, I would

305

confront her right now."

She paused. "The letter I read claimed that I could be an illegitimate daughter of King Edward or, as Cai has told me, the Prince of Wales' daughter, in which case the King would be my mother's cousin and my enemy. Which is it to be?" Wencilian flared up.

Brother John had never seen her so angry. "But, dear Wencilian, I can understand that you are so confused. I wish I could help you. I wish we could be sure. It could be that you are an illegitimate daughter of the King, and this Brother Gregory is trying to kidnap you to claim a ransom."

"Would the King care that much, though? Kings have children everywhere, so I believe. I would have to be of some importance, to somebody. It really makes more sense that Brother Gregory is speaking the truth. He gave me a ring which belonged to my mother, a wedding ring. It has a date – 1278. He tells me that I was born four years later. That is the year, this Father Thomas writes, that the Princess of Wales was born. Cai told me too that I have a mark on my left shoulder, which is true. He saw it when I was a babe."

Wencilian's face was flushed and her body hot and wet with perspiration.

They heard footsteps approaching and then the outer door of the infirmary, with its familiar squeak, opening. Time had been forgotten.

"Wencilian, I must leave."

As Brother John embraced her, tears flowed down both of their cheeks. They knew this could be the last time they would talk together.

"May God bless you, Wencilian, now and for ever."

"Brother John, what are you doing here?" Sister Beatrice looked startled as she swept past him near the infirmary entrance.

"Just delivering some tinctures, Sister. I hope they will be of use to you. How is the young girl, Margred?" He thought it best to engage her in conversation whilst Wencilian composed herself.

CHAPTER 48

Sempringham Priory

Brother John felt God had not quite deserted him on this day. After leaving Wencilian, he walked straight to the monks' infirmary to seek Brother Gregory out. He found him alone, watching the patients.

"Brother Gregory, I must speak with you at once."

"Ah, I thought you would appear before long."

Cai steered Brother John towards his quarters at the rear of the room. "Please keep your voice low; not all my patients are deaf or incapacitated. I know you don't trust me, Brother, and I can't blame you for that. You care for Gwenllian; I respect the fact that you have cared for her since a babe. You will miss her, but please don't stand in our way. The future of my country could depend on us. I am offering you a chance to come with us, if you want to."

"Come with you! I have been in this place for forty years. In any case I would slow you down, I am not as agile as I used to be. How can you convince me that all you say is true and that you will not harm her?"

"If you come, you can see that what I say is true. If you stay, I have no way to convince you totally. I have shown you the seal of Llywelyn. I have nothing else which can prove my story is true, except my love for Gwenllian and the fact that I will lay down my life for her if I have to."

"It's true that you don't try to distract me with false promises. You seem to me an honest man, but can you not talk openly with the Prioress? I think she is near to discovering who Wencilian really is and I know she cares for her; she may listen to your story. She receives money for her though and she may not be keen to let her go."

"How do you know about the money, Brother John?"

"I overheard, one day, the Prioress in the confessional box, but I have never spoken of it to anyone, before today."

"Before today?"

"I have just told Sister Wencilian what I overheard. I felt she now needed to know."

"It is true the King sends money to ease his conscience." Cai explained. "Do you really think that the Prioress would displease the King and the whole Church, putting herself at great risk? If she or anyone gets any hint of this, you know well that Gwenllian would be punished, locked away somewhere else or even worse, killed, yes killed, Brother John. The king killed most of her family. Do you think he would spare her if she were caught escaping? Do you think he would risk another Welsh rebellion? You have no choice, Brother, but to come or to remain silent if you too love Gwenllian."

Brother John was stunned. What Brother Gregory had said was most likely true. He now had no choice. Whatever course of action he took would put her in danger, but remaining silent at least gave her a chance.

"Why, oh why did you come here, Brother? Damn you, why did you not leave her in peace, here, where she is not unhappy with the only life she has known."

"Ah, I have wished the same sometimes, Brother, believe me. But I am doing the right thing, for her and for her country. There is no turning back now."

"Then promise me that you will guard her with your life. If I hear of any harm befalling her, I will leave this place and seek you out, even if it kills me."

Brother John knew it was an empty threat, but he had to show some force and make some protest however lame it may really be. He turned and marched down the corridor to the cloister. He heard a bell, but knew not what time of day it was.

His heart was thumping, he was sweating and his head felt strange. He had to get to his cell and lie down.

Cai sat at the small table in the corner of the infirmary. He did not mock Brother John, for he was a threat to their mission, but he knew he could do him no physical harm nor would even be capable of it. He felt sorry for him and wished he had never had to put him in such a position. They were both united in their concern and love for Gwenllian. Resting his head in his hands, Cai felt guilt sweep over him; he could not deny it. He was about to disrupt the life of not just Gwenllian, but many others who had shown him only kindness. He felt guilt for deceiving innocent people, but there was no other way.

A patient called out to him, "Brother, help me please."

Cai walked over to the elderly monk who writhed in pain on his pallet.

"One of your draughts, Brother; that will help me with the pain, please."

"Of course, just give me a minute." Cai replied, tucking the sheepskin cover over him.

He walked to the still room and heard Brother Gilbert's footsteps, returning from mass. He had taken his time, he thought, no doubt stopping off at the kitchens for a tipple and a gossip with the cellarer. Cai mulled over the conversation with Brother John. He was certain now that Brother John wouldn't talk, so at least he could inform Brother Gilbert of his impending departure. He would claim to have been summoned by the Abbot of Cwmhir. He would explain that he had accidently intercepted the messenger.

Tonight, after Compline he would have to speak to Gwenllian. He needed reassurance that she was still determined to go. When they had last spoken they had planned for the following night, Lammas Eve, as much as they could in the scant time they had found to whisper over the wall. She had tried to explain where the exit from the tunnel was located. He would wait there, hiding in the foliage if he could, then under the cover of darkness they would creep to the edge of the forest where Hywel would meet them. It sounded straightforward, but it all depended on Gwenllian being able to safely access the tunnel.

Explaining to Brother Gilbert was not as easy as Cai had anticipated. He had to placate him with a promise of returning when he could. He also had to agree to inform Father Roger straight away. In fact Brother Gilbert wondered why a messenger hadn't delivered the message to Father Roger, which would have been normal procedure after all.

"I encountered the messenger at the gate whilst taking a brief walk for some air," Cai said, thinking quickly. "But you are right. I will go to Father Roger right now."

There was no one in the chapter house, so Cai drew up a chair to the large centre table and quickly wrote a message on a small piece of parchment he found on a corner desk. The message he signed from the Abbott of Cwmhir Abbey, and he sealed it with the seal in his pouch, Llywelyn's seal, and hoped that Father Roger would not look too closely. He had read the message so the seal would naturally be broken and the Prince having been a patron of Cwmhir, he may well have had his name on the seal as far as anyone knew. He was thankful he had kept that seal safe.

In the event, Father Roger did not ask to see the message.

"Well, you have stayed longer than you planned to, I'm sure. We shall be sorry to see you go. You have been a great help to Brother Gilbert. I wish you well, Brother. I don't know who will replace you, we are losing two canons this summer to go to university and have no replacements for them. We are so low in numbers compared with the nuns. It seems that the religious life is more inviting for females, or maybe there is a lack of men out there to marry," Father Roger commented with humour.

Cai felt at ease in his presence. The Prior showed no hint of being suspicious of anything at all. Cai returned to the infirmary, his mood boosted a little. So far, all was well.

CHAPTER 49

Sempringham Priory

On Lammas Eve, the convent was more vibrant than usual. Gwenllian collected the supper from the kitchens to take to the infirmary. The lay sisters who worked in the kitchens were buzzing around chattering excitedly. The aroma of meat and freshly baked bread diffused into the atmosphere an aura of warmth and hope, hope for the year ahead. The harvest had been good this year and no amount of discipline could quell the joyful mood.

It would be these fleeting moments that Gwenllian would remember most of all, when she left this place. As she and two young nuns walked back to the infirmary to distribute the food, a wave of guilt overwhelmed her. She could not even say goodbye to any of the Sisters she had spent so much of her life with. What would they think? Would they worry, would they not care that much? She would even regret leaving Sister Beatrice and Sisters Agnes and Marie Claire, they had been a part of her life since she could remember.

"Are you coming to supper in the refectory, Sister Wencilian?" one of the young nuns enquired.

"If I can be excused, I will. Thank you, Sister, I can manage now."

Alice came to her side to help. There were ten patients to see to, but if Alice, Leoba, Sister Beatrice and herself could get them fed and settled, they could all go to the refectory for the Lammas supper.

Gwenllian whispered to Alice, "We are leaving tonight. Gather a few belongings. Before Vespers we will leave them in the Lady Chapel in a safe place. After Compline, we will leave. Wear your cloak. Be ready."

"Wencilian, I didn't think you were totally serious. What is going on? I can't just leave, can I? Where will we go? We have nothing." Alice was breathing rapidly and looked pale.

"It's alright, Alice. Trust me. We have help. We will be taken to a safe place, although it may not be easy. I'm sorry I haven't told you much ... I had to be sure and I didn't want to put you in danger. I don't want to force you to do anything against your will, but if you want to leave this place, are you prepared to follow me and trust me? I have found out things about my family that have shocked me to the core. When we are free, I will tell you, Alice."

"I'll do anything to leave this place. If you go, I go."

"What are you whispering about over there, Sisters?" Sister Beatrice approached them. "If we get all these patients settled, we can all go to the Lammas supper together."

"That is exactly what I was explaining to Alice," Gwenllian replied. "We should all go if we can. I was speaking low so the patients would not hear me."

Sister Beatrice shuffled away without comment. She was beginning to trust the judgment of Sister Wencilian more and more these days. As she walked away, she smiled to herself; she was pleased with Wencilian and she had certainly lightened the load for herself.

Alice was confused, but knew she would not have the chance to question Wencilian again until much later. Whatever she had planned she would have to go along with. Gathering her things was not difficult as long as she wasn't seen; she possessed very little – the nun's garments she stood up in, her cloak, the ring, a change of undergarments and a shawl which her mother had made for her, would all fit into a small linen bag, the one she had brought with her when she was admitted to the convent. They were going to be conspicuous in nun's tunics and if they removed their head dresses, surely they would be even more noticeable with shorn heads. She just prayed that Wencilian knew what she was doing and where they were going.

Then Alice thought of her family. "I won't ever be able to go back there," she muttered aloud to herself. "My family could suffer an awful disgrace if I leave here."

That realisation made her pause, she would lose either way, staying or going. Staying she knew would be even more intolerable without Wencilian; going could cause distress to her family, and whatever decision she made would cause herself grief.

Tonight there was to be a short reading after Vespers in the chapter house, followed by the Lammas supper in the refectory with meat and sweetmeats and freshly baked bread.

Taking her place at the table next to Alice, Gwenllian savoured the aromas which drifted around her and thought of the Last Supper of Christ which he had shared with his disciples knowing the fate that was about to befall him. He had not flinched from his fear even in the face of possible betrayal. She needed that courage now.

Isobel served her with mead, winking and smiling. "You enjoy yourself with this, Sister Wencilian. It's not often you get the chance. How are you? We have not spoken for a while?"

"I am well, Isobel, thank you." Placing her hand over Isobel's, she said earnestly "You have been a good friend, Isobel."

Isobel searched her face, wondering whether she should be worried. Something was afoot, she sensed it. She thought about the night they had helped Mira run away. There was a similar air of intensity around Wencilian tonight, but nothing could be mentioned here. She glanced at Alice sitting next to her and the strange little postulant with the white face. They were both quiet and serious, unlike most of the nuns who were enjoying the feast and the freedom to natter which was rarely granted them. Maybe there had been another death in the infirmary which had upset them.

Isobel returned to her duties; she would catch Wencilian later if chance allowed.

In the monastery, the monks and canons too were celebrating, with rather more gusto than the nuns. Father Roger had joined them and presided over the long refectory table. The rules on silence had also been relaxed, but as the level of noise rose Father Roger was becoming agitated. He knew they all needed to let off a little steam now and then, but he disliked any unruly behaviour. Now was a good time for an announcement.

Banging on the table, as the silence increased he began, "Brothers, we share on this night the blessing of the harvest and give our thanks to God for all we receive. You have all worked hard to provide for the Priory and the wider community. Tomorrow we will share with that community by inviting the villagers to partake of food and drink after the Lammas Day mass."

He paused. "I would like also to thank Brother Gregory for his help during his time here. Some of you may know that he is leaving us tomorrow. Hopefully he will return again in the future. May we wish him well on his travels. May God go with him."

Cai reluctantly stood to the cheers aimed at him. He had hoped not to draw much attention to his departure, but was secretly pleased that his time here had been of some use to the Priory.

Brother John shot him a fierce look from across the table. Cai hoped no one had seen it. He had to make an effort to keep his voice steady as he spoke.

"Thank you, Father. I am glad to have been of service here and I thank you all for your hospitality. I hope that circumstances may allow me to return in the future."

He sat, feeling that was as much as he could say in total sincerity. He had intended to part from the festivities at midday and avoid this, but he felt he owed Father Roger a flimsy thank you if nothing else.

He gulped down his drink, and then steadied himself, a glass of mead would steady his nerves but too much could impair his judgement. He ate as much as he could manage; he might not be eating much in the next few days or longer.

He thought of Gwenllian. May the God and Goddess protect her, give her courage. Seren, use all your strength tonight to help us. Let this harvest be successful for all and the future of our country.

The bell rang for Compline, the monks rose to file to the church, the time was approaching. As soon as darkness fell, he would grab a few hours' sleep then he would be gone from this place.

CHAPTER 50

Outside Sempringham Priory

Cai stood in the light of the half-moon behind a clump of trees and waited. He barely dared to move. Gwenllian and the postulant could arrive at any moment. Darkness was falling. He hoped they would be able to time their escape to catch the last remnants of light but with enough darkness to conceal them. Was this the right place which Gwenllian had described to him, not far from where the tunnel met the forest edge?

Hearing a rustle of leaves, he leaned out to see a shadowy figure stumbling around on the soggy ground. The rain that last evening had increased the ever present dampness of the earth on the edge of these fen lands. He wouldn't be surprised if there was a storm soon following the heat of the last few days. Who was this? It was not Gwenllian, the figure was too stocky and for a moment the moonlight reflected from a bare head. It was Brother John. What on earth was he doing? Had he decided to come with them after all?

Cai held his breath. Any slight sound would carry on such a night. Maybe Brother John's presence here meant that he must have kept his word. Cai tried to scan the surrounding area from behind the shield of the trees as best as he could. The flat land could not hide much and he could not detect any figures in the distance. If Brother John had betrayed him he would have to be prepared to fight, but one man would not be any match for whoever was out there. Whatever happened, he vowed he was not going to lose his princess for a second time.

Then, from within the woods, behind him, he heard the crumple of feet on bracken and twigs, the crisp crunch of wood breaking. Heavy feet, not those of a young nun, approached behind him from the deeper forest. His heart thumped loudly; he drew his knife from the folds of his tunic. The footsteps stopped. His own breath pierced the silence. If they couldn't see him, Cai was sure they would hear him. The dim glow of a moonbeam lit up a man's face, not more than twenty yards from him. Already drenched in his own sweat, relief flooded through him, fear abated, for before him stood Rhys and behind him, Hywel and Owain.

Rhys laughed the deep belly laugh Cai had not heard for so long. "Ha, look at you! What a state you are in! Did you think we wouldn't be here when you needed us, bard?"

The three men stepped forward to embrace him.

"Shh, keep the voices down. I'm so glad to see you, but we are being watched," Cai whispered.

Rhys stepped away to the edge of the woods for a moment and returned dragging something behind him.

"What, by this?"

He laughed again, hauling a protesting Brother John and dropping him at their feet.

"It's alright; he is on our side. Don't hurt him."

"What are you doing here, old man?"

Brother John gasped for breath, holding his chest as he tried to stand, clinging to some dignity.

"Rhys, leave him. Let him speak."

Cai hoisted Brother John up carefully and brushed the twigs off his cloak.

"Well, speak man!" Hywel now commanded.

"I … I came to say goodbye, goodbye to Wencilian. When Brother Gregory announced yesterday that he was leaving today, I knew I had to follow him as it would be the last time I would see her."

"Her? What is Gwenllian to you?"

Cai stood in front of Brother John. "Brother John has been close to Gwenllian since she was a young child. He certainly means her no harm."

"Where is she? Is she coming?" Hywel demanded. "We need to leave as soon as possible."

"She'll be here and she is bringing with her another Sister, a young postulant, who she claims is special and cannot be left in the convent."

"I don't believe this, Cai. What is going on? You will be too conspicuous on your travels."

"Gwenllian will not leave without her, but we talked, albeit briefly, and we agreed that you will escort the young postulant, Leoba, to the mountains and leave her with Seren until Gwenllian arrives. From what I gather, that may be the best place for her."

"But Cai, I may not be going there immediately. Did you think of that?"

"I'm sure you can find her somewhere safe, Hywel. Gwenllian would not leave without her."

Hywel cursed under his breath, whilst shaking a bag to spill a jumble of cloth onto the ground.

"It's fortunate that I brought along two garments for Gwenllian. She will have to make do with one now."

The two men had momentarily forgotten Brother John, who stood behind them. Cai turned to see Rhys clasping him strongly on the arm and holding a knife to his throat.

"Please Rhys, release him. He will not betray us, I am sure."

"You are too trusting, Cai. Being a monk does not necessarily make him an honest man."

"You can trust me, I will not betray you," Brother John pleaded. "I just want to know that Wencilian will be safe."

"I will be, Brother John." A softly spoken voice came from behind them all.

"Gwenllian, how long have you been there?" Cai approached her and took her hand in his, leading her into the circle of trees.

Leoba followed, clinging onto Gwenllian's heavy cloak. Alice crept behind.

"Just a few seconds, long enough to hear that man insult

Brother John."

She spoke bravely, but Cai could see fear in her eyes.

In the dim light of that small forest clearing Gwenllian witnessed something unbelievable. Hywel, Owain and Rhys dropped to their knees and bowed their heads, and then Cai did the same. They were in the presence of a princess, their Princess of Wales.

Tears fell from Rhys's eyes as he spoke. "Forgive me, Tywysoges, I am only here to protect you. I meant no harm. I am so happy to see you. We have waited so long for this day."

"Indeed we have," echoed Hywel, standing and approaching her. He took her hand to offer a kiss. "Tywysoges means Princess in our language and you are our true Tywysoges, returned to us. Don't be afraid; we will care for you, but for now we must not linger. You are to go with Cai. The ship is waiting. Owain and Rhys will guide you, but your postulant will have to come with me. But what is this I see – another nun behind you!"

"Sister Alice. I could not leave her. She comes with me."

Gwenllian was still in shock. She had stepped out of the boundaries of the Priory into the frontier of a new existence, but had not been prepared for all this. These men obviously worshipped her, adored her, but they really knew nothing about her. One thing was sure, they would do her bidding and protect her, but she knew nothing of the world of men. She was glad Alice had agreed to come; it gave her strength, even though Alice was the one she had thought would need more protection.

"I have only clothes for two women," Hywel muttered, knowing he was defeated.

"I have some spare clothes in my pack," Owain volunteered. "One will have to pass as a boy. That should be no problem with shorn hair."

"Excellent," sparked Hywel. "Alice is the tallest, the clothes should fit, although it would be easier if it were Leoba; she could pass for my apprentice. I think that would be better, for we are travelling overland. It may be hard for Alice on board the ship if she has to pass as a man, and the convent at Chartres is expecting your daughter, Cai. She will just have to explain Alice as her maid. Please get changed now; we cannot wait. Cai, I have clothes for you."

Gwenllian was not sorry to throw off her nun's tunic, but she kept her rosary and warm cloak. She had never worn a woman's robe before. This one was not splendid, but it was a delight to the eyes after the plain nun's garb. She slipped it over her undergarments, feeling the soft silk slither along her fingers. On the chest was a frill. Her fingers fumbled with the ties and buttons along the front. The colour was dark, but indistinguishable in the faded light. The headdress and veil covered her shorn head.

She looked at Alice, who beamed with delight as she touched soft fabrics that had been forbidden to her since she left her family.

"Wait, Wencilian, what a picture you look ... a true Princess. I am honoured to see you as you should be, but I will miss you. Please take these with you; I have no use for them." Brother John pressed two gold coins into her hand. "There should have been four, but those thieves robbed me of two."

"I remember that day well, Brother John, but where did you get them from?"

"I brought them from my home. My father said to me that I should not give everything to the Church. He said I might need them one day. I have always kept them hidden."

"I can't take them from you, Brother John."

"I will never leave this place now. You may need them. Keep them safe."

"You are a saint. You will always have a special place in my heart. God bless you, Brother."

Gwenllian was reluctant to leave him, but urged on by Cai, Owain and Rhys, she and Alice followed the men through the forest path which would lead them to the small boat, waiting in the marshes, which would then take them to the ship, which would steer them to their new life.

A shriek above them caused the women to stumble a little. Cai and Gwenllian looked up to see Boden sweeping alongside them.

"See, he will not leave you either, Princess. He will journey with us. 'Tylluan Gwenllian' – 'Gwenllian's owl' in our language," Cai whispered closely to her.

"Tylluan," she whispered back.

"You are learning fast, my Princess."

CHAPTER 51

On board ship

Above her, a small lantern bobbed in the sharp breeze. The hand that took hers was strong and coated with coarse brown hair. Her eyes travelled along an arm, a torn linen tunic and a broad shoulder half exposed to the morning air, up and into the shy hazel eyes of a young sailor. Each new touch, each new sight, each new sound was a discovery.

"Welcome aboard, ma'am." The young man nodded to Gwenllian as he steadied her up the gangway. Alice followed, wobbling a little with the movement of the plank, closely followed by Cai, who seemed to stride up as if he did it every day.

Once they were on board, an older man stepped forward from behind the young sailor. To Gwenllian he looked strange, dressed in a brown tunic that was covered by a white tabard embellished with a big red cross. He bowed to the women, but addressed Cai directly. "Welcome. Please follow me to the deck shelter at the bow. The women will be safe there and out of sight."

By way of explanation, Cai whispered to Gwenllian, "Come, we must follow the Templar Knight."

They moved towards the front of the ship as quickly as they could. Even in port, the ship swayed with the prevailing wind. Gwenllian and Alice stumbled in their long skirts, grabbing first onto the ropes that stretched down from a wide stretch of canvas that was wrapped darkly above them on a beam, and then groping along the side of the ship to keep their balance.

Until her flight from Sempringham, Gwenllian had never set foot off dry land, apart from the brief time in Robert's boat on the fen crossing the swampy channels to Hilda's house. Now, still remembering the swaying and slopping of the small boat they had taken through the marshes under the light of a watery half-moon, she clung onto Cai's cloak as they entered the dark of the wooden shelter at the bow.

She knew they needed to be out of sight as soon as possible, for they may have been followed. All night they had wandered through the maze of waterways that branched across the fen; every splash of the oar, every knock of the rowlocks sounding loud in the stillness, every distant baying of a dog raising the hairs on the back of their necks.

After hours of rowing, the moon had passed below the horizon, mist shrouding them from the stars and settling on their garments. Gwenllian and Alice shivered, missing the warmth of their nun's tunics.

At last a hint of daylight had shown them the way to the east. The air carried a new scent, a tang. Gwenllian breathed deeply and looked up into the gloom – above her the distant cries of seagulls and ahead the plaintive calls of another bird.

"Can you hear that? The peewit?" Cai put his hand to his ear. "We are near the sea."

Gwenllian nervously peeped beyond the door of their shelter in the bow. In the early morning light, the deck was busy with men at their tasks. She searched among them, unable to shake the sense of being followed from her mind. She wondered if the alarm had been raised at Sempringham or if they had not yet been missed at all.

All around them, men prepared to hoist the great canvas from the beam. Others took their place at the oars below. They shouted loudly at each other. Gwenllian did not understand some of the words, but she knew they were most probably curses. She was relieved that the ship was about to leave the port; the sooner it did, the safer they would be, away from England.

They had boarded at Bishop's Lynn amongst the hustle and bustle of traders and townsfolk. Their ship was loaded with wool, grain and salt, bound for Dunkirk. Surely, no one would look for them on a trading ship such as this?

When the wind started to fill the canvas, the men put down their oars and joined together to pull with all their might on the ropes. The canvas rose up into a wide square sail and the ship drew away from the shore, waves slapping beneath the keel.

Gwenllian and Alice stepped into the gap in the flapping canvas curtain which covered their shelter. They peered out at the vastness of the ocean. Dawn was breaking, pink streaks slashed across the pale grey sky. Gwenllian glanced at the receding land, the world she was leaving behind; it was her familiar world, but the life in the Priory had never felt familiar to her. Her stomach lurched suddenly from the motion of the boat and in part with fear. Had she been reckless to trust Cai and come on this journey of madness? She squeezed Alice's hand. At least she had a friend. She felt Alice tremble and put her arm around her shoulder.

Cai was talking to the men with the red crosses on their tabards, the Templar Knights. He crossed over to Gwenllian and touched her gently on the arm. "I know my Princess that this is all so strange for you. Have courage; you and Alice need to rest for a while. We, all of us, have barely slept at all for many a night, I'm sure."

Cai ushered them back into the shelter.

Gwenllian held his sleeve. "There are many questions I have for you, Cai."

"I know, and there are many things I want to tell you, but rest now. There are benches here with sheepskins. Wrap up and sleep for a while; then I will fetch you some food and we will talk when you are ready."

The morning breeze was steady and the sea a gentle swell, no more, but Gwenllian awoke feeling nauseous and stiff. Sitting up she noticed her silk surcoat was torn in parts, no doubt from the scramble through the outskirts of the fenland to reach the little boat which had taken them to the port. The ship swayed and timbers creaked. An aroma of fish mingled with smoke drifted into the shelter. Her stomach heaved and she grabbed the pot which she assumed had been put in the deck shelter for their relief and vomited.

Alice groaned as the sound awoke her. "Where am I? Wencilian what is wrong?"

"I think it's the sea sickness, or maybe lack of food, Alice."

"I too feel a little nauseous. I had a nightmare and was so scared, Wencilian."

"I think we are safe now. No one will find us. We have left the land far behind. I need to go on deck and breathe fresh air. Come Alice."

Cai was on deck helping a young sailor cook fish on a brazier that was lodged between large stones. Loud male voices resonated all around. The young women hung onto their skirts with one hand and reached for a halyard rope for support with the other.

"I hope you feel rested, ladies." Cai addressed them politely, and then turned to the young sailor. "I will tend the food, young man, you fill your lungs with fresh sea air."

With the sailor gone, Cai gave full attention to Gwenllian and Alice. Here, he told them, they would start as they meant to continue. He would pose as Gwenllian's father travelling on business. He would be known as Jeffery of Gloucester and she would be known as Isobel, travelling with her companion, Mirabelle. Only the Captain and two of the Templar Knights who were to accompany them knew their real identity and if anyone else questioned who they were, they would be quickly silenced.

When the young man returned to tend to the cooking, he smiled at Gwenllian and offered her a fish on a wooden platter, to which she turned her face away and made for the side of the deck.

Cai and the young sailor chuckled, but not unkindly.

Cai then took her arm. "Perhaps some bread may be preferable, daughter, until your belly adjusts. Come, sit in the shelter. I'll fetch some bland food and drink. Come, Mirabelle."

When Gwenllian and Alice had eaten a little, their stomachs settled. They sat in the deck shelter and listened, speechless, while Cai began the tale of Gwenllian's Welsh heritage.

Cai spoke slowly and chose his words carefully. There would be a tremendous amount of information for Gwenllian to absorb and he knew she was feeling quite delicate and not just because of the sea voyage. There would be plenty of time for her story to unfold in the months to come. But she was eager to know the truth which had been kept from her for eighteen years.

"Your great grandfather, my Princess, was King John of England, and his daughter, Siwan, was the wife of Llywelyn ap Iorwerth, Llywelyn the Great, Prince of Wales, grandfather to your father."

"Such a noble background I have. I laugh to myself now to think that I believed I was a pauper's child, abandoned and unwanted. But Cai, tell me first about my mother."

Cai knew he would have to tell her all that he could remember about Eleanor at some stage, but it hurt him so much to think of her. And, when he did, the memories were so intertwined with his beloved Celeste and poor Morwena and the dreadful fate of Dafydd and his young sons. Catrin, at least, he knew was safe and happy; that was a miracle indeed.

"Cai!" Gwenllian prompted.

"Sorry, my Princess, I was lost in memory for a moment."

Gwenllian saw the look of distress on his face. "I'm sorry, Cai, if you would rather wait until another time, I can have patience; after all I knew nothing of my identity or my family until you spoke to me. But promise me you will not call me 'Princess', I don't know how to be a princess, just call me 'Gwenllian'. I am Gwenllian."

Cai took her hand. "You are Gwenllian and I am sorry that for a while you must be 'Isobel' and have your true identity hidden yet again. It's only for your protection and only for a short while. When you enter your homeland, I can assure you, you will feel like a true princess."

In a moment of quiet, they realised that beside them Alice sobbed softly into her cape.

"Alice, my friend, I fear I have neglected you a little. What is wrong?"

"I'm sorry. I am truly happy for you – you must know that. I am just thinking of my family; I may never see them again. What will they think of me now? You have people waiting for you, people who will honour you. What is to become of me?"

"Alice, you will always be by my side. None of us truly know what the future holds. I am as apprehensive as you. You know more of how this strange world works than I do. You must guide me in the ways of the people. I am so glad you are by my side for I don't think I could have come without you, but I am sorry to have torn you away from the Priory and the chance to see your family."

"Once a year, that is the only time I would be allowed to see my family and then it would pain me, I know that. I am being foolish, Wencilian."

"Gwenllian, call me Gwenllian, but only when we are alone. For now we are Isobel and Mirabelle."

"And," Cai added, "it is too late to return now. That life has gone. Cherish the memories, Alice, but look to the future now. We will look after you. Come, ladies, on deck with me."

Cai led them around the deck shelter and to the bow of the ship and held them both to steady them, one on each arm.

"Do you see that land in the distance? Your new life stands before you now. Breathe deeply the fresh sea air. Is it not liberating to feel the force of the wind, the spray of the sea on your face, to feel the anticipation, the excitement of new life? Magic is in the air. Catch it, keep it in your heart."

As he spoke the face of Seren flashed before him and he knew, for the first time since he had arrived at the Priory, that they would be safe.

"Many years ago, Gwenllian, your mother stood on the bow of a ship like this feeling just like you, both vulnerable and strong, a noble lady on a voyage to a new life. She was on her way to marry your father, but her ship was taken by King

Edward, her cousin, and she was captured and taken to Windsor Castle, where she was held for three years. Your father had refused to pay homage to Edward and was declared a rebel. Eventually he was forced to submit and signed the Treaty of Aberconwy, which reduced his lands, but enabled him after some time to marry your mother."

Cai paused, then gripped the women tightly to him as the bow rose and slashed into an oncoming wave.

"The wedding at Worcester Cathedral was spectacular. I was there, mingling amongst many who held riches and power in the land. When we rode back to Abergwyngregyn, where you were born, the people cheered and welcomed your mother. There was peace for a while and they were happy. We were all happy. They were good days."

Cai turned to Gwenllian to see her face wet, the salty spray of the sea on her cheeks mingled with the salty tears of grief.

"Let's go back to the shelter. We need to prepare. The captain says there are a few spare articles of women's clothing stored on board. We will soon reach the port and we have a long journey overland when we arrive ... plenty of time for my story to continue and plenty of time to share memories, laughter and tears."

CHAPTER 52

The Convent at Chartres
September 1300

The cool shade of the cloister was welcoming after the midday heat. Gwenllian fanned herself with the blue silk cloth she had bought from the market. She had been in the convent for nearly one month with Alice, but this visit to the market was the first time they had ventured outside. Although they were free to come and go as they pleased, Cai had warned them not to venture too far, too often, and of course only with an escort.

Mother Superior had encouraged them to enjoy the market, with an escort of course, for ladies of their position should not go out alone. She had thought it may cheer them up. It would take their minds off worrying about their father who had set off straight after leaving them here, gone to conduct his business.

Gwenllian did not like this deceit, but it was necessary. Cai's business here was, it seemed, to search for Celeste and to secure a safe house for them. He had told her of his love for Celeste on their journey to this place. He had also told her a lot more of her history, her family and her possible future, all of which was totally enticing and absorbing.

Hilda had been right, she certainly was of noble birth. Her great grandfather had been King of England, her father the last Prince of Wales. Her mother was the only daughter of Eleanor of England and Simon de Montfort, Earl of Leicester. If not for Cai she would have remained in ignorance, imprisoned. How could she have been so deceived as to her real identity?

This convent at Chartres was a welcome respite, not only from the arduous journey overland on horseback, but from the turmoil in her mind. The three knights who had accompanied them here had laughed good heartedly at her first attempts to ride a horse. She and Alice both adapted to riding fairly quickly, but adapting to her freedom was another matter. It would take her time to adjust to this new world she found herself in and assimilate all the information she had been told. There would be a lot more of it too, she was sure. Cai was wise to leave them here for a while. Leaving the convent at Sempringham through the tunnel, escaping over the fens, the long sea voyage to Dunkirk, and then the ride to Chartres had barely left her time to catch her breath.

The coolness of the cloisters and the familiar sounds and rhythms of the daily routine were like a harmonious melody which soothed her. Here, she could adjust slowly without the feeling that her old life had been ripped too harshly from her.

Alice was her constant companion and they shared a pleasant room within the guest house. In the quiet moments, she would repeat to Alice what Cai had told her about her true family, as if each time she could believe it more and more.

As far as any of the Sisters here were concerned, she had travelled with her father and her maid, who was also her companion, while he conducted business on behalf of the well-respected Templar Knights. Her mother had died several years before and her father refused to leave her alone in England. If she was to feign grief, she didn't need to, for Cai's sad story of her mother dying after giving birth to her had filled her with such sorrow that her grief was raw. Alice too was mourning the loss of her family and bearing the guilt of leaving them behind, for ever.

The nuns were kind to them. They seemed a bit more jovial than the nuns of Sempringham, maybe it was the warmth of the climate … that, she enjoyed tremendously. She smiled when she saw the nuns file to the church for each service. She could attend when she chose, and out of respect she chose to attend several times a day. But she was no longer a nun – she was a young woman with a future ahead.

330

They called her 'Mademoiselle Isobel' and her companion 'Mademoiselle Mirabelle', and as for Gwenllian and Alice, they conversed well with the Sisters in French. It was only to be expected that many English women of their class would be versed in Latin and French, but they had to be careful not to reveal that their education had been too extensive – that could arouse suspicion.

Today, at the market Gwenllian had used one of Brother John's coins in order to purchase cloth for Alice to make them new dresses. She felt that the Mother Superior might think it odd that they had little luggage and only one change of clothes, which they had found on the ship.

Alice was determined to hone her skills as a seamstress and was delighted to have something to occupy herself. She started work straight away and Gwenllian was relieved to see her content, rarely fretting any longer about what she had left behind. Alice had lived in the outside world; she had a family and she was being exceedingly brave, with a new zest for life ignited inside her since they had arrived in France.

When night fell though, as Gwenllian lay on her pallet, her thoughts would wander back to her old life. She often thought of Brother John and prayed that he would be safe and not punished for her actions. She wondered if they were searching for her or if the Prioress would suffer for letting her escape. How could they cover up the fact that two nuns and a postulant were missing?

It was at least fortunate that the King's chancellor had been recently to do his inspection. He may not be back for several years. The King, she had learned, was in Scotland on another barbaric campaign based on avarice and greed. It was fortunate that his attentions were elsewhere. She was beginning to realise that there were many evils in this outside world.

Sometimes in the deepest night, the dream would come to her again – the horses' hoofs, the shouting, the full moon and the shriek of the owl. But she no longer feared the dream; she treasured it, for Cai had told her of the night he escaped with her from Nanhysglain and she had realised that the dream was a memory, the only memory her mind had retained of her life in her country. Cai had explained that the trauma had embedded the memory deeply into her spirit and maybe that was good, for it was meant to be. And the shriek of the owl may have come from the mother of Boden, who flew with them when they escaped that fateful night. Whatever happened, that owl must have followed her all the way to Sempringham Priory. She could see Boden now, sleeping, perched in the rafters of the granary at the side of the guesthouse at Sempringham. He had flown with her until they had reached the boat which took them to the ship which brought them here. But he would go no further. That was the sad end of their time together. The Priory was his home.

Cai had told her that his folk believe that these beautiful birds are sacred. He told her that owls are the symbol of Blodeuwedd, a Welsh goddess who, created to fulfil a man's desire, eventually takes back her power and becomes a woman who is strong. She had a beautiful castle, a devoted husband, a secure life. But her refuge became her prison and she fell for another man. As a punishment she was turned into an owl, her silent flight and screech cutting through the forest. She became wise, independent. Cai told her Blodeuwedd symbolises transformation and balance. He told her not to be afraid. When they reached the mountains of Eryri she would understand; she would be at home.

Had Boden and his mother been sent by this strange goddess, Blodeuwedd, or by an angel, or by the spirit of one of her ancestors, or had he been just an ordinary bird, reared by hand and attached to what he thought was his family? There were many mysteries in the world that Gwenllian had yet to understand.

Tired after Compline, Gwenllian and Alice prepared for bed. The heat of the day and the excitement of visiting the market had taken its toll. Gwenllian wondered if the dream would come tonight, but it was only seconds after she lay down on her pallet that she fell into the blackness of a restful sleep.

After a few hours she awoke and was sure she had seen Brother John standing by her bed smiling at her. Was he bidding her farewell? Had that been a dream or was it real?

Sempringham

The Prioress Elizabeth smoothed down the clean tunic that the lay sister, Isobel, had delivered to her that morning. Isobel had lingered as if to ask her something, but had obviously changed her mind. The Prioress had no idea what it could have been about. Maybe she had some information regarding Sister Wencilian. She would seek Isobel out later; she would never give up trying to uncover the mystery of Wencilian's disappearance. She was the only one who could find out now, for today was a solemn occasion. She had been allowed, with Sister Agnes and Sister Marie Claire, to attend the funeral of Brother John.

Brother John, she was sure, knew what had happened to Wencilian. He had tried to speak to her when she visited him in the monk's infirmary, but the few words he could utter were unintelligible. He had been found, so she was told, collapsed on the floor near Father Roger's office, his robes wet and covered in mud, as if he had been outside the Priory onto the fenland.

It was later that day when she discovered that Wencilian was missing.

Poor Brother John lingered in a semi-conscious state for several weeks. Brother Gilbert had said that his heart was very weak and he had been struck by some type of palsy, but what had triggered that, no one would ever know.

The Prioress just prayed that her deceit over the disappearance of Sister Wencilian and Sister Alice would not be discovered in her lifetime. When she heard that Brother Gregory, the strange travelling friar had left, she feared the worst. Sister Ignatius had reported her suspicions about him and, compiling all the information she had gathered about Sister Wencilian, or should she say 'the Princess Gwenllian', she realised a plot of some kind must have been carefully planned. Why she was not quick enough to unravel it, made her gravely doubt her own capabilities, but she had made a quick decision.

She let it be known that the young Sister Wencilian, on command of a higher authority, had been transferred to the Gilbertine nunnery at Sixhills. The Sisters were all informed of this and would ask no questions. A young novice, who had unusually been in the Priory since the age of ten and had just taken her vows, would receive the name of 'Sister Wencilian'. The King had certainly never set eyes on the former Wencilian, and Father Roger, who had only ever seen her once, would barely remember her she was sure. Her position was safe for now, but if ever she were found out the consequences would be worse than she could imagine. For if they discovered the truth, then she would be held accountable.

Sister Alice, well, she had been transferred with Wencilian, but what she would tell her family next year when they visited, she had yet to decide. The saving grace was that Alice had said she refused to see them ever again because of her sister's betrayal and her family's reluctance to consider her wishes that she did not want to be a nun.

As for the young postulant, Leoba, she must have gone with them as well. Mother Elizabeth had not reported her missing, to avoid attention. She was of little importance and still a heathen she was sure.

Wencilian did play on her mind though, not only for the danger she had put her in, but she would never rest until she knew the full story. She was also sorry; she had been fond of Wencilian and prayed that she would be safe. What if this Brother Gregory had abducted her and taken her God knows where?

Elizabeth's confessions were more regular. She confessed any minor misdemeanour in an attempt to alleviate the guilt. Her dreams were cursed with demons mocking her and often in the mornings she cried, not for the demons, for she knew they were illusions, but for the child she had left behind and for the hope she had fostered, the hope that Wencilian might have been that child.

There was a knock on the door.

"Please wait outside, I will be ready in a short while."

She knew Sister Marie Claire and Sister Agnes would wait patiently outside her office, and Sister Ignatius would be there too, but waiting rather impatiently to fill the shoes of Sister Marie Claire when the time came. She had had to promise her this. Sister Ignatius didn't know the whole truth, but she could make life very difficult for her. It was almost blackmail, although no such words had been spoken. She hated that and she hated her, and on this day she was not sure if she didn't hate God and this place she was in. She took a gulp of her best wine and pulled the black veil over her face before she opened the door. Today was a day to think of dear Brother John, a man whom she believed had a genuine heart, rare amongst men.

CHAPTER 53

Montargis, France
September 1300

Cai was weary and hot. He was not used to the heat, especially dressed as he was in tunic, hose, boots and cloak. He remembered how comfortable his monk's robes had been. He wasn't quite sure where he was, but his horse was thirsty so he had stopped in the small village to find water and food. It was a fine horse the Templar Knights had supplied him with, but he missed his Ianto, who he hoped was happy at Philip's house.

When they left the ship at the French port, the Templar Knights had escorted them to the convent near Paris, and then the knights disappeared as if they had never been. Cai had lingered for several nights, lodging close by the convent to make sure Gwenllian was safe and settled.

There, even in the restrictive atmosphere of the convent, she seemed to delight in her new freedom, for she was not entirely bound by their rules, being a guest. He had not felt so buoyant and happy for many years. He had succeeded, Gwenllian was free, although he knew the journey was not yet over. He could serve no further purpose for now by lingering around her, and he could not be there in France and not seek out Celeste.

Celeste had been a servant and companion to Eleanor since about the age of thirteen, but she was not a lady of low birth; her family owned land near Montargis, and that was where he was headed. He realised that she could be married, in a convent herself or even deceased. Or she may have not made it back to her homeland at all. All these doubts surfaced from time to time in his mind, but he pushed them away, for he had an underlying faith that he would find her and he would not go to his grave without discovering the truth. Philip had, in part, kept his promise. He had found out that her father still lived and there was a chance that Celeste could be with him.

Hywel had supplied him with some coins and spices for his journey and a spare set of clothes. This journey had been far more comfortable than his last one, resting in a taverne or occasional monastery, but as a merchant, not a monk.

He had been on the road though for several weeks and was getting weary and looking a bit shabby. He was also very near to his destination, so he needed to find accommodation to rest and smarten himself up.

He thought of Hywel and wondered if he was back in Eryri with the strange little postulant. He thought of Seren. Another month or two and winter would be casting its cloak upon the mountains, snow would settle and passing would be very difficult. He could not take Gwenllian there until at least next spring. He loved those mountains, but the climate was harsh. Would it be too harsh for his Princess? he wondered.

A man approached him. "You look weary, Monsieur. Where are you headed? I have not seen you in these parts before."

Cai looked up at the younger man, who eyed him suspiciously.

"I am seeking somewhere to rest for one night. I am headed for Montargis," Cai replied confidently in French, although he knew his accent would not pass him as a native.

"Well, you may be in luck. I have a large house and my wife caters for travellers. We can offer you a comfortable night and accommodation for your fine horse."

"That is generous." Cai had little option but to trust the man. He did not know if there were any other villages before Montargis; he was now so close he believed. He did suspect though that being in a family home he would have to make conversation and possibly face a barrage of questions. But it could provide an opportunity for information. "I will accept your invitation."

"You won't regret it, Monsieur. Forgive me, I have not introduced myself. I am Estienne de L'Estang and my wife's name is Cateline. I was a stranger here myself several years ago. I was passing through and had not intended to stay, until I lodged in what is now my very own house and set eyes on the lady who is now my own dear wife."

Extending his hand, Cai replied, "I am Jeffrey from England."

"Only Jeffrey?"

Cai cleared his throat. "Jeffrey Walter, from Gloucestershire." An innocuous name from a broad area. He hoped this would not raise any suspicion and that Estienne would not recognise his Welsh accent.

Cai could not say that he regretted his host's invitation, when he set off early the following morning, washed, changed and having spent a comfortable night – Cateline had served him an excellent meal of salted venison and spinach tart. His host had known a little of Celeste's family, her father and brother, but he did not mention Celeste. Nor did Cai, he did not want to arouse any suspicion. He was on business, plain and simple.

His horse was rested too and had a sprightly gait as she trotted along the wide track which led down into Montargis. He felt optimistic, but nervous. The heat of the day was rising and he could already feel sweat collecting on his back. He knew from his host's description what type of house to look for. Indeed it was more than just a house, it was a small chateau set on a low hill on the far side of the town surrounded by sloped terraces of vines.

He stopped in the town for wine and to collect his courage. A little bit of local gossip may be useful too, he thought, but it was nearing midday and the town folk were busy at their work, or keeping out of the heat, taking their noon day meal.

He found a small taverne and sat in the shade, collecting his thoughts. Should he just appear at the house? If Celeste was married, his sudden presence could be disruptive, to say the least. If he sent a messenger though he might not be accepted; after all they knew nothing of a Jeffrey of England. She may not even be there. Estienne de L'Estang had not mentioned her, but then women were not always considered important enough to mention. No, he decided he had come all this way, he had helped to free Gwenllian, he would ride in bravely but choose his words carefully.

As he approached the chateau, he noticed that it was not in good repair. The vines were almost ready for harvest but no one was working on the land. The place had an air of neglect and disquiet about it. He rode around the outside and still he saw no one. Perhaps it was abandoned. He prayed not. That would be a cruel fate to meet after having come so far. Finding what seemed like the main door, he hammered loudly. After several minutes it was opened by a young woman, whom he took to be a servant, but when he looked more closely at her face he saw the resemblance. She was no servant. She had to be a daughter of Celeste. Her auburn hair hung freely around her shoulders, her eyes were the same striking brown.

Cai swallowed, speechless, then stuttered. What a fool of a bard, he said to himself.

"Bonjour Mademoiselle. I am Jeffrey from England. Is the Seigneur at home?"

"What is your business, Monsieur?"

Before he could answer, another woman appeared in the shadowy entrance behind her. Her head was covered by a bib, but there was no mistaking her beauty, faded a little however from when he had last seen her.

As the girl took a step back, the woman moved forward and time stood still for him, the years which had separated them dissolving away. But she seemed a little confused, moving her head from side to side in an effort to understand what or who she saw in her doorway. Then recognition swept over her and she clasped her hand to her heart as if to ward off a terrible realisation.

"What is your name, Monsieur?" Celeste asked, reverting to some semblance of decorum and formality.

"Em, Jeffery Walter, Madame. I have some business to discuss, Madame, if I may. I have travelled a long way."

"Langette," Celeste turned to the young girl, "Please go and prepare some refreshment for our guest. Bring it into the solar."

Turning to Cai, she beckoned him to follow her along the hall into a small side room where stairs led up a comfortable sunlit room. She closed the door and stood searching his face. "Cai, I am being bold, but am I mistaken or is it really you?"

"I am almost speechless, but yes, it is me. Celeste, I vowed that if it was the last thing I did on this earth it would be to find you. But I could not assume that you would even recognise me, let alone admit me into your home, for I do not know any of your circumstances. I can barely believe that you stand here before me."

"Cai, how did you find me and why after so long? Quiet, I can hear Langette on the stairs."

The girl entered, nervously peering around the door as if scared of intruding.

"Merci, Langette. You may return to your studies now."

"The girl?" Cai enquired.

Celeste turned away from him to look through the window. "My daughter. She is nearly eighteen years old." She spoke quickly, nervously. "I have a son, he is sixteen and trains in my uncle's house. When he is of an age he will return to oversee the estate here. As you can see, it is a bit run down. I have to care for my father who is very ill. We cannot afford servants, or …"

Celeste broke off and turned to Cai. Seeing his concern, she offered him a chair. "Sit, please, Cai." She then continued, "The King offered me safe passage back to my family after the capture of Gwenllian, on the condition that I never returned. I was imprisoned for weeks. I didn't honestly know what became of little Gwenllian, or you, or Catrin, or poor Morwena. I was intending to get back to England somehow, but discovered that I was carrying a child. Yes, Cai, you may as well know – your child, Langette. My father married me off as soon as possible, to a good man."

"Is your husband here, Celeste? I cannot believe I have a child."

"Wait, hear my story. No, my husband is not here. He died several years ago. We lost his land. That is when I came back here to be with my father.

"She is so like you, Langette, but she must never know. She only knows one father, my husband. Oh, how I missed you for so many years and thought that you must be dead. Where have you been, Cai, and why are you here now?"

"I never gave up hope of finding you and I will tell you the tale if I am permitted to stay for a while, but I will tell you that Catrin is safe, married to Philip now, with a child. I don't know what became of Morwena, but Gwenllian, Gwenllian is safe, lodging within a convent near Paris. I brought her here and will take her back to Gwynedd when it is safe."

"She is so close! Why did I not know?"

"It has only been a few weeks, Celeste. She was kept in a convent in England. There is so much to tell you, cariad, so much. Come here to me, let me hold you a moment."

"I don't know what to think, Cai." Celeste leaned into him as the tears flowed.

"Then don't think, my love, don't think for a moment."

"The air is so fragrant when the sun goes down. Is your father settled? Maybe you can show me around the grounds." Cai babbled nervously. "What have you said to your ... our, daughter? I could hardly take my eyes off her during supper. I hope I did not unnerve her. She says very little."

"Cai, so many questions. I have said that you were a bard in the court of Llywelyn and a close confidant of the Prince. She knows the story of Eleanor, Gwenllian and the Prince. It kept her entranced for many a night when she was a little girl. You can be yourself, but not her father, for now anyway. I'm sure she will be in awe of you. It is like her childhood fairy tale come true."

"Is there hope for the future, for us?"

"When I look across this terrace, sometimes instead of seeing the town of Montargis, I see the mountains of Gwynedd. I see Llywelyn and Eleanor riding to the Llys at Abergwyngregyn, so happy after their marriage. They were good days. Then I fight to keep away the images of my dear Eleanor after giving birth to Gwenllian, her life fading. She will never be forgotten in my heart. You see that building beyond the river? That is the priory where Eleanor spent ten years with her mother, the Countess Eleanor, after the death of her father, Simon de Montfort. It was from there that she left with me to sail to Wales. That fateful journey ended in our imprisonment, but I think you have heard that story many times. Now here I am back in my childhood home. How the wheel turns, Cai. From what you have told me so far, we have our little Princess back and she is going to need our care. Perhaps she should be here with us until it is safe for her to return to the mountains of Gwynedd. Do you think she would be safe here?"

"I think we will have to risk that. We can keep her safer than strangers in a convent, I'm sure. She needs some freedom and it will help her adjust. She has a companion with her, Alice. They will be good company for our daughter. So, can I assume your consent then?"

"Consent?"

"To us."

"Let us see if the wheel turns in our direction again, Cai. Now I must check on my father. Goodnight, Cai."

"Nos Da, cariad."

It was a hot and sleepless night for Cai and he guessed that it would be for Celeste too. All the broken pieces of his recent life were melding together, but there were still cracks to mend. He was starting to feel whole again, albeit a little fragile. He sank into the comfortable feather mattress. How would the wheel turn, he wondered? No matter how much anyone planned, humans were always at the mercy of fate. That much he knew.

CHAPTER 54

The mountains of Eryri

The mountain peaks reflected a soft pink light over the grey of the impending night sky. The moon was rising as Seren walked to her secret grove. This was where she could be truly alone with her thoughts, her feelings. If anyone else knew of this place, they would not dare approach, for here she was in communion with her God and her Goddess and here she would receive their answers, their wisdom.

She knelt on the soft earth before the blue oracle stone, huddling into her thick cloak. The ringing stone which echoed the voice of her ancestors had stood in this place for thousands of years, before her time. It listened, it spoke and emitted the low murmuring sounds she had been trained to hear. But for a moment there was silence. Then the only sounds she was aware of as she closed her eyes were the soft rustle of the leaves on the gnarled Welsh oaks surrounding her and the distant howl of a lone wolf.

The mist was creeping around her; in seconds the atmosphere changed – autumn as approaching in Eryri. Soon, once again, her folk would be cut off by the winter snows. Ever changing, ever new, yet so much remained the same. But in the consistent rhythm of life there was new hope.

Now was a precious moment filled with subtlety … Gwenllian had been freed. Hywel had returned and told her the tale and some of it she had known, she had seen with her gift of foresight. But the girl who had returned with him was not Gwenllian and that she had not foreseen. Gwenllian was still not in her true home, but somewhere in France, in a convent, safe.

She had proved herself to be brave, a true warrior spirit, like Gwenllian, the last Priestess of Ynys Môn, and like the warrior Princess Gwenllian ferch Gruffydd; those who had gone before her, those who had risked their lives to save their people.

Cai had put the ancient words into song many a time:

'Thrice will cometh Gwenllian,' the old prophecy has foretold.
'Thrice will she sacrifice her blood, Gwenllian,
both beautiful and bold.
She will lay upon the earth and cry for all those taken,
Her noble tears will give birth once again to our nation.'

Gwenllian, it was a noble name; Eleanor had chosen well, but in doing so she may have sealed her fate. Maybe that could not have been avoided anyway, Seren wondered. Would sacrifice be the fate of every Princess of Wales or would Gwenllian be the last? Perhaps one day they would all become legends.

How this story would end she could not foretell, but she knew in her heart that it would not end for a long time yet, not in her lifetime. She knew that her strength was fading and it would make her so happy to stand face to face with Gwenllian and embrace her, to welcome her to her true people. The last rituals had taken their toll, sapped her energy but she would do it all again for her people, for Gwenllian.

Looking into the stone, she could see Gwenllian walking stoutly up the mountain pass in the spring with Cai by her side. She would have to wait, but their Princess would come home to them. Until then they would survive the harsh winter with hope in their hearts.

For now she had to be grateful. Her daughter had returned to her and she had a granddaughter to be proud of. The mountain grove of Eryri would survive too for many, many, winters and years to come. They were strengthening. She offered a prayer and blessing to the God and Goddess. Their knowledge had survived since the ancient times and would one day illuminate the world.

Hywel was resting with them, here in the mountains. He had work to do – the manuscripts he had gathered on his travels and the Llywelyn manuscripts needed preserving. They contained the only written knowledge of her people and the priesthood, and if the manuscripts were not to survive for future years, there would not be those who would have the knowledge, speak their truth and work their magic.

The young girl Hywel had brought with him was a natural and was ready to begin her training. Her ways were different, of the old Saxon tradition, but she had the gift. Leoba had sat with her and Luned many nights around the fire and told them what she knew of Gwenllian and life in the Gilbertine priory where she had been kept, and what her own mother had taught her of the old ways.

"The caged birds had flown and were singing," she had said. Her voice was indeed sweet and melodious, and apart from the cold, she assured them she felt completely at home with her new family.

Seren saw the fire in her eyes and her spirit in flames when she sang and danced with the young novices. Leoba had been sent to her. Together with Luned, she would spark renewed dynamism within their sacred community, which would send waves across the earth. And those who received the waves would know, know that the Druids of Eryri were powerful again. The Priestesses of old had foretold that their tribe would never die, but only lie dormant through the dangerous times. "Nourish the daughters, cherish the daughters, for they in turn will replenish the earth," they had said. "Preserve your knowledge; keep it secret until the time of fear and persecution is over." The words of the ancients were never forgotten by those who trod this path.

When she had discovered Cai that day on the mountain path, desperate, clinging to life, Seren had known that something momentous had occurred. Later, as he had recovered, she discovered the story of the capture of Gwenllian. There was a blanket of sadness which covered all her kin. Gwenllian had been their inspiration, a young and tiny soul, one which would regenerate their country when she had grown and blossomed. Some gave up hope, but not the Druids of Eryri. They believed and never lost hope, weaving all their power and magic into procuring her freedom. Now she was free, but there was still much work to do.

For the moment though there was peace and satisfaction and there had been a great deal of celebration since Hywel had returned. The late summer had been kind. Warm weather, ripened fruits, good hunting and the certainty of the future had blown a new breath of life into those harsh mountain habitats.

Seren lay down, weary now. Looking into the oracle stone always depleted her energy. The walk back to her hut would be too strenuous, especially as darkness had fallen. She would sleep here tonight, protected in her secret grove. As her eyes half closed, she saw Cynan. Then she saw herself as a young girl, laughing, skipping up the mountain pass with her mother, the spring flowers pushing through the cold solid earth around her. That's how Gwenllian would arrive, she was sure, only it would be Cai holding her hand. As she drifted deeper into the night, her own hand reached out now to her mother, who stood beside her beckoning. Behind her was a line of Priestesses in their blue robes, swaying to and fro, almost translucent. Seren heard the call of Ceridwen, beckoning. Her reply was barely audible. She muttered to the night breeze and the owl above. "Ceridwen, I hear your call; as the maiden returns, I, the crone, must pass into your abode."

Her soft breathing faded, as if lingering between the known and the unknown. If anyone had passed at that time, they would have only seen the High Priestess sleeping under the beauty of a new crescent moon and heard the hoot of an owl as it flew between the ancient trees above her.

CHAPTER 55

Montargis, France

I could stare at that view for endless moments … the town of Montargis, where my mother lived in exile with my grandmother. Were it not for Cai, I would never have come to this place. Blessed Cai, so happy now that he has found me and found his love. I stand on the top of the terraces; behind me is the place I now call home, the house of Celeste and her daughter.

I am happy here with Alice, Langette, Cai and Celeste. They are teaching me a lot about the world, yet it is quiet and peaceful here. They were right to say that living here would help me adjust to life outside the Priory, although the journey to this place gave me an overload on the senses. I think if I had been much older, I could not have tolerated it.

But this won't be my final resting place. I have to make the dangerous journey to my homeland, sometime in the spring when the winter snows there have melted, so Cai has told me.

I think I may prefer the warmth of the climate here. In the evenings sometimes, we sit outside and Cai tells me so much about my homeland and my family. We have shared many laughs and tears. The harsh winters at the Priory took their toll. There was always dampness, a damp mist which seeped into every crevice of that stone structure. Yes, it was a fine building and it was my home, although the folk who inhabited it were not

347

my folk. I never felt that they were and now I know why. I was not born to stay there, but I am not ungrateful for that time; I was treated well and educated, although feeling that I was always a caged bird wanting to be free, like Boden. When I watched him fly, many times I had the urge to crawl through that tunnel out into the wildness of the night. And I finally did.

Sometimes I dream that I am back in my cell, the semi-darkness casting shadows around me. I hear the bell ringing for Compline and join all the nuns reciting 'Salve Regina', some with pure devotion, some because of habit or fear, and some because they know no other way, like me. I see the dim lights of the fen dwellings flickering, then consumed by the watery mists. I see the faces of Brother John, the Sisters and my dear Boden.

Then I wake into the strangeness and joy of this new life I have been given. Every day is filled with new discoveries. I feel like a young child exploring the world, seeing the beauty of the summer fading into the vibrant tints of autumn, running through the fields, tasting the ripened grapes and then the fine wine made from them, which is a delight.

But I know that there is a lot of suffering too in the world. Cai tells me of the Druids of Eryri and the sacrifices they have made. He tells me that I am destined to train with them. He tells me of the battles that my father and uncle fought, and the losses they incurred, the final loss of their Principality, their homeland, their identity. He tells me of the betrayals of his own people and the evil that some men do. I think of my poor little cousins imprisoned in a castle so far away, and my girl cousins locked up in a nunnery, like I was. Will we ever free them? I don't know, but I am glad that I have not remained ignorant of their hardship and pain. If I ever reign as Princess of Wales, I will make them heroes and celebrate their bravery.

I think too of the woman called Hilda, who told me I was of noble birth. How much did she know? Her life slipped away before she had the chance to tell me. How could anyone possibly imagine that all of my family history, my real identity, had been hidden from me. I knew that secrets abounded in the Priory, but even to this day find it hard to believe that those who knew could be so cruel. I know the Prioress was searching for my true identity, but Father Roger, did he know? If he did, I suppose I cannot blame him for keeping it secret, as no doubt he was acting on instructions from King Edward himself, and may have been threatened into silence. Can I forgive them all? I am not sure.

I feel close to my mother here, but someday soon I will journey to the place where I was born. I shed a tear as I imagine my dear mother holding me in her arms while her own life slipped away. My father sacrificed his life for his country and my mother sacrificed her life for me, but before she died she blessed me with my name. My name is Gwenllian, Princess of Wales – Gwenllian ferch Llywelyn, Tywysoges Cymru.

GLOSSARY

Abergwyngregyn . . . . the mouth of the white shell river

Alban Hefin . . . . Midsummer (the light of summer)

ap . . . . son of ...

awen/Awen . . . . literal meaning 'flowing spirit', in Druidism 'awen' is also the 'inspiration of the sun' and a symbol often engraved or tattooed on objects or bodies.

fach . . . . small /little, but used as a term of endearment, as in 'Catrin fach'

caeth . . . . captive/slave

Cai . . . . an ancient Welsh name meaning 'rejoice'

Calan Mai . . . . May day

> **nos Calan Mai** . . . . May eve, parallels Beltane

cariad . . . . love/darling/sweetheart

Carneddau (pronounced Carnethi) . . . . a mountain range behind Abergwyngregyn. (Bera Mawr is the highest summit.)

Catrin . . . . a popular girl's name meaning love or loved one

Ceridwen . . . . a Welsh Goddess derived from 'cerru' meaning cauldron. She has different spellings and meanings, but generally she is the crone, the bringer of wisdom

crwth . . . . a medieval Welsh stringed instrument

Cymraeg . . . . the Welsh language

Cymru . . . Wales

Diolch byth . . . . thank heavens

drycraeft . . . . Saxon tradition of magic

ferch . . . . daughter (daughter of)

Ianto (Yan-toh) . . . . a Welsh form of John/ Ifan. Can be used
as a term of endearment

Llys . . . . Court

Lughnasadh . . . . Celtic festival at the beginning of the harvest
Season

maerdref . . . . a component part of a complex which included
the Llys (court) worked by bond tenants holding
their land in tenure

mawr . . . . big

mynydd . . . . mountain

seren . . . . star (also Seren used as a girl's name)

tad . . . . father

Tywysog . . . . Prince

Tywysogaeth . . . . the Principality

Tywysoges . . . . Princess

tylluan . . . . owl

Ynys Môn . . . . the island of Anglesey

A bit of help in pronouncing the Welsh alphabet:

b, **d**, **h**, **l**, **m**, **n**, **p**, **ph**, **t** . . . . pronounced as in English

a . . . . as in 'mam'

e . . . . as in 'hen'

c . . . . as in 'King'

ch . . . . as in 'loch'

dd . . . . as in 'that'

f . . . . as in 'vase'

ff . . . . as in 'farm'

r . . . . well trilled

ll . . . . between a 'cl' and a 'th', a sound you really need to hear spoken,

ng . . . . as in 'sing'

rh . . . . as in 'through', well trilled